W9-CTK-775

## HAIR-RAISING PERIL IN THE TEMPLE OF DOOM

As soon as I awoke I wished I had not, for I could feel in great detail the agony of my scalp as each hair in my head tried to rip from its native soil as it strained upward, and the horrible tension in my neck as my body was pulled in the other direction by its own weight. The red hot glaze before my eyes vanished briefly when I blinked and saw Amollia dangling just across from me. Her short curls would not allow her to drop as far from the iron ring to which they were tied as did my captive braids...

I saw a shutter fly open, and suddenly a stick was thrust forward, striking Amollia in the ribs, setting her swinging and shrieking. A moment later I too received a clout that tore loose part of a braid, so that blood and tears simultaneously coursed down my face as I rocked to and fro...

"Isn't that a shame?" Chu Mi's slimy voice hissed to Aster. "Such nice little women. Such good friends of yours. See how much they hurt? Don't you want to give us what is ours so we can pull them in before they are quite bald and dropped into the river for the crocodiles to eat. . . . ?"

Bantam Books by Elizabeth Scarborough
Ask your bookseller for the titles you have missed.

BRONWYN'S BANE
THE HAREM OF AMAN AKBAR
SONG OF SORCERY
THE UNICORN CREED

# THE
# HAREM
# OF
# AMAN AKBAR
## *or*
# *THE DJINN DECANTED*

## *Elizabeth Scarborough*

BANTAM BOOKS
TORONTO · NEW YORK · LONDON · SYDNEY · AUCKLAND

To all of my feminist friends who have become interested in the lives and culture of Middle Eastern women through Middle Eastern dance, and to all of my teachers of that dance, especially Jeannie and Naima. Also to all of my men friends who have had harems, now have harems, or would like to have harems, I affectionately dedicate this book.

THE HAREM OF AMAN AKBAR
*A Bantam Book / October 1984*

*All rights reserved.*
*Copyright © 1984 by Elizabeth Ann Scarborough.*
*Cover art copyright © 1984 by Steve Hickman.*
*This book may not be reproduced in whole or in part, by mimeograph or any other means, without permission.*
*For information address: Bantam Books, Inc.*

ISBN 0-553-24441-8

*Published simultaneously in the United States and Canada*

Bantam Books are published by Bantam Books, Inc. Its trademark, consisting of the words "Bantam Books" and the portrayal of a rooster, is Registered in U.S. Patent and Trademark Office and in other countries. Marca Registrada. Bantam Books, Inc., 666 Fifth Avenue, New York, New York 10103.

PRINTED IN THE UNITED STATES OF AMERICA

O      0 9 8 7 6 5 4 3 2 1

# *Chapter 1*

In the second year of the reign of the Boy King, Aman Akbar commanded his djinn to begin casting into the ether for wives suitable to the station to which our illustrious lord then aspired. An ambitious yet kindly man with a taste for the exotic engendered by the fashion of the day, Aman specified to his djinn servant that a woman for his harem must be comely and well learned in wifely crafts and also be of noble blood among her own people, but must not be so beloved that loss of her would greatly grieve her kin.

Perhaps you will think that such an arrangement was all very well for Aman Akbar but detestable for the women involved. You would, for the most part, be wrong, though the error is certainly forgivable unless you, as I, had been the third daughter and middle child of the overlord of our tribe. We Yahtzeni are fighters first (by inclination) and herders secondarily (by occupation). Thus good men are a rarity among us, for the attrition rate is great.

Our foes are distant relations to my mother. They live primarily in the upper portions of the hills and raid every spring and fall, killing many men while stealing sheep and women. We try to raid back, but are not such good climbers as they, and lose even more men in such raids. Meanwhile, the women left behind still bear children, and these children have in later years seemed more often to be girls than boys, so that the girls among us, by adolescence, have no marriage to look forward to, but a life of perpetual girlhood and servitude to their parents and the tribe. The only possible distraction any of us can as a rule anticipate is to be captured, enslaved, ravished and married only when we bear male children to our captors and are thus proven worthy of protection.

By the time I, as third daughter, was born to my father, he had begun to despair of sons and in his sorrow became unhinged enough to teach me to fight with the curved bronze dagger and lance, to hunt with bow and arrow, and to capture and ride wild ponies, as he would have taught a son. My mother thought him mad and kept telling him no good would come of it, and the surviving older men in the tribe taunted us both and regarded me as uncommonly wild and strange. Great was my mother's relief when she bore my brother and I could be tethered to the spindle, flocks and loom, and taught the healing potions and prayers she considered essential to a daughter's education. Still, my early training as my father's son stood me in good stead when the camp was raided, my father sorely injured and my sister—somewhat gratefully—carried off. My own distaste for my people's enemies' marriage customs was explicitly expressed with my dagger.

Thus by the time I first felt eyes upon me as I sat spinning, watching the sheep, I was already considered unmarriageable among our people and thought to be of an unnaturally fierce disposition.

Rain was sparse that season, and the sky, promising snow, looked like a felted blanket. Our sheep ranged far and wide to find forage and I with them. I'd found a comfortable rock, just high enough for my spindle to rest against my thigh. When I felt the eyes upon me, I stilled my spindle in mid-whirl and clasped it to my hip. The hills around my flock teemed with wolves and bear, as well as mother's disgruntled relatives. I set aside the spindle and grabbed my dagger, fearing the two-legged beasts more than the four. Had I known what was truly behind my unease, I would have been terrified beyond any comfort to be gained from the knife.

Later I would be glad that I had had to wear my new robe that day, for the tattered one my mother had sewn for me for my womanhood dance had been torn

beyond repair in the last battle. Even before that, it
had been worn to transparency in places so intimate I
was almost embarrassed to wear it in front of the sheep.
The threads for my new robe were finer spun than
those in the old one, for my skill with the spindle had
increased in the years separating the making of the two.
I had dyed it a rich rust color by soaking it in a bath of
iron wood. Escaping the camp to roam with the sheep
put me in a festive mood. That and the chill sharpening
the morning prompted me to add to my new finery the
felted vest I had been embroidering for my sister before
her capture—it had the fleece of a black lamb inside
and the yarns were various yellows and soft pinks.
Aman says that he found the contrast between my
finery of that day and my ferocious aspect in battle most
erotic—Aman talks that way sometimes. For although
he has lived all his life in Kharristan, he has always
been a keen watcher of the market place and also is the
possessor of a vivid imagination. He finds the strange
people who flock to that center of the civilized world
endlessly fascinating and their diversity intriguing. Thus
he was prepared to find me beautiful instead of merely
odd.

I am told the djinn complained that I was unworthy—
what noble woman, he protested, would be so careless
of herself as to bind her hair into leather-held braids
instead of twining it with pearls? Which shows how
much the djinn knows about feminine adornment—my
hair is almost white and pearls would ill-become me.
He also deemed my substantial nose hideous—but this
is typical of the djinn, who has lived a sheltered existence,
for the most part, confined in his bottle. Therefore his
views often tend to be prudish and conservative. Though
a great one for taking others places, he has generally
taken no part in the life of those places, thereby managing to stay relatively untouched and unenlightened by
his travels. However, on the occasion in question, his
priggish complaints fell on unheeding ears, for Aman
replied, "Her nose is curved like the beak of the hawk
and is a fitting complement to the glitter of her eyes—
know you, o djinn, that the hawk is a noble bird and

proud and also, I think, useful." There was further discussion of the sort Aman indulges in when carrying out
these quasi-poetic analogies of his, about soft feathers
and delicate coloring but even when he is being smooth-
tongued and soft-headed he can be acute. You notice
he did not pick a frivolous bird to compare with me.

All that morning I felt skittish as an unbroken
pony, disturbed, though I knew it not, by invisible
scrutiny.

The new pasturage was a sloping mountain meadow and the way was long and tiresome. I quickly shed
my vest, the pleasant coolness giving way to prickly
discomfort as the sun and I climbed together. By the
time I reached the stream where I planned to watch
while the sheep grazed, sweat dewed my forehead and
stuck my new garments to me at the armpits. The
bubbling water looked refreshing and I smelled goatish.
I did not wish to spoil my new clothing by stinking it up
on its first day in use, so I shed it gratefully and waded
in. The icy waters revived me for but a moment before
I began shaking with a cold that struck through my
body as though to cut flesh from bone. I shot from the
water, blowing through my nose and lips like a horse,
hugging myself and shivering in my blued hide.

"Who can account for the taste of my master?" a
voice whined, seemingly from above. I looked up sharply
and dove for my clothing, not to cover myself so much
as to find my dagger, still tangled in the silken sash.
Despite the unfamiliar accent, I feared I had been
caught by our enemies and was determined to sunder
as many as possible from their lives before they could
sunder me from my maidenhood.

"Yes, yes, Rasa Ulliovna, by all means cover thyself,"
the querulous voice continued. I was so startled to hear
it speak my name that I abandoned my blade to search
again for the speaker. Once I saw him, I ceased to
worry. Such a one, I thought, I could handle with my
two hands. "Do you obey me, girl," the djinn commanded more sternly. "We have much to do before I may
deliver thee unto the master."

"You, pip-squeak, will deliver me to no one," I

replied, snatching my gown over my head in one jerk so as not to let it blind me any longer than necessary. "How dare you spy upon a princess of the Yahtzeni at her bath?"

"Thy pardon, Highness," the entity replied, rising from the rock on which he balanced like a ball and doing his best to bend at his nonexistent waist. "I sought a private time with thee. The draperies of thy bathing tent were invisible to mine eyes." In spite of his mockery, the djinn seemed genuinely disconcerted for, as I have mentioned, he is prudish. "Thou hast no need to take fright of despoilment by the gaze of mine eyes. I am an ifrit, not a man, who sees thee in thy rather unpalatable nakedness."

I knew not the meaning of the term "ifrit," nor of the terms "djinn" or "genie," for there are no such creatures in the lore of the Yahtzeni—even at that, the entity obviously was not one of my usual enemies. While several of them might have had good cause to learn my name, none of them were apt to use the djinn's fancy mode of speech. Nor would any of them for any reason I could think of short of madness or the threatened torture of loved ones attire themselves in his strange clothing—billowing trousers of scarlet silk, an indigo tunic, and a vest of a color I had never seen except in some sunsets—a brilliant blue-green, like the stones of which I have become so fond that Aman has declared them my talisman, in particular. Around the circumference of the being's copious midsection wound a sash of golden cloth. The same cloth wrapped his head like a bandage. He wore no weapons, and his feet faded into a wisp of mist settling like a low fog across the rock. This last factor would have made me cautious, had I dwelt upon it, but the djinn's bland unwhiskered face and soft corpulence assured me that if he was an enemy, he was scarcely one with which to reckon seriously. Still, he might be able to summon friends, and I had my sheep to tend.

"Begone," I told him, flashing my dagger, "or I'll let the air out of you." And then my dagger flashed no longer, but vanished from my fist. At that I trembled like a child and shrank from him, knowing I had made a grave error.

"That's better," the djinn said smugly, and vanished to reappear beside me, all of him, that is, but the feet.

This time I observed his lack of visible support with great reverence, prostrating myself before the nonexistent detail and groveling, which is the only course of action prescribed by Yahtzeni lore for dealing with demons. "Forgive me, fearsome one," I managed finally. "I knew not that I was in the presence of such as yourself."

"Nevertheless, thou art," the djinn replied, "and wasting my time too, I might add. If thou wilt be so kind as to separate thyself from the earth as thou didst from the water, I shall undertake to enchant thee at once so thy master may behold thee in thy dubious splendor before this day has ended and another begun."

"Master?" I asked, puzzled despite my terror. "Do you mean my father? I have no other master."

"*Have* had," the djinn corrected, somewhat wearily. "And a deplorable state of affairs that is too. But never fear, that also shall be remedied by my powers and by thy master's will. For the great Aman Akbar hast looked upon thee and found thee pleasing, though God alone knows why, and has bidden me to bring thee to him this day."

"That's all very well," I said, my awe lessening as I grew used to this peculiar being. "But I'm not at all sure I want a master. I'm a chieftain's daughter, not a slave—what sort of man is this Ak—it sounds like a sneeze to me. And even if I did want to go, what of my sheep?"

The djinn snorted, his jowls wobbling. "Thou art even more foolish than thou lookest, O woman, to think of sheep and talk of slavery when high honor hast been awarded thee. Speak not of such matters to the instrument of thy deliverance from squalor and ignorance. For thou art to be installed in the harem of Aman Akbar, richest man in Kharristan save only the Emir himself, and—er—hero of a thousand adventures. I do his bidding in seeking thee out for this privilege."

"Some privilege," I answered, sitting up straight to pull on my leggings. "You spy upon me like a lecher and seek to carry me off—to go to some strange man and his harem, whatever that is, with no talk of marriage—and certainly none of a bride price. And I suppose that in order to accommodate you and your master I am to let my people's sheep just scatter among these hills? And who will do the work in our tent with my sisters gone, my father injured, and my mother growing daily older and more feeble?"

The djinn cast his eyes downward, as if to gather patience, and sighed a sigh that parted the mist where his feet should have been.

"Thou art a willful woman as well as an ugly one, and I pity my master. But he would have thee and is not a man known for unfairness. Thy sheep shall return to thy father's fold of their own accord. And I suppose I may provide thy father with recompense for the loss of thy labor if that is the way of thy people—though only crass barbarians would have it so. Properly, the master should demand of thy father a dowry for relieving thy poor parent of the burden of thy appetite and rattling tongue."

"Demanding of my father would do no good," I said. "The flocks and the horses belong to all in my tribe, as does the work of my hands."

"I see. A cask of jewels should be more than adequate. I'll send them along with the sheep."

"Horses," I said boldly. "My people have no need for trinkets, but horses would lighten my mother's load and help at the herding and moving the tents. Ten should do nicely."

"*Ten!*" the djinn sputtered, but in a thrice produced them in a manner I found wondrous. I made no further protest as the beasts, black, necks arching, stampeded the sheep down the hill away from us and toward my father's camp. I swelled with pride at the bargain I had made and hardened myself to accompany the djinn.

Ten horses was the highest bride price ever paid for any woman among my people and indeed, as the djinn had suspected, the custom of paying any such price had fallen into disuse because of the lack of men. The djinn, perceiving my ill-concealed look of triumph, muttered something about the price being high enough to buy twenty more tractable houris, but then he snapped his fingers, the mist of his feet solidified into a rug, and when he had seated himself upon it and convinced me to do the same, he spoke a quick incantation and we rose into the air in a most astonishing fashion.

That the djinn should use an unusual mode of travel did not surprise me. I would have been disappointed had such a powerful being suggested we walk or ride one of the new horses. But the higher we flew, the more the mountains and glacial clefts drew my eyes over the side, and when I looked away, I had to whip my head back quickly so the wind would disperse the tears that formed as I saw my familiar plains shrinking to a thin yellow-green line. I spied the camp of our enemies and leaned so far over the edge of the rug, trying to spot my sister, that it tilted dangerously. The djinn threw out his arm and a magic force pulled me back and straightened our course again.

We flew over more mountains, beyond which were broad fields and seas and other mountains and great cities, and yet more plains and mountains; all of this in an eye's winking.

As we soared higher, it seemed to me, we should have seen yet more wonderful sights, but this was not so. Above the clouds were none of the palaces and gardens and herds of the gods, nor even the warriors we had lost in battle sitting around sharpening their knives and axes, waiting to make the next thunderstorm. Or if they were there, they were invisible to me, for all I saw were the tops of clouds, nothing more.

The djinn sat silent, legs and arms folded, and would not speak to me. After a time the clouds thinned to a gauzy film, muffling us for a moment in its fleece before our conveyance sliced through it. I saw that we had been among the shrouded peaks of very tall mountains. From these we dropped into foothills, through which flowed a pair of rivers, between which was set a great city—round, scalloped with domes and prickled with spires, glowing pale amber by the light of the sickle-shaped moon rising above it.

"Kharristan," the djinn said, hovering briefly to savor my astounded reaction at the sight of what his culture had produced. The cities I had seen were those walled towns we visited from time to time to trade our fleeces, horn buttons, weavings and yarns for knives, needles, certain foodstuffs and occasionally for dyes we did not possess. Once or twice I had gone with father to trade with the servants of powerful men at the back entrances of their fine houses; there I saw a fine bolt of silken cloth, a porcelain bowl with figures painted on it, and a portable goddess chipped from marble. But mostly what I had seen were rude collections of straw and mud or mortared stone, surrounded by walls of the same—evil-smelling, foul traps for the whey-faced city men who dwelt in their own filth—as my father was fond of saying. None were like this mountain of moonlit walls, golden spires and billowing domes whose deeply shadowed and gracefully arched windows and doors made it look airy as a snowflake.

Muddled as I was by moonlight and the exhaustion of my unusual activities that day, I failed to notice the other magnificent palace in Kharristan, which seemed to me to be all one great and beautiful building. The djinn flew us to Aman Akbar's residence as soon as he felt I had had sufficient time to be duly impressed and yet not enough respite to regain my composure, which he seemed to delight in upsetting. I didn't even recognize it as a residence. Even though we settled down among walls to get there, I thought we'd landed in a vacant pasture in the middle of the city, for there were flowers blooming, trees and an animal blowing water out of the middle of a rectangular pool. The weather was no longer winter, as it had been at home. The wind rushing past my cheeks as we landed was as warm as human breath. My woolen robe began to prickle once more against my skin.

Aster, about whom I will say more later, would make sure to tell you what kind of flowers bloomed there, and how many of them, and also would remark that the trees were different than the sort I was used to. She would also tell a good many other things which are beside the point and probably, on the whole, not entirely truthful. What was important was that Aman Akbar was waiting for me beside the pool.

Deep in the brain of every woman who has ever lived, there has been the dream of Aman Akbar or someone like him. Not that I had previously imagined a man who looked like him—never had I beheld anyone so dark and yet so fair at the same time. But a man whose touch is soft as a horse's muzzle, whose breath is sweet as clover rather than sour with the remnants of his last meal, a man who smells of well-washed cloth and whose hair mirrors any available light—aiyee! He was so much prettier than I was I could hardly speak for gawking. When he reached out to take one of my hands I hid them both in my skirt, ashamed of the dust deep in the knuckle creases and the scars of many brambles and many battles crisscrossed in pallid patterns along the backs of them and up my wrists and arms. His hands were well-shaped and long-fingered, the skin the color of honey, soft and smooth, though I felt the roughness of callouses when he succeeded in capturing my uncooperative wrist.

Not that beauty and good grooming were all that there was to his charm. In my experience, a man's cleanliness is less often to his own credit than to that of the woman who scrubs his clothing and carries the water for his libations. But there was also about Aman Akbar an air of wonder—at his surroundings, at the djinn (though this was tempered by such haughtiness as befitted the master of such an establishment), at life, and oddest of all, at me. His eyes were blacker than sloes but were wide and warm. His smile was at once sweeter and more tender than my mother's and more understanding and protective than my father's. Not that my parents ever smiled, either of them. Our people aren't generally great smilers. But his was even better than theirs would have been if they did that sort of thing. I felt that here was a man who would never cuff me for losing a sheep or breaking a water jar because I was more precious to him than anything else. Needless to say, I took to him immediately.

He said something to me in a low, soft voice. I recognized his name and mine though when he said "Rasa" he spoke the word with such melodious tones that it sounded totally unlike it did when I heard it screamed across the plains or over the cookfires. The way Aman said it it should have meant "first blossom of spring" or "face of the new moon" instead of "wild grass" or "weed"—which is its true meaning. Other than the names, however, I didn't understand a word he said. I nodded hopefully, nonetheless. He blinked, smiled sympathetically, and gave the djinn a command.

The latter rolled his eyes and bowed with a great show of reluctance, muttering, "But what is the use of foreign wives if you teach them to speak? Is not the chief virtue of such women their inability to scold or gossip?"

"The Lady Rasa is to be the heart of my heart, the light of my soul, o ifrit. How then shall I gain her confidence if she cannot understand a word I speak? I must not only win her love, but must also acquaint her with her new surroundings and the one true God and His word."

"It is done. Every word that passeth from thy mouth she hath understood. However, I can still arrange it so that she can understand all thou sayeth but cannot speak herself," the djinn said hopefully. Aman looked sternly upon him. The djinn shrugged and abruptly dissolved into smoke and blew away.

"Where did he go?" I asked, as much to see if the demon had done as he was told as because I was interested. He had. Aman stroked my hand in a pleased fashion with his thumb as he answered.

"Back to his bottle, beloved, to wait until I summon him again."

"Are you a great magician then, to be in control of

such a demon?" I should have thought of that before. This bargain I had made would not be so clever if my husband were able to kill me with a fire-bolt the first time I angered him or would change from his present virile form into something vile at bedtime. A Yahtzeni woman usually lost a few teeth after marriage, but I had figured that I, being a largish girl, would be able to handle any of the men in our tribe or our enemy's. Had I inadvertently overmatched myself?

"No more than any other man of extraordinary wit and courage," he said, puffing out his chest and gesturing grandly before darting me a quick sidelong look to see if I was sufficiently impressed. I was simply puzzled, and must have looked it, for he relaxed and grinned, patting my arm. "What I mean to say, my darling Rasa, is that winning the services of the djinn required a great deal of both—and considerable luck. Though it was all in watching people, really. I noticed that a certain very wealthy man seemed to be searching for something and guessed that the object of his search must be a thing of great value, else why would he bother with it? With a little shrewd maneuvering, I managed to beat his agents to the thing, which turned out to be an old bottle." He smiled, his teeth flashing like the edge of the moon. "No Kharristani in his right mind would ignore such a treasure. Some old bottles contain nothing, some contain old wine, but many— and these are the important ones, the ones of which we all learn when we are but children, contain captive members of the race of the djinn, who must grant the person who holds their bottle three wishes."

"Why?"

His hands spread and his eyebrows rose, a gesture more graceful than a shrug. "Thus it is written. Some say the bottle contains not only the djinn's form but his soul, and to preserve it from harm the djinn performs his magical services."

The whole thing had an unsavory sound to me but I hated to be critical so early in our relationship. One could see, however, why the djinn wouldn't necessarily be a cheerful or willing servant.

Aman Akbar was leading me into the palace, not through the back entrance either, but through open-sided passages roofed with arched ceilings and supported by white pillars carved with trailing vines. The warm night air was laden with the sweet-spicy smells of flowers I had never seen before and the sliver of moonlight danced our shadows before us. Inside, a lamp lit itself and dipped in front of us before leading us onward. I gaped.

Aman Akbar looked pleased as a six-year-old boy who has mastered his first slingshot. "You will notice that when I ordered this palace, I ordered it all with the utmost in magical labor-saving devices—no servants anywhere. I have only to step across the threshold and magic provides for my every wish." He placed a hand on the back of my neck and turned me this way and that to admire first the feathered fans with eyes in the tips that waved up and down the moment we were within range, the books that invitingly turned their own pages, and the bathing room, where steam hissed from the walls and jets of water leapt up as if trying to catch us when we skirted around them.

Here Aman Akbar said, "Perhaps you would like to refresh yourself after your long journey, my dear."

"In *here*?" I asked, for I am used to less aggressive water, except in flood season.

"It *is* the bathing room," he replied sensibly, and mopped a fingerful of perspiration from my brow. This mortified me. Aman Akbar wasn't sweating and I was sure no one else around here ever did either. He smiled again that sweetly reassuring smile and pushed me toward the clutching fingers of water. "Go. You will enjoy your"—and here he gave a significant pause that indicated what he was about to say was not entirely what he meant—"evening meal more when you have bathed."

I certainly would. Fighting all that water was bound to work up an appetite. On the one hand, I was tempted to make it the fastest bath ever taken and on the other hand, remembering the activity indicated by the pause preceding the mention of the evening meal, I was tempted to take quite a long time, both to be thorough enough not to be embarrassed before my elegant new lord and also to put the damned thing off as long as possible.

But I tried to cooperate. I really did. I was beginning to agree with the djinn that being chosen by Aman was an unusual honor and I had no wish to respond to such distinction by being disobedient the first time he asked something of me. So I stripped, and folded my clothing as close to the door and as far from the water as possible.

The baths of Kharristan may be famed throughout the world, but I simply couldn't cope with them in my travel-bemused condition. No sooner had I stepped into the quietest looking apparatus there, a deceptively tranquil pool, than the waters turned into a whirlpool, and the demon at the bottom tried to suck me under. I sustained a rather major bruise scrambling out of there, and stood panting, looking over the edge. Perhaps this was a test of bravery Aman was demanding of me, to face these water demons? I had never heard of such a custom, but one never knew about strangers. Nobody I knew ever sent feetless demons on flying rugs to fetch brides either.

Approaching the baths as such a test was not an appealing prospect without knowledge of how they worked or the use of my dagger. Being naked didn't help either. I decided the only thing to do was to submit myself to them, as to the gods, and hope for the best. That, as has been often explained to me, is the sort of thing the truly brave do when the battle is lost, their lord is slain, and the enemy is as numerous as drops of water in the sea—an unfortunate comparison, from my standpoint.

Marching bravely forward, I endured the suffocating steam and the needlings of the water jets, and when nothing more horrible happened, turned so they could reach other areas of my body, in order that they should see that they might do their worst and I would be undaunted. Discouraged, the steam dissolved and the water jets fizzled out after a time and sent instead a

flurry of rough sponges, flying through the air, attacking
me from all sides, scraping and polishing my hide,
bruising old bruises and scraping the scabs off my knees
and elbows. Hot water followed, but I endured it,
stoically, though the cold water almost made me scream.
After that, heavy towels swarmed upon me, smothering
me, insinuating themselves under my feet and into
personal places in an obscene attempt to make me
falter. This activity was followed by the assault of the oil
and perfume bottles, which heaped their contents upon
me, to slide around on my skin until I was marinated
in the stuff.

Then, incredibly, everything simply shut off. The
pool smoothed and a cover pulled itself over it. The
towels retreated to the alcove, where the light of the
lamp beckoned me, shining on the soft blue folds of a
lightweight gown to replace mine, which now hung
drying on a silver peg. It was a pretty gown, and cooler
than mine, so I donned it and followed the lamp and
my nose—for I could already smell the odor of roasted
meat and other, unfamiliar scents, that nonetheless
conjured up fairly accurate pictures of the steaming
platters surrounding Aman Akbar.

# Chapter 2

"You forgot the belt," he said,
disappointment giving him a child's pout. "The dress
looks more like a tent that way."

It was a rotten thing to say to someone who had
barely escaped from water demons for his sake. I hadn't
seen any belt for this gown—which did unfortunately
resemble a somewhat diaphanous tent—and even if I
had I probably wouldn't have paused to primp. I was in
a hurry to get out of there. I hunkered down on my

heels, so I wouldn't tower above him and also so he could invite me to eat.

He patted a cushion beside him and, as further inducement, picked up a tender-looking morsel from the nearest platter and extended it to me, waving it just under my nose. I settled back against the cushion, and grabbed for the meat, but he withdrew it, insisting with an intent, amused gaze that I open my mouth to receive it. I felt my face grow hot with embarrassment. Only small children are fed thus among our people. Or the sick. But this was no doubt another of my husband's weird customs, so I closed my eyes, opened my mouth, and received the meat, which was so delicious I practically swallowed it whole. After that, he nodded to the platter and pointed to his mouth whereby I gathered that I was supposed to feed him. I wished heartily he had not lost his tongue all of a sudden and gained in its stead something of a self-congratulatory smirk, but I gathered that this too was customary and tried to forbear. So until the silver platters were considerably less burdened we silently fed each other kumquats and rice, pistachios and lamb, oranges basted with honey, and lovely fruit drinks called "sherbets."

By the time we were down to peeling the grapes, a messy process not facilitated by fingers greased with mutton fat, the silence gave way to a great deal of giggling. When my last grape shot out of its skin and ricocheted off Aman's nose, I was considerably more comfortable than I had been at any time during that day.

When the giggling diminished to an occasional gust, he snapped his fingers twice and little bowls of scented water appeared under them. We used these to wash off the mutton fat, and the bowls bobbed and disappeared. Simultaneously a subdued din of whinnying horns, out-of-tune strings and palpitating drums began throbbing out what was the most disorganized piece of music I had ever heard. But it was certainly suggestive and I had only to look into the eyes of Aman Akbar to know what the suggestion was.

He took my hand again, saying, "I know one form

of entertainment, my love, for which we need no magic other than that of our own producing."

By this speech I knew that he wished to do with me what men do with wives and slaves. Knowing that I had sold myself for a good price, I resigned myself to keeping my part of the bargain.

Every Yahtzeni child knows about the marital activity—no one who lives in a tent with six to twenty other people could fail to be aware of such, though the participants usually try to disguise what they are doing with curtains and blankets. Still, such attempts are unsuccessful with sufficient frequency that now I was able to assume the mating position I had learned by watching my mother, who, like the rest of my people, knows all there is to know of love that sheep can teach.

For a moment Aman Akbar made no move in my direction and I cringed inwardly wondering if our differences in customs had not created another embarrassing misunderstanding. Perhaps I would need to introduce him to some sheep too? But then he tapped me playfully on a nether cheek. I looked around to my backside to see the occasion of his delay and he smiled at me and, taking my shoulders, pulled me back into his arms and taught me many things unknown to sheep, whose bodies would not permit them the pleasures ours proceeded to enjoy.

Afterward I fell into a profound and dreamless sleep. Dreamless, that is, until the wailing began, softer than the howling of wolves but louder than wind. I couldn't tell if it was dreamed wailing or real, but either way it was bothersome. My mother always puts more stock in people's dreams than reality anyway, assigning all manner of portents and omens to them. I woke enough to feel Aman Akbar roll over, groaning, to fling an arm across my shoulders.

Of everything that had befallen me since meeting the djinn—the trip, the palace, the water demons, the meal of strangely flavored foods—only this man seemed real. This I felt not only in the almost unpleasant warmth of his well-tended flesh next to mine, but from the sweat that did after all moisten that skin, and the callouses that roughened his elegantly shaped feet and hands. Similarly, the matters with which he sought to impress me—the palace, the djinn, his flowery speeches, his boast of "extraordinary wit and courage," his lovemaking—meant less to me than his manner. He, the handsome, wealthy lord of all of this magnificence, wanted very much to please me with all of these things, wanted very much for me—a stranger, a foreigner, of significance chiefly to my enemies—to like him. I found that I did, if not for any particular reason except perhaps that he was uncertain that I would. A Yahtzeni wishing to impress a woman would have picked up a horse with one arm and her with the other and not thought to solicit her opinion on the matter.

Aman began to snore. Gradually the wailing died away. I offered myself the groggy explanation that it was only natural that a palace built by demons was haunted by ghosts.

Wailing of a different nature awakened me the next morning. This sound had a spiraling, chanting quality about it and seemed to be emanating from a latticed window on the wall farthest from our mattress, of which I was now the sole occupant. I rose, pulling the blue dress over my body, sticky from the night's exertions and already perspiring somewhat in the first early simmer of the day. The streets below me were silent, and the few people visible across the city seemed to be napping upon rugs. Several streets over, the singer with whom the chanting originated serenaded them from a tower. With my new understanding of the local tongue, I could even make out some words. I heard the same sound four more times that day, and later learned that this singing was the call to prayer.

What I could see of the city, deprived of its moonwash, looked in the hard glare of sunlight more like the ones I was used to. The amber color was lent it by the bleached mud bricks of which the walls were fashioned, and these were much besmirched, chipped and soiled. Not only that, but with so much heat everything smelled to the heavens and the flies were awake, even if the people still slept. I liked the splashes of gay colors and the bright striped patterns that cropped up on blankets and clothing, wool drying in the sun, rugs and shop canopies. Perhaps Aman Akbar would let me buy some of the wool to fashion him a cloak—we Yahtzenis use mostly vegetables dyes, and the bright crimsons and indigos made even my fingers itch to weave them. I might as well like it. Now that I was a proper wife, I would no doubt be doing a lot of that sort of thing.

The light filtering through the window caught an answering glimmer from the mattress. A slender bangle, all of gold, where Aman had lain. An additional wedding gift. For all my ignorance I could not have done too badly or he wouldn't be rewarding me, would he? I slid the bracelet onto my arm, then removed it again and dropped it onto the pillow. I needed a bath more than adornment. I wasn't about to face that chamber of horrors from the night before however. The strange symmetrical pool in the clearing where Aman had first met me was more to my liking. Provided I could find it again, I'd bathe there. On the way, I'd brave the water demons long enough to collect my own clothing and maybe find the belt missing from the blue dress.

The water demons had been properly quelled the night before, it seemed, for now there was no trace of them, just the covered pool and the room, with my robe still on the silver peg, the sash that matched the blue dress beneath it, and a white robe of the same weight but a finer, shinier material, on a shelf beside them. The fans at the doorways were likewise quiet, and that pleased me less, for the morning had waxed from warm to nearly unbearable. None of the books saluted me either and I began to wonder if the pool would be there. It was, though the animal in its center no longer spouted water. But the flowers and trees still abounded providing perfume and delicious shade covering at least half the area. I washed thoroughly, dressed in the white robe instead of my heavier homespun, and looked around.

A pleasant spot to break my fast, I thought. But though certain tantalizing spicy smells shimmered across the tiled rooftops of the rest of the palace, no food appeared before me in response to my wishing. I tried unspoken wishing, spoken wishing, and finally cursing when I realized that only Aman's wishes produced food, as well as all of the other amenities missing this morning. He had not, evidently, thought of everything—but then, of course, he had lived alone before and wasn't used to considering what another person would do while he was gone. It was not really a problem, for the remains of the feast from the night before still littered our wedding chamber. Returning to the room, I retrieved the food and carried it back out to the fountain. I saw no more of Aman Akbar that day or the next, and none of the night intervening.

As a warrior I had fairly good nerves. As a wife the same nerves were wrecked by noon-time. Had he gone out to herd sheep? Or into the town? I slept but little that night, pacing the chamber, running out to the garden periodically to see if he was only just arriving, listening to the street below for his voice, which I wasn't really entirely sure I would remember.

The room was stifling. I slid the bracelet, the ring my lord had given me, up and down my arm in a fitful manner, trying to decide what I must do. Surely such a rich man didn't herd or hunt and if he were delayed on business, why didn't he send me a message? Why not take me with him? I would have liked to see the city, even if it was too hot.

When he was not there by the next day, I considered going into the town to search for him, for I was becoming frightened for his sake. Thieves and murderers prowled city streets, my father said. Worse men than my mother's cousins. What if my new husband had met with one of those? Then what would I do? I knew no one in this strange land except he and the djinn, and the latter was not likely to be much help without his master.

But as the day wore on, and I once more expected

to see him appear by the pool or in the street outside
my window at any time, I told myself that though this
city seemed threatening to me, to him it was home. He
had lived here for years without my protection, and
would no doubt be less than grateful for it if I interrupted
him while drinking with other men, gambling, doing
business, or whatever it was that kept him away. Such
absences were not an indication of bright days ahead for
us, but so far what he had done regarding me had been
otherwise exemplary. Nevertheless, I promised myself
that if he missed the evening meal (which I too would
miss, for the leftovers from the dinner of two nights ago
were now little more than cores, seeds and fly-blown
scraps) I would go searching for him, as well as for
something to eat.

I was in the process of keeping this resolution,
having redonned my own robe, attaching to my sash a
knife I found in the room of books, when suddenly I
noticed that the pages had begun turning, the lamps
were lighting, and, sure enough, down the corridor, the
eye-tipped feather fans were waving in salutation as
Aman Akbar strode through the arches and pillars
beyond. He was more beautiful than ever, clad in a coat
of green embroidered thickly about the hem and facings
with blue, scarlet and gold. Full blue trousers belled
out beneath. Upon his feet were curly toed slippers of
gold-embroidered scarlet. These matched the bandage
which wrapped many times around his head. This
bandage, called a turban, was in its turn bedecked with
a brooch of blue jewels set in gold in the shape of a
flower and from this sprouted three white feathers, so
that he looked tall and stately. Upon his face was the
tender smile, though it seemed to me weary, and in his
hand a silk-wrapped parcel.

"My Lord!" I cried, running up to him and then
stopping, uncertain as to whether I was expected to
take his coat, bow, embrace him, or make some other
obeisance. I knew what my people did, but I was
unfamiliar with the ways of the rich and powerful in this
land, and even my lenient husband might take offense
if I behaved improperly. He, however, solved my dilemma.

"Beloved," he sighed, opening his arms and folding me therein.

"Where were you?" I asked, and from the hard look with which he favored me gathered that my perfectly reasonable question was not permissible. I tried to cover it up, "I mean, if you were herding, is it not my duty to relieve you and to bring you lunch at midday or—or does the demon do that?"

The hardness fled from his countenance and his brown eyes melted with sympathy. "But, darling, you fretted for me. You must not. My business often takes me away unexpectedly, but I am well-provided for when away from your side. See you here, I've brought you a gift." He extended the parcel of yellow silk. I unknotted it, and a pendant of gold dangling one of the blue-green stones tumbled into my hand. Aman tenderly placed it around my neck saying, "Ah, how well it suits you. I see you found the bracelet. Are you pleased?"

"I am and I thank you but—"

"What do you fancy for dinner tonight? I had in mind partridges roasted with honey and almonds and perhaps a sherbet of pomegranate and rice with dates."

And so this night passed as pleasurably as the first had, with the difference that Aman, once refreshed by his meal, grew loquacious, and began to tell me more of the city and its people. Some of this talk was entertaining, and some seemed simply an unburdening of his mind, for he was in a rage about the conditions under which the new Emir forced the city's poor—Aman's old friends— to dwell. The royal guards had become the scourge of the common people, whose homes they looted at will. Nor did the armsmen scruple to carry off women, assault holy persons, or rob the cups of beggars. The Emir, save for enriching himself, paid no attention to affairs of government but was concerned only with accumulating objects of magic, beautiful women—even those betrothed to others (Aman waxed especially indignant over that.)—and the wealth rightfully belonging to old and respected families who had served the former

King well for generations. Aman's own father, he told me, had been an adventurer in the service of the King, and had won a measure of fortune and prestige. This modest legacy was left for Aman when his father died, to be his when he reached manhood. But when the King conquered Sindupore, he found it necessary to settle the capital in the still-troubled heart of his new domain, leaving the other great cities in the control of various governors. Among these were several like the Emir, seeming chiefly to qualify for their posts by being too untrustworthy or inept to be of use to the King within the new, turmoil-filled frontier. Under these governors, taxes were raised and possessions confiscated until the fortune of Aman's father had been reduced to nothing, and Aman had been forced to labor at the most menial of tasks to support himself, until he found the lamp.

I found this discourse most enlightening, but remembered that my father said that every man who was not governing was likely to feel privately that his lord was unfair at times and I discounted somewhat Aman's discourse because I thought his complaint was quite possibly of such a nature and also because I was preoccupied with my own questions, still unanswered in spite of all of his words. Not that the words were not spoken with what appeared to be deep sincerity. Aman Akbar was at his most appealing, making great effort to relate these matters to me so that I would understand them and think well of him for the manner in which he had elevated himself above his harsh circumstances. And so I did think well of him, for he was most charming, most persuasive, and listening to his soft and throbbing voice was no strain upon my ears. Even so, there was something slippery in the way he told his tale, a hint of evasiveness in the quick darting away of his eye, the sudden change of subject just as I thought of a question to ask. I felt rather as if I were being sold a horse I had not yet seen but was expected to buy just on the weight of the testimony of its owner.

He had been lying on his back, gesturing to the

ceiling, popping a grape into his mouth occasionally, but suddenly rolled over and looked at me closely. "You're very quiet, my darling Rasa," he said.

"I could hardly add to your eloquence, my Lord," I replied. The words came out wryly rather than flatteringly, as I intended.

He let forth an inelegant hoot of laughter and hugged me. "I *have* lectured you somewhat, haven't I? But you are so easy to talk to, as I knew you would be. When I first saw you leap over that campfire to slay that rascal who had one of your comrades pinned down, I said to the djinn, 'That's the girl for me.'"

"When was that, my Lord?" I asked. "Why did I not see you?"

"Because I wasn't actually there, my darling. If I had been, do you think I would have stinted to leap forward and aid you and your noble father and thereby win your regard? But the djinn did not actually take me to the places—place, where I saw you. Instead, he cast the image of the events occurring in your camp upon the waters of one of the garden pools and thereby let me choose you for my bride." Looking deeply into my eyes, he lifted a strand of my hair and curled it between his fingers. "I am so happy that you agreed to come with the djinn, or I would have been obliged to embark on a journey to seek you out and win you in less expeditious ways. Your lands lying so far from my own, we might have both been very old by the time we came to lie here together, but I would have done so, nevertheless. Women of high birth I have seen aplenty, with the djinn's help, and women whose beauty inflames my senses. But none of them moved with the fierce grace of a cornered lioness as you did, nor did such loyalty and courage shine like moonbeams from any other pair of eyes. I knew at once that you would be my friend as well as lover, that you would support and even guide me in all of my dreams and plans."

Perhaps he also knew that I would be so overcome with pleasure at his praise that I wouldn't question him for a while about what those plans and dreams of his were. In any case, we were both too taken up with the spirit of the moment to pursue conversation further and all of my questions slipped my mind for the time being.

One of the more innocuous of these questions was about the wailing that came only at night—more faintly when I was alone than when Aman was with me, but occurring at about the same time. When the wailing came that night, we were very involved in amorous activity, and when I might have asked what the sound was, my mouth was otherwise engaged. Aman completely ignored the noise. His disregard for it convinced me that it was as normal and commonplace an occurrence as the prayer-caller. So I gave it no more thought until the following night. It was fainter then, and farther off, but no less annoying. The self-pitying tone of it seemed to mock me as I once more paced our wedding chamber alone, gnawing on a partridge bone.

I hasten to emphasize that it was Aman's evasive attitude and not fear which prevented me for so long from further investigation. For though he talked more about the stories, customs, and religion of his people, and plagued me for similar information about mine, he never alluded to where he spent every other night and all of his days. If I so much as looked inquisitively at him, he, clever fellow, would ask me to tell him more of my battles against my mother's cousins, and I would grow so engrossed in my own memories and presenting them entertainingly and in such a way as to reinforce his good opinion of me that I again forgot my questions. In this way a week passed, with Aman feasting, talking and dallying with me every other night. When he was present, everything was brighter, more intense, more distinct, even the wailing. When he was away, I wandered aimlessly through the long days, ate sparingly of food I ceased to taste, and wished for a spindle or even a loom to help me pass the time. Nights alone I thought of the nights with him and wondered that even the wailing was less robust when he was gone.

By the end of the week boredom, curiosity, the wailing and the inability to speak what was in my heart and mind to my lord, even while loving him more each night, drove me to desperation. The next night we spent together, I made certain to awaken when he did and followed him.

I lost him almost before he left the palace, for I had to wait until he had left the room to don my own native gown which was not as transparent as those provided in the room of water demons and therefore less likely to attract attention on the streets. This delayed me sufficiently that I was unable to see him in the halls or labyrinths. However, passing the room of water demons, I heard the hissing of steam and water and also singing in my lord's voice more distinguished by lustiness than tunefulness. I hid myself behind a pillar and waited until he emerged, clad now all in crimson, with silver plumes in his turban and a necklace of silver links across his broad chest.

He passed me and entered the library, two doors down on the opposite side of the corridor. The wooden doors to most of the rooms are seldom kept closed, in order that the air may flow more freely throughout the palace and lessen the heat, and so, by repositioning myself near the pillar opposite the room, I could see Aman crossing the room to a shelf. With a touch of his finger he caused the shelf to pivot. Out it swung, betraying an empty space behind it, from which my husband extracted a vessel made of some shining substance, green and cloudy. This bottle he carefully tucked into his sash. Replacing the shelf, he gave the volumes a little pat and strolled jauntily from the room, past the rectangular pool. The animal spritzed a salutory spray of water in his honor and continued spritzing until he had passed. By the time I felt it safe to follow, the animal's mouth was empty, only the glistening rivulets upon its metal hide bearing witness that the beast had come to life momentarily. I quickened my step in case the doors too worked only for Aman Akbar. I would have to be very stealthy to sneak through right behind him without being discovered, but he gave no indication that he had the slightest suspicion he was being followed. So intent was I upon keeping him in sight without tripping or stubbing my toe on something that I paid little attention to my surroundings.

Some will ask why I followed Aman Akbar, despite all I have written of his mysterious disappearances and appearances, of his bland reassurances of safety while declining to discuss his whereabouts. Was I not betraying his trust by doing so? I can only answer that I was not. On the contrary, I was adhering to the very code which engendered in me the loyalty for which he had expressed such admiration. I saw my duty as a wife differently than women of this country are wont to do. For I was trained not as a wife, but as a warrior. My husband was not only my husband, but my lord, my ring-giver, as well. Among women, so often removed, forcibly or otherwise, from their own people, loyalty to the over-lord is hardly advisable, since if one is taken in a raid, bears children to and marries one's captor, one's former overlord will become the enemy of one's children. Therefore, the allegiance of women is directly to their husbands, who in turn represent the family at council. It is an arrangement born of necessity from years of captivity and enslavement. With most women, sworn against their will to men not of their choosing, the duty ends with bearing children, herding, the usual domes-tic sort of thing. But for me, raised to fight for my father who was also my overlord, my duty to my husband included the same services, should he require them. At least, that was how I saw it. If he was still in trouble, and his reluctance to talk about it stemmed from a desire to protect me, I must discover the source of and remedy to his problem. Therefore, I braved the streets of Kharristan for his sake. And also because I was curious—and wanted to sample the wares of the bazaar and possibly have something fresher than leftovers dur-ing the next two-day absence.

First, however, I wished to learn where Aman Akbar spent his days. To this end I followed him through streets just beginning to bustle with people preparing for their day. On the way out, Aman paused at a little room near the gate and pulled from it a rug, which he slung over his shoulder. It looked very incongruous to see such a finely dressed man carrying a burden through streets lit with oil lamps on poles and as yet unilluminated by the first glimmerings of dawn. The first two men I passed gave me hard stares and one deliberately threw the contents of the water basin in which he had been washing himself at my feet, splashing mud onto the hem of my robe. I glared hard at him and debated long enough about the advisability of making him drink the water, mud and all, that I lost sight again of Aman Akbar.

At the next corner I spotted him, his step quickening as he reached a cobbled street leading toward the tower where the singer practiced his craft. Sure enough, before I was able to close the distance between the two of us, the singer began his song and Aman hurried even faster, disappearing into the building attached to the tower.

Several other men also went into the building, and all of these also gave me very hard looks, then turned up their noses and stalked inside, carrying rugs like Aman's. I thought about following, but since I didn't seem to be welcome, and because if anyone made trouble, Aman was sure to discover my presence, I decided to wait for a moment to see what happened. Nothing happened. When the singer ceased his song all was quiet except for one great voice and the mumblings of several others. These were prayers, I realized suddenly. Aman had said the singer was calling the people to prayers and I had followed my husband when he went to pray. He was a very devout man—and from what I had experienced of the character of the other men that morning, the only good-natured man in all of Kharristan. I hoped his gods appreciated him. Very well then, I'd give the market place a look and be on my way to wait dutifully at home until his prayer vigil was completed.

The streets were not silent for long. Suddenly a landslide of people tumbled around me, jostling, elbowing, shouting, and running as the business of the city began. Baskets of melons, trays full of jewelry, big clay pots full of little clay pots, bolts of cloth, racks of copper jars

came out of hiding and lined the street. Bright canopies
unrolled to shade the merchants, and the fragrances of
spices and perfumes mingled with the stench of the
streets. People cried to each other and to their beasts,
donkeys and peculiar-looking hunchbacked beasts with
deceptive smiles on their ugly faces and a predilection
for biting and kicking. These beasts wore woven saddles
with tinkling bells and carried burdens nearly as large
as themselves. A few people stared at me rudely, and
still I could not understand the reason for their hostility,
until I noticed that the women in the marketplace, of
whom there were few, wore cloths over their faces.

Perhaps they were expecting a dust storm? Or
perhaps all of the women of this race were very ugly, so
hid themselves. In which case I did not see why so
many people cast offended eyes at my person. Certainly
among *my* people honest women did not cover their
faces without some special reason.

Besides the merchant women with the cloths over
their faces, small bundles of black draperies darted
about, dodging animals and bargaining with the sellers
of fruits and silks at the tops of their voices. I would
have done the same, for I had come to do so, at least in
part. However, I had forgotten that I had no coin with
which to buy and no wools with which to barter, and short
of selling my bracelet or pendant, which I did not wish
to do, I would be unable to pay for the goods I found so
attractive. Regretfully, I turned away and headed back
the way I came.

Or tried to. My route was altered abruptly by the
changing of the Emir's palace guard. One moment I
was standing between the booths of a purveyor of dates
and almonds and a silk merchant whose bales of
shimmering wares had drawn my eyes as surely as the
sea draws a river to it. The next I was in serious danger
of merging with the paving stones as nearly forty men
on black horses galloped straight through the center of
town, scattering people and produce with jangling
abandon. When the dust cleared, I raised my head and
wiped my eyes and rose from where I was wedged into
a muck-filled corner between wall and street. I ven-

tured forth, looking after the last of the flying hooves, wondering what all that had been about and why none of the other folk seemed to be moving again yet. My ears still rung with the noises of the first procession, and so I heeded not the din of the second until it was almost upon me—the disturbance in the air, more than the clatter of hooves and the jingle of harness caused me to turn and look and flee for my life straight down the street ahead of them, dodging and ducking and racing just ahead of the horses until I was able to fling myself through an arched gate and cower against the wall until the horses thundered past.

This portion of the city, not visible from my window in the palace of Aman Akbar, was not so different from cities I had seen before. The streets were full of refuse and excrement, dried and odoriferous splotches and runnels coating the bricks just below waist level, and sore-bedecked beggars in all states of disrepair contending with sellers of dung-cakes for the attention of passersby not noticeably more prosperous than themselves.

Through this morass I wandered, past the next gate, and the potters who plied their craft nearby, and on to the next. Here I spent a goodly portion of the following hours, overcome with longing for the familiar home I had left as I watched the weavers at their horizontal looms doing the same work I had always hated. Had I had upon me any coins I would have tried to purchase one of the combs they used to beat the new rows of knots back against the already completed pattern. The combs were ornately carved and tinkled with silver and jeweled charms which I felt sure must impart some magical qualities to the rugs in progress.

I tried to strike up a conversation once with one of the youngest, to ask her about the dyes, and if their sheep were like ours, and why they cut and knotted their weft rather than wove it in a long thread as we did, and how they spun. But the girl, after one shy glance up over the top of her veil, ignored me. The others shifted positions, so that their shoulders were to me. They spoke in fast, loud voices to each other, giving me no opportunity to speak to them.

I've since learned that many women go unveiled in the market place, mostly foreign like myself, although a few of the desert tribes scorn to hide their women's features, even in public places, but that day I saw none of those and almost began to wonder if I was as deformed as the looks of my husband's countrymen seemed to imply. Their attitude toward me put a damper on my friendly feelings, and I wandered back toward the gate of beggars, feeling that perhaps after all a day spent in the company of dormant water demons and leftovers from love feasts was preferable to the society of haughty foreigners.

Prayers had been called once more as I stood watching the weavers. The populace again prostrated itself. I felt as though I were in a deserted city haunted only by the wailing ghost in the tower.

The sun was high and hot now. Instead of business continuing as usual, most of the merchants rolled down their canopies, the beggars crouched against their walls, and the craftspeople disappeared within doors to wait for the heat to pass. I, mad stranger, sweltered in my woolen robe. The top of my head burned as if I were carrying a dish of hot coals upon it. Except for the occasional tinkling of bells, a snore here and there, a footstep on a distant street, and the buzzing of the insects flecking the abandoned produce, the city was quiet, until I passed close by another gate.

Thus the brutal tone of the raised voice struck me all the more forcibly. For some reason, my first thought was of Aman Akbar, and that he had encountered danger after all. Perhaps this was because I had just been debating whether I should return to the tower containing the prayer-caller in order to ascertain that my beloved was indeed spending his days piously, or in some other harmless activity. The sound of impending conflict seemed a guarantee that he was not and I hurried toward it, snatching up a handy chunk of stone on my way.

Aman Akbar was not there, but others were, and one of them was clearly in trouble. A burly man wearing the uniform of the armsmen who had all but ground me into the dust was manhandling the first bare-faced woman I had seen all day. Perhaps because she was no great beauty she saw little reason to hide her face, which bore the red imprint of a large hand on the left cheek. Both of these people were turned slightly away from me, and intent upon each other.

"Slave-slut! If you weren't too good before when you belonged to the wine-seller, what makes you think—?"

"I'm no slave now. I'm free, and making a good living without the likes of you—" she spat back. "Leave me alone or I'll curse you such a curse—"

Her threat seemed feeble under the circumstances but the armsman took her seriously. His fingers flew to her eyes and when she tripped backwards against the wall he shoved his hand into her face. She might as well have tried to claw a tree away.

In even the most private quarrel there comes a point where intervention is necessary purely to keep people from doing harm they don't mean to each other in the heat of battle. I hefted my rock, brought it down on his thick head, where it probably wasn't going to kill him, and stepped aside to let him fall. The woman shook her head, gave me a quick penetrating look, which I answered with a modest grin, and hoisted her skirts and trotted away.

As I dropped the rock and walked away from the armsman's inert body, I found I was thinking longingly of the rectangular pool with the spitting metal animal in its middle.

Unfortunately, I had neglected to leave a gate ajar and found myself locked out. This did not please me but there was no help for it, and however little I had used it of late, I possessed the stalking patience of a good hunter. I hunkered down in a shadow so as not to be observed by those who disliked me for my mode of dress, and spent the rest of the day watching for the return of Aman Akbar, so that I might enter after him. If he did not enter, where then would I spend the night? Foolish man, I thought, to live alone, with no guards and no one to attend either of us. What if I had become ill or injured? I was hot, dirty and hungry by the time I saw him approach, a blur of brilliance two streets away. I was preparing a wrath to match that I imagined he might entertain if he learned of my adventure.

Nor was I alone in looking for my beloved, for across the street from the spot I had worn clean with the now-dirty soles of my feet, two others watched: a fellow in a turban striped green and gold, and one in a guardsman's uniform. Now, how long had *they* been there? Though both of them studied the gate to our palace, neither seemed more than mildly curious about me, until Aman Akbar appeared. Then I had a fear that they would reveal me to him, and I stepped into hiding in a shadow. However, when I followed the swaying plume of my beloved's headdress inside, and the magic servant closed the door behind us and I glanced back once, the guardsman smirked at me and the man in the striped turban rubbed his knife-pointed beard.

The curiousness of the presence of those men and their reactions to my lord and myself was presently wiped away by the curiousness of the actions of my lord himself. For he did not, as I expected, proceed through the garden, past the rectangular pool and to the room of water demons, but instead walked to a far wall, and tugged upon a length of trailing fuchsia, whereupon the wall opened and closed behind him.

After a long enough time that he was not likely to hear my footsteps and a short enough time that I was not likely to lose sight of him, I followed, yanked upon the vine myself, and the wall opened again. On the other side was a garden similar to the one in which I had stood, except that the pool was circular and contained another sort of metal animal and the flowers were all different shades of red, crimson, scarlet and pink. I went after him, through similar carved pillars, under similar vaulted arches, the journey confusingly ending as he stepped into the room of the water demons, with steam hissing, tub swirling, and perfumed jets spurting even as they had been when first I beheld them. I saw all of this through the door, which he was careless about closing. I was aided, now that the light of the day was dimming, by two solicitously bobbing oil lamps, hovering near the door, waiting for him to finish. By their light I saw after a time that the room was not the same as the one to which I was accustomed, for the tiles were gold and blue, rather than rose-colored marble, and the tub was of a different conformation, and the little alcove for keeping clothing was in a different location. The man, however, was the same handsome, honey-skinned Aman Akbar and at that I wondered exceedingly.

This part of the house was but in a few details a replica of that part in which I was housed. Soon the aromas of roasted mutton and saffron rice told me that the activities here might be similar to those in my own abode. As Aman emerged from this second room of water demons and I ducked from pillar to pillar pursuing him, I was nearly knocked down by the trays of food wafting in his wake into a room whose door was open and across which a curtain of jeweled beads shimmered. As my husband approached the door, a shapely and supple hand which seemed carved of black marble parted the beaded strings and took him by the arm, pulling him within, leaving the trays of food to follow alone.

Alas! *All* activities were the same. The beaded curtain was not entirely able to conceal that Aman dealt with the owner of the ebony arm even as he had dealt with me on other nights. I tried to decide whether to rush upon them and kill them both with my bare hands, a sad alternative even had it seemed plausible, or to demand an explanation, which seemed shameful. Or perhaps I would simply slink away and confront him tomorrow—for of course this was where he spent the nights out of my company. Of all possibilities this last was the most impossible. Thus torn between going or staying, I was lingering by the curtain when I heard the wailing.

It seemed more edifying to investigate the eerie

noise that had been haunting me since my first night in the palace than to listen to the more earthly noises of whose origin I was all too sure emanating from the room before me. No light bobbed forward to assist me. The magic controlling the palace was well aware of its master and did not extend itself to accommodate others unbidden. So I groped back down the line of pillars alone, until I came once more to the garden, and there, pacing back and forth by the pool, was a black-clad figure, darker than the night surrounding her, her skirts swishing and bracelets clinking as she moved, and all the while the wails emitting from her proclaiming her kinship to wolves.

I could see her feet, but still I was not sure that she was a natural person, and not a ghost or a demoness of some sort. Having made an unfortunate error with the djinn, I was cautious in this regard. I hid and watched, squatting on my heels in the concealment of pillars and night shadows as the woman swept about like a crow with broken wings. I almost decided she was indeed supernatural, for the power of those lungs to keep wailing was so extraordinary to my weary mind it seemed beyond human ability to sustain such a racket.

But about this too I was disillusioned, for I heard the shushing of soft footsteps behind me, and shifted my gaze to see Aman Akbar, bobbing lamps preceding him. He was barelegged and bareheaded, clad in a hastily tied robe. His expression was pained but neither frightened nor angry. At his approach the wailing stopped, as did the pacing. The black-garbed figure waited for him to reach her, whereupon she embraced him with a certain injured chilliness, visible in the stiffness of her shoulders, the angle of her head and elbows where the wide sleeves slid above them.

Then as if seeing him had destroyed her, the woman sank to the gound in a black heap and sobbed. With weary patience, he knelt beside her.

"Mother, this has got to stop. Every night you disturb my rest. Every night you do without the sleep you need to plague me like this. What ails you? Won't you tell me? Are you ill?" All of this he asked as if he knew the answer and dreaded it.

"Ill?" she spat derisively. "Not ill. Sick rather, sick to my stomach when I think of my son who was the light of his father's eye ignoring his own beautiful bride to languish in the embrace of unclean and unbelieving foreign harlots."

"Mother, we've been through all this before. I tried to find Hyaganoosh but she has moved. She has a better situation in life now and is not interested in the contract you made when we were children. What would you have me do? Carry her off against her will? I like these women—you would too if you gave them a chance. Amollia is the soul of sweetness and is very good with animals—"

"That wild beast of hers nearly took my eyes the first night she was here!"

"It hasn't bothered you since though, has it? She has it under control, and she loves it, and I won't make her part from it. And I'm sure you'd find Rasa a great help if you'd only consent to meet her. She and Amollia are both perfectly nice girls even if they're not relatives. They're ladies in their own lands and better born than you or I or Hyaganoosh for that matter—"

"Don't you dare talk against your poor cousin! The things that child has had to endure while waiting for you to find a station in life so you could do your duty by her! No wonder she was enticed away by the Emir! Why, her mother would—"

"Her mother is with God and her father also," Aman Akbar said with pious reproof equal to his mother's. "All of this was written long ago, so I fail to see why you work yourself into such a frenzy. Hyaganoosh is in a place where she may gain high station and for my part, I have acquired wives who among their own people were born to even higher station—"

"Then they should have *stayed* among their own people," the mother snapped. "Hyaganoosh is the daughter of your father's own brother and has a face like the full moon and she deserves to marry her cousin, the richest man in Kharristan—"

"I know, I know. But you forget that her cousin is not the richest man in Kharristan. He is second to the Emir, to whom he pays exorbitant taxes and owes allegiance and in whose graces he holds a negligible position since tricking the bottle of the djinn out from under his Eminence's nose. I have the bottle and the brides of my choice and the Emir and Hyaganoosh have each other—"

"*Aiyee!* To think I raised a son who would sell his own true love for riches and an uncouth ifrit who doesn't even know how to run a household properly!" And she wailed even louder and said a lewd expression neither easily nor graciously translatable.

"Furthermore," she said, "it is unworthy of you to say that Hyaganoosh is with the Emir willingly, for I have heard among my women friends that she is most unhappy, and was coerced by him. *I* was told she was faithful to the troth you two plighted, but her faithfulness availed her not and she was carried away by force—"

"And fails to enjoy the luxuries and fine dresses he lavishes upon her? Pah! Did it occur to you that your women friends would hardly tell you otherwise of this relative of my father's you dote upon, especially if it will add more fuel to the disapproval with which you favor your poor abused son these days? I thought you would like being rich, mother. I only got the genie for your sake." His voice dropped to a caressing murmur and I saw him stroke her cheek. "It pained me so to see you carrying those heavy piles of dung patties out to sell—"

"It gave *me* something to do," she replied, jerking her face back, regretting it immediately, and reaching back out to touch him. But it was his turn to repulse her and he rose now.

"Go back to her!" the old woman screamed, and black eyes flashed fiercely for a moment from beneath the black draperies and I saw a nose not unlike my own and a bony, determined chin rise to face the retreating back of Aman. "Go back to your foreign tart! Abandon your family! Shame your cousin! Pour grief upon your old mother's heart! It is all I deserve. I'm only a poor

honest woman—not an exalted high prince who can sit
around in the bazaar and talk all day and debase myself
with sinful pleasures by night—"

"Goodnight, mother," Aman said softly, and I saw
something glitter against his cheek as he passed by my
hiding place. The old woman continued to rant and wail
long after he had disappeared.

# Chapter
# 3

The heat awoke me the next
day, beating in through the latticed window as if in a
serious attempt to burn through the delicate strips of
wood separating the diamond shapes. The street noise
was almost as appalling as the heat, and to my chagrin I
found that the food left from the feast two nights ago
was all but inedible. I felt much better when I had
thrown an orange across the room and watched it
splatter against the carving of stylized flowers decorat-
ing the wall. As if in remonstrance, the prayer-caller
began wailing noon prayers. The realization that I had
compensated for a sleepless night by dozing the morning away did nothing to improve my mood.

My mind felt as rumpled as my bed and my face
was swollen with tears and sleep. I still felt like applying the nearest blunt object to all within this confusing
household but was also aware that in doing so I was no
doubt sealing my own doom. What galled me most, I
suppose, was that in selling myself into this arrangement,
I had inadvertently fallen into domestic problems as
painful as those I had sought to avoid by evading my
mother's relatives. The gods do not like to have their
plans thwarted, I suppose.

My husband now occupied the place formerly held
by my father and chief: His will was law. But I didn't

care for those laws—they went against me, they confused and angered me. Furthermore, he had lied. No leader should lie to his people and no husband to his wife. Maybe he'd try to beat me (though I doubted it), but I'd face him with his lies. Thus decided, I stomped with satisfying ferocity down the corridor, picked up a fresh gown in the room of water demons (all but *daring* them to rise up and fight me) and stomped out to the pool, stripping off my new clothing and flinging it onto a pile with the old. I paddled around the rectangular pool on my hands and knees, letting the lukewarm water refresh me as best it could.

The first intimation I had that something new prowled my familiar garden was the growling slightly to the left and above my right ear. I elbowed myself back slightly and risked a look up. A round, bewhiskered face with malice in its golden eyes, a curving cat's grin not quite concealing fearsome fangs regarded me from the raised edge of the pool. Just past its sleekly muscular shoulder, I beheld a space in the garden wall where no space ordinarily was—the doorway to my rival's quarters. What had the black-clad hag said about a beast? If this was the beast, I began to think more kindly of her judgment, for I cared for its presence in my household no more than she.

The cat blinked, wiggled its hindquarters and jerked its tail twice. I backed toward the metal animal in the middle of my pool. We stayed thus for a time, eyes locked, the cat's acquiring a somewhat mournful expression at my inexplicable reluctance to come out of the water, which it plainly shunned, and allow myself to be devoured.

The sun was very hot indeed and I could feel my hide blister through the water. My face was moist with my own perspiration and I rinsed it briefly, not wanting to take my eyes from the predator. The cat settled onto its front feet and watched with a certain detached interest.

Someone knocked timidly upon the front gate, and the cat's head snapped up. The knock was followed by other, equally timid knocks, and by smothered laughter, after which someone grew bold enough to knock loudly. Before I had time to wonder who was there, the black-clad figure of the night before, a small spare woman with a nose not unlike my own, rushed through the now not-so-secret entrance to the adjoining garden. I cringed deeper into the water and hoped the cat, now out of sight, had gone to chase the newcomers or, better yet, had escaped through the front gate while it was open. A quick peek over the edge revealed that the damned creature instead was curled atop my clean robe, kneading its rapier claws and growling to itself in a pleased fashion.

Meanwhile, Aman's mother gathered the women inside the garden and divested them of their outer garments. Beneath their cloaks they wore bright dresses of the same loose cut and a great deal of clanking jewelry. Most of them were older, but a few younger women and children were among them.

Leaving only enough of my head exposed that I could see and hear, I waited as the women strolled past. They exclaimed over the flowers and the fine artistic detail of the tiles and carvings, and greeted each other.

"So, Um Aman, how are you doing?"

"Well, Naima, thanks be to God. And you?"

"Well, also, God be praised. And your son?"

"He is also well, thanks be to God."

"And your son's ifrit?" This last was a departure from the normal inquiries.

"He is also well, in the manner of devils and plagues, and has cursed me with other devils. But I won't discuss that now." She looked around her as if sensing my presence and ushered her friends through the door, saying, "May God preserve us all."

A woman clad in unevenly dyed crimson stopped and placed her hand on Um Aman's arm. "God has done well enough by us, Samira, but he has given you wealth and a certain position to maintain. Are you sure our visit will cause you no trouble? Your son is a rich man now. He—"

"My son is a fool," Um Aman spat, then, evidently

repenting her forthrightness, said more gently, "But not such a fool as to deny his mother the comfort of the friends of her girlhood. Our home is yours. You honor us both with your presence. Forgive me, Khadija, all of you. Aman is a good son. A good provider."

One of the women giggled. "I don't like to be critical, Samira, but if he took his other duties as seriously as he does providing for you...."

"You're right, of course. Otherwise I would not have sent for you seeking your advice."

"What are friends for if not to support a poor widowed sister in time of need?" another guest said sympathetically, to be interrupted by an impish and rather breathless laugh.

"Has he brought home another one yet, Samira?"

The group passed through the garden wall and from my sight.

Which returned me to my original dilemma of escaping the cat. Except that the cat was no longer on my clothing. From behind me a languid voice said laughingly, "If you plan to stay in there until we're the same color, you'll be there a long time, my friend. I'd forget it, if I were you. Aman Akbar likes variety in his love life."

I swirled around in the water, stubbing my toe against the metal animal, and the same ebony hand I had seen the night before reached down to assist me.

Even to those accustomed to the sight of black women—which I was not—Amollia is striking in both beauty and bearing. She is tall and straight as one of the pillars supporting the palace and black as a shadow on a starry night. She and her cat carry their heads with similarly proud and half-amused bearing. Her eyes seem to say she has seen everything, has been neither impressed nor disappointed by it, and is looking forward to seeing more. That day she was wrapped with a cloth the color of curry, heavily embroidered with gold and wore her own weight in jewelry on her neck, arms, ankles and ears. Her hair was short and curled like the fleece of a black lamb.

Ignoring her hand, I stood, snatched up my clothing,

pulled my robe over my head and stepped across the edge of the pool. The cat made no move to stop me.

"Who are you?" I demanded. "What are you doing in my husband's house?"

"I might ask you the same thing," she said, the tips of her teeth showing dazzlingly white against the dark plum color of her lips. "But that would only complicate matters unnecessarily. I am Amollia Melee, daughter of the Great Elephant of the Swazee, wife to Aman Akbar. I take it that you are my co-wife. Welcome, sister."

And she opened her arms to embrace me. I failed to understand her attitude. I didn't feel in the least like embracing her.

My lack of enthusiasm did not deter her. "Have you eaten?" she asked. "Wait—let me guess. Leftover kumquats and cold rice, right? I've made do with the same fare on the nights he spends with you. It's possible he just forgets about everything but what he's doing at the time, or it may be his strange idea of economy. He's frugal in his way, is Aman. Must get it from his mother, I suppose. *She*, however—" she stopped and gave a brief, dainty lick combined with a sidelong look at me. "I suppose you *are* interested in something fresh, hot, and tasty to eat, are you not?"

I nodded.

"Aman says you are a warrior. Are you very brave?" A demon probably not too distant a relative from the djinn played in her eyes.

I shrugged and watched her warily.

"Very well. Come along. We'll tackle the lioness unarmed. She has a mean mouth but she feeds it well. Perhaps she can be shamed into feeding ours too."

Curiosity warred with pride and won out. "How came you to know so much about this household?" I asked.

"About the old one and about you? Is that what you mean? Why, Aman told me, of course." And did not tell me. That stung like the bite of an enemy's arrow. "He introduced me to the old woman and—ah—that's why he didn't introduce *you* to her. She was not what you would call ready to welcome me into the bosom of the family. As for you, Aman discussed the matter with me before deciding to bring you here."

"He did?"

"Assuredly. I told him I didn't want to have to put up with that cranky old woman and this great big house all by myself. Besides, what would people think, a man of his stature having just one wife? What if he wishes to entertain somewhere outside the palace? With no slaves or servants in our employ, who would help me with the work? And anyway—" she sighed and looked at me with a pleased and even fond expression "—I am the one hundred and thirty-fifth daughter of the Great Elephant and used to having all of my sisters and all of my mothers around me. With Aman gone during the day and no one but my leopard Kalimba for company, that old woman drives me mad with her silence. I am most glad to have you here. I would have sought you out sooner, but Aman said he felt it would be best for you two to get to know one another first, and for you to grow accustomed to your new surroundings before you met me . . . particularly before you met his mother. But I think he would have prolonged the time of dealing with us separately as long as possible."

"Why?" I asked, feeling distinctly disoriented all over again.

"Because men don't like for the women to compare stories, of course. One at a time, they stand a chance of cajoling or browbeating us into letting them have their way in all things, but when we join together, there's very little in which they dare oppose us. Still, Aman is a good man, a kind husband. And he has *that* mother to contend with, so we must be extra loving and patient with him. If we do not handle her properly, she will be the scourge of our lives. So, if you're quite ready?" And she linked her arm with my reluctant one and together we crossed my garden and hers, through another gate into yet a third garden where the women were assembled by a charcoal brazier from which emanated succulent smells.

I knew open warfare already from my life among

my own people. From Amollia I learned subterfuge. A common foe makes allies of the most unlikely persons.

As we neared the group, Amollia's noble stride shortened to a demure shuffle and her proud chin bent into her neck, so that she gazed humbly at the ground. I followed her example and together we stood with seeming timidity on the outskirts of the group.

One of the women tittered behind her hand and Um Aman glared in our direction. A benefit of casting one's eyes downward is that one thus deflects the full impact of such a glare.

Perhaps Um Aman realized this, for she said, "These strange-looking creatures are the very harlots my son has brought as concubines into the home he built for my old age."

"I understand from my Faisal that Aman claims to have two foreign *wives*, Samira," said the eldest among them—the one our revered mother-in-law had addressed as Khadija.

"Have you been invited to the wedding, you who are my oldest friend?" Um Aman replied bitterly.

A number of children clung to the skirts of the behind-the-hand titterer, an understandably weary-looking young woman. A girl of perhaps four years with a great quantity of the contents of her nose smeared across her cheek said, "Mama, why are those ladies so *ugly*?"

"Hush, child, or they'll put the evil eye on you," her mother whispered, enveloping the child in her tattered and dirty skirts, effectively cleaning the face and shutting it up at the same time.

"It's true though," another of the younger women observed critically. "They are ugly. Um Aman, I'm surprised that a man like Aman Akbar has no better taste than to marry a woman so dark and one with a nose like that!"

Um Aman immediately turned on her. "And where did you learn so much of taste? My Aman has most splendid taste—look at this palace! I've heard the former King's favorite wife was very dark, and if you ask me, the nose on that washed-out strumpet is her best feature. Aman says they're both princesses too. Better born than any of us." Though she said this with rather perverse pride, she stabbed us with another glare. "They'd better not give themselves airs around me, though. I won't have it."

"They don't say much, do they?" the third of the younger women, a plump-cheeked and saucy sort, remarked. "Do they talk at all?"

At this a rather plain woman whose long braided hair was liberally streaked with gray looked up from her embroidery. High in one cheek a dimple winked encouragingly as she smiled directly at us. "Would you talk, Miriam, with everyone making such rude comments about you? Is this how we repay Samira's hospitality, insulting her son's new wives? Poor things, so far from their homes. Their mothers must miss them terribly." She turned to Um Aman and said gravely, "It doesn't seem to me that they're giving themselves airs, Samira. Quite the contrary. They seem very modest and shy and quite cowed. People who don't know you often fail to realize what a kind heart you have, my dear." She smiled at us again and Amollia modestly, shyly, and in a cowed manner licked her lips and allowed the most delicate droplet of drool to form at the corner of her mouth. "They're hungry too," our defender told Um Aman.

Um Aman's gaze, formerly fierce, dropped abruptly and she leaned across to the platter containing the couscous. With a sharp straightening of her elbow, she proffered it without looking at us.

Thus we partook of hot food rather than leftovers and met those women with whom Um Aman shared her problems. The only other interesting fact about the encounter was that Um Aman kept referring to us throughout as Aman Akbar's concubines and insisted that he had no wives until he had taken his cousin to wife.

The party ended just before mid-afternoon prayers. By that time everyone had had an opportunity to discuss other ungrateful children with whom they were acquainted, and Um Aman seemed to feel much better. Amollia rose to her feet and with a soft jingle of jeweled limbs headed for the gate leading back to her garden. I followed quickly. Aman Akbar could be coming home any time now. And tonight if he followed his previous pattern he would be looking to stay with me.

Amollia walked straight through her own garden and trailed the departing visitors into mine.

"Pardon my intrusion, sister-wife," she said pleasantly. "But I thought I would at least greet our husband with you this evening. He should know now that we two are acquainted. I think we should also speak to him about having the magic feasts shared between us so that one of us need not make do with leftovers when he lies with the other." She smiled. "This is one advantage of having co-wives. Together we may perhaps exert more influence over our husband than either of us might do individually."

Aman Akbar, however, had his own ideas about his family banding together. Amollia and I posed companionably, sitting side by side on the edge of the fountain, pretending not to notice when the metal beast started spouting as our husband entered the garden. The cat spread across Amollia's feet, kneading its claws in and out while she told me some of the jokes the minstrels from neighboring kingdoms told of her father, the Great Elephant. Her former home sounded merry and exciting compared to mine and I found I laughed more often than I wanted to and began to wonder why Aman Akbar had summoned me to wife when he already had such an amusing creature on the premises.

Aman entered the garden and greeted us, taking one of each of our hands in each of his and kissing them in turn before seating himself on Amollia's far side. He twinkled uncertainly at us. "So," he said. "So."

"Even so, husband," Amollia smiled. "Rasa and I have been discussing our household and thought we would greet you together this night. How has your day gone?"

"Well, thanks be to God," he said, taking refuge in the formula. "And yours?"

"Well, indeed. We joined your honored mother

and her friends in her garden this afternoon and profited much from her wisdom."

"You did?" He tried to sound pleased and incredulous at once but the incredulity had a decided edge over the pleasure.

"Indeed," I said. "She is a very fine cook, your mother." I thought I was being pleasant too by failing to mention that she was also a very disagreeable woman, but the twinkle in our husband's eyes was extinguished in two rapid blinks.

"Good," he said. "Good. I'm glad you're all getting on so well."

"As a matter of fact, husband, Rasa and I were thinking that perhaps if it would not tax the magic of your bottle too much, we would like to be able to share our dinners with you so that—"

He blinked once more and smiled his most dazzlingly tender smile. "What a wonderful idea, my clever darling. We shall all eat together. Shall we sup here in the garden? Afterward, I think the djinn shall entertain us with a new surprise I've been considering."

We had music that night, some of the thin-noted throbbing love songs of which Aman was so fond, and a song or two from Amollia's homeland, which caused her to leap to her feet and dance a sinuous dance that made my jaw ache with the wish to remind her that tonight was supposed to be mine and that we were in my garden. But though Aman looked as if he were enjoying himself and he talked at great length about a funny fellow who had accosted him on his way to prayers, he remained distant. We ate the almond-stuffed lamb and rice and all of the standard sweets without saying too much. When Amollia attempted playfulness with grapes, our lord smilingly declined and chewed his, skins and all.

When he had finished he wiped his hands on a towel with pile thick as a beaver's pelt and pulled from his sash the bottle I had seen him with previously.

Closer up the bottle looked more disreputable than ever, just a scratched, discolored old bit of crockery, dust still smeared upon it in places and dirt caked for all time into its dings. Stuck in the mouth of it was a broad bit of stuff that seemed like wood or bark of some sort and on top of that was a melted-looking seal of greenish, tarnished silver which had endured some attempts to polish it. Dangling from this seal was a bit of broken chain.

Aman's long fingers stroked the chain for a moment.

Amollia laid her hand upon his arm and said solicitously, "You must let me repair that for you, beloved, or you might lose the top sometime."

He looked as if he would do so only if he had been five years dead and said, "You are so thoughtful, dear one."

And he pulled the cork out of the bottle, nearly choking us all on the cloud of acrid smoke that boiled from it.

The smoke set to work arranging itself and solidified into the form of the djinn. The djinn straightened his turban and tugged at the hems of the two sides of his vest and said, "What is it now, noble master? I thought not that thou wouldst spend thy last wish so soon but perhaps these women tax thy beneficence beyond measure. Is it thy pleasure that I return them whence they came?"

"Not at all, O djinn," Aman replied. "I wish you to fetch forth that last candidate you showed me before I decided to wait."

"Dost thou refer to that princess from the Central Empire? Master, I think there is a thing thou shouldst know concerning that one."

"I know only that she has touched me most deeply," Aman Akbar said as passionately as he had ever said similar words to me. "And for my final wish I would have her come and be my loyal and loving bride, an ornament to my home and the friend of my bosom." And he clapped his hands and the djinn's feet once more solidified into a rug upon which he sat, folding his arms grimly as he flew away.

Aman Akbar turned and looked meaningfully at us. Amollia carefully knelt beside her cat and scratched its ears, avoiding looking at either of us. I wondered which of them to kill first. He for taking offense and retaliating in such an underhanded way or she for provoking the situation at which he apparently took offense? I did not understand these people. Nor did I understand myself at this time. What did I care if the silly man was offended when his own actions quite naturally caught up with him? Why should I even want such a man to share my bed? Was I not better off without him? Surely, somehow, I could manage to find my way back to my own land, to my father's camp. But I found I didn't want to. It was rather crowded here for my taste, true, but no more crowded than in my father's camp or that of his enemies. Aman bewildered me, but I had become most attached to him and wasn't about to give him up easily.

He stood up suddenly to greet the djinn, who sailed over the well on a carpet burdened with a small black-haired figure in an embroidered blue silk jacket and white trousers, a tidy roll of belongings tied to her back. Surely the djinn had been gone no longer than it took to peel an orange and just as surely our trip from my home to Kharristan had taken most of a day. Again, I did not understand, but at least the djinn, unlike his master, was magic and was supposed to be beyond my understanding.

The girl leapt off the carpet while it was still at the level of the shoulders of the metal animal in the pool and flattened herself in front of Aman Akbar, her hair fanning prettily across her back and the tiles.

Aman Akbar looked triumphantly from Amollia to me and touched her lightly on the head. "Come, my dear, rise up and tell us who you are." He confronted the ifrit, whose middle was bent in a bow as if awaiting applause. "I assume she can understand me."

"Dost thou never learn, O master?" the djinn sighed. And added, in a resigned tone, "She can."

"Indeed I can, O master, and let me assure you your every word will be to me a sacred command." She scrambled into a kneeling position and regarded him with tilted eyes both large and shining set into a round-cheeked face with a distressingly tiny nose and a pointed chin. Above either ear was a large pink flower with many petals.

"There now, my darling, you are a princess and while your humility is becoming it is quite unnecessary with one who loves you even as he loves his own life and two women who will cherish you as a dear sister and who will help you in every possible way."

"I am a wha—? Oh, yes, so I am." She smiled at him. "But actually, my people aren't that formal. 'Princess' sounds so stilted, don't you think? My lord and master could certainly call me by my given name, which in your tongue means Aster. And my revered sisters need not use my title. Lady Aster is respectful enough—I'm sure the difference in our stations is moderate."

Aman Akbar beamed at her. "As gracious as she is lovely. My dear, I'm sure you must be exhausted from your long journey. Let me return my servant to his bottle and I'll escort you to your quarters."

"May I remind thee that although my services as already delivered remain thine, great one, my obligation to thee is now fulfilled and thou must needs leave me to rest in my bottle?" The djinn looked highly pleased about this.

Aman Akbar looked only mildly vexed, but replaced the stopper in the bottle with alacrity once the djinn had smoked himself back inside.

"And now, dear ladies, I'm sure you two have much to talk about now that you're such good friends and won't mind if Aster and I repair to our marital chamber."

"Not at all, O husband," Amollia said with a voice softly docile and even affectionate. And to Aster she added, "Little sister, may you find all to your liking. If you have any questions or problems, please feel free to avail yourself of our assistance."

I thought Amollia would do well to speak for herself. I also wanted to remark that Lady Aster shouldn't mind a little noise in the night. That it would only be the mother of her new husband lamenting her son's knuckle-headed behavior. In fact, I had half a mind to join the old hag in her nightly session. Instead, Amollia showed me the darts with which her people used to hunt and we played a game with them until the call to morning prayers.

Aster's quarters were to the left side of my own, while Amollia's were to the right. My self-appointed friend returned to her own empty bed as the wailing of Um Aman was replaced by the wailing of the morning prayer-caller, leaving me to try to bear the heat alone. And to wonder why my lord should have acted as if he had been betrayed when indeed I was the one who had been misled.

I yearned to speak with him when he emerged from Aster's garden into my own, and I stayed beside the pool waiting. Yet he did not come and I began to wonder if Aster's rooms contained a separate exit to the streets.

I had a poor idea of the layout of the palace. Buildings larger than a good-sized tent were too vast for my taste, and the succession of rooms seemed an unnecessary labyrinth. But when prayers came and went with no sign of Aman Akbar I became worried. Was this new one then so skilled in love as to separate our husband from his devotions to his god? If so, how long was it until he cast me out? If he came that night to my section of the palace, I would be reassured. Meanwhile, I did not eat or sleep but sat beside the fountain enduring the heat of the day, letting the flower scents soothe me and the light breeze cool my fevered mind.

The face peering over the top of the wall appeared sometime around midday, when most of the people of the city took their rest. I had been breaking off blossoms from the garden and floating them in the pool to amuse myself when I heard a faint scrabbling noise. Looking around and up, I barely managed to glimpse a quick succession of knife-pointed beard, wide-open mouth, precisely trimmed mustache, beakish nose, pocked cheeks, popped eyes, thick brows bowed into hoof tracks of surprise, and green-and-gold striped turban before the apparition was gone.

I remembered the face. But to whom it belonged or what its purpose could be in spying on me, I could not guess. I rose and ran to the gate to call out. The gate was locked, however, and though I pried and pounded and prodded I could not find a way of forcing it. When I turned from it yet another apparition faced me, the black-clad form of Um Aman.

She flung herself between me and the door as if she were afraid I was going to injure the wood.

"What are you trying to do now, foreigner? Disgrace my son again?"

"I? Disgrace your son? Old mother, it seems to me it's the other way around." She glared at me but her glare seemed to lack some of its earlier conviction and I thought about asking her why, if she didn't like the way her son behaved, she had reared him to have such odd ideas about how to run his home. Instead, I asked, "Have you a friend of the family with a face like a rockslide, a pointed beard and a striped turban? One who is fond of entering over the wall?"

She narrowed her eyes suspiciously. "Of course not. Only a scoundrel would climb another man's harem walls. Who is this man, strumpet? Your secret lover?"

"Certainly," I spat. "And I was telling you about him because I wanted to introduce him to the rest of the family. Old woman, I have tried to honor you for the sake of my husband but you are not a sensible person. I tell you, I do not know who this man is but I wonder at his intentions toward my husband. I saw him watching this house two days ago when I—"

"When you what, girl? How came you to gaze upon another man?"

I shrugged, seeing from her angry gaze that a lie was in order. "I saw him from my window."

"Did he see you? Unveiled?" The woman made much of the last word, hissing it with a sharp intake of breath that made it sound as horrible as "decapitated" or "impaled."

"I don't think so," I said. "What does it matter?

Honest women of my people don't need to hide their faces."

"You may not have noticed, harlot, but you are no longer among your people. As long as you are among mine, and God grant that will not be long and that my son soon discovers your true nature and sells you to the slavers for such little value as he can gain from your worthless person, you will not go out unchaperoned and will cover yourself with a respectable abayah as is required of any decent wife." And she pulled her cloak over her head and her veil across her face so that she again resembled a bale of black laundry with eyes.

"I thought you said I'm a concubine," I reminded her. With a contemptuous swirl of black draperies she departed and I once more had to amuse myself.

I whiled away the hours imagining tortures I could subject the lot of them to. I belatedly included Amollia, toward whom I had started to entertain a sneaking fondness, when she failed to appear to keep me company even as morning became afternoon and afternoon fled with evening upon its heels. How could she, having caused me to find disfavor with my lord, have the temerity to sleep when I needed to speak to her? Nor could I go wake her without risking missing Aman if he left his new paramour's arms long enough to perform the rituals he had never, dammit, neglected for my sake.

Our conversation with him had, as it developed, had more effects than the addition of Aster to our number. When time came for the evening meal and I reached for a last smear of lamb grease left among a few kernels of rice on one of the platters, the platter suddenly whisked itself away and three other, smaller ones appeared, each with a meal-sized portion of seasoned duck, nutted rice, and assorted fruits. This was accompanied by a cool brass jug sweating with a refreshing condensation of sweet moisture and filled with a delicious drink far surpassing the fountain water I had been drinking throughout the day.

My pleasure in this repast was not great, however, for Aman did not appear with the sustenance, and from this I gleaned that he was passing a second night in the arms of his new love. I grieved. The sun sent a glory of vermillion streamers across the sky, pinking the distant domes. The fountain tinkled, the breeze blew and I patted my full belly and settled down beside the fountain in the lush grass. Perhaps he'd come out for a stroll. But I doubted it. From sheer exhaustion I drifted into sleep.

The grass stirred against my cheek and tickled my nose and I woke, seeing at first only the blur of movement, and then, in the starlight, the legs and curl-toed slippers responsible for the movement. The fountain behind me spurted more energetically than had been its wont all day, with Aman Akbar now near rather than merely in the immediate vicinity. As he turned down the path to the outer gate, I rose and followed him—quiet, if I do say so myself, as Amollia's cat.

Obviously he did not wish to attract notice. No less strange than his behavior, however, was the unusual silence in the night. It seemed unfair. Um Aman had wailed nearby when Aman was making love to me, and in Amollia's courtyard when Aman was with her. Why had she not plagued him with Aster as well? Perhaps she had finally strained her stringy old throat. That thought provided me with at least some satisfaction.

My satisfaction diminished and I suspected she might have had the last word after all when I saw Aman creep out the gate. There was what looked like a gaping black hole or a great shadow with no object to cast it in the middle of the wall beside the gate. A last quick look over his shoulder from Aman caused me to brush against this shadow, and discover the substance of it, which was cloth. The cloth of the same black draperies about which I had earlier been admonished. I swept up an armful of them and squeezed through the closing gate as Aman's back retreated down the street, rounding the corner beyond our palace wall.

Um Aman's stature increased considerably in my eyes as I struggled to don the disguise afforded by the draperies while attempting to walk and keep an eye on my husband at the same time. The veil does not hook on either side of the head covering but is rather a portion of the head covering itself and must either be held in place with one's hand (I tried, to no avail, to tuck it over my ear, causing the whole business to bare my head.) or secured with one's chin.

I was fortunate, in this venture, that Aman Akbar, a rich man who could well afford a fine stable of steeds, was not partial to conducting his errands on horseback. Perhaps he did not know how, being a man from humble origins in a city where humble men walked or went nowhere. Except for the encumbrance of the cloak, I followed him easily enough through the shadowy streets, grateful for the marvels of municipal lighting I had noticed the first morning I followed him.

We passed the palace where Aman prayed, and followed the market street through which I had been chased by the soldiers, coming at length to another long white wall, above which rose tiled domes and spires and through whose latticed windows soft colored lights gleamed. The heady perfumes of night-blooming flowers lifted across the walls, teasingly.

I melted into a shadow as from his sash Aman drew the bottle and from the bottle the cork. Smoke billowed and the djinn loomed above him. "I told thee that finishing thy harem was thy final wish and to bother me no more."

"Ah, that would be so," our husband replied, "if indeed my harem was finished. But as my mother keeps telling me, the house and my other women are but a setting for the central jewel, my cousin, Hyaganoosh, dwelling within these walls."

"I thought thou disliked women of thy own kind, despising them as uninteresting."

"I've changed my mind."

"Thy shrew of a mother got to thee, did she not?"

"My mother has nothing to do with it. She is a wonderful woman who has always done everything for me. Why should I deny her the company in her own household of this girl she treasures so much if it will shut her—give her pleasure? She's just reminded me of what a charming girl my little cousin used to be. If only you can get me into Hyaganoosh's chambers, I'm sure I can convince her to come with me as my bride."

"What will she think of thine other brides?"

"Well, as my mother has pointed out, while those women are married to me according to the customs of their peoples, I am not exactly married to them according to our own ways. Thus far they are, by our law, concubines. Surely Hyaganoosh will not object to them as such, and if she does, I will take some of the treasure you have given me and build them a new house, and she need never know. But by law I am allowed four wives and four wives I intend to have, God willing."

"Oh, very well. Never let it be said I do not give full value. But thou hast been wily indeed in extracting several wishes for the one and though I must say it has been a pleasure to serve a master who uses his power over me with such cleverness, think not to prolong thy hegemony by so much as a wistful thought hereafter. I intend to sleep a good long time when thou art done with me."

"O djinn, would I trick you? Only deliver me to the chambers of my cousin and let me win her heart and you shall be quit of me."

I was ready to be quit of him right there, after that perfidious speech, and would have told him so except that no sooner had he finished speaking than the smoke drifting at the djinn's ankles belched upward, enveloping both master and servant. When it had dissipated from the ground, so had they. A wisp of gray curled up over the wall and across a wide open area to disappear between the carved marble vines of a centrally located window. After a short pause I heard a faint surprised squeak, and then nothing.

Though I strained my eyes and ears, from that position beyond the wall, I could see or hear nothing intelligible. The squeak was followed by a hush, the hush by a distant creaking, and the next noise I heard did not drift out the window but rather seemed to be from somewhere on a level similar to my own. It was also a fainter noise and more muffled, sounding like a giggle. I heard little more for several hours, during which I imagined all I would say and do to Aman Akbar and also to Hyaganoosh if he brought her forth. I also imagined what they might be doing there in that palace, but the truth of that I was not to learn for some time. Still I could hear in my mind, if only there, Aman's blandishments to his cousin, and her coy protests. They naturally had to speak softly, for the measured steps of a sentry patrolled the other side of the wall by which I waited. Only that sentry's pacing kept me from doing some of my own, for I feared alarming the guard to my presence and that of Aman, for whom the wrath of a guard was entirely too gentle.

I slept not at all. I swear it. Nevertheless, shortly before dawn, my eyes, which I had been resting, snapped open and my head, lolling on a stiff neck, jerked up. A short distance from me a gate crashed open, flung wide by a soldier with a stick in his hand.

"Go on, now, out with you, accursed one! And thank your donkey's gods for a lady's soft heart that you weren't flayed alive! The Emir takes his rose garden seriously!"

Only stillness answered at first and the guard retreated from the door for a moment. The swish of his switch sounded three times, and the third time was followed by indignant and heartsick braying as an ass whiter than the whitest lamb galloped out of the gate and down the cobbles. I leaned incautiously away from the concealing shadows to watch. The guard, following the donkey out the gate a pace or two and slapping the stick against his palm in a satisfied fashion, spotted me.

This armsman was a far more considerate fellow than the one who assaulted the woman at the gate. He gestured to me, smiling, and pointed down the road after the donkey, calling, "You there, woman! There's a nice bit of livestock for you if you care to lift your heels before prayers. Get a move on! Chase it! Its owner will never have the nerve to claim it after it invaded the harem gardens. Only put a rope around its neck and you can beg from donkeyback from now on."

There was little I could do but pretend to agree, and run after the donkey while putting as much distance as possible between myself and the guard. Aman Akbar would have to extricate himself as best he could. Perhaps indeed the djinn had already smoked both Aman and his cousin back to the palace. Perhaps had even installed her in my chambers.

I began to chase the donkey in earnest, not a difficult task since the beast and I appeared to have adopted the same route and the white of its coat was easy to follow even in the dim light of a new morning. A woman with property of her own was someone to reckon with, someone with bargaining power. Whatever trials the new object of my husband's affections might mean for me, I meant to face them riding rather than walking. The gods were with me for as I pantingly neared Aman's palace, I saw that the gate had swung open and the donkey's tail was disappearing inside. I sped after it and stood, gasping for breath, in the courtyard, as the poor animal likewise stood with heaving sides, its eyes rolled back so that they seemed as white as the rest of it.

Aman had to be around somewhere, else why would the door be open, but I could not see him. I hurriedly slipped off the abayah and hung it where I had found it. The most prudent course of action seemed for me to return to my own chambers and pretend to sleep, for these people were entirely capable of claiming that I was guilty of treachery if they discovered I had been out at night. I would tend the beast first, however. The poor thing had dragged its hooves over to the pool beneath the spurting fountain and was lapping at a rate that would surely sicken it.

"There, my dear, there," I said into one long ear, tugging it gently. "Come away now and let Rasa rub you down."

But instead of submitting gratefully to my attentions, as I might have expected, the beast let forth an ear-

splitting bray that rocked me backwards on my heels.
"EEE-*YAW*!" it said.

I stretched my hand forward while keeping my
distance otherwise, and the animal lunged at me, braying
loudly and plaintively.

"EEE-YAW, EEE-*YAW*!" it repeated, its brown
eyes rolling and its hooves pawing at the tiled paths. I
wondered momentarily if eating roses made donkeys
crazy. Braying continuously, it backed me against the
fountain and eee-yawed at me, punctuating its noise with
sharp tosses of its mane and angry thrashings of its tail,
all the while showing its great white teeth and hopping
up and down on its front hooves so that I felt my
exposed toes in great jeopardy.

Just as I thought I would be obliged to take a swim
to escape the creature, it reared up and bounced back
down again facing away from me and galloped off through
the hyacinths to the hidden gate to Amollia's garden.
Amollia and the cat stood there framed by the swags of
flowering vines. The donkey galloped headlong for them.
I shouted a warning, but the beast was already upon
them. It stopped, dirt and shreds of ruined rose bushes
spraying beneath its hooves, and continued its braying
at her. Its voice was growing fainter now, but no less
insistently plaintive.

Amollia looked puzzled and tried to pat it, whereupon it ran back to me, still braying. The bray faltered
to a wheeze.

"There, there, old dear," I said in my gentlest
horse-taming talk. "Don't take on so. Come and have
that nice rub-down. You're home now. No need to carry
on." It gave one last heartsick bray and laid its long
head against my midsection, a great shuddering sigh
running from eartips to tail.

I took a deep breath and let it out again and patted
the beast's forehead. It brayed very faintly and looked
up at me sadly before it began again to drink, this time
more slowly, its sides heaving.

Using the end of my sash, I began to wipe the
froth from the beast's sides.

Amollia quietly joined me. Her robe was long and

decorated with paintings of leaves. Her face wore an expression of mingled bewilderment and exasperation.

"What possessed you, sister-wife, that you not only sneak from your husband's house in the middle of the night, but also prove that you have done so by bringing that ass home?" The ass looked up with dripping muzzle and gave her such a wounded expression that she gave it an apologetic pat and at once began using the hem of her gown to help me mop its sides. "You do realize that among these people that kind of behavior could get your body separated from your head?"

I lowered my voice, so as not to stimulate the beast again. "What makes you think I went anywhere?"

"I suppose the ass knocked at the door and you were simply practicing these people's laws of hospitality by admitting it? I saw you leave and I know you were up to—"

The cat Kalimba had been sniffing, perilously, first at the donkey's hindquarters and then at its muzzle. Rather surprisingly, the cat rumbled in a contented manner the whole time it sniffed and even more surprisingly the donkey made no objections. As we spoke, the cat settled itself, paws curled and eyes slitted, in the shade of the donkey's belly. A gate brushed open at our backs and Kalimba immediately pounced forward, growling.

A blinking, yawning, tousle-haired Aster emerged from her own garden. Her hair flowers were folded into droopy semi-circles dangling over her ears. Her silken pajamas were rumpled. "Whose animals?" she asked, as familiarly as if she were not an unwelcome stranger.

"The cat is mine and the donkey is Rasa's," Amollia said smoothly.

"I didn't know our husband would let us have personal pets," Aster said. "What am I to have for mine, do you suppose? A peacock, perhaps? Or a panda? Or maybe one of those horrible-looking hump-backed things I saw out the window this morning? If Aman wants to get me one too and asks either of you what I'd like, tell him a cricket, will you? They're easy to take care of and one never feels too aggrieved if they die."

The donkey gave her a squeaky bray and trotted toward her but she dodged it. It brayed once more, sadly, and turned back to us.

Aster eyed it speculatively. "Not a bad-looking beast. Did it follow you home, barbarian?"

"Home from where?" I asked innocently.

"From following my husband, of course. I watched you leave, so you needn't deny it."

What I had thought was a private excursion turned out to have been fairly public after all.

Amollia said calmly, "Rasa was only trying to protect our husband. He had been behaving strangely."

"This humble person could not agree with you more, elder sister," Aster said with a quick bow. "And I certainly am not one to betray secrets. I but wondered, barbarian, that you have so little love left for your current life that you should speed toward another with such haste. City streets at night are dangerous, you know, especially for those who are where they should not be. But you need not fear my tongue. Why, in my last life but one I was a magistrate known throughout the province for my discretion—"

"There is nothing to tell," I said. "And nothing to hide. I suspected our revered mother-in-law had finally convinced Aman Akbar to seek the woman Hyaganoosh—"

"And so she had," Aster nodded agreeably. "I—er—chanced to overhear them when the old bat interrupted my wedding night to exhort with her son."

"So I followed him," I finished, a little lamely.

"Ah," Amollia said. "And once you were there what did you do?"

"Nothing. I waited, and when the donkey was driven out from the courtyard of the Emir, I followed it back here. I merely wanted to see this Hyaganoosh."

Amollia rolled her eyes at the dawn-streaked sky. Aster pointedly studied her fingernails. The donkey snorted. "Well," I said, "if he had left her alone for a short while I could have told her how terribly crowded it is here and how hungry we get while waiting for Aman."

"That wouldn't bother her, I'll bet," Aster said. "If

she's tai-tai, number-one wife, he'll change things to suit her."

"I had," I said stiffly, "planned to exaggerate."

"Ah," Aster said, nodding wisely. During this exchange the donkey looked from her to me as if following a fighting match of some sort.

"And did you speak to her?" Amollia asked.

"I think I heard her squeal," I said. And I told them all that had happened, and how the guard's intended kindness had forced me to leave before Aman returned.

"You would have had a long wait," Amollia said drily. "He has yet to return."

At this the donkey gave another short wheezing bray, which even to the animal's own long ears must have sounded feeble, for it desisted at once as if shamed and hung its head.

Aster patted it absently. The cat at its feet growled low. "That's where the old woman is now. She came round shaking me awake early this morning and asked if I had seen her precious son. When I said I hadn't, she put on her crow robes and went to search for him. I can tell you, she doesn't look nearly so pleased as she did after she spoiled my wedding night."

"Don't be too sure that was a wedding night," I told her, and repeated what had passed between Aman and the djinn concerning us. *That* stopped her preening.

"But at least Aman doesn't intend to set us aside," Amollia said. "And this is not truly his doing, but his mother's. His cousin has had her whole life to win him, but had it not been for the old one, he would never have pursued her."

I thought of my father's tents and of the new horses my alliance with Aman had won him and of the life of my sister, a slave to her captor until she bore him a son. Being the least of Aman's concubines was better than her life, in many ways. Yet I was not so sure. I would almost rather face all of my mother's cousins single-handedly than watch Aman stroll away with one of the others again. But at least by now there were so *many* others that I was unlikely to be lonely when he did so.

The donkey had wandered off and seemed to be trying to go indoors toward our chambers, but I felt no inclination to stop him. The cat prowled after him.

"He would be very foolish to cast me off," Aster said confidently. "He paid twice what father was offered for me by the people who run the flower boats."

"Flower boats?" Amollia asked. "What *are* you talking about? Are flower boats some sort of royal honors that a princess should be sold to them? Princesses don't get sold to anything, except perhaps husbands. Or so it is in my country."

"In mine, birth means little," Aster shrugged. "Station in life is the thing. My family in this life was once noble but my esteemed grandfather committed a slight indiscretion with public funds. Since then, my family has existed as a troup of traveling players. A princess is only one of the many roles I play. Fortunately, it was the one for which I was costumed when Aman saw me. My father had already made a deal with the manager of one of the boats—that's where the best and prettiest girls are sent to dance and sing and please men."

"That's barbaric," Amollia said. "Our people would never do so. Rather they would marry you into the harem of an established man who could protect you."

"Oh, our men marry several girls sometimes too," Aster said airily. "Only there are too many girls."

"But why do they not dispose of the excess ones at birth?" Amollia asked.

"They try," Aster said. "But you can't always tell who's going to be excess. You were lucky to be so valued among your people. I am surprised they let you marry so far away."

"Oh, they don't know I'm gone and won't unless they take a count," Amollia answered. "They'll assume I've run off into the jungle with Kalimba, and think it no particular loss either. For in truth I am the ugliest of all of the daughters of the Great Elephant. You see, I have never quite persuaded myself the time was right to submit to my beautifying tattoos."

"Modesty is a becoming ornament," Aster said piously.

"Happily, Aman seems to be of the same opinion," Amollia said. "I was more than pleased to be spoken for by a man who doesn't want me to carve my skin with knives and rub magic ashes in it. That he also granted that I should keep Kalimba with me, when any man of my people would have insisted I turn her out into the jungle or make a robe of her, was a greater boon yet. True, having only three other women with whom to share wifely duties will seem bleak but—"

The ass galloped out from between the arches leading to my quarters. Chips flew from the tiles broken under the flying hooves as the beast clattered past us and skidded to a halt beside the gate. The gate creaked open. I ran after the beast. Though reason told me the gate had to be opening for Aman and no other, I surreptitiously clutched a knife I had once found in the library. The gate had opened before without Aman, and the fountain had sprayed. The magic wasn't working according to its custom and Aman wasn't behaving according to his either. I, however, was going to behave according to mine.

Footsteps plopped on the road outside, only one set first, light and hurrying, more halting than Aman's and not as firm. Then others, which were very firm indeed. These did not approach from any distance but commenced as soon as the first walker neared the gate.

"You there, woman, wait," a man's voice commanded.

"In God's name, sir, who are you to bother an old mother returning from an urgent errand?" The voice corresponding with the first set of footsteps was Um Aman's.

"Do not be alarmed, madam. We are the appointed representatives of the Emir Onan and we wish a word with you, no more."

"What could such exalted personages want with me?" she asked. Fear was in her voice and her weight creaked the door open farther.

"Actually, it is with Aman Akbar, master of your house, we wish to speak. We would have spoken with him earlier today, in his customary place in the cafe in the bazaar, but he has not been seen in any of his usual places of business."

"He has had—er—pressing business," Um Aman said. "No doubt he is now sleeping soundly in his bed as any good man might do. Perhaps I could take a message?"

"That is unacceptable. A personal response from Aman Akbar is required."

"My son is not available, and any official who would disturb such an important man at this hour would do well to look to his job. My son is not without influence."

"You had better hope he is not without money, old woman. There is a small matter of unpaid taxes on this estate and at least one unregistered female slave being harbored on the premises."

"You must be mistaken. My son has no slaves."

"She has been seen." His voice was muffled for a moment as he consulted with the other in whispers. "What do you think? A night in the dungeon for this insolent old bird until her influential son satisfies His Eminence?"

The donkey took a step closer to the gate and it swung open, all but spilling Um Aman into the garden. Knocking the animal aside, I threw myself upon the gate and succeeded in closing it most of the way before the official could get more than a foot in the door. The foot was crushed with what must have been considerable pain to its owner as Amollia, Aster, Um Aman and the donkey joined me in keeping the gate closed.

"Open up, I say! Aman Akbar, if you are in there, you are called upon to account to the Emir!"

Aster suddenly disengaged herself from the rest of us and, standing well back from the door, spoke in a voice much lower and stronger than the breathless little girl tones she had formerly used, the new voice holding some hint of Aman's fluid accents. "In the name of God, do not disturb a man in his own home. My beautiful new wife is ill and I have been tending her this long night through. My friend the Emir is well aware of my good reputation and—and—the tax payment is on its way to him even now by messenger service. He will reward your zeal with blows if he hears of your discourteous treatment to my mother."

Her speech so moved the donkey that it croaked agreement. Pikes magically concealed in the topmost portion of the wall revealed themselves in bristling array, as if armed men wielded them. They were balanced there seemingly by ghosts but so angered was I then by almost everything that had happened since my arrival in this country that I snatched down one of the pikes and thrust the tip through the opening in the door. The ghost formerly holding my pike had sense enough not to resist and our would-be oppressors were no less sensible. The foot withdrew instantly.

Hasty consultations were held on the other side of the wall. In greasy tones, one of the officials said, "Your pardon, Aman Akbar. We will depart for now and see if your messenger has reached the Emir. If he has not, perhaps we can expedite his progress."

"Indeed," Aster growled. And two sets of footsteps marched double-time down the street again.

Um Aman was as grateful as could be expected. "How dare you impersonate my son?" she asked. "Where is he? What have you done with him that he cannot speak for himself?"

Amollia ignored the woman's flailings and the red color her face was turning and put an arm around her shoulders. "Old mother, we do not know where Aman is. Did you hear no word among your friends?"

The woman sagged slightly and her cheeks seemed more sunken than before. "No word." Then the wrath in her eyes rekindled and she shook off Amollia's arm. "But how can you pretend he is not here? The magic is functioning. It functions only when Aman is here."

"I do not know. We also had thought that he was here but if you can produce him you're doing better than any of us," Amollia replied reasonably. "Perhaps he arranged for the magic to work in his absence."

Um Aman shook her head stubbornly. "He never

does so. Before *you* came he was gone all night once or twice and had I not insisted on bringing my own brazier and housekeeping implements from our hut, despite him telling me I need not, I would have gone hungry. He is a good boy, but poor at considering details. No doubt that is why we have incurred the wrath of the Emir. Had he but mentioned to me the taxes, I would have seen to it that they were paid. But now you—you have lied about it and they will probably come and take us all to the dungeons and I will never see my son nor the light of day again!"

At this the donkey once more seemed to go mad, emitting great hoarse wheezing "EEE-AWS" until we had to hold our ears. The beast frantically knocked against the old woman until he had her backed into a corner. She tried to beat him away, raining blows upon him with her gnarled hands. Kalimba snarled at her, and Amollia, who was already trying, with Aster's assistance and my own, to pull the donkey from her, now had to try to restrain the cat as well.

Quite by accident, she hauled Kalimba back across the donkey's legs, raking them with the cat's claws. Rather than further agitating the ass, this seemed to shock him to his rightful mind again, and he backed away from Um Aman, shuddered one last time, and with a docility that spoke of a broken spirit—or heart—allowed me to lead him away. Thinking that all that braying surely had dried his mouth, I led him to the pool. He walked so sadly that my anger quite fled and I patted him and spoke to him gently. He lowered his head to drink, but then shook it, as if he could not take a mouthful, and raised it again, regarding me from the depths of miserable, frightened eyes of a familiar melting brown. Perhaps I would have recognized those eyes sooner, but there was no hint any longer of Aman's triumphant twinkle.

The metal beast in the pool was more discerning, however. Once more as its master approached, the fountain began spraying in a maniac, sprightly fashion so that its droplets spread to the edge of the pool. The donkey's sides heaved and Aman's sad eyes looked out of his ass's face once more and I sank to my knees and embraced him.

Amollia and Aster approached too, Amollia with halting steps and Aster saying, "But, but, but—" as if she were a bird with one song.

Um Aman did not see the resemblance at first. But finally she stopped being indignant and muttering imprecations long enough to truly look, and then she wailed as even she had never wailed before. "Witches! Murderesses! What have you done to my poor son?"

# Chapter
4

I'll say this for Um Aman. When she has made up her mind to do something, she is a woman of action. Shortly after morning prayers, Amollia, Aster and I were bundled into abayahs and, with Aman Akbar trotting beside us, hustled through the streets to the gate of the dung-sellers, through a wall and into a courtyard, where we soon stood among a crowd of Um Aman's cronies watching a wild-eyed woman veiled in her own greasy hair having fits around a doomed chicken.

We took a proprietary interest in what the woman and the chicken had to say to each other, for they were the judges of the council of women Um Aman had selected to determine our fate.

I would have thought she'd have been more interested in finding out how to turn Aman Akbar back into a human or at least in paying the taxes, but, as usual, when something goes wrong, the first priority was to find someone to blame. Also, as usual, the someone was bound to be the outsider—or outsiders—and in this case, it was my co-wives and me. At least Amollia had her cat, still perched upon the back of Aman Akbar who was protected from the claws by a very fine rug plucked from the floor as an improvised saddle blanket. Amollia looked as serene and sociable as if she were attending a celebration at which she was an invited guest but stayed close by Aman and Kalimba. Aster's eyes twitched from one woman to the next, and one doorway to the next. She had kept up a stream of nervous chatter most of the previous night until threatened with extinction by drowning in the fountain if she didn't shut up. Part of Amollia's serenity, I suspected, was exhaustion. None of us had slept for fear of being murdered by Um Aman or carted off to the dungeons by the tax assessors.

Um Aman had disappeared a short time before the prayer-caller sang his earliest song and had returned with the abayahs. We arrived at the gathering with a number of other women and children, some of whom I recognized from Um Aman's party. Moments after we settled against the side of the house farthest from the racks of dung cakes drying in the first rays of sunlight, a ragged boy arrived with the woman now confronting the scrawny chicken.

Um Aman consulted with her briefly, and then turned to the others, interspersing questions and explanations with all of the standard references to their god's wisdom and mercy.

We did not exactly stand among them—no one wanted to be near us. No one looked at us, though there were frequent wondering, puzzled, and frightened glances at Aman Akbar. Until batted away by their mothers, several children made a game of running forward to touch him and scampering quickly away again. The mothers stretched their fingers out at us in a sign of warding off, not the same as that my people use against demons, but obviously with the same intention. We had been promoted overnight from nuisances to menaces.

The fits of the woman with the chicken were evidently a preface to some sort of rite, for she stopped suddenly, huddled in the dust shivering in her sweat-soaked gown, her ankle-length hair unbound and dust

streaked where it had swept the ground. The chicken—a
rooster actually—now fed unconcernedly near her head.
She crouched there for a long time in the midst of
everyone and the other women spoke very little. She
was not only resting, it seemed, but in some sort of
trance. It ended when her arm whipped out, grasping
the unfortunate rooster by the neck.

This signaled a few of the other women to start
drumming on whatever was handy: the floor, overturned
water jugs, children. The entranced woman writhed to
her feet and, flopping fowl in hand, began emulating
the movements of her prey, all in time to the improvised drumming. This was no solo performance. Several
of the others, at one time or another during the dance,
rose and followed her movements, or created their own,
mostly involving a lot of jerking and flopping. Some of
the contortions of head, abdomen, arms and upper
body appeared impossibly boneless. But the basic steps
did not appear complicated, and the women who neither danced nor drummed trilled an eerie cry that
rivaled the prayer-caller's and clapped their hands in
complex counterpoint to the drumbeats. But though
the other dancers rose and danced and collapsed again
throughout the morning, the woman in the middle
began to show that she was a person of special power,
for her dancing continued and she never quite killed
the rooster until the end.

Actually, the ritual probably usually has another
ending. But Amollia loves to dance and the cat loves
chicken. Amollia's people decide many important matters by dancing too. She, more than Aster or myself,
was duly solemn and respectful throughout the ceremony.
But as the day wore on, and the heat rose, and the
rhythm of the drums and hands reverberated through
our skulls, and the trillings ululated high and mournful,
and the hair of the shamaness snapped like a banner to
the music, Amollia's eyes glazed over. Her hands twitched
all the way up to her shoulders and into her torso and
soon her feet began to move. Before I quite realized
what she intended doing, she was in the middle, danc-

ing with the others. The main dancer tried to salvage
the situation. She snapped the chicken's neck immediately,
the drumming stopped, and Amollia retreated back to
our corner, still looking dazed. The others looked horrified.

The main dancer threw the chicken down and
gutted it, wiped the knife she had used on her skirt and
set it aside. With movements she had no doubt learned
from the spirits with whom she had been communing
she raised her eyes and poised her hands high, preparing
to sink them back into the chicken. She was too slow.
Kalimba leaped from the back of Aman Akbar in a blur
of spots, secured the chicken, and retreated between
our husband's hooves to enjoy the treat and any attendant portents in peace.

Someone screamed. Aster's foot shot out and Um
Aman, dagger in hand as she dove for the cat, sprawled
on the ground. Someone grabbed Aster and someone
else assisted Um Aman. Dragging Amollia with me, I
sat down in front of Aman Akbar, shielding the cat from
the crowd. I drew my own knife and prepared to
defend myself from the women, who seemed to regard
the death of the chicken as a signal for our deaths.

Fortunately, the shamaness saw the matter differently.
"In the name of God, desist. This is a holy animal and
the black woman also carries holiness within her. Did
you not see how the spirits entered her?"

Had Um Aman not been supported by the body of
a friend, you could have blown on her and knocked her
over, so shocked did she look. "Holy? But clearly she
and these others are possessed by evil."

The dancer drew herself up, her hair a tangled
mess, what was visible of her face smudged with dust
and flecked with chicken blood. Her dignity was
undeniable. "You argue with a seeress?"

"No, no, God forgive me. But this is the woman—"
and she said the word even more poisonously than she
usually said *slut* "—who directed my son away from his
true bride."

"And the pale one with the knife? And the little
maiden beside her?"

"Other foreign *women* who directed—"

"Who directed your son away from the girl you chose for him?"

"Yes, until I was able to persuade him, God be praised, of where his duty lay."

"And when was this?"

"One night ago."

"And when did he become a donkey?"

"One night—" she broke off.

"Aiyeeah! You call yourself a believer and yet cannot accept that which has clearly been written? Only by the compassion of our most compassionate God have you been granted these blessed vessels of great holiness and this cat, who shall aid them in devouring the evil afflicting your son as surely as it devoured the cock. These women would have protected your son from the very evil to which you hounded him."

"But they are not even believers!" Um Aman protested.

"Have they been instructed?"

"No. There has been no time—"

"Then how can you condemn them? You have failed in your duty toward them as well as your son, but God seems to favor you nonetheless. Do not abuse His mercy." And with that the woman clapped her hands and the hostess brought forth a basin of water in which first the dancer and then all of the others washed themselves before midday prayers. Two women came forward with bone combs to help the dancer dress her hair. She pushed it back with both hands and began washing her face as they tugged at the tangles. As soon as I saw her face I had to look very carefully elsewhere. For though she had surely known me as soon as she stepped into the courtyard, I saw her clearly only at that moment and recognized her as the woman on whose behalf I had clobbered the armsman.

We ate with our hostess, a widow who had no men with whom to concern herself, and departed for our home in mid-afternoon. On the way Um Aman spent a few coins for food, in case Aman Akbar could procure from the palace magic only nourishment appropriate to his new body.

We need not have hurried, for we returned to find our gates barred against us with the seal of the Emir splashed across them. Um Aman began to wail again, and Aman himself to bray piteously. Um Aman wiped her face on her sleeve and gave a final sniff. "And that woman said God was being merciful. What does she know? My son an ass, the door of my home barred against me, three new mouths to feed, and all of us beggared."

"Shhh," Aster said, her eyes shifting from right to left over the top of her veil. "There could be guards nearby. Beggars we may be, but you and I, old mother, have been beggars before, eh? Be glad that we're alive and free—for the time being."

Though Aster's wise words did not exactly cause Um Aman's face to be transformed by glee, some of the anguish did depart from the old woman's eyes.

"Perhaps we could talk with this Emir or even with his wives," Amollia said. "After all, if he is the ruler, he must dispense justice and surely he will see how unjust it is to take everything when—" She stopped as Um Aman and Aster both gave her pitying looks. "No, perhaps he wouldn't."

We departed before the Emir could impound our persons as well as our house. Even in abayahs a group of four women with a donkey and an exotic cat is not an inconspicuous party. The widow received us again at her home with good grace and declared that she hated eating alone anyway.

We brought with us the few purchases we had made in the market, and these paid our way that night. But by the way our hostess scraped and sent the children to borrow as she prepared the evening meal and from the small amount of couscous and bread she was able to produce for each of us even with our additional contributions, it was evident that she could ill afford company twice in one day.

Um Aman looked as if she might weep again. "A wonderful meal, Sheda. I could never make couscous like you."

"Ah, Samira, it is nothing compared to yours. And when I think of the other delicacies we had at your house that day!" She smacked her lips appreciatively but her eyes were anxious as she looked at her children.

We could not stay here.

She spread mats for us on the floor, and nothing would do but that Aman Akbar sleep with the children. When the others were quiet, however, our husband rose in his new sure-footed way and, pulling the door curtain aside with his teeth, walked into the courtyard, his head hanging low. Amollia, whom I had thought to be sleeping, rose at once and followed him outside.

Though it seemed to me that it was no use to borrow a bed if you didn't sleep in it, and I was more than a little tired, I could no more sleep than they could and crept outside to stand beside them. We said nothing to each other, but in a very few moments Um Aman joined us, followed, belatedly, by Aster, who had been asleep from the look of her but who didn't want to miss anything.

"We must free him somehow," Amollia said quietly, stroking Aman's ears.

"That is very easy for you to say, blessed one," Um Aman said with spiteful emphasis on the last words, "but how? We cannot even buy food and Sheda may come to harm for offering us even this small measure of comfort. And if we are taken, there will be no hope for Aman Akbar. Oh, I had a feeling the Emir would not believe you," she wailed—but softly, for fear of waking her friend's family—at Aster. "I should have taken the time to dig up the bag of gold coins Aman gave me to make into a necklace. Then we would at least have enough to eat and start some small business while we figured how to free him."

Amollia bit her lip and I wanted to smack the old woman for her oversight—none of the rest of us had bags of gold to forget, after all.

But Aster shifted her lower jaw and scratched her

nose speculatively and said, "You'd have to dig it up, eh? That means it's buried, I suppose?"

"Why else would I have to dig it up?"

"What I mean to say, revered mother, is that it is probably buried where the tax assessors are unlikely to find it. Is that so?"

"Unless they are able to steal the hiding place from my mind, yes."

"Then what is to prevent us from digging it up again?"

"Nothing but the barred doors and the Emir's seal and the walls," the old lady said. You would almost have thought she didn't want her gold back.

# Chapter 5

We moved along side streets known to Um Aman to avoid any guards the Emir might have placed upon the gate. Aster was quite agile, but she was too short to reach the top of the wall, even by standing on Aman's back. Amollia, however, vaulted up with no problem, though she scandalized Um Aman by kilting the skirts of her abayah far above her knees. Once she and Aster were safely atop the wall, they were able to help Um Aman, whom I had to assist with a boost from behind before joining them.

While Um Aman departed for her own quarters, the rest of us wordlessly headed for ours. Amollia's portion of the palace was nearest to Um Aman's, but the visit to her former chambers was brief, for before Aster and I had crossed her garden, she ran back down the pillared passageway, shaking her head. "Stripped, even to the beaded curtain. They've taken everything."

But they hadn't taken it very far.

The metal animal of the fountain lay dead in the

grass, its spray forever dried, while beside it and behind it and piled high above it where once the cool
waters had rippled, the furnishings of the palace were
heaped in a foothill of treasure, carpets and cushions,
cooking pots and half-melted wax candles, gold and
silver ornaments. Starlight glittered off the occasional
jewel while above it all sat the djinn. The smoke from
his nonexistent nether appendages cast eerie drifting
shadows across the courtyard as the light breeze played
among its tendrils. He looked extremely morose, as if
the surfeit of richness beneath him gave him indigestion.

Aster hailed him as if it were midday in the center
of a city where she was not likely to be cast into a
dungeon if anyone heard her. "Old Uncle, how glad we
are to see you! Now that you have returned, we are safe
and you can help us change our husband back into his
proper form."

The djinn shook his head. "On the contrary, Madam,
it is my sad duty to foreclose upon the treasures I have
bestowed upon thy husband, my former master, and
deprive his estate of its trappings to the greater glory of
my new master."

"Is this how you people value honor?" I asked.
"You should die before deserting your lord when he has
fallen low, defend him with your life rather than feeding
upon his belongings like a carrion crow."

"Thou hast but a poor grasp upon the more delicate aspects of the situation, O wan-faced one," the
djinn replied with an arrogant lift to each of his chins.
"In the first place, the ways of my people are not the
ways of thy people, God be praised for His mercy and
infinite wisdom. My life is eternal and I will lose it for
none so long as my soul remains intact inside its sealed
bottle. Whosoever possesses that bottle is necessarily
my lord, and him I must obey whether I will it or not."

"And just who controls your soul now, demon, and
so cruelly demands our home when the whole of your
magic is at his command?"

"Alas, for my sake as well as thine own, woman,
none other than the Emir himself commands me, he

who owns the beauteous Hyaganoosh, downfall of thy husband."

"Downfall of us all then if that is so," Amollia said. "Do you mean to tell us that Aman's own cousin betrayed him to the Emir?"

"Oh, no, ebony lady. Rather she concealed him from the Emir by causing me to turn him into an ass. The Emir would not have bothered to waste a wish thusly, but would have dealt with thy husband by other means." He ran a finger under his lowest chin, meaningfully.

"If she's the one who made an ass of my husband, why do you say the Emir is your master? I think myself that you have been in that bottle too long," Aster said. "In your next life, you really must pray that you are something less reclusive."

"In this life, I hope in the future to avoid females with mouths as full of words as the desert is of grains of sand," he replied curtly, then sighed and folded his arms across his belly. "But for now, listen, and be enlightened and perhaps this tale may be told abroad as a lesson to all about the treachery of women. It happened thus and should you tell it further, be so kind as to give proper credit by saying first that it is . . ." And he wrote his title in fiery script in the air above our heads so that we could not mistake his meaning.

## "THE DJINN'S TALE"

"*It so happened that my master desired to complete his harem, as full of exotic and strange women as a zoo is of animals of similar origins, by adding to it the civilizing influence of the girl of his mother's choice, a beautiful follower of the True Belief who was, as is proper, his paternal cousin.*

"*However, this cousin, being of high beauty and low birth, had already been noticed and selected by the Emir of the city, the only man as wealthy as Aman Akbar, and, alas for my poor master, far more powerful. For wealth alone does not make power. Rather it is the* knowledge of how to use one's wealth to exert one's will over others that makes a man powerful and in this the Emir was already far more skilled than his rival. In other ways, though, Aman Akbar was cleverer for he had obtained his own wealth by outsmarting the Emir and all of his men, preceding them in the discovery of the bottle containing the magnificently magical djinn who now tells this story. Fortunately for Aman Akbar, the Emir was never certain who tricked him out of the bottle, and also was unaware that the lovely peasant girl he had added to his household was the beloved of that same trickster. Aman Akbar knew both of these facts only too well, and also was prudently knowledgeable of the unwisdom of seeking to deprive his mighty rival of a second treasure. It was for these reasons, I believe, that he contented himself with his foreign ladies and sought to forget she whom his mother considered his true bride. However, in the end courage and filial duty prevailed over wisdom and good sense, as happens in so many similar tales, and he set out to win the beauteous Hyaganoosh.

"To this end he walked to the Emir's palace, inconspicuous as any casual citizen out for a stroll. With him he carried the miraculous djinn—that is, myself—and my bottle. By walking, rather than flying with his djinn as befits the master of so powerful a being, he avoided attracting the attention of those who would have said when the girl was discovered missing, "Ah, yes, I saw Aman Akbar and a djinn flying on a magic carpet toward the Emir's palace shortly before the girl disappeared." It is in my mind that he was not entirely convinced that he would be able to persuade me to include his desire to acquire Hyaganoosh in his harem as part of his third wish and intended to try to win her without my help if I denied him. But deny him I did not, for he was extremely wily in the phrasing of his wishes so that each individual wish contained several subwishes which I was obliged to grant in order to gratify the primary wish. When he wished for wealth, he included within wishes for the types of wealth he desired, not only the appointments of the palace, jewels for his women, fine clothing and gold and silver coin in his treasury, which should have been enough for most men, but additionally he wished to gain a wealth of knowledge, obtaining by my magic the interest of wise men who instructed him in matters of history and law. When he wished for the palace, he wished for the magic to run it so that servants would not deplete his wealth. And likewise, when he wished for his harem, he wished to select the women individually, listing within his wish his requirements. A shrewd man, as I've mentioned, though as it was proved, not shrewd enough.

"I had already warned him that the woman from the Central Empire was the fulfillment of the last portion of his last wish, for I considered with her arrival that his harem was complete. What man in his right mind would burden himself with more? But since a man is allowed four wives by law, and I too, as a fellow believer, wished to see him enjoy a suitable spouse, we compromised. I agreed to aid him in at least gaining the girl's chamber so that he could use his own powers of persuasion to win her.

"Kindly granting him my most impressive means of entry, and one also more convenient for entering through lattices than the standard carpet, I transported him in a cloud of smoke to the room which she, by virtue of her beauty, had been given to occupy alone until the Emir found time to bestow upon her his—er—grace. When my smoke vanished, I watched from my bottle. And ah, I must say in spite of it all that she possesses a beauty worthy of even such trouble as befell my poor former master and myself!

"For her hair was black as night, and her eyes like jewels bright, her skin a beam of light, her breasts a—"

"Lecher's delight?" Aster offered. "Get on with it, Old Uncle. We women are little impressed with each other's charms, and even less are we interested in the charms of this rival, except as they pertain to our husband's destruction."

"That's the trouble with infidels," the djinn complained. "No sense of poetry. No doubt it was because it had been so long since my master had seen a good-looking woman that his usual glib tongue deserted him, and before he recovered it the girl emitted a sweetly modest scream of protest—"

I forbore to mention that I had heard it as a squeal, and not all that sweetly modest.

"My master and I rushed forward to embrace her, to quiet her fears and keep her from alerting the palace guard all in the same masterful and eloquent gesture.

"When Aman removed his lips from her own she did not scream but, as befit one of her situation, required further information. 'Just who do you think you are to—' she began. Then, upon recognizing her true love and intended husband, moaned, presumably with rapture, and said, 'Aman. Is it you?' And when he averred that it was indeed, she said, 'Well, that's a relief. At least you're family. What is that in your sash that's gouging a hole in my ribs?'

"Quickly, my master removed the offending item, which was, as you may guess, my bottle, and handed it to her, impulsively, overcome with love at her beauty and the tenderness of her greeting. 'I—I brought this for you, my beloved. A wedding present.' The scamp! If he could no longer command my services, he intended to use me anyway first to win this incomparable beauty and then to have her, as his loyal and loving wife, wish of me what was needful and good for both of them.

"The gentle creature was not impressed however, and held my bottle from her between thumb and forefinger, so that I feared she might break it. 'Thank you, cousin, it's—it's—very nice. Let's go down to the garden and I'll pick some flowers to put in it right now.' And before he could stop her she raced past him lightly as a gazelle and had all but gained the garden when to our common chagrin, we heard footsteps and the Emir calling, 'Oh, Hyaganooooo—oosh, my little poppy seed, my little—' No, I will refrain from repeating that one, since you females have already said you have no interest in a catalog of your rival's charms. The girl was frightened, naturally, for if she was caught, it would *mean death for both her and my foolish former master.*

"*Aman, you are a great ass! What if*—' *and she fell down the last step to the garden as he, in a panic, rushed past her, and the cork, which was loose in my bottle, fell out and I came forth and granted her wish.*"

"Djinn, you are very devious," Amollia said, wagging her finger at him. "That was no wish, just an accident, and for that you transformed Aman Akbar?"

"Lady, it was the girl's wish or she would not have said so. When someone expresses themselves in such a fashion and uncaps my bottle, who am I to inquire as to how they choose to say it? And never have I seen anyone so relieved as she was when Aman Akbar turned into a donkey just as the Emir appeared. By that time I was safely back in my bottle. I do not think that the startled girl, in her fear and trembling at the prospects of being caught, realized quite what had happened or who her benefactor was in preserving her and her cousin from her master's wrath. It should be noted that when I was listing her attributes, before I was so rudely interrupted, at no time did I describe her *wit* as being surpassing bright.

"The Emir, however, is very quick indeed and immediately demanded to know what she was doing risking her delicate lungs in the night air, whose animal was that in the garden, and from whence had she obtained the bottle. She cast her eyes modestly down and handed him the bottle, caressing his neck and chest with her free hand. 'Oh, my lord and master, how relieved I am to see thee!' she said, and raised her eyes wonderingly and batted the lashes thereof with a fury worthy of the sirocco. 'Seest thou! Someone has admitted that beast to thy garden! I heard a noise and looked out my window, and observed that this beast was among thy roses, defiling them and also devouring them, and I thought of nothing but thy loss and hastened down to drive it away—'

"And the Emir pretended to be convinced and said, 'My brave darling!' and the lady continued, 'But it would not heed me and I cast about for some object to

*throw at it and found this old bottle lying upon the
ground. I think the beast may have kicked it out from
under a shrubbery.'*

*"A bottle in my shrubbery? I'll have the gardener
flogged,' the Emir said.*

*"But as he threatened, he leaned over the girl's
dainty foot and scooped up my cork from the ground
and thereby contained me, else I would have found
myself flogging a gardener for him. He—the Emir I
mean, I know nothing of the gardener—is a man not
unlearned in the arcane arts, and knew for certain
what his concubine had delivered into his hands when
he saw the seal of Suleiman upon the cork."*

"So now you live with the richest, most powerful
man instead of simply one of the richest, and our Aman
wears a donkey's tail!" Aster said. "I suppose that
makes you happy, may you be a worm in dung in your
next life."

"You wrong me, lowborn princess," he replied,
looking almost as sad as Aman. "For, irregular as was
thy husband's household, it was more amusing by far
than my present employment, and in a life as long as
mine, amusement is no trifling matter. This new master
may be a prince but he vouchsafes me no journeys to
foreign climes to procure rare types of ugly foreign
women, nor does he permit me to run his household
with my magicks, preferring outmoded prosaic methods
instead. Indeed, he shows little appreciation for my
powers, for all that he has coveted them, but seems
chiefly pleased that he has deprived someone else of
them. Not only is he wealthy, but has, I suspect, access
to magic from other sources, to regard mine so poorly.
Where thy husband took greatest delight in using my
skills, this one sets my bottle in a niche in the wall until
he may spend my power as he would an insignificant
silver coin. The sole task he has set for me is to gather
for him thy husband's holdings, for though he knows
not that Aman is the donkey, he knows that Aman is
missing and his household helpless and has invented

this new tax specifically to bring down the upstart whose glory threatened to dim his own.

"Imagine! Me! One of the most powerful beings of the cosmos reduced to the station of tax collector! But thus it is, and I am so reduced by the will of my new master, and you see before you the fruits of my labor, upon which I was merely taking a brief rest when you encountered me. Also, his seal is upon the door and that too is his will and therefore I must say to you, though it grieves me to do so, 'Scat!' and 'begone!'"

"One moment, demon," I said. "If indeed you harbor tenderness for our husband, tell us then, what is to prevent us from finding this Hyaganoosh and persuading her to undo the wrong she has done us?"

"Naught but a piddling desert, an insignificant sea and a bit of a mountain range, O strange one," the djinn replied. "The Emir was not entirely convinced by the story his fair one told him, I suspect. And though he cannot prove her treachery, he has chosen to send her away as a gift, from the looks of the entourage accompanying her. Probably to the King. The Emir has not been in high favor since the King's father banished him from the capital to administer these lands. Again for suspected but unproven treachery. The King is a boy on the verge of becoming a man and very susceptible to such gifts. It may work."

"I don't suppose you could help us snitch your bottle and then fly us over to where the woman is before you have to go back to the Emir, could you, venerable Uncle?" Aster wheedled.

The djinn was both mournful and indignant. "I can perform no such tasks on thy behalf, lady, while the Emir holds my soul sealed in my bottle. Strictly speaking, I should not have spoken at all. However, it is partly upon my head that such unsuitable beings as yourselves have been loosed upon this city and I felt it no more than my duty to warn you and to explain what befell my former master. Furthermore, my new master will kill thy husband if ever he learns the truth of this matter, even though Aman Akbar still wears a donkey's hide. The lot of you will be sold at market, I suppose, since no one in his proper mind would believe you are lawful wives—if the Emir believed that you were, he would probably put you to death as well. Therefore, avail yourselves of my wisdom and get you far from the reach of this Emir, and take your braying spouse with you."

Um Aman jingled across the garden behind us. If she discovered the djinn, she would rapidly undo these vestiges of goodwill he offered. If he discovered the gold she carried, he would be bound to take from her the gold that represented what hope we had left of a future.

Amollia fell quickly and noisily into a genuflection, all of her jewelry setting up a tremendous and concealing clatter. "Your advice is welcome as always, immortal one," she said. "But pray, do not let us hinder you in your work, but rejoin your master and allow us a moment or two alone to weep our women's tears for the life here we have lost."

"It would also help," I added, "if you could neglect to mention to your new lord that we're here."

"Hearing and obeying," the djinn replied and winked out, along with the treasure upon which he had been seated.

It took Aster's truly civilized, highly developed understanding of how to evade obedience of inconvenient laws and persons of authority to devise a plan to deliver us from our predicament. It also took the cooperation and connivance of Um Aman's cronies to implement the plan, and a great deal of Um Aman's hoarded gold.

The women did not have to be asked to come to the widow's home the next morning. As soon as prayers were over, they arrived en masse, their eyes shining with curiosity above their face coverings. Each in turn kicked her shoes into the courtyard before settling her behind onto the mud bricks of the yard. Once settled in this fashion, the women gazed up at us expectantly, waiting to hear our tale of woe regarding the loss of our home. By then, of course, everybody knew about our misfortune, since one woman's husband's second cousin's son had seen the sign on our gate in passing.

Aster's plan delighted them, and frightened them a little at the same time. But now that they had it straight from the mouth of the seeress that we were good and blessed women, most of them seemed inclined to enjoy our audacity and the chance to buy something beautiful, even if it was not for themselves. And truly, there was nothing wrong in such a plan, for were not wronged women supposed to be allowed to apply to the wives of the ruler for justice? That was within the law and surely it was a good thing to help a friend receive what was due her. It was doubtful that even the Emir would deny a mother and wives their rights if they followed the proper procedure, and if he did, and Um Aman and the foreign women came to harm, why then, the cronies had done their duty as friends and would have a large party to lament the woes of one of their number and a new story to tell for years to come.

So with Aster's carefully edited version of what she intended us to do ringing in their ears and Um Aman's gold burning in their palms, they set forth upon their individual shopping sprees to the stalls of the best of the silk merchant's, the carter's, the jeweler's, the cobbler's, and those other establishments where our needs might be obtained. Also, there were those truest friends of Um Aman's who were willing to loan jewelry of their own to help us make a more fitting appearance, despite the very real possibility that it might never be returned to them. Before they left, when preparations were completed, and while they were still seated, I saw Um Aman tuck a coin in the sleeve of each of their abayahs, and if the leathery lines around her eyes glistened with dampness, still her face was determined.

The women returned that afternoon with their booty, and the next day and the next their free hours were spent in the courtyards of first one and then another, so that no one in particular would be implicated in case of trouble (Aster's suggestion), sewing, embroidering, and otherwise fashioning the silk and jewelry into garments and curtains for the litter being produced by the carter at our order.

At last Khadija, the oldest of Um Aman's friends and the best embroiderer, shook the kinks out of her reddened fingers and passed the garment she had been sewing over to Aster. Her daughter did likewise and her pretty young granddaughter, who had chattered with excitement during the whole three days' worth of work, licked the last of her needle pricks and added her shimmering contribution. Certain children received in front of the doors of wealthy houses other items which had been ordered. When all was in readiness we four gathered in the house of the seeress, who lived near the Emir's palace. Earlier that day we had accompanied the other women to the hammam baths, where we had bathed and oiled and perfumed ourselves with ointments and fragrances purchased and borrowed, but all of fine quality, before donning once more our own dusty clothing. Now we flew around an equally dusty room, for the seeress did not see such insignificant things as dust in her own home, and fastened, pinned, tied, polished, adjusted, combed, brushed, draped and patted our costumes into place, finishing with the help of the seeress and Um Aman by applying kohl to our eyes and rouge to our lips and cheeks and beautifying henna symbols to our palms and fingers and faces—the latter were for Amollia and me. Aster said it was more high class to do without the henna.

For Amollia and I were to be the serving women, walking beside the palanquin while Aster, dressed as a great lady, rode within. Um Aman was not overly fond of her own role, which was to wait for us at the caravanserai in case we needed to bolt. Then too, if we did not return, she would have Aman Akbar to care for. She could not risk prison, rotting inside the Emir's dungeon while on the outside her son could be bought and sold as the beast of burden he appeared to be. After more than a few stern words, she departed. Aster climbed into the palanquin, Khadija's out-of-work male third cousins picked up either end, and we paraded out of the back alley which was all but deserted now in the midday heat. From there we had only to round a corner to the main gate of the Emir's palace.

Amollia coolly announced to the guards that we— Aster that is—had been requested to visit the wives of the Emir of Kharristan by the newest wife of her own husband, the King of Persia, who was, she said, related to one of the Emir's ladies. They could announce that the Princess of Wu, wife of the King of Persia, had arrived.

The Emir's ladies were delighted to see us, which was hardly surprising. During the days Aman Akbar had left me alone in the harem, I would have been glad of visitors too.

We tried to make an interesting spectacle of ourselves. Amollia and I each carried a ceremonial-looking but quite functional spear, embellished with paint and colored feathers and so on. Our abayahs were bright blue, as per Persian custom, with gold at the sleeves, the edge of the veil and hem. Aster wore a scarlet brocade jacket with a pattern of gold and rubies (Well, they looked like rubies.) and all-but-transparent red-and-gold-striped trousers with lots of jewelry on her feet and hands and Khadija's grandmother's ruby earrings hanging to her shoulders. Her hair hung straight under a golden turban with red plumes.

The Emir's women, more sensibly, wore very little indeed, for it was the hottest part of a hot day. My own garments were soaking and I deeply hoped nothing untoward would happen, for I wasn't sure I retained the strength to deal with it.

Amollia and I stood by the door and tried to keep straight faces while Aster was offered the softest cushions upon which to sit and the nicest of dainties upon which to snack. We waited for her to make her move and wondered. For one so talkative she had been vague on a number of rather important points which now began to occur to me. All she had said, really, was that if we would follow her plan to get her inside the harem, she would obtain the bottle and all of this rested on her faith that wealthy, bored, fashion-conscious women of one country were very much like wealthy, bored, fashion-conscious women of any other. Since I had never known anyone of that description, I had to take her word for it but she certainly sounded as if she knew what she was talking about, so I didn't object. Amollia seemed to have faith in her, but Amollia seemed to have faith in everyone. Um Aman, as I've hinted, invoked her God with great vociferousness for blessings for our success and gruesome vengeances if we failed.

The Emir's wives were uniformly raven-tressed and dark-eyed except for one copper-haired woman who appeared rather miserable but who wore many more jewels than the others. Though many of them were extremely pretty, they had in common a listlessness, which may have been due to the heat, a dullness around the eyes, and a certain bloated quality bespeaking lack of exercise. Among them, Aster, about whom there was nothing dull, listless or static, looked more like a goddess than a princess. She played it to the hilt, gazing down upon the others from her lofty height a full head shorter than any of them, even sitting.

Her gracious silence and unspoken disdain of her surroundings caused them to jabber and show off all the more to impress her. Women of my tribe wouldn't have taken kindly to such an attitude, and would probably have stoned her for her airs, but these ladies were well-aware of the advantage to be gained from a person of importance. Aster casually clapped her hands and had Amollia crawl forward to present one of the necklaces we had had made and though it was of mediocre workmanship and not all that costly, the recipient, the Emir's second wife, seemed sure that if it came from Aster it was rare and costly. At any rate, she admired it a great deal, keeping any misgivings she had to herself.

The others passed it around and I crawled forward, tangling myself badly in the folds of my garment but otherwise managing to conceal my distaste for crawling, and presented Aster with another casket of earrings and lesser jewels. These she laid on the floor, allowing the wives to pick over them like children scuffling for candy at a festival.

A very young one gigglingly admired the effect of her new pearl ear-drops in a gold-backed hand mirror. "Are all the ladies in Persia wearing these, Princess Aster? And what about your women guards? I think that's frightfully novel, to have women guarding you. Would they be strong enough if some man absolutely couldn't control himself—you know, if he happened to glimpse your beauty or something, and tried to assault you?"

"If Amollia and Rasa couldn't handle him, my little pet, Kalimba, would have him for dinner," Aster sniffed smugly, reaching out to pet the cat, attached to her wrist by a length of gold-colored metal. Kalimba, not caring that she went better with Aster's outfit than with Amollia's, growled warningly, and Aster's hand quickly returned to her lap. "You see, she's showing off how fierce she is."

"Ooh, I think it's rather dangerous, but rather intriguing too. What do you do with the cat when your husband comes to your chamber?"

"Why nothing. Don't you customarily have your leopard lying by your side when your husband loves you?"

"I don't remember," the second wife said with more wit than I'd have given her credit for. "However, Onan did once give me a jewel box with a cat upon the lid that looks just like your pet. Would you like to see it?"

Aster indicated with a sweep of her lashes that she would, and one of the younger wives scurried off to fetch it.

"*Charming*," Aster pronounced, examining the emerald eyes, the topaz spots on a coat of solid gold.

"Do you really like it? It's quite old actually. It looks exactly like your cat, doesn't it?"

"It certainly does," Aster admitted, as if she were just being pleasant. "Why, the eyes are the exact shade, aren't they?"

"That they are. You must take it. I insist."

"How very gracious," Aster said, accepting the box and snapping her fingers. Amollia glanced uncertainly at me, gave a slight shrug of one shoulder, dropped to all fours again and crawled forward to receive the trinket.

"Just which of the Persian King's wives *are* you, Princess Aster?" a brash young thing inquired.

"His favorite," she said without hesitation.

"The guard mentioned something about a new wife having a relative here?"

"Ah, yes, that was the point of my visit. This poor little thing who came to us from one of the—less conventional—routes. She's so terribly homesick. She asked if while I was here I wouldn't visit and see her cousin Hyaganoosh. Which of you might that be?"

"What a pity!" the second wife said. "She has left this palace and been sent to another establishment in Sindupore. It was a promotion, you understand, but sudden."

"Amana will be so disappointed," Aster said. "She specifically asked me to see her cousin and tell me what her rooms were like, if she had a garden to enjoy, what sort of presents her husband had given her. Such a child! Still, I suppose I can invent something reassuring."

"Dear Princess Aster, if it will ease your kind heart, we'll be only too happy to conduct you on a tour of the harem."

Aster allowed that it would ease her kind heart a great deal.

"Lovely," she said indifferently, when shown the pools, the gardens, the thick dark-red carpets so intricately ornamented and piled upon one another, the gold-inlaid tile work, the gold and silver fixtures, the luxurious appointments throughout. "Cozy little place. How charmingly quaint to have such a profusion of—things. I'm afraid the current trend in Persia is toward a certain elegant simplicity. Oh, quite stark actually, compared to *your* sweet little palace. Take those lovely rugs there. Now, for a person of a certain . . . individual bent, those would be just the thing to have exactly as you have them, but the floors at home are kept bare except for the marble tiles, which are shined to a high gloss with the elbow grease of Nubian slaves. And a room may have but a single ornament, say a vase like this one," —She ran a finger around the lip of a vase I recognized suddenly as having stood a few days before in the library of our palace—"adorned only with a spray of winter branches. *That's* the sort of thing I mean. They're doing it in all the best houses now, I understand, from Mesopotamia to Baghdad. How delightful to see such . . . traditional ideas still prevail in some parts of the world."

"It sounds a strange fashion to me," a younger wife said, wrinkling her alabaster brow.

"Not really. It is simply a matter of a certain sparseness, I suppose you might call it," she said with a world-weary sigh, "a lack of the usual cushions, rugs, jars, lamps, and bottles, replacing all of these little knick-knacks with uncluttered elegance."

"Isn't that rather bare?" one wife asked.

"My dear, that's just the point, don't you see? You *have* heard surely that in order to have more it is sometimes necessary to have less?"

That wife looked baffled but another said slyly, "You did say you are from Wu, did you not? Because all of this seems very inscrutable to me."

Aster laughed. "My dear, I couldn't agree with you more. But it *is* the way things are done in Persia and the other centers of fashion these days.

"I seem to have missed this trend," the second wife said, and the worry in her voice slipped through only slightly. "I do wish our husband would keep me informed of such matters when he goes abroad. It is so much to his advantage that his household be foremost in Kharristan with the current styles."

"The best ideas *are* slow to filter into the provinces," Aster said beneficently.

A concubine sitting near my feet drew her veil across her mouth and whispered up to me, "How in God's name can your mistress afford all that bareness? Where does she *put* her household things?"

"That's a simple matter," I said, suddenly inspired and beginning, finally, to understand Aster's plan. "She gives three presents for each gift she receives and each gift she gives is of twice the value of the one she receives. It keeps her busy, trying to maintain that stylish bareness, but as a result her rooms *are* fashionable and her generosity renowned."

The recipient of this information considered it for a brief time, then turned to the woman beside her to whisper.

Someone buzzed softly into the second wife's ear and she asked Aster, "You truly like these carpets, milady? You don't think they're—too much?"

"Certainly not. Why, they really—um—add something." She sounded as if the something might be rust, perhaps, or mold.

"Then, oh light of grace and beauty, you must take them with you as a token of my esteem and that of my husband's house! You there, girls, roll up these rugs for Her Highness. Our master would not like her to report to her husband the King of Persia that we were neglectful of her household needs, and everyone knows that the rugs to be found in the markets here in Kharristan are of superior quality."

"I'm overwhelmed," Aster said. She continued to be overwhelmed with golden platters, a bit of jewelry she yawningly admired in one room or the other, an ornamental sword, and various vases, but I could see that disappointment and restlessness were overtaking her pleasure in this charade. It didn't seem to be producing the results for which she had hoped.

"And this is Leila's room now," the second wife led us, huffing and puffing under the weight of the treasures acquired in the last room, to a charming chamber with a familiar latticed window overlooking a rose garden. The red-haired woman sat possessively in a corner and looked embarrassed. Aster scanned the room with the eye of a wolf selecting the weakest but tenderest lamb. "It used to belong to Hyaganoosh."

This was obviously also the room where the Emir now spent his nights. Though the chests carved from precious gems and scented woods probably provided storage for most of his clothing, lengths of silk and gauze trailed negligently across the floor. While Aster loudly and fervently admired every box and container in the room in hopes, I suppose, that the bottle might have been stored in one of them, the cat paced restlessly at the end of its chain and began toying with the end of one of the silken lengths, batting at it. Aster's voice grew louder and more brittle and the women began to look affronted. Amollia's face was wary. Aster was definitely overdoing it. The women had no authority to give her the Emir's personal belongings, and despite her assurances that she would be sending them a few things by messenger from her Persian palace as soon as she returned home, some of them were beginning to look with regret at the items they had given her. Only the cat seemed natural and unconcerned, peering out from beneath a self-made veil, probably one of the Emir's sashes, and batting an obligingly roly-poly article between her front paws. No one else was watching, and since I was too encumbered to bend down and examine the object, I snagged it with the butt of my spear and rolled it toward me. The cat didn't like that, but her chain didn't reach far enough for her to argue with me. The cork to the djinn's bottle! What was it doing rolling around on the floor? And where was the bottle in which it belonged and the accursed contents of that bottle? Even as I wondered at these matters, I dropped the rugs and embroideries I carried with the pretense of rearranging my load and when I picked them up again, scooped up the cork as well hiding it in my own sash inside my abayah.

Aster was making her goodbyes by then, pretending to take careful note of the names of each wife in order to know to whom to address the gifts she wished to send. Amollia led the way out of the chamber perhaps a bit sooner than Aster was ready to leave, and I was right behind her. The Emir's ladies were looking decidedly peevish. The open litter was as welcome a sight as a cave in a thunderstorm and Amollia and I rushed toward it as fast as pomp permitted, and tossed our burdens inside, while Aster and the second wife chatteringly followed behind. We would have been safe enough if the Emir hadn't chosen that moment to return home.

# *Chapter* 6

I do not think that the separation of men and women is a good idea, the way it is done here in my husband's country. It makes some of the men a little crazy. The Emir rode into the courtyard with a number of his guard, all of them on gleaming black steeds, and his eyes did everything but fly out of their sockets when he beheld the unveiled Aster among his wives.

At first I thought he must know who we were and what I had found, for he leapt from his horse's back as if he were a far younger, trimmer man, except that he caught his foot in the horse's silken trappings. That alone saved us. For while he was fumbling, Aster bolted for the litter and the cousins of Khadija trotted off double fast through the still-open gate before the guards realized that anything was amiss. As we passed them I heard the Emir babble, "But who is she? That shining one? I must have her! Who is she?"

He followed us a few steps and I looked back, expecting to see the guards wheeling to bear down on us as we gained the street. Instead I saw the Emir's second wife, hastily veiled before the guards, throwing herself around his legs and crying, "Stop, Dawn of My Day, cease pursuing our guest, for she is the Queen of Persia and you would insult her husband."

I didn't hear any more than that for the litter bearers whipped us around the corner to the seeress's house and ran off down a back alley. The three of us dragged the litter inside, pulled off our finery and donned our old clothing, covering ourselves with dusty, well-used abayahs. By the time the hoofbeats of the Emir's guard shook the walls of our refuge, we were peacefully sitting on the roof, helping our hostess sort her inventory of charms and chicken bones. The litter had been chopped up for firewood, the fine gowns folded and hidden with the other treasures behind the bedding.

Indeed, we felt ourselves very clever and free from detection until suddenly a column of smoke descended upon us and the seeress covered her face with her veil and prostrated herself. The djinn stood before us, glowering. Aster fell into a coughing fit. Too much smoke, no doubt.

"You certainly get around," I said to the djinn.

"I am not the only one," he said severely, and a little plaintively. "O wives of my former master, why must you always be the agents of complication and chaos?" I wondered if our Yahtzeni demons were nearly so prone to whining and self-pity as this creature.

Aster recovered and smiled winningly at him. "On the contrary, O being of everlastingly long years, we were bent upon doing you a good turn and delivering you from your captivity."

"Or at least making it possible for you to be the captive of someone more appreciative of your powers," Amollia added judiciously.

"Whatever was in thy tiny woman's mind, thou hast botched it, for now I am bound to deliver thee to my master, who having seen thy face is overcome with the passionate desire to possess thee."

Aster considered this only a moment before waving it airily aside. "Out of the question, Old Uncle. The Lady Aster, the dutiful wife you see sitting here before you, has never had the so-called honor of meeting the illustrious and felonious person who employs you. How can he therefore be so enamoured of her?"

"Don't be coy with me, habibi. Thou wast within his dwelling but a short time ago and he saw thee unveiled. I told Aman Akbar that failing to train his women in the proper veiling procedures would—"

"But it was not I in his courtyard," Aster said, "but

a Persian Queen. The only resemblance between us is that we are both—ahem—very beautiful and virtuous married ladies."

"It was thee I saw crawl into the palanquin, O gem of infidelity. Thinkest thou I do not recognize the plague of impiety and impropriety I have loosed upon this land in thy form and the forms of thy accomplices?"

"Ah, but I tell you, dear djinn, that you are mistaken. Ask any of the Emir's wives. They will tell you we were nowhere near the palace today, such humble women fallen so low as we are, all but widowed."

The djinn placed both pudgy hands on his turban as if his head had expanded to fill it and moaned. "But he has required of me that I fetch thee—"

I crawled between the djinn and Aster and pointed at him. "You heard her, demon. We aren't going. Haven't you done us enough harm?"

"Rasa," Amollia said reprovingly. But the djinn stared at me and shook his head again, while Aster continued with the voice of sweet reason, though she had to peer around me to meet the demon's piggy little eyes.

"Dear Old Uncle, do you not understand that you have been asked to fetch to your master a Queen? You cannot bring him a low-born foreign woman, no longer a virgin. Like many men, your poor master has fallen in love with an illusion that not even a djinn can supply. Go to him and say the lady has already left for Persia and seek no more to dishonor your former mistresses."

The djinn gave her a perplexed look and me one so full of anxious confusion that he appeared ludicrous. "You heard her," I snapped. "Go."

"Hearing and obeying," he replied, and smoked back over the rooftops.

We left with the caravan that same afternoon, hired camels and Aman Akbar carrying Aster's booty. We were now officially rug-and-silk merchants, though we had enough variety of goods to open any sort of stall we cared to. If our appearance was shabbier than that of the other merchants in the caravan, no one commented.

In fact, four unaccompanied women excited a great deal
of unsolicited solicitousness among our traveling companions, who seemed to be trying to look through our
draperies to see if we were worth adding to their own
collections.

We rode in little houses called howdahs atop the
backs of camels. I suppose the idea was that being in
the howdah would not only shelter one from the sun
but would also serve to ameliorate the effects of the
camel's rocking gait upon one's stomach. Not so. I am a
good horsewoman but I am not a good rider of camels, I
confess. I preferred for the most part to walk along
side, though I suffered from the sun despite my abayah
and sandals. By the standards of my own country my
skin was well-weathered and tough, but I found I was
ill-prepared for this climate: my skin burned and peeled.
My temper soured and curdled. Aster declared I was
more than a match for Um Aman at her worst. But if
my temper put me in a poor mood to deal with my
friends, it put me in an excellent one to deal with foes.

But even Amollia's good nature was somewhat taxed
by the journey. Animal lover that she is, she made a
perfunctory attempt at befriending the camels, but said
she found their personalities only slightly more amiable
than mine.

Thus we traveled for several days with the caravan,
under the delusion of protection, four helpless, weak,
and for my part, heat-sick females. We saw waves of
sand, and waves of heat, and supercilious camel smiles,
and dung-dropping camel behinds, and endured the
speculative eyeball rollings and half-jeering remarks of
our companions . . . until the brigands livened things up
by sweeping down upon us and causing a carnage that
quite revitalized me, despite the heat.

It happened suddenly. One moment there was
nothing but sand as far as the eye could see and the
next a flapping white line, like a flock of geese on the
horizon. The man leading the camel ahead of ours
shouted and flung out a hand, and several others shouted
also and drew swords. I had retained the ornamental
weapon given Aster by the Emir's wives and drew it

too, just in time. The dots on the horizon rapidly grew into horses and men. The blood from the rider of the lead camel of our caravan was already spurting from his neck before my sword was drawn. All around us animals and men churned the sand and camels scattered in all directions. Single members of the deadly flock detached themselves and gave chase to the faint-hearted souls who had suddenly decided to seek another route, while the main body attacked those who stood against them. I cleaved a limb or a neck here and there but the sword was dull and unless I could pounce unexpectedly upon a brigand, I found myself without adversaries. Even the foes I wounded seemed disinclined to take me and my blunted sword seriously. By the time I looted a decent scimitar from one of the bodies, what was left of the caravan was in the hands of the attackers.

Depending upon how you look at such things, good fortune or ill dictated that we women were regarded as booty and were taken prisoner rather than slain outright, as were those of our companions foolish enough to fight for their goods.

The problems for our foes began when they attempted to take possession of us. A brigand seized Amollia, who struggled. This displeased the cat, who leaped upon the brigand, whose companion drew a scimitar and sliced at the cat. Both cat and its prey were saved only when Amollia wrenched herself from the grasp of her assailant, causing that man to fall, cat and all, to the ground. Whereupon Amollia whistled loudly and the cat bounded away and sailed over the nearest sand dune.

Our husband bucked and bit those who would steal him, behaving as might any self-respecting ass under similar circumstances.

A flying bundle of draperies dragged Aster backwards from her camel at the beginning of the raid and I didn't see her till sometime later. Um Aman sensibly chose to throw herself onto the sand and pray through the whole thing.

I for my part cheerfully waded in to exchange

hacks and slashes with a great many fellows who no longer could afford to ignore me. What added to my cheer was that, perhaps due to Um Aman's prayers, I avoided being wounded in the exchange. The sons of dogs did outnumber me, however, and while I was defending myself with my excellent second-hand weapon, a pair of the wretches took me from behind, one grappling my knees and the other yanking my head backwards and laying hold of my veils and hair. I was severely irritated. Say if you must that all things are fair in love and war, but having just fought a great deal of the latter, I was in no mood for even more of the former, which, unless I missed my guess, was what these thieves had in mind for us all.

My suspicions were confirmed when a brigand lay his forearm across my throat, pressed his cheek next to mine, breathing noxious fumes laden with something akin to essence of well-aged goat urine and camel milk mixed with blood (a common drink among that sort of person. It smells even worse than it sounds), growled, "Aha, this one fancies herself a man. Shall I slay her like one?"

"What? And waste all that? By God, the sun has broiled your wits at last," the other replied and snatched my abaya askew from under his comrade's meaty arm.

'Twas my gallant spouse saved my honor, or at least delayed its loss long enough for me to save it myself.

With a stricken bray and hooves spraying sand, Aman Akbar galloped into the clutch of ruffians surrounding me. His hooves clouted them like clubs of iron and his back arched and straightened, a catapult of bucking to power his mighty kicks. All the while his awesome voice rent the desert air with its shrill clamor of ass's indignation.

More with the thought of escaping being stricken by those hooves myself than of actually obtaining freedom, I ducked below the shock-loosened arm of my chief captor and sprinted across the sand—straight into the perfumed arms of the limpid-eyed, moon-faced gentleman who had been sweeping forth to peruse the results of the raid.

"Kill the damned donkey!" a voice behind me bellowed.

"Never mind him! That thrice-accursed woman's attacking the Khan!"

I was not. I was tripping upon my disarranged draperies and he, in his attempt to rise, was tangling them with his own and with the sword still in his scabbard. Having heard the brigand threaten Aman Akbar, I tried to free myself to race back to his defense, but as I finally extricated myself momentarily from my new complication, I saw that Amollia had preceded me. Like a great black falcon she swooped into the fray, smashing the circle surrounding our husband and throwing herself upon the man who clung to Aman's stubby mane and held a blade to our poor husband's jaw. Blood stained Aman's pale coat already but with great deftness Amollia pried the blade from the brigand's hand and sent it flying.

She wasn't able to prevail for long. In an instant another brigand flung himself upon her, and Aman Akbar shot out from under all three, galloping off to attack from yet another position. In this endeavor Kalimba joined him, her spots again streaking to stripes as she launched herself at the men with whom her mistress was locked in combat. Her ferocious scream was such, as they say in this land, to turn the hair of children gray.

And now, her prayers finished, Um Aman joined the battle. The nails of her hands raised like talons before her, her veil slipped down over one cheek, its beaded string dangling from her chin, she rushed forward in defense of her beleaguered son. The brigand atop Amollia all but lost his eyes, saving himself only by twisting aside in time to swing his arm across both of hers, rapping her across the ear.

He in turn was rapped by Aster, who sprang forth as if from nowhere, leaving a brigand behind her clutching futilely at the torn black robe she had discarded as easily as a serpent shedding its skin.

Beneath it she wore a simple blue robe, and had gathered its long sleeves into her hands. These sleeves she swung with such momentum that I saw they had weights in their tips, and using them as cudgels she felled three of the men, including the one who held her robes, almost before anyone knew she was there.

My heart sang within me. This was more like it! From a complete rout, it looked as if we might be winning. At least we were fighting. Screaming my father's battle cry I bounded forward, only to be yanked back, my own sash jerking tightly across my middle.

"Hold, my impetuous beauty," the voice behind me said with maddening calm and even gentleness. "In the name of God the compassionate and compassioning, I bid you hold."

"Hold yourself," I replied, twisting so that I might smite him. He skipped nimbly out of smiting distance. "I have a battle to fight here."

"So I see," he said, and inserted two fingers between his lips, blowing a loud, piercing whistle. "Cease, by God, as your commander I bid you, cease this warring against women and beasts!"

"They started it," one of his men protested.

"By God, we did not—" Um Aman began angrily. But the commander whistled again, silencing them all.

"Hearing and obeying," the men mumbled with various degrees of meekness, and the one who had obtained a firm grip around Amollia's bosom lowered his arms until they sedately encircled her waist instead.

"For shame!" the leader scolded. "Do you think we are common brigands to—"

"As a matter of fact . . ." I began. He glowered at me.

"You dishonor the principles for which we fight. Rich merchants to fatten our war chests are one thing. Women fighting for their lives and virtue—"

"And *winning*," I growled. I was angry at having to stop while we were ahead.

"Are another. Ah, ah, ah, ah!" He shook a finger admonishingly at a fellow with a scar cutting diagonally across a face that probably hadn't inspired songs to its beauty before but now gave him the fearsome aspect of having two noses, "Touch not the loyal ass, nor yet the lion. These noble beasts but defended their helpless mistresses, thereby preserving us from committing a great wrong. Ladies, lay down your weapons. Come to my tents where you may cool yourselves in the shade while we tend your wounds."

Accepting an invitation was not the same thing as being captured. I realized, when the hot blood that rose in my veins during battle ceased surging against my throat, that we could not have won. There were vast numbers of these men and we had escaped murder at their hands only because of the benefit they hoped to gain by reason of our sex—whether to slake their own lusts or to sell us as slaves. Their master seemed of a different mind and I saw no reason to antagonize him. We could not fight indefinitely nor could we flee into the desert without camels or water so it seemed best to accept his hospitality.

Um Aman took this to extremes. Upon ducking into the dimness of the man's tent, she immediately threw herself across the rich carpets spread on the sand and sprawled beside a lady who was turning a handmill. The startled woman fell back on her heels and Um Aman grasped the handle and cried, "I lay an *ar* upon you to protect my family and the family of my son. A thousand virulent curses smite you if you dishonor us."

In doing this, she evoked another of the customs of her people. A woman whose protector is absent may claim protection from another man by doing as Um Aman did, throwing herself upon the mercy of her host. Though women ordinarily did not choose to appeal to those who murdered their escorts, I suppose, the custom was not without practical merit. For the appeal to the man's nobler instincts was backed by the promise of messy, painful and inconvenient occurrences which would befall him should he fail in his duty toward his involuntarily acquired obligation.

Our host was clearly put out. "Where is this son of yours that he cannot protect his own family?" he demanded.

"You know very well where he is, oh my chosen protector," Um Aman replied smugly. "He is tethered outside with your animals."

"Tethered?" the two-nosed brigand asked, horrified. "Great Khan, I swear to you, we slew all the men but we didn't tether anybody! No one, that is, but the ass."

Aster hung her head with a childish sadness calculated to melt hard brigand hearts and said, "That is no ass, that is our husband."

The leader, called Marid Khan, sat down abruptly, missing the cushion he had aimed at and rubbing his hip as he regarded us. He bit into an apple and chewed for a while before asking, "And what manner of women are you, helpless ones, to be married to and the mother of an ass?"

"Whoever they are, Marid Khan," one of the men commented as he dressed the scratches inflicted by Um Aman's nails upon one of his fellows, "they fought as tigers."

"One of them *is* a tiger," Two Noses pointed out and addressed Um Aman directly, "Is she your daughter too, old woman?"

"Enough," the Khan said, gesturing us all to sit, for women had begun pouring into the tent bearing with them viands whose odors immediately dispelled any desire I might have had to make or listen to lengthy explanations.

Marid's chosen profession required a lot of moving, and with this we, as new members of his tribe, were expected to help, as well as with the spinning, weaving, cooking and other tasks. I felt comforted by the familiarity of these tasks, much as I disliked them.

We traveled in not only dangerous but exalted company, for not only was Marid Khan no ordinary brigand; he was a rather extraordinary rebel prince. His people had roamed the desert freely in the time of the Emir's predecessor and had traded peaceably with the city folk. Marid himself had been sent to Kharristan as a boy to be educated and to learn courtly manners. But upon the ascension of the Emir Onan to the governorship of Kharristan, the favored position of Marid Khan and his people changed for the worse. Around the same time, problems developed between the throne and

Madrid's people. Some aunt of Marid's had disappeared from the King's harem and the mutterings were that she had been slain.

Marid's stance as leader of his people was to enrich them and gain honor and status in the kingdom by relieving the city of much of its excess wealth. What he would do once he was rich wasn't really clear, but everyone was delighted with the loot obtained by robbing the caravans and so far no one had thought to question his plans beyond that point. He was, after all, a relatively young leader. To make war and gain prosperity seemed like a good start.

The men of this tribe were not the only warlike ones. The women were constantly quarreling among themselves, a practice they discontinued only long enough to torment us. I had begun to think that all women in these lands liked the idea of sharing husbands, but rapidly learned I was in error. Amollia's amiable attitude toward polygamy was far from universal. Though men liked to have as many wives as they could afford, the women felt that the only way to ensure being first in the affections of their husbands was to be the only spouse. Three apparently unattached and unrelated young women were therefore most unwelcome to the other women. The wives were afraid their husbands would decide to take one of us as an additional wife. The single women liked us even less, for Marid Khan was very eligible indeed and might decide to choose one or more of us over the girls who had hopes of winning him for themselves.

Nor were they wrong, for before long I noticed Marid casting longing looks in Aster's direction. One evening shortly thereafter, when she was over-long fetching a waterskin, I found her near where the animals were tethered. She was engaged in a hair-pulling, face-scratching contest with three of the unmarried women who shared our tent. This was not my sort of fight, and I would have left her to it except that one of the others pulled a knife. I had no trouble disarming her without harm to anyone, but she made a great deal of noise and a crowd gathered.

Um Aman, Amollia and Marid Khan were among those gathered. Marid Khan grunted something harsh to the other women and they ran off.

"Is this how you protect us, mighty prince?" Um Aman demanded.

Marid Khan was not accustomed to reprimand. "The girl had no business out here alone anyway."

Aster had lost only a small patch of hair while gaining four parallel scratches down one cheek. She seemed to feel that by being the last one left at the scene of the battle she had won for she tossed her tangled hair and watched with glinting eyes while her adversaries departed. Now she turned to Marid Khan and tried to look piteous. "I was but being a dutiful wife and taking a bit of fruit to my poor husband, mighty Khan," she protested.

"Don't start that again!" Marid warned her. "It is you women who are under a spell, not that simple ass. You are to stay away from that beast, do you hear me, or I will have it killed."

"The *ar* I placed upon you covers my son too," Um Aman reminded him.

"*Ars* cover people, not livestock," he told her. "Mind what I say."

We had to return at once to the sleeping tent, but when everyone else was facing one direction, Amollia turned briefly and pointed, and the cat who followed her like part of her skirts streaked back to the place where Aman was tethered.

The four of us settled close to one side of the tent that night while all the other women hugged the opposite side. We shared the largest of the carpets we had gleaned from our visit to the Emir's palace. Marid Khan had granted that we keep it, along with our personal jewelry and other small loot Aster managed to conceal in her sleeves. Um Aman quickly fell into a muttering sleep, but Amollia, Aster and I waited until the other women slept. We were far from certain Aster's assailants would not repeat their attack in the night. Outside, the last few cooking fires winked out one by one.

When the tent began filling with smoke, I thought for a moment one of them had gotten out of hand, for I did not at first recognize the djinn in his vaporous form. But very quickly the smoke solidified into his familiar rotund figure, and he bowed.

"Greetings, infidels," he said to the three of us. "I must say you have certainly led me a merry chase."

"You have great nerve to speak of us leading you, djinn," Aster replied, whispering. "I hope you are proud of yourself to drive poor frightened women from the comforts of the city by reason of your master's greed and lust."

"Slant-eyed one," he said. "Thou hast so far heard nothing. Indeed, it is through benevolence that I seek thee out—to warn thee that thou and thy comrades had best adjust yourselves to the fact that soon my master will discover all of the import of your thievery."

# Chapter
7

"Thievery!" Aster cried indignantly. "You forget yourself, djinn. If you think our transactions with the Emir's wives were thievery, you obviously know nothing of the craft."

"Let us say then," the djinn began, steepling his pudgy fingers and rocking back and forth on the smoke below his billowing trousers, "that you removed from the house of the Emir certain items."

"Gifts freely given us by his ladies," Aster shrugged defensively. "Trinkets. Tokens of their esteem. Nothing more."

"Aha!" the djinn cried. "The faithless wenches *gave*

you their husband's treasures, did they? No wonder it has taken him so long to wonder where all of the missing items have disappeared to. Summer cleaning indeed! I knew it all along. Fortunately for both you and his wives, the Emir has followed his usual pattern of disregarding my great wisdom and has yet to ask *me* to locate that which he deems lost." His small eyes narrowed to become even smaller and he said in a rather oily tone, "You have been very foolish little women, but you are new to our land and its customs. Therefore I will once more be kind to you and suggest that I can see that you are no longer interfered with. If I must wait until my master commands me to deliver to him his property and the thieves thereof, it will go hard on you. Whereas if you give me that same property to return now, we can avoid exposing your tender and ignorant persons to this man of strong power and weak character, for I can assure thee, in particular, Lady Aster, that once he learns who has purloined his possessions he will demand the addition of thee as interest on his loan of them to thee or else have thee put to death."

"You seem to know his intentions rather well even though, as you claim, he has not consulted you," I remarked.

"Service is my life," the djinn replied modestly. "Therefore, if I can quietly return to the Emir these things you hold—"

"If we save you all that trouble," Aster said, overriding him. "It seems to me that you should do something for us in return."

"*Aiyeeah!* Why did my former master choose to marry horsetraders of every nation? Foolish woman, I seek to do thee a service!"

"And so you can. In return for those items you want, which will cause us considerable trouble to take back from Marid Khan (if indeed we can get them) and which must be worth something if the Emir desires them so much, you must revoke Aman's curse."

"Only she who invoked it may revoke it," he said primly.

"Then you must help us reunite Hyaganoosh and your bottle long enough that *she* may cause you to lift the curse from him."

"That would be just," the djinn agreed. "Particularly if she transferred the curse to you, stubborn creatures that you are. However, I can do no such thing, even if I wished to do so, while the Emir holds the bottle."

"But you can come here on your own, without his knowledge," Aster said, swinging her arms in a wide swing. "I find this very strange."

The djinn gazed at her owlishly. "Dost thou really? *I* find *that* very strange. For thou of all people should now realize that once a wine is decanted, the full flavor cannot be recaptured until the spirits are resealed once more in the bottle." Had the heat of the desert overcome the djinn, that he should speak to us of wine when we were talking of magic? It seemed so, for though he had been about to say more he suddenly stopped, wafted lightly backwards and began to fade. "Excuse me, thou art correct, of course. What if my master called me and I wasn't there? Why—er—naturally, I must be going. But consider our bargain and I will try to speak of this with you later—" and he quickly dissolved and cleared the tent.

We had no chance to forget the so-called bargain, nor to honor it, for the matter was taken from our hands. I thought I felt a disturbance in the tent during the night, but so weary was I by the time I finally slept that the faint rush of air and moonlight, as of the tent flap raising and lowering, disturbed me not. Nor later, as it must have been, when something touched my lips and instantly soothed me into a deeper, more profound sleep. And not only I but the others Marid Khan had sworn to protect slept like the dead while around us our shelter was removed so that when we awoke it was from the heat of the sun baking down upon us. Tent, carpets, cushions and camp had all stolen away in the night, taking everything but our clothing and the rug we were lying upon, even the animals—including Aman Akbar and the cat.

Um Aman opened one eye and began to wail more

loudly than ever she had done outside my bedchamber when Aman and I were making love. "You wretched girl!" she shrieked at Aster. "Now see what you've done! They've cast us out! I ensured our protection and you have offended our hosts and ruined it all."

"A thousand pardons, old mother," Aster yawned, wincing slightly as she stretched her bruised arms and blandly surveyed the vast, empty desert. "I should have let them beat me senseless, I suppose?"

The inside of my mouth tasted of a strange bittersweetness, and my lips were coated at the center with a sticky substance. Amollia picked at her teeth with her finger and examined the finger afterward. "Umm," she said, nodding to herself. Aster and I stared at her, waiting for an explanation. Um Aman continued to wail. "This little bit of red flesh and seed—" Amollia said. "How strange to find the fruit of slumber so far from home."

"How strange indeed and how inauspicious," Aster said, sighing and pulling her legs up under her to sit crosslegged on the rug.

"Ignoble and cowardly is what it is," I said contemptuously. "I thought better of the empty-headed wretches when they tried to fight openly and honestly, as decent folk should."

"You wouldn't have if you'd gotten the rough end of their camel prods," Aster assured me. "But I'm surprised Marid Khan didn't miss us. No doubt he'll be heading back this way as soon as he discovers we're gone."

Amollia shook her head sadly and lay back down on the rug, drawing her knees up to her chest. "Not if they told him about the djinn."

Apparently not all of our tent mates had slept through the visit of our husband's former servant. Marid Khan feared Um Aman's curse. How much more would he fear a djinn? Enough to abandon to starvation, heat and thirst four already less-than-welcome guests? So it seemed.

Aster sighed. "I suppose there is no hope for it but that we must start walking back to the city. Maybe we will find a water bag someone has forgotten on the way.

Maybe even some other travelers who will take us with
them if we give them our rug. Maybe—"

"Maybe we'll get lost," Um Aman wailed.

"Once more, a thousand pardons, venerable one,"
Aster said. "I failed to realize that we are now safe and
comfortable. Perhaps in your aged wisdom you would
like to tell us that over the next dune is another city
whose ambassadors will be coming along shortly to
carry us within its walls in all style and luxury? Or
perhaps you know where there is a great river nearby
that will be flowing past us any moment now?"

Um Aman's reaction to the mockery was predictable.
After she slapped Aster smartly, she began wailing
again, though more hoarsely by now.

Amollia patted her shoulder and made clucking
sounds but the old woman shook her off. "I'm not
weeping. I have better sense than to waste the water of
my tears on the jibes of a tart like that one. You girls
are all so young, and you don't know the ways of the
desert as I do. No worse calamity could have befallen
us. I have been a good woman all my life, a pious
woman. Why has this happened to me? Oh, I wish to
God we were safely out of here in some green and
pleasant place where my poor son could be reunited
with his loving mother without fear of harm from Emirs
or djinns or any of this rich man's nonsense!"

Until then, I confess, I had not taken the local
religion seriously. I had seen Aman Akbar in the prayer
house and certainly Um Aman said loudly and often
how she felt about her god—but until that point I had
had no idea how the god felt about her. Most of ours
didn't pay us much attention, except to let us win a
skirmish or live through the winter with fewer deaths
than usual if our sacrifices pleased them and we performed
every word and gesture of the rituals correctly. If
things go badly, we assume we've fouled up the formula
somewhere or that the sheep sacrificed wasn't fat enough
or had some hidden disease, or our enemies were
offering a better one or more powerfully rendered
prayers. But never, never in my lifetime or in any of the
stories of my people was there an incidence of someone

but invoking the name of a god and—whoosh—the god picks up the rug the worshipper is sitting on and whisks her off to safety. And not only the worshipper but all of the non-worshippers with her. I began to think kindly of this god.

Actually, it didn't exactly whisk but rose gently from the desert, considerately, for it was a large rug and there were four persons for it to balance without spilling. It remained level at all times but rippled very slightly beneath us.

When Um Aman perceived what was happening, she paled somewhat but showed her mettle by immediately, if carefully, prostrating herself and beginning to pray in earnest.

Despite the hot breeze of our passing, we baked between the sizzling sky and the equally sizzling sand beneath it. This was worse heat than any I had endured in my life. It was far hotter than the city of Kharristan, hotter even than the clay ovens my mother made to bake her bread, hotter than the flames of cooking fires, or so it felt to me. Winter I understand well, and the warmth of summer has always been welcome to me, but this kind of heat was not fit for human life. Fear, blood and pain I can and have endured. But this heat drew the life from my body, sucked the vision from my eyes and sounds from my ears and sent the world spinning around me. I swooned.

At least I was not the only one to succumb, though all of the others were a good deal more accustomed to such heat than I. When I awoke only Um Aman was still alert but then, she was still in the throes of her recent religious experience, not only in body, as we all were, but in spirit as well. But she seemed to be having second thoughts, for now she was stretched out full length on the carpet, and squinting over the edge. I did not need to do likewise. What was below us was to be seen not just over the edge of the carpet, but extending on every side but one. Where before had stretched sand as far as the eye could see, now stretched water, a great blue sea of it. Um Aman's god did not do things by halves.

To the water, however, an end was in sight. For growing ever larger was a narrow ridge of brown, topped with green. Sea birds skimmed the air above us, mewing cattily, and as the distant land grew less distant, the roar of the water striking it grew more intense, competing with the bird cries. Aster stirred, opened her eyes, grimaced, and closed them again. Amollia woke as the rug climbed upward, perpendicular to the sheer cliff.

We gasped, shrieked and shuddered in turns as the carpet presented us with new concerns. Was it going to succeed in dodging *all* of the taller trees of this thickly forested land? Would it find a clearing, or just land us in a tree top to fall or climb down as best we could? Would we perhaps be mistaken for a large bird of prey and be shot down by some conscientious archer? Would we ever touch ground again? Once there, would we be able to find anything to eat or drink? The last question especially began to concern me, along with another, more private matter suggested with forceful urgency by the incessant swish and pound of the water below.

The rug settled downward through greenery sparked with flame-colored flowers and scented with a pungence that was a mixture of floral perfume and decay. The heavy fragrance, the raucous cries of the wild birds, the chirrup and chatter of other wild things hung in air denser than that in either the desert or in my own home near the steppes. I found it easier to breathe.

Easier yet did it become when the rug drifted to a stop as softly as a fallen leaf in front of a mud-brick structure baked a chalky white by the sun. It was unimpressive in size but the graceful lines of the facade were not those of a rude dwelling clumsily thrown together for shelter.

Flowering vines crawled up its sides and a walled terrace spread out before it, the stones gleaming like bones in the sunlight. Between the stones crept moss and the first trailings of new vines. I saw things slither into the shadows as the rug touched earth.

"Now where in the seven levels of hell do you suppose this is?" Aster asked, whistling.

It was the wrong thing to say, and ungrateful, after we had been delivered from the desert so expeditiously.

"Shut your ignorant mouth," Um Aman said. "This is a shrine, a holy place."

"Well, wherever it is, it's on solid ground," Aster replied, stepping very quickly across the outer border of the carpet and onto the terrace. "And this poor orphan is going to make sure she stays here should another fit of piety overcome you, mother-in-law."

I leapt off behind her and joined the slithery things in the shadows and tall brush long enough to relieve the most pressing matter concering me. Um Aman meanwhile was commanding the others to roll up the sacred carpet.

I pushed through the bushes and was stepping back onto the terrace when the first small stone struck me a glancing blow on the shoulder. My warrior's reflexes were somewhat dulled by the events of the day, but when I saw that the stone was followed by a shower of others on a day otherwise too clear for a hailstorm and heard my companions shout, I dove for the bushes again.

"Demons!" Um Aman shrieked. "Demons have possessed the shrine!"

Aster dropped to a squat, covering her face and head with arms and elbows, but Amollia took my example and scrambled out of range into the foliage.

"They're not demons!" she yelled back, half-laughing. "They're only monkeys. Look on the roof! Just monkeys throwing stones." But she stopped laughing a moment later as one of the stones struck Um Aman squarely on the top of the head. The old woman keeled over and lay very still.

We both called to Aster but she was clenched tightly into herself. I plunged through the shrubbery and in two bounds reached Um Aman. Amollia burst from cover as I did, and between us we unpried Aster and shoved her toward the bushes while we dragged Um Aman with us.

But as we retreated, the monkeys, little bullies, advanced, screaming imprecations, waving their hairy arms, jumping up and down, and mugging in a way that might have been comical except for the stones. They leapt from the roof and hopped toward us, each with a sloping, lopsided gait alternating standing on hind feet while supporting themselves with the knuckles of their hands, when they weren't using those hands to lob stones at us. I almost lost an eye to one, and my shins, stomach, arms and back were pulverized before we reached the trees.

Who would have supposed you could hear a hand-clap amidst all the noise and confusion? And yet, when it came, it was louder than every other noise, and for a moment not only the monkeys stopped chattering, but the sea birds ceased crying, the ocean ceased roaring, and all of the sounds of that thick and teeming forest stilled.

Who could clap such a clap? The god of the carpet himself? Another djinn? A chieftain, perhaps, like Marid Khan? I turned, expecting to see someone like that. Instead a short, dark woman, obviously out of breath, stepped out of the trees and panted, "There now. There now. Friends."

The monkeys stopped and looked at her. And she looked at them, familiarly, as if they were indeed friends. She put a hand to the breast of her simple orange garment, which looked like a sort of turban for the body, wrapped and draped to cover anything strategic. When she had regained her breath somewhat, she shook the gnarled walking stick she carried in their direction. "What have you been doing in my absence, eh? Trouble again? Can't I leave you alone for a single afternoon without you cluttering up the courtyard? For holy animals, you've got no respect." And she leaned over and began picking up rocks until we slunk back out of the bushes and she looked up at us, unsurprised. "Visitors. That's it, of course. No wonder the racket. How did you get here? Must have flown. I've been camped on the path to the village since yesterday evening."

"Who are you?" Aster asked.

"I'm a holy woman. What do I look like? I keep

this shrine for Saint Selima, these monkeys are sacred to her, and if you'll pardon me, I've had a busy morning talking to a cranky tigress. Help me pick up some of these rocks, will you? Can't have a cluttered shrine."

Amollia stayed her hand as she stretched it toward another rock. "I beg your pardon, holy one, but our mother-in-law was injured by your guardian beasts."

The holy woman looked shocked and perhaps a little pleased. "Really? You mean they hit something?" She examined a rock quizzically. "Well, well."

Dropping the rock, she accompanied us to where Um Aman lay. I started to grab the old woman's arm to drag her into the shrine and the holy woman slapped impatiently at me. "Not that way. You'll kill her. We must carry her *on* something."

"The rug," Aster said, snapping her fingers, then looked from Amollia to me uncertainly. "That is, if you think we can trust it to stay on the ground."

But Amollia had already taken the hint and unrolled the carpet beside Um Aman.

I waited for the holy woman to direct us as to the best means of transporting Um Aman but the shrine's keeper was staring instead at the carpet.

"God *is* merciful and compassionate," she said.

"Careful with your praying around that rug, with all respect, wise one," I cautioned. "It might take off and fly again like it did with us."

"With you? You flew upon the sacred prayer rug of Saint Selima?"

"That's how we got here."

"My prayers were answered," she said.

"You were praying to get us out of the desert too?"

"I was praying that the carpet, stolen from the floor of the holiest of all holy places in Sindupore, would someday find its way back. The Saint wove it with her own hands, miracles in each fiber, unlike some of those other rugs which were simply woven by ordinary mortals and later enchanted by magicians and sorcerers who had to depend upon an overlaying spell to make them fly. Not only is there holiness in every knot, but the carpet is large enough for even the largest of beasts to pray to God properly." She shook her head wonderingly, then knelt beside Um Aman. "But what are we standing here talking for? I thought you wanted me to help this woman."

When she had bandaged and prayed over Um Aman and made her comfortable on one side of the shrine, the holy woman, named Fatima, brought forth a basket of fruit, a loaf of bread and a skin of water, upon which we pounced without hesitation or apology.

"So," she said when we were done, "you must be very devout to have activated the sacred carpet of Saint Selima."

"The carpet flew for the pious mother of our unfortunate husband, holy one," Amollia said. "We are not of your people."

"Obviously. Nor of my faith either, is that what you're trying to tell me? Don't be shy. It's no great shame to be an infidel. Everybody has to start somewhere." She dug around in a corner for a moment and returned with a clay bowl full of sweets. "Saint Selima is very popular here." She thrust the bowl out to me. "You're the lightest, the tallest, and the least like us. The most infidel-looking of all. You first. Pick a sweet. The choicest. Go ahead." I tried to demur, for her overbearing liberality unsettled me, but she pushed at me again so I took something melting and sticky and popped it in my mouth.

Then she said. "If you aren't believers and your husband's mother didn't know she was bringing the sacred carpet back to its maker's resting place, then I take it devotion didn't bring you. What then?"

"Desperation, holy one," Amollia answered.

"Ah," she said wisely.

"You see, holy one," Aster explained, "the Emir from whom we acquired your saint's rug—and don't ask me how he got it—also drove us from the city after one of his wives turned our husband into an ass."

"An ass?"

"A white one," Aster nodded.

"It would be," Fatima said. "Such transformations used to be common in these lands. They are not particularly difficult to undo, however, if you can get the person who invoked—"

"The curse to revoke it? So we've been informed," Aster said drily. "But the problem is that the djinn's bottle is still with the Emir, our husband is still with Marid Khan in the desert, the woman who cursed him is somewhere called Sindupore, and all we have left is this." She fished in her sleeve and brought forth the stopper to the djinn's bottle, which I had given her to hide when we were forced to surrender our other loot to Marid Khan.

Fatima took the cork from her. "But, my dear, this is a very great deal. Without this cork, the djinn cannot be contained in his bottle. While the Emir holds the residence of the ifrit's soul, and can control him somewhat by threat of destroying it, he cannot fully avail himself of the djinn's power until he holds the cork bearing the seal of Suleiman."

"So that's what that smoke-footed fiend was going on about with his riddles about wine," Aster said.

"No doubt that is also why he was so suspiciously helpful," Amollia added.

"No doubt. As for the woman...where in Sindupore did you say she was?"

"First we have to find Sindupore," I reminded her.

Fatima shook her head.

"Do you mean to say we are here?" Aster asked. This time the holy woman nodded.

"Perhaps," she said, "I can be of more help if you tell me the whole story."

When we had told her all there was to tell the day was well into afternoon and it was raining hard in the courtyard outside. Our tale took longer than usual to tell because she insisted on verifying each point with each of us, and would hop up and go attend to some chore—picking up rocks until it started raining, spooning water between Um Aman's lips, chasing away a monkey, just as we got to the important parts, and whoever was talking would have to start all over again.

"And that is all?" she asked brightly, small plump fingers interlaced over her crossed legs, round face nodding from one of us to the next, seemingly inquisitive but perhaps slightly bored. Certainly not surprised or overcome with awe, dread, pity or disgust at our circumstances. I began to feel more hopeful.

"That is all," Aster said. "And for this humble person it has been quite enough. I begin to long for the flower boats of Willow Lake."

"Have you some means to help us, wise one?" Amollia asked. "Could you cast bones or examine chicken entrails as the seeress in Kharristan did to help us find Aman Akbar once more?"

"We-ell, no, I'm not much for bones. Saint Selima was much more interested in living creatures than dead ones and I would be risking my share of paradise to cut open a poor chicken just to ask stupid questions about that which is already written anyway. However, I have something perhaps better."

"Better than prophecy?" Aster asked, the doubt clear in her voice. It was plain that she was thinking, as I had often had occasion to do myself, that priests and shamans were always quick to assure you that you didn't really want them to do the real magic you *did* want them to do when they could do for you some trick they had meant to do all along because they already had their quite unmagical preparations made to perform it.

Fatima, however, quite literally made no bones about magic having connection with the help she planned to offer. "Oh yes, I have much more reliable help than prophecy. I have monkeys."

"We want to find him, not stone him," Aster said.

But Fatima had already padded on her bare feet back to the threshold and, thrusting her hands outside into the rain, clapped them once, hard.

Thereupon it rained monkeys as well as water for several moments. She spoke to these monkeys slowly and seriously, explaining what she wished them to do, pausing only to make sure her descriptions of Aman Akbar and other principal persons were accurately detailed, and soon they scampered from the doorway and their chattering was lost as they sprang into the forest and disappeared. "All the jungle will soon know of your search. We have only to wait."

"It is a pleasant place to wait," Amollia said in a tired, dreamy voice. "Very like my home. We were having the monsoon rains there when I left."

My eyes followed hers to the dull, faintly yellow-gray skies, the tossing fronds and branches blurred by the slanting silver-beaded veil splattering into the puddles on the terrace. I failed to see why anyone would be sentimental about such weather.

After three days, waiting became tiresome. Um Aman, when she opened her eyes, was not truly awake. She drifted in and out of sleep filled with nightmare mumblings and thrashings. She made less sense than usual when she was awake, and was, incredibly, even nastier and more hostile than she had previously been.

Fatima appeared unconcerned. "That she wakes at all is a good sign. Be patient."

But it became increasingly difficult to be patient, for clearly we were in Fatima's way. Her morning was normally spent in prayer, contemplation, gardening and hearing the supplications of pilgrims to the shrine. While we stayed with her, we were the only pilgrims. Afternoons she was accustomed to spend tending the shrine, sweeping, washing and cleaning up the dung of Saint Selima's sacred animals. With us there, she cut her contemplations short to care for Um Aman. Afternoons, during the rains, too many of us crowded inside the little shrine for her to have enough room to do any sort of work, though if the rains weren't too heavy or started late, we all tried to help clean up the dung of the many rats, monkeys, mongooses and other small . . . and sometimes not so small . . . animals who visited the shrine.

"Is this position of yours hereditary?" Aster asked Fatima as we sat around staring at each other one afternoon. Fatima's hands were filled with a half-finished basket, while I sharpened my knife and Amollia infused fruit juice into Um Aman. Fatima missed a stitch with her river grass, hissed, and raised her head, her lips pursed with irritation at yet one more interruption.

"Hereditary? Hereditary? What do you mean hereditary?"

"I mean, was this Selima an ancestor of yours or something? Is that why you have this job keeping her shrine?"

"No, of course not. She was a saint, a great teacher, a miracle worker and a friend to animals. You've already seen how she can make prayer rugs fly and how all animals honor her. She could talk to them, you know. And since this shrine is filled with her essence and I have lived here these many years, I can also talk with them. But not because I'm a relative or any such nonsense as that. My own folk aren't even from this land. They're nomads."

"How came you to dwell here then?" Aster asked, tilting her head at an angle that looked as if she had practiced it specifically to lend her an air of childlike innocence and charm. She was bored and already knew all she cared to about the rest of us. Our hostess provided her with hope of diversion and she wasn't going to be put off easily. "Did the saint give you this house as a reward for your work?"

"No, no, nothing like that. When I served Selima she had no house. We roamed the jungle and ministered to the animals and prayed all the time." She gave up and set the basket aside, looking wistfully past us through the open door and out into the jungle. "My feet hurt constantly when I began to follow her. All those years I spent sitting on my behind made me soft. But I come from people who are great walkers and it was a real pleasure to be associated with someone like Selima after all the nastiness of the seraglio!"

"Where was that?" Aster pried.

"Oh, where I used to live. My father made an alliance, and I was part of the agreement, along with several camels and some pretty good horses and bolts and bolts of cloth," she sighed.

"It didn't suit you, living there?"

"No. No, indeed. I didn't care for it and in fact,

when I was heavy with my child, I almost died simply from sadness. But that's when the Valideh, the woman who ran the harem, invited Selima to speak to us. Hearing her changed my whole life. As soon as my child was born and I was free of my obligation, I found her again. I was her devoted disciple until she died. Then I built this shrine with my own hands—well, I did have a little help from the men in the village, but I paid them with some of the jewels I had from the old days in the palace. It's not a bad life. Interesting even. Her bones being buried beneath the shrine still provide us with miracles occasionally, so steeped in holiness was she, and the animals are much better company than I was used to before I became her disciple."

"But what of your child?" Aster asked.

Fatima pressed her lips together and gave Aster a penetrating look under which she shifted uncomfortably. "The harem favorite was barren. My child was given to her to raise as her own."

"He must have been a horrible man, your husband," I said. Not even my mother's relatives would do such a thing.

"Not at all," Fatima said lightly, fussing again with her basketry. "Considering his position, his isolation from all for which God had made him responsible, the poor advice he received, and his ill health, he was a very good man. I was sadly grieved to hear of his death but almost . . . almost I am glad of what happened. My life has been more useful since I left the harem. Here I can help. Not all of the people in this land are believers, for it has only been enfolded in God's compassionate care since we trounced the former King in battle four years ago."

She sighed and smiled nostalgically. "The country-side smoked for months and there was a whole wall built by the harem of the heads of the former King's supporters. I do the will of God and Selima more peacefully, of course. I try to make the best use I can of what God has been good enough to grant me in the way of worldly items and also use certain talents taught me by the saint to keep the people safe from the

animals and the other way around. It can be very tiring.
Snakes will forget themselves and crawl into the homes
of men, where one or the other are apt to perish from
the contact. Tigers grow old or become weary of chasing their usual swift prey and snatch children from the
village instead, if one doesn't speak most severely with
them and see that they are provided with other fare."

"A useful talent," Amollia said. "I only hope it can
help us find Aman Akbar."

It is not a wise idea to speak of hope in the shrine
of a saint any more than it is to speak of wishes around
an uncommitted djinn if you would prefer not to have
swift and unpredictable results. Hardly had Amollia
finished speaking when we were deluged with a throng
of wet monkeys, who swung in from the jungle, pattered
across the terrace, and began simultaneously jumping
up and down and chattering at Fatima in what little
space there was in the shrine.

Fatima grunted and turned to us with a satisfied
nod. "They have news of the woman who transformed
your husband. She and her escort traveled through the
jungle, on the road leading to the capital at Bukesh but
a short time ago. This was reported by the beasts who
dwell in the jungle this side of the mountains. Those of
the agricultural area nearer Bukesh have not yet replied."

I sheathed my knife and rose to my feet, outraging
an oversensitive monkey upon whose tail I trod with
my bare foot. "Then we must go to the capital and find
her. The djinn said she was probably intended as a
present for the young King."

"You surely don't mean to go now?" Aster asked.

I did. The odor of the room full of wet monkeys
was sufficient to make me anxious to go even if their
news had not been.

"But Rasa, you can't go alone," Amollia said. "And
our husband's mother cannot travel, so at least one of
us must remain until she can."

"That is not so," Fatima said quickly, absolutely
beaming at me. "I can look after her well enough
without you. Since Selima's carpet brought her to me,
you might almost say it's a mandate from the saint

herself that I do so. In the usual way of things, I would counsel that you follow God's will and not seek to interfere, but since you're unbelievers, you're not likely to do that, are you? Besides, maybe it is written that you are to go."

"A certain seeress in Kharristan has said as much, holy one," I volunteered, and drew a glare from Aster.

"That seeress didn't figure on us three unprotected women having to march alone through a jungle full of hungry tigers and rock-throwing monkeys," she objected.

"Why, you must think nothing of such dangers, my dear Lady Aster," Fatima said so cheerily I began to prefer her less effusive moods. "Have you not been the guests of Selima's shrine, and am I not keeper of that same shrine? Do you seriously think I'd encourage you to go abroad in the jungle so dear to Saint Selima without some talisman of her protection?"

"We *are* unbelievers," Amollia reminded her, quite unnecessarily, but Fatima ignored her.

"I would especially not ask you to perform for me the one small favor I had in mind without assuring that you would live to perform it."

"Ahh," Aster said gloomily. "A favor."

"You need not sound like that, my girl. It isn't a large task for a person such as yourself, who tricked the Emir's wives into giving up the carpet of Selima, and who has stayed a step ahead of a powerful djinn all this time. I desire only that you take the King a couple of gifts for me. Having a real errand at the palace from a bona fide saint and her chosen representative may even help you gain the company of this Hyaganoosh you seek. First, I want you to give the King this," and she stripped from her neck a thin gold chain, upon which was a charm of a hand, broken in half. Aster accepted it.

"And second, I wish you to pluck a lemon from a tree that grows in the mountains."

Aster smirked as if this was what she was expecting. "A special tree, wise one?" she asked with mock innocence.

"You might say so," Fatima nodded.

"Now I wonder how I came to know that?"

"It isn't all *that* special," Fatima said. "Any one of

the trees in the garden of the King of Divs will do. All you need is one little lemon to give to my s . . . to the King."

"Couldn't you have one of the monkeys do it?" Aster asked.

Fatima sounded genuinely shocked. "The monkeys are sacred to Saint Selima!"

"As opposed to the three of us who are unbelievers and therefore expendable, you mean? Even so, wise one," Aster grinned and dropped the necklace around her own neck. She seemed more cheerful rather than less now that her fears had been confirmed, which I suppose just goes to show how much some people like to be right.

But if Fatima was sending us into danger, she at least provided us with food: melons, oranges, dates, nuts, bread and rice, wrapped in cloth packages. All of this we dropped into netted bags that hung from our sashes. She also gave us a piece of silver to lodge us when we reached the city, and the promised talisman.

The talisman was disappointing in appearance, for it was nothing but a soiled and tattered rag. Fatima swore solemnly, however, that it was a scrap of the headcloth actually worn by Saint Selima during the last few years of her life. It was, Fatima assured us, redolent of the saint's essence.

"Most assuredly it is redolent of something," Aster agreed, and handed it to Amollia. "Here, you take it. It doesn't suit my coloring."

"You are not to wear it, infidel," Fatima said impatiently. "You hold it forth, thus." She demonstrated with a monkey. "And allow any beast you meet to sniff it. The beast will then smell the scent of Selima and will understand what is in your heart and you, as bearer of the cloth, will understand what is in the heart of the beast."

The monkey was leaping up and down ecstatically and chattering, but since that was not uncustomary behavior for a monkey, I was not persuaded.

But Fatima was adamant. "With the aid of this cloth you will be as safe in the jungle as if under guard, which in a way you will be. You should have no trouble reaching Bukesh with time to spare to run my little errand. It is not only of importance to me, you understand, but also for the good of the kingdom that the King receive the lemon and eat it personally. Did I stress that? He must eat it personally." She paused and sighed, as if it were she who was going to perform a difficult and distasteful task instead of us. "It has, you see, a certain knowledge of bitterness beneficial in the extreme to one whose life has been too sweet."

Aster ignored the poignancy in the voice of our benefactress. "We'll do as best we can for you, wise one," she said. "But you realize we may never reach this lemon grove of yours. For one thing we have an old enemy after us—the djinn of whom we told you—even now he might be ready to pounce upon us. Also, we might get lost and never find the lemons at all. And if we did, maybe we wouldn't outsmart the gardener and he'd put the guard on us. And what makes you think the King will see us? Since we're women, we probably would have an easier time applying directly to the headwoman in the harem for justice, as Um Aman's friends advised us to do in Kharristan."

But Fatima would hear none of it. She had far more advice and instructions than kernels of rice to share with us. We need not worry about the djinn, she said, for djinns couldn't fly over salt water, as we had. We were perfectly safe therefore from our old enemies, at least the supernatural ones. To avoid new enemies of the same sort and also to avoid getting lost, we needed only to be very sure to always take the right-hand path wherever there was a choice. If we followed the right-hand paths, she maintained, we would also come to the exact spot at the foot of the mountains where the Div King's minions would not trouble us, and we could pick our lemon and be on our way. As for being received by the King, send him the charm Fatima had given Aster. That way we would be bound to see Hyaganoosh *and* be able to carry out the little favor. Of course, if that was too much to ask, Fatima could always find some hovel in the village where we might be taken in as long as we were willing to work in the rice paddies for our keep. She would naturally have to have back the head-cloth of Selima and the other gifts.

Heartened by such encouragement and advice, how could even the most ungrateful and incredulous unbeliever fail to hasten to assure her that all would be done even as she directed? Shortly after morning prayers she waved us down the path to the village.

# Chapter
# 8

The first thing we noted about the village—and this with great relief—was that none of the women wore veils or abayahs. This may have been because these folk were not believers, as Fatima had indicated, but it seemed more likely to me to be because the accursed garments were simply too ungainly for traversing the steamy, overgrown jungle paths. Without Um Aman around to protest on the behalf of propriety, we removed ours likewise.

Amollia strolled on ahead of Aster and me, swaying with her stately, graceful walk down the single muddy street. She was dressed in her own native garment, not the golden one in which I had first seen her but a plain white cotton printed with rusty brown designs and wrapped in a fashion similar to Fatima's gown. Her jewelry clinked lightly as she walked. Aster, still in her indigo trousers and jacket with the long weighted sleeves, frisked from one side of the road to the other, using the necessity of avoiding work animals and their drivers as an excuse to peek into the various hovels and garden plots and thus appease her unabashedly vulgar curiosity. I still wore the lightweight, pale green gown I had worn away from Aman Akbar's palace, and followed cautiously, trying to keep feet and hem out of the reeking piles and

ıddles in our path. Altogether we made a spectacle as
ılorful in this remote village as the procession of jugglers,
robats, dancers and musicians that sometimes had
ıraded past my latticed window on their way to some
vel or other in Kharristan. Little wonder that heads
ırned as we passed. Little wonder that almost immedi-
ely we acquired an elephant.

It happened thusly. A recalcitrant oxen being disci-
ıned by a child of perhaps six years was taking its
ıastisement none too calmly, thus necessitating our
ısty removal down a small side street. Whether it was
e sound of loud and long lamenting or the curious
ght of a gray hump rising beyond the thatched rooftop
at piqued our—meaning Aster's—interest, I am
ıcertain. However, upon investigating, we saw that
e lamentations were issuing from a man seated in a
atched lean-to adjoining the house. The lean-to con-
ıined only a rough table upon which were scattered
me tools—a fine-bladed saw, an awl, a block of charcoal,
ırious pipes tipped with clay, an anvil and a small,
ılit oil lamp of the type the holy woman had used.
ıese things he ignored, instead holding his head in his
ınds and weeping, tears streaming between his fingers,
fts of hair standing straight out from his beard and
ıturbaned head.

Beside the lean-to, an elephant shifted from foot to
ot as if embarrassed. With its trunk, it snatched
atch from the roof and shoved the thatch into its
outh in an almost absent-minded fashion.

The elephant was far better attired than the man.
pon its back it bore draperies of many-colored silks,
nbroidered with gold thread and jewels, and upon its
ıad it wore a matching harness. Both adornments
ere trimmed all around with tiny golden bells that
ıkled merrily as the elephant ate and the man wept.

"My word, business must be very bad for that poor
an to be so upset. Perhaps we should ask if we could
ılp him," Aster said to me, her voice raised even
gher than usual so that the man would overhear and
ıght explain himself if he cared to.

He did.

"On the contrary, lady, business is much too good
he said mournfully. "And please, I beg you. Do not he
me. It is help from another well-meaning lady whi
has brought me so low. Oh, that that monkey-lovi
female had never come out of her shirine long enou
to give me that accursed ruby!"

"You don't seem to be a grateful sort of fellow
Aster sniffed, twitching her trailing sleeves disdainful
away from his threshold.

"How can I be grateful for my ruin?" he waile
"Soon the beast will demolish my house, my wife
garden, and then, who knows, the whole village. A
who may stop it? Besides which, it will all be my fault

"Perhaps you had better explain yourself," I sa
severely. I wanted him to understand that I was in
sympathy with his complaint against our mutual benefa
tress. But on the other hand, we might be able to te
the headcloth by using it to cause the elephant to cea
doing whatever it was doing that so upset the man.

"I was formerly a maker of brass vessels and ine
pensive nose rings for ladies. Always I had fancied
could do great works of art, if only I had the prop
materials. I had heard of the woman at the shrine
Selima—who in this place has not?—but had not m
her until one day my youngest child was snatched aw
by a tiger. Fortunately, the lady was nearby and persua
ed the tiger to abandon my child in favor of an oxen
though I confess, we could have done more easi
without the child than the oxen. To express my gra
tude for her interference, I presented her with one
my nose rings, a creation I had made up especially for
gentleman who, as it happened, had more taste tha
funds.

"Say what you will about these religious fanatic
some of them are well-born and that woman has a ve
fine eye for workmanship. She admired the object ve
much, though she said she must refuse it as she ha
given up such things when she sought holiness. S
further asked me what a man of my talent was doi
wasting himself in this village. I answered that I ha
often wondered the same thing myself, but that I w

too poor to better myself. If only I had gold and fine gems. I was sure I could make jewelry and vessels fit for the King himself. She looked very interested when I said that, and later brought by a ruby stone and some old gold settings from which the gems had been removed, saying that she had no further use for such things.

"I was astounded! Sure that my fortune was made, I dreamed and planned until I had the perfect design in which to use the materials fate had placed in my hands. The work went swiftly, for, as I suspected, I was always meant to deal with fine materials.

"And as luck would have it, a caravan passed through and an emissary from Jokari bought the bracelet for enough rupees that I should not have had to work for a year. Not only that, but I imagined the honor the King would heap upon me if only he should chance to ask the maker of this special treasure. Naturally, I knew it would be but one trinket among many, but it was so outstanding that I had hope of attracting his particular notice.

"And, alas, I did. A month ago a caravan returning to Jokari arrived, and with it instructions for me to present myself at court to be recognized and favored by the King. I had to spend part of my commission on a fine suit of clothing to be presented in, and more in travel expenses. And once I arrived in Bukesh I had to buy lodging and gifts for my family and friends, did I not? But though I spent the last of my funds, I was not downhearted, imagining the riches the King would bestow upon me.

"But when I was granted an audience with His Magnificence, did he give me gold? No. Jewels? No. Robes of honor—well, I suppose had he not been distracted by affairs of state and his pressing need to take his afternoon nap he would no doubt have done so, but he did not. No. What he gave me was this elephant!

"An elephant, mind you! How am I to feed an elephant? How do I maintain it? Why, keeping up with shoveling its dung alone will leave me no time for my chosen labor."

"But the beast is clothed in fine cloth and jewels

and little gold bells!" Aster pointed out. "Surely you can sell those and—"

He shook his head sadly. "Alas, I cannot. His Majesty explained to me that I was being given care of this elephant because the beast is a noble veteran. Its trappings are its own possessions. I could not even ride it home without it rolling its eyes most fiercely at me. The beast is to live a life of luxury—at my expense! I cannot even sell him, as such an act would be judged ungrateful and a treason to the throne. No, I am ruined, doomed, while this beast literally eats me out of house and home!"

"I see," Aster said. She seemed for once to be at a loss for words.

Amollia meanwhile had paid little heed to the man but had gone, headcloth in hand, straight to the elephant. Its one small eye regarded her anxiously, almost entreatingly, as she stroked its crinkled gray trunk. The beast had stopped devouring the man's thatch, a great boon since that form of dining had been most distracting not only because of the noise it produced but also because of the showers of scorpions and small serpents falling at intervals as they were dislodged from their resting places. The elephant now calmly ate a large portion of the pistachios Fatima had provided for our journey.

"Is there no way we could convince you to let us have this beast?" Amollia asked, fixing the man with her black-eyed stare so that he stammered and forgot to weep.

"L-lady, I only wish I could. But I cannot sell him. To do so would be treason."

Aster's tongue leapt once more into action. "Sell him, no, of course not, for we have already heard how attached you are to this marvelous creature. But perhaps we could *rent* him?"

"Rent? Rent—hmm . . . yes, rent. An excellent idea. I see no objection to that, if you truly wish to have an elephant to walk with you on your journey, for he will not allow you to—"

I think he started to say "ride" but was compelled

to stop at the sight of the great animal kneeling and
with its trunk gently assisting Amollia to mount herself
upon its head.

Amollia pulled one of her massive silver bracelets
from her arm and a necklace of raw amber from her
neck and flung the jewelry to the man. "This should do
it," she said.

"For such a great beast as that? Playmate of my
children? Wonder of all the village?" He tried to sound
indignant.

She jerked a golden ring from her finger and
tossed it on the pile. "My last offer. One more word and
you keep the elephant."

"Take him and blessings upon you," the man said,
quickly grabbing up the jewelry. With Amollia's beads
twined in his fingers, he steepled his hands together
under his lower lip and bowed. Before the rest of us
mounted, he insisted we remove the trappings so that
he could retain them "for safe keeping."

We were off to a fine start. We had only to turn
right at each fork and ride our elephant and we would
no doubt proceed speedily to the lemon tree, pluck
Fatima's gift for the King, who would in his newfound
wisdom and gratitude send forth his men to rescue
Aman Akbar and require Hyaganoosh to restore our
husband to his proper form. Perhaps he was a truly
beneficent King (if not a far-sighted one, as the incident
of the jeweler and the elephant suggested) and he
would restore to Aman Akbar his property, maybe even
reward the rest of us with some treasure.

I liked riding on the elephant, though I was
positioned upon his high broad back and the posture
was awkward. Amollia had the best place, right behind
his ears, with Aster, whose legs were the shortest,
behind her. I had to straddle the beast and alternated
between having my legs stuck straight out in the air
with my skirts rucked up to my knees or bending my
knees sharply up to my chest and resting my heels on
the roll of the animal's sides. But to ride him was finer
by far than walking.

Where the road was crowded, with people going to

and from the curious hillside fields Aster explained
were rice paddies the people fled from our elephant's
great feet. Even the oxenlike water buffalos, massive
animals good at growing rice, Aster said, gave us wide
berth. Yes, I liked riding upon this elephant very much,
and I began to wonder if I could get the King to send
my father such a beast. That would show my mother's
cousins a thing or two!

As for the elephant, he seemed happy enough to
be in our company. I find I have been referring to him
as casually as if I had known such creatures all my life. I
had not. Amollia supplied us with much lore concerning elephants and entertained us for a time with stories
about those she had known. But even before that,
when she had first approached the creature as if he
were a valued and respected friend, I had felt no fear or
antipathy toward the outrageous-looking animal.

For all his ponderous appearance, so swift was our
elephant that we had passed most of the settlements by
mid-afternoon and were heading into a forest of lush,
thickly intertwined greenery. Here the road forked, both
tongues darting into the trees.

Amollia stopped the elephant and looked from the
trails back to us. "This is very strange," she said uneasily.

"How so?" Aster asked. "It is as Fatima described
it to us. She said there would be a fork in the road."

"Yes, but why just as the road enters the jungle?
Cutting one path alone through such a tangle and
keeping it clear is difficult, why cut two? Surely the
paths do not go in such different directions until later
on and if so, why does one not skirt the edge? I saw
nothing at the village of such importance that it need be
so conveniently connected—"

"You forget what the metalsmith said about the
caravans," Aster reminded her. "No doubt the paths
connect to trade centers and the caravans come from
some port located more auspiciously near the shoreline.
Naturally commerce would demand—"

The rest of her argument was literally drowned out
as the monsoon arrived, promptly and abruptly. That
day the rains began in no gentle, drop-by-drop dribble,

but with a sudden opening of the heavens which deposited a sea of hard rain upon our heads in a continuous pounding deluge.

Amollia shouted over her shoulder to us, "The elephant wishes us to dismount."

"Why?" I shouted back, not caring for the idea.

"So it can roll in the puddles," she screamed in reply, rotating her middle finger to show how the elephant would roll. "Elephants like getting wet as much as they like eating."

"I do not!" Aster cried. "Ask the elephant to take us into the jungle where we will be safe from the storm before he—"

With a roar and a crack the rain-silvered trees were illuminated by a jagged bolt of fire which flashed from the heavens to strike the ground immediately to the right of our good beast. Forgetting his bath and his riders and all sense of decorum, the elephant bolted.

I was thrown back with a jolt that sent every date, nut, and kernel of rice I had consumed in the last four days flying back up into my mouth. For a moment I tottered on the beast's back, but another bounding step threw me forward again and threatened to topple me. I grabbed for Aster, and clung to her waist. She in her turn clung tightly to Amollia, who had laid an earlock on the elephant and who was shouting what were meant to be calming words at the beast's head. Only my skill at clinging to horses' backs—quite a different matter from the one at hand—kept me from losing my grip and falling to my death beneath the thunderous feet. By the time he stopped, I was no longer interested in elephants.

We slid from the beast's back like wax drippings sliding down a candle, and my joints had all of the steel of the same melted wax.

The beast's flight had brought us to a river bank, and the three of us sank onto thick grass while the elephant disported himself in the water, his terror forgotten in his pleasure at seeing so much water. We cowered beneath the trees and watched his antics wearily.

Aster laughed weakly as the beast sprayed its head

with a shower from its trunk. The rains had lessened their force now and no longer stormed around us but pattered gently down in a soothing manner that served to relieve the heat. The grass gave up its warmth in steam that carpeted the forest floor.

"Pitiless pachyderm," Aster said. "He nearly killed us."

Amollia shrugged, "The lightning might have killed us. Never have I seen that kind of fire from a monsoon! But see you, between the rain and the river, our friend has found elephant paradise."

While the elephant bathed, we each ate a cold rice ball and one of the pomegranates with which Fatima had supplied us. Afterward, Amollia displayed a new talent for climbing trees, climbing a palm with what seemed a single liquid motion. Flashing us her strong white grin from the shade of the broad fringed leaves, she wrenched loose several and threw them down for us to use in fashioning a portable rain-shelter, which we could hold above our heads as we rode. We also passed our first night beneath it.

Just before we slept, Aster opened one eye and rolled lazily onto her side so she faced us. "Do you suppose we took the right?" she asked.

"Hmm?" I asked.

"The right. Do you suppose this is the right fork? I'm wondering if when the elephant stampeded, he took the right fork or the left one?"

Amollia reached out and touched the foot of the beast, who was dozing beside our resting place. "Being an elephant," she said, "he no doubt made his own road."

I dreamed all night of riding the elephant, my bones jolting even in my sleep. I hesitate to mention where the blisters which disturbed my slumber were located, and resolved that the next day I would walk until the blisters upon my feet matched those elsewhere.

In the morning the rain might never have been, except that the path was muddy, though the heat had already sucked the moisture from it so that in some places the dark brown had already turned light and dusty. Brilliant flowers bloomed among sparkling leaves, bright as emeralds.

I walked a few paces behind the elephant all morning and though the view ahead was not the sort of which bards sing, I felt the better for having momentarily come down in the world. Around midday we came upon water once more and the elephant wanted to bathe again. Amollia and Aster also dismounted.

I sat down upon the river bank and watched the elephant, who found to his delight that he could wholly submerge himself in these deep waters and did so, only the tip of his trunk protruding. I thought about swimming across to the other side and seeing what lay ahead, but felt too lethargic. Amollia and Aster took the opportunity to stretch their legs, exploring a little path that wandered off to the left of the one we were on. The flowers bloomed in even greater and gaudier profusion than elsewhere, and the exclamations of my companions that floated back to me with the bird songs and chatterings of monkeys above the low music of the water indicated that the flowers were even more beautiful farther on.

When I felt the first spit of rain on my arm, I knew that more time had passed than any of us thought, and I rose reluctantly and started down the path after my wayward co-wives, thinking to meet them returning. However, when I had walked for several minutes, it occurred to me that I was wasting time, since I had the use of a perfectly good, if rather waterlogged, elephant, and could enlist his aid in apprehending the strays. With this idea in mind, I trotted back down the path, but when I came to the spot where the elephant had been bathing, he was gone—ears, tail, trunk, tusks and all.

Cursing the inconstancy of elephants and people who were never around when one needed them, I once more ran down the flower-bordered trail, and began calling. Soon the din of the rain beating on the roof of the jungle muffled my cries, even to my own ears, and I ran dumbly on, and sometimes blindly too, for here

along the river the overhead protection was not ver
great, and I cursed myself for several varieties of a
idiot for neglecting to bring along my palm-leaf paraso

Thus I failed to notice the strange, idol-ridde
edifice until I had almost run past it. Only when
heard myself hailed and turned to see Amollia's gri
flashing at me from the stone doorway did I see wha
the thick vegetation had all but concealed.

It looked like no dwelling I had seen in my ow
country or in Kharristan, and blended as well with th
jungle as if it had grown out of it. Its tallest towers ros
only to the tops of the tallest trees and were curve
from top to bottom and ridged with rings of carved an
pitted stone. The structure was not a single rectangula
building, but a series of interconnected towers, tall an
squat, capped with domes or open to the sky, an
reminded me of nothing so much as a patch of elaborate
ly carved toadstools. Drawing closer, I perceived tha
some of these carvings were hewn into a series
scantily clad women of a shapeliness I had never see
duplicated in real life and could never hope to attain

Amollia's grin widened. "Wait until you see th
ones inside. They're enough to turn you into an ol
woman, just looking at them!" Nor did she exaggerate
for the carvings on the inside of this outlandish plac
were indeed more depressingly fantastic than those o
the outside. In these the voluptuous stone figures wer
twisted with inhuman bonelessness around each othe
in the performance of an astonishing variety of sexua
activities. Almost more interesting was the fact tha
these antics were illuminated by the flames of hundred
of candles set into various recesses in the walls. Upo
the floor lay fine carpets thick and spongy as moss an
in colors richer than those of the flowers along the patl
Stacks of fat pillows were strewn about the room. Silve
and gold trays filled with fruits were beside each stack
Down one wall of the largest tower room a stair of shinin
water cascaded into a pool whose bottom was pave
with an infinitely intricate web of tiles as gorgeousl
colored as the carpets.

"What is this place?" I asked.

"Judging from the carvings and the furnishings," Aster said, "it is assuredly a retreat for some pasha who keeps a private harem in the jungle, away from the sight of his regular wives. He's probably taken them all to a bazaar somewhere on a big shopping spree."

"If they look like that, I don't think I want to meet them," I said, sitting down on the stone threshold so as not to get the expensive furnishings wet. I felt a little dazed by the splendor, and also by my jaunt through the jungle in search of these shameless voluptuaries, each of whom sank down upon a pile of cushions and proceeded to peel herself something.

"Throw one of those here," I said irritably. "If we're to be slain for trespassing, I want to die well-fed."

"The door was open and we no sooner walked in than we saw the candles," Aster said through a mouthful of plum. "Probably the servants are off somewhere praying. Everytime I can't find someone in this country, that seems to be what they're doing."

"Wherever they are, they should be very glad that we are here and equally glad we are willing to stay awhile," Amollia said with mock seriousness, waving her hands outward in a fluid gesture that encompassed the entire room. "Otherwise, with all of these candles alight, who knows what damage could befall this house?" She sighed, snuggling deep into a pillow and closing her eyes. "No, they are very lucky indeed we happened along in time to be of assistance."

I could have pointed out that if we all slept, whatever damage might befall the house would befall us as well, but instead I made myself as comfortable as possible against the door frame and followed her example, as Aster also soon settled herself to do. The rain was still pelting down very hard, and after eating I found I was incredibly sleepy.

I had no sooner closed my eyes, however, than I had a nightmare. Confused images of the fruits, the candles, iron rings and a donkey tied by its hooves to a spit tumbled over and over in my head. Finally, all of this receded to be replaced by a black-shrouded figure, whom I took at first for death but saw, as it approached, to have the angry eyes of Um Aman. She was shaking her finger at me and shouting silently. Perhaps this was her way of telling me she had recovered from her wound and was back to normal. She seemed to be quoting something from what I knew, in the way one knows in dreams, to be a prayer book—something about wives—I was about to make it out when I heard another voice and snapped awake, drawing my dagger even as I opened my eyes.

My first thought was of Amollia's last words and I looked over to see her still soundly sleeping and unimmolated by vagrant candle flames. Aster was sitting halfway up, her eyes focusing beyond me.

Following her gaze, I found myself staring at what was surely a Yahtzeni prince. Behind him were two other princes, and, though all were clad in warrior garb, each of these fellows was in aspect as varied from the other as the three of us were from each other.

If he who stood grinning down at me, making no move to parry my dagger, was not a Yahtzeni, then he was surely of a related tribe. Red hair bristled fiercely from under his leather helmet and fringed his face. He was clad in a sleeveless tunic of embroidered sheepskin and leggings also of sheepskin. He wore ornaments of bronze upon his arms and down his chest in the manner of armor. A sword was strapped to his hip and a full quiver of arrows and a bow were slung over his brawny shoulder. His eyes were the cold blue of our mountain streams.

To his left stood a man as black as Amollia. His face and arms were covered with patterned scars like tattoos carved into his skin. He was clad in a robe of blood red girded with a spotted hide that looked suspiciously like that of Kalimba and he brandished a white-tipped spear. He was taller than the man of my race, and finely muscled. His smile gleamed through the rain—not the smile one uses to greet guests but the smile of a hunter congratulating himself on a recent kill.

The third of these fellows was smaller and appeared to be of the same race as Aster. He was clad in subtly

woven silks of misty sea green, over which was linked a
sort of wooden armor. His black hair he wore long and
his thin beard and mustaches he also wore long. Though
slight of build, he was no less handsome and muscular
than the other two. Like Aster, he was also apparently
prone to curiosity—for he was straining to see around
the redhead's shoulder—and to talkativeness, for it was
he who spoke first, though to his comrades rather than
to us.

"What have we here? Three wild roses taking root
in our chambers? Three pearls beyond price so far from
the sea?"

The redhead grinned down at me so heartily I
thought I heard his teeth grind. "Two ewe lambs and a
very wet shepherdess more likely from the look of
them," he said.

Amollia roused up with a languid smile and said
graciously, "We hoped you wouldn't mind. But we were
passing and noticed you'd left your candles burning.
And it being monsoon season and the rains having
started—"

"Gracious lady!" the man of her race said in
Kharristani so fluent I wondered if he too had been
tutored by the djinn, "Please do not apologize. Your
eyes light this poor dwelling far more than all of these
puny candles. You must stay with us. Share our meal."

"Yes," the silken-clad fellow added with a warm
glance at Amollia. "Though our home is but a sty of a
place, hardly fit for such rough dogs as we, we would
be sorely aggrieved if you did not grant us the honor of
your company."

I was dubious about this invitation, even then, for
they looked as dangerous as they did handsome. But,
we had entered their home without permission, and
they were blocking the door.

We spent the best part of the afternoon eating,
drinking, and engaging in pleasant, if rather limited,
conversation. The black man joined Amollia among her
stacks of cushions, the Oriental prince sat beside Aster,
and the red-haired fellow fairly swept me from the
stony threshold, paying no attention to my protests

about my wet clothing, and deposited me upon silken cushions similar to those enjoyed by my friends. Aster's friend clapped his hands once. Half of the candles extinguished themselves. He clapped again. A brimming tray of mutton and rice seasoned with saffron appeared before us, along with bottles of strong drink, the first I had sampled in these lands.

Nor did these princely beings expect us to wait until they were done, as had Marid Khan and his men, but like Aman Akbar fed us morsels with their own fingers. I noted with amazement and approval that, in spite of my new friend's rough manner, his hands and fingernails were clean.

Even better, though he had the looks and manners of those accursed relatives of mine, he smelled much better. In fact, he smelled not at all of the wet wool, horse sweat and smoke of dung fires that cling to my people even after repeated baths. I confess I wondered briefly what his mother was like and how many women he already had.

At once I felt guilty, remembering poor Aman Akbar, and stole a peek away from the rugged face above me to see if Aster and Amollia noticed what had to be my obvious disloyalty in thought, if not yet in deed. Neither appeared to notice anything but the countenance of her companion. I would have to look elsewhere for moral guidance.

I cleared my throat and said to my warrior's beard, "Good of you to offer to put us up. I am Rasa Ulliovna of the Yahtzeni. We three are the wives of an important and wealthy man named Aman Akbar—"

"I know," he said shortly, though by no means in an unfriendly fashion, for his arm tightened around my shoulders as he spoke. He gave the impression that he was simply a man of few words.

I tried again. "What is your name and how came you and your companions to dwell together?"

"Some call me Dag, but you can call me 'beloved,'" he answered with another squeeze. After that, he was long on the squeezing and short on the conversation. His idea of wooing seemed to be a variation on Yahtzeni fighter practice—he would thrust and I would parry, all the while laughing as if he were privy to some joke I was not, which did not particularly move me but did provide me with ample opportunity to hear the conversations on either side of us.

Aster was giggling as her new friend snapped his fingers and changed her hairdo, twining the black locks into a tall crown interlaced with pearls and pink rosebuds. With another snap he provided her a golden-backed mirror with which to admire herself.

"You shouldn't!" she protested in a teasing and half-hearted fashion. "I hardly know you."

"What is there to know, my little peony blossom?" he replied, stroking his mustache between thumb and forefinger. "I am handsome, witty, talented, educated, and have a fine house—"

"Oh, then the three of you don't own this place together?" she asked with a coy look from under her lashes.

"Well, yes, but only as a gesture of brotherhood—because we're such fond friends and everything. But this is only one of our hunting lodges. Each of us lives by himself in a great palace with many pavilions and enough servants to populate a small city. There I could give you anything you want." He snapped his fingers and a skewer full of mutton chunks and vegetables jumped into his hand. "Here we are forced to rough it."

I applauded not because I hadn't already seen much better but because I was sure I was expected to applaud, the magician having caught my eye as he amazed and astounded Aster.

"That's not so much," Dag grumbled, his pride apparently injured by the fickleness of my attention. "We can all do that stuff. Wish for something. Go on. Anything. Wish for something."

What I really wished was to be home again with Aman Akbar in his original form, minus Um Aman and the others, with Hyaganoosh nothing more than another silly name, but I had the feeling that that particular wish would not be well-received by my host. So I scaled my aspirations down somewhat and said, imitat-

ing Aster's teasing tone, "If you can truly do as you sa
fetch me that old rag Amollia has in her sash."

He snapped his fingers and nothing happene
whereupon he first flushed, then scowled mighti
Changing tactics, he pointed his thumb at Amolli
who, without looking away from her escort or indicati
in any way she knew what she was doing, took th
headcloth from her sash and tossed it over her shoulde
to me.

"There is something strange about that rag," Da
said, still scowling. He withdrew his arm from m
shoulders when I tucked it into my own sash.

I found I did not care to explain to him th
properties of the rag—not until I knew him better
any rate. I therefore changed the subject to the on
always certain to fascinate any Yahtzeni warrior—himsel
"You're remarkable!" I exclaimed. "How came you b
such skills?"

"My brothers and I are all great friends of a—er-
very powerful magician."

Amollia's friend had noticed our little byplay an
decided to get into the act too. He flashed us a dazzlin
smile and I saw that his teeth had been filed to points

"Some of us are greater friends than others, howeve
What you lack, beloved brother, is flair. Watch this
And from nowhere great ropes of gems and ornat
bands of gold and silver dropped over Amollia's hea
onto her neck while bracelets far shinier and mor
massive and ornate than the one she had used
purchase—excuse me, rent—the elephant clasped then
selves around her wrists and ankles. Long open-wor
pendants studded with rubies and sapphires and eme
alds swung from her earlobes while a matching trinke
adorned her nose. Her eyes crossed as she tried t
admire it all.

"Don't be too impressed by this, my little panther
her friend said. "This is nothing compared to what m
brothers and I have to offer the maidens we love if on
they agree to brighten our lives by marrying us. Isn
that so, brothers?"

"I was about to say something of the sort myself," Aster's friend said, bowing slightly.

"How about it?" Dag asked with a wink, and ventured a cautious squeeze of my knee.

Amollia rose with jingling dignity to her feet and said firmly, "My sisters and I need to confer. Will you please excuse us?"

Before Aster and I could rise, our suitors politely withdrew into an adjoining room.

"What do you mean we 'have to confer'?" Aster asked. "What's to confer about? Chu Mi was just getting ready to produce a new gown for me."

"That is exactly what we need to talk about," Amollia said, studying her with a solemnity at odds with her own festive appearance. "I think there is something strange going on here. A prince for each of us? Did you take their proposals seriously?"

Aster considered, her finger tapping her pointed kitten's chin. "I take a new gown seriously. There's nothing so strange about that. And if we each went our separate ways with these men, it would solve the problem of who was in favor with Aman Akbar. I'd say it was a good opportunity for a smart girl to be the pet of a rich husband of her own people."

"You can't mean to abandon Aman now," I protested. I felt very sorry for Aman, even if he had brought most of his trouble on himself. I was glad he wasn't around to hear his last favorite speak of him, that disastrously romantic man, in such discouragingly practical terms. I didn't agree with her about the advantages of having a husband of my own people either. I was not really ready, for one thing, to be initiated into the joys of sheep-style lovemaking.

"I didn't say I was going to abandon him," she said defensively. "I just said I could see where it would be a smart thing to do."

"If you're thinking, little sister, to use this situation to rid yourself of competition, consider how much harder it would be for you alone to free Aman Akbar from his curse," Amollia said.

Aster looked glum. "I just thought of that."

"You might also consider that the three of us at least seem to be able to get along. A new husband might marry other wives less compatible. So, for that matter, might Aman, should you succeed in ridding him of the curse after having rid yourself of us."

Aster shrugged. "All right. All right. I was only pointing out that on the surface it seemed a very good opportunity. I didn't really expect either of you to take advantage of it any more than I intended to. Personally I'm in favor of letting them down easy and leaving as soon as possible. I find I have developed a certain dislike for magicians—too much like djinns for my taste."

In that she was closer to the truth than she knew.

They seemed to have expected our demurrals and in fact, I caught what looked like a flicker of glee passing between Dag and Chu Mi. It was gone at once. Chu Mi took Aster's arm and said, "If you must go, you must. But I have for you a parting gift. Come with me to the next room and I will give it to you."

She shot him a brief, hard look but then greed overcame her sense and she followed him. As soon as the door closed behind them I heard a sound I had heard only a few times before in my life and all of them recently, that of a bolt sinking into its slot. But I had no time to contemplate the meaning of the noise, for all of a sudden it seemed that the heavy timber of the bolt had descended not into its slot after all, but into my skull, which without warning burst apart with pain.

As soon as I awoke I wished I had not, for the pain that had caused me to lose my senses was no better. In fact, with my senses returned—or most of them—it was, not unnaturally, much worse. Now I could feel in great detail the agony of my scalp as each hair in my head tried to rip out its own native soil as it strained upward. The horrible tension in my neck as my body was pulled in one direction by my hair and in the other by its own weight. My eyes would not open fully, half shut with the tugging of the skin around them. I knew at once, however, as does every little girl whose mother or sisters have ever braided her hair what was happening to me. My hair was being pulled. Hard. The red-hot glaze before my eyes vanished briefly when I blinked and I saw Amollia dangling just across from me, a little higher than I was but in similar straits, though her short curls would not allow her to drop as far from the iron ring to which they were tied as did my captive braids.

"They take rejection badly, don't they?" she whispered huskily. Her whole face threatened to pull inside out and her eyes slanted at an angle far more acute than Aster's.

My own voice emerged only with difficulty. "I think we made the right de—cision. I'd never want to marry a man who considers this . . . sort of thing . . . persuasive."

But persuasive was exactly what this treatment was meant to be—though we were not the ones being persuaded. No sooner had I spoken than between Amollia and me something banged and I saw the edge of a latticed shutter fly from a point near my waist to one near Amollia's hip and heard a scrape as it struck stone on the other side. Suddenly a stick was thrust forward and struck Amollia in the ribs, setting her swinging and shrieking simultaneously. Her cries would have been heartrending to me except that before I could have my heart rent, my head was instead once more all but rent, for I too received a clout that tore loose part of a braid so that blood and tears simultaneously poured across my face as I rocked to and fro.

Chu Mi's voice sliced through my pain. "Isn't that a shame? Such nice little women. Such good friends of yours. See how much they hurt? Don't you want to give us what is ours so we can pull them in before they are quite bald and drop into the river for the crocodiles to eat? Or perhaps the great Simurg will pick them up in her talons and rip them off the wall and carry them home to feed her young? You wouldn't want that to happen to your friends, would you? So give us what is

rightfully ours and spare your friends their pain an
yourself the sight of it. You have no use for the obje
after all."

"I'll have less use for it when you're done with m
I'm sure of that," Aster said angrily. "Who are y
really? What do you want?"

"Oh, no, clever one. Oh, indeed no," Chu N
laughed. "You won't get *me* to name the unnameabl
You may sit here and think about it and watch thos
two swing and surely it will come to you. It is only m
tenderness toward you and your beautiful long blac
locks that keeps you from sharing their fate."

Silence. Then Aster, leaning far out, her head an
torso barely glimpsed from the corner of one of my poc
tortured eyes. "Oh, Amollia! Rasa! Dear sisters! Ar
you all right?"

"Very well, thanks be to God," Amollia said in
dry, pained imitation of Um Aman and her friend
"And you?"

"Aster," I gasped. "What do they want?" I was nc
thinking very clearly at that time, as my brains wer
being sucked out the holes vacated by my hair.

"Oh, that. The cork, of course, Rasa, didn't yo
guess? But don't worry. I don't care what they do t
me, I won't give it up. I'll be brave as you would be i
my place and never let them have it. For then wha
would they do to us?"

I was wishing she would consult me about what
would do in her place instead of just assuming sh
knew, when the wall under my right shoulder slithered

# *Chapter* 9

I have mentioned the volup
tuous figures carved into the stone walls of the buildings

Since beyond us stretched the trunks and greenery of the jungle and below us, according to Chu Mi (for I could not look down), flowed a river, it was safe to assume that we hung from one of the outer rather than inner walls. I shifted my limited gaze to the right, only my training at confronting that which frightened me keeping me from shrinking from what I knew, from the touch I had already endured, was there.

I was slightly mistaken. No fully live snake had crawled out of the wall to add to our pain and the certainty of death. Rather, the most distant aspect of the carving touching my shoulder, that of a dancer bearing across *her* shoulders a hooded cobra, was changing. Or at least the snake was. Had it not been for the touch I would have assumed I was enduring a waking fever dream born of my anguish, for the stone warmed in color and writhed in sections, until gradually it did indeed bear the semblance of a living snake, flicking its tongue in and out as it slithered across the dancer's more-than-supportive bosom and onto my shoulder, where its darting tongue all but touched my cheek.

My breath stopped.

"Yesss," it hissed and I found I was making little whimpering sounds.

I felt rather than saw Aster strain forward in an attempt to look around me. "Rasa? What is it? Is it the bird? Is a crocodile trying to bite your toe? Chu Mi says they can jump this high—"

"*Must* you repeat everything you hear?" Amollia gasped. I barely heard any of it. I was busy being petrified. Then Amollia must have managed to lever herself into position to see me for she emitted a faint yelp which she strangled at once for fear, considerate creature that she is, of startling the snake into striking. Slowly and carefully she said, "A stone snake is licking Rasa's face."

"Poor thing," Aster said resignedly. "Maybe it's an indication of what her next life will be like—"

The snake had borne all it could bear. "If you stupid females do not stop your screeching and babbling I will quite forget the good impression I was forming of you for showing such fidelity to your husband and abandon you to your doom after all."

Had the pain not kept me alert I would have swooned again from relief. "Djinn?" I asked.

"Shush! What good does it do me to disguise myself if thou bellowest my nature to all within hearing?"

"But how came you here?" Aster asked, leaning so far forward that she struggled for a moment for balance and had to withdraw a fraction back inside.

"I prefer not to say," the snake replied, folding its hood primly round its head.

"You're probably responsible, aren't you?" Aster hissed back.

"Silence, I say. Thou needst not carry on so. A djinn must do what he must and I am the servant of the bottle even if thy taking ways have allowed me unaccustomed freedom. Can I help it if your conduct was far more commendable than anyone would have thought of three infidels? I tried to give yon Divs shapes which would tempt you into doing my master's will rather than horrify you but you were not so easily led astray. Oh, bravo, dear ladies! Bravo!"

"Your praise is as touching as your confidence in us, O djinn," I replied. "But get us down." This I hissed back at it so vehemently that now it was the snake who drew back its head.

"Oh. I couldn't possibly interfere directly," the snake replied. "That would be contrary to my present master's wish. However, I can give you the benefit of my advice, and am inclined to do so, now knowing what laudable characters you have—for women. And I certainly cannot allow you to perish without telling you how proud I am of you for being strong and defending your honor and turning down the temptation of luxury and delight, choosing instead to endure great woe and pain by denying the Divs that which they seek."

"You see?" Aster hissed emphatically. "I *knew* he was responsible."

The snake ignored her.

"On the other hand, resistance in this matter is absolutely useless. My master would have from you the cork to my bottle and even you ignorant females must see that he will have it sooner or later."

"Whose side are you on anyway?" Aster demanded. "First you warn us away from the palace, then you make a half-hearted attempt to force us to return with you to the Emir—"

"I did not!" the djinn replied huffily. "Obviously, if I had in any fashion attempted to force you, you would have gone. Though I was not certain that my cork was in your hands at the beginning of that interview, I knew I had been at liberty an uncommonly long time. Therefore, my main task at that time was to comply with the letter of my master's wish, which, as you pointed out, was not possible, even for one of my power. I felt the power of the seal Lady Rasa bore on her person toward the end of that meeting however. Later, when my master had discovered the loss of it but did not yet know where to look, I took advantage of his disorganization to make a foray of my own to your tent to try to persuade you to give it back voluntarily."

"And when that failed, you turned upon us with your minions?" The resentment in Aster's tone was not nearly sufficient to cover mine. She sounded merely pouty. I was wishing the djinn back into his old form, whereupon I would somehow find the strength to hoist him by certain particularly tender parts of his person from the ring upon which I hung.

"Not mine, lady! Oh, no. I merely advised a stratagem whereby the Emir's ally, the King of Divs, might use his subjects to assist the Emir in obtaining the cork from thee. And a gentle, honeyed stratagem it was. What point was there, I asked, in using unnecessary brutality? Only she who held the seal could give it, and she had to give it freely, for it cannot be taken by force. Hadst thou acquiesced to the wooings of the Div, Lady Aster, thou wouldst have been deprived of the seal of Suleiman the moment thou removed—whilst thou—well, the Div would have obtained it when thou hadst laid it aside."

"And what would have happened to us then?" Aste asked.

The djinn-snake swelled a little. "Well—er— suppose the others would have been abandoned in th jungle and thou delivered unto my master, who cove thee yet. Or perhaps all of you would have been give to the King of Divs for his service. How should I know I cannot think of everything. Be assured it would hav been a gentler fate than that which inevitably awai thee now. For myself, I spent a great deal of tim detouring overland to reach this place. It was very ba of you to seek to avoid me by crossing the ocean th way."

None of us apologized.

"But now, Lady Aster, thou must for the sake Lady Rasa and Lady Amollia give up the cork. It is no use to you whatsoever. It serves only to bring upc you the wrath of my master and his powerful allies. Yc do not know the ways of Divs. They can turn then selves into anything. Anything. At the present momer the Emir is high in the favor of the King of Divs, whom he secretly pays tribute, for he sent him th beauteous Hyaganoosh. And my master will not re until the cork is returned, for so long as it is out of th bottle, he cannot fully control me. Unless he wishes expend one of his wishes and formally command me, may come and go at will. And he has already used tw of those wishes!" The djinn chortled a little at that.

"I wish you had told us all of this before," Aste complained.

"While I could not act forcibly against you, neith could I willfully disobey he who holds the bottle. An at the time, I thought you no better than he. Now th I know what faithful and devoted wives you are—"

"If you approve of us so much, release us fro here!" I said, and as hard as I tried to make it soun like a command, to my roaring ears it sounded mo like a whine.

"Apologies, Lady Rasa. I cannot. As I explained, cannot act against the Emir directly any more than can act against you. It is a very delicate matter." Th snake's tongue flicked in and out in a finicky manner, as if illustrating the delicacy. "One can't expect infidels to understand. But I would give the Divs the seal, Lady Aster. They cannot force it from you but they can do very bad things to Lady Amollia and Lady Rasa. Very bad things indeed—oh, my goodness!" The snake's color began to dim to stony pitted gray again, and only the eyes remained lit and the tongue lively for a moment as the hiss dried to powder. "I am fading. The Emir must be calling and therefore I must go. Even if he has no wish, I must be present in case he does have. May God protect you, even if you are infidels. You'll need it."

"Wait! Can you do nothing?" I cried as the last life in the stone snake fled and the heavy thing weighed now upon my arm, increasing the burden upon my poor scalp. And, making matters worse than ever, the smoke accompanying the djinn's exit from the creature's mouth and nostrils tickled my nose and caused me to sneeze. I almost swooned again from the pain.

Aster's torso twisted out the window again and she looked up at me sympathetically. "Heavens, you poor thing. You look like your skin is going to pull off your neck any moment now and drop the rest of you into the river." One needs such sympathy in times of peril. "I'm certainly glad we didn't agree to marry them. Not only are they wicked but they lied about who they are. Probably aren't princes either. Oh well, at least it's comforting to know they can't do anything really awful."

"To you, Aster," Amollia's scratchy voice reminded her. "They're killing us."

"Ummm. You may be right. So they are," she replied, and she did sound sorry.

"Go tell them you'll give them the cork," Amollia croaked.

"What? And lose all my bargaining power? Then we'll all be in the same pretty fix."

"Don't give it to them. Just tell them you will. Keep them occupied for a while."

"I don't see how. If I say I will give it to them and I do, that will take very little time, and if I don't, that

will be obvious too and they'll just come back up her
and hurt you some more."

That happy thought provided me with inspiration
"Say you . . . hid it magically. Make up some long ritua
by which you must retrieve it. It can last all night 1
necessary." I doubted that I would have been capable o
manufacturing such an act, but Aster was a professiona
actress—and charlatan as well, no doubt. She ought t
be good for something.

"Well, I'm not sure—" she began.

"Go," Amollia said. "Or our deaths will be on you
head and there's *no* telling what you'll be in your nex
life."

Aster left and below we heard her voice, loud an
fast, selling our captors her story. Meanwhile Amollia'
hands raised out of my line of vision.

"Be still," she said. "I'll have myself loose now—

I heard the clank of her bracelets on the iron rin
above the patter of the rain into the river below. Th
storm no longer came in gusts, as it had previously, bu
drizzled gently.

"Ahhh," she said at last, and her body shifte
upward. After a moment she said, "Rasa, I've untie
my hair from the ring. I'm holding it with my hand
now. Try to hold still, for I am going to climb into th
window long enough to unwind my sash and bind i
around you to tie you by the waist to my ring. That way
when I unfasten your braids, you won't fall into th
river before I can catch you."

Disinclined to nod, I groaned instead. I still di
not understand how, even if she freed me this time, th
two of us would be safe from the magic that had put u
there initially. Our enemies had only to snap thei
fingers again, or whatever it was they had done before
Still, with a respite from the blinding pain, perhaps
would think of something. Or perhaps Amollia ha
more of a plan.

She began swinging back and forth from the ring
kicking to try to reach the window ledge. I was glad sh
had warned me ahead of time, for it saved me painfu
flinching. She succeeded on the third try. From withi

the room came the sound of rustling cloth and jingling
jewelry. "Courage, barbarian. When we are free of this
place I shall teach you the tricks of hairdressing known
only to my people." She was silent for a moment before
I felt her reaching toward me, her fingers brushing my
waist. Even that slight movement stirred the stone
snake on my shoulder and I spun slightly, dangling,
half-swooning from the fire radiating from my head
down to my deepest self. I thought then the roaring
rush was in my head, and the heavy, deep, drumlike
beat also. So pervasive was the noise I barely heard
Amollia's scream, though her mouth was close to my ear.

I heard enough of it to open my eyes, which
suddenly were filled with feathers, each the size of a
spear and colored with a brilliant green brighter than
new grass and a yellow sunnier than the sun itself.
Unfortunately the gale wind generated by the beating
wings made up of these feathers rocked me back and
forth so painfully that I could not really appreciate their
beauty. I was almost relieved when the giant foot—like
a chicken's if a chicken had talons as long as a man's
legs—wrapped itself around my waist, for it served to
anchor me for a moment and ease the anguish of being
buffeted about.

Somewhere inside my tortured scalp I understood
the low chucklings emitting from the great bird belonging to both foot and feathers. They meant, roughly
translated, "Aha! I was right to hunt here again. Yet
another morsel ripe for my plucking. My young will be
well-fed."

A curved orange beak rushed toward my face and I
felt only one more flash of fire as it snapped shut before
the awful pressure on my head released and I felt
myself carried upward. The wind and rain cooling my
poor head relieved me so that I passed once more from
waking, heedless of my new danger.

I awoke with the divine ancestor of all headaches.
The scenery did nothing to improve it. Feeling my poor
tender scalp with small pats of my finger tips, I learned
that my braids had loosened. The ends had been chopped

a good foot shorter and the bound end hacked aw
Even so, the weight of it hanging hurt my scalp an
coiled up each length and laid it most gingerly atop
crown.

I lay slumped in a hut-sized structure composed
twigs and grass, containing several eggs that wo
come to my waist when I stood—which I had
intention of doing. For beyond the low, ragged edge
the nest a cliffside plummeted in jagged jumps i
purple haze and dark-green jungle glistening with ra
Above me was a leaden sky with a range of icy cr
biting into it. For the first time since I left my ho
country, bothered by the heat, I was not.

From the extreme dinginess of the sky and t
soaked condition of my clothing, I guessed I had be
in the nest for some time. My skin was warm howev
probably because the mother bird, while sitting on
nest, had had to sit on me as well. I was fortunate t
she preferred to save me to be fresh, live food for
young instead of snacking upon me herself.

How much time had passed since she left the nes
knew not, but she had done her work well while s
brooded, for now, in her absence, the eggs began
hatch.

The noise was almost more than my poor tortu
head could bear. When at last the first shell split do
the middle and pieces broke away with a crack lou
than thunder, I would have screamed except, of cour
to do so would only have made matters worse.

As it was they deteriorated rapidly. A hide
creature with the puckered pink skin of a stewed chi
en dotted with a sparse sprinkling of down poked
bald, pop-eyed head out of the crack in the shell a
opened its yellow beak, showing a pointed rosy tong
"GARAK!" it said. I wept, cringing from it, covering
ears and my vibrating scalp with my hands as bes
could.

I thought it meant to eat me as it shoved its fa
toward me, but when I uncovered my head enough
look into its watery pop eyes, it cocked its head rath
forlornly and seemed piteous right up until the time

rent my brain again by repeating its squawk. "GARAK!"

Still, the noise had a questioning, helpless quality to it. Not that I cared. It was, under the circumstances, no more helpless than I. But if I could only make it stop that horrible squawking before my head came off, I thought I might make my own last moments somewhat happier. Under the headcloth tucked in my sash the remnants of Fatima's food dangled in their net bag. The creature watched me avidly as I untied the bag, and when I extracted a bit of dried bread it went wild.

"GARAK! GARAK! GARAK!" it cried, its cries increasingly loud until I was ready to jump from the nest to a mercifully quick death. Instead, I flung caution aside and risked my hand by using it to stuff the bread into the fledgling's craw.

I was rewarded with a moment of blissful silence, nothing but a shadow of the former pain pounding my pate. When the creature once more opened its mouth, I popped in a rice ball. In this fashion I continued to deliver myself from its noise—first the bread, then the rice balls, and finally the dates, the pomegranates, the bananas, the oranges and the nuts until all were gone. Blessedly, by then so was the young creature's appetite until at last it kicked aisde the remainder of its shell, hopped out upon the shards, and relaxed, its head resting fastidiously against the headcloth on my lap, as if using it for a pillow. The bird made small, bearable, chirping sounds. These lulled me into another short nap myself, from which I was awakened by the beating of wings.

I thought then that perhaps the time had finally come to jump. The food was gone and when the small bird's hunger returned, it would add its din to the present cacophony and my head would crack open like its egg.

The chick twitched to alertness as its mother's shadow folded over us.

My hand on the headcloth of Selima, I once more understood the mind of this bird as I had done, though too distracted to wonder at the matter, while dangling from the temple wall.

"HAAATCHED, precocious one?" she asked. "You were supposed to eat that morsel, not sleep upon it." By this she meant me. "I see I must chew it for you if you are to have some before your siblings hatch."

Once more her monstrous beak swung down, casting the shadow of doom upon my countenance. But before she could do her worst, her child all but finished me off with its protests. "GARAK! GARAK!" it cried, pecking and beating at its mother with its well-formed though yet small and featherless wings. This time I understood, to my astonishment, that the garaks addressed to the giant bird meant, "Away, monster! Leave my mother alone!"

The mother bird emitted a confused squawk and flew off, landing a few soaring circles later with some odoriferous carrion with which she tried to pacify her offspring. The baby bird, full of my provisions, would have none of hers and defended me staunchly.

The mother bird glared at me, a glare I returned, and for the first time she seemed to notice that I was alive in the sense that she was. "Why, you yellow-crested, puff-chested, featherless wall-clinger!" she shrieked. Her name for me was so complex I admit its meaning might have eluded me even given the understanding imparted by the headcloth, except that she repeated it with each shriek and hence I became well aware of my image in her great green eyes. "You have stolen from me the love of my first-hatched! I would tear you into worm strips except that I would have to kill my child to do so!"

When she had squawked herself hoarse and me into a throbbing recurrence of my headache, I said reasonably and very very quietly, using the politest language I had heard among these people—for I had great respect for that beak and those talons, "It grieves me to have caused my esteemed hostess so much pain, mighty—er, jade-crested, golden-feathered, emerald-winged gem-among-birds." I had not become the wife of a consummate flatterer without learning something.

"Do you really think so?" she asked. "That is a very pretty name, but I am, of course, the Simurg."

"I am—er—the Rasa," I replied. "And as I was

saying, O Simurg, most beauteous and beneficent of birds, when your charming offspring awoke from its shell and cried out to me for food, my pity was aroused and as you were away, I fed it in your stead, for am I not a mother too?"

"You are?"

"Oh, yes. I have sixteen children at home and the eldest yet a toddler." Consorting with Aster had also left its impression upon me.

"The poor things! Why were you not with them instead of hanging around on walls?"

"Oh. That. You see, it is—er—this way," I stammered. I could not imagine the bird would believe or be interested in the truth—she seemed a simple, home-bound creature, if you discounted her more murderous attributes—so I told her something within her understanding. "My kind gathers food thus. We wait hanging there upon that building, looking like part of the wall, until—um—until snakes writhe past on the statues or a fish swims by, whereupon we pounce."

"Is that why I've so often found tidbits hanging there?" she asked, obviously pleased at the new information. "My dear, your instincts are leading you astray, I must warn you. Your kind has such terrible camouflage I think you will soon die out if you don't find new modes of food gathering soon."

"Ah, you are wise as well as beautiful," I said. "And do you know, we don't seem to catch much that way either."

Another "garak!" interrupted our conversation as a new chick emerged from the shell. The Simurg's expression of interest in me changed to one of covetousness but "my" hatchling glared at her and flapped its small wings menacingly.

"I believe you are a well-intentioned creature," the Simurg said reluctantly. "But I simply cannot have this. I need to be gathering food for my young and I cannot be bothered about you staying here and having them all think I'm nothing but some sort of delivery pigeon. Come, back to the ground with you. And remember what I've said about hanging around walls."

"Hearing and obeying, mighty Simurg," I said, adding the djinn to my list of impersonations. I surrendered my person to her talons whereupon she scooped me up, and flew almost straight down, barely braking with her wings in her haste to be rid of me, depositing me at the foot of the cliff. From high above I heard a last mournful squawk which now sounded less like "garak!" and more like, "Maaa!" But it died away as the Simurg set me free, my feet again touched solid ground, and the bird's beating wings overcame all other sounds.

Ah, safety. Now all I had to do was traverse the miles of tangled jungle between me and Aster and Amollia—if they still lived. At least I had the headcloth, and had only to ask the animals to find my way back to the temple.

Evening was rapidly approaching, however, so I sat down against a tree at the foot of the cliff. I wished I had not given the baby Simurg all of my food. I wished my scalp did not ache so much and wished the rain would stop or that I had the means of building a fire. What I did not wish for was to meet another snake, but that was what I got, nevertheless. I was not distressed for I had had good luck getting information from snakes previously, if one counted the djinn. Therefore, as the serpent descended the tree, its head weaving before my eyes as it investigated what manner of creature I was, I matter-of-factly raised the cloth to its snout and asked it in the name of God and Saint Selima how I might return to the "hunting lodge" in the jungle.

The snake gave me to understand that it was not at all religious and that if I did not desist shoving the rag in its face I would receive a richly deserved venomous reward. But at least the snake didn't bite me immediately. Heartened by this concession, I ventured to ask further where I might find food.

"I haven't the faintest idea," the snake replied. "I'm not even entirely sure what something like you would eat. I don't see why you must molest me when there are others of your sort in yonder cave. Why not ask them?"

To hear of the presence of other humans from the lips of a snake (if indeed snakes may be said to have lips) struck me as faintly ominous. Any human of which it spoke did not seem to me to be one whose acquaintance I particularly wished to make, but who was I to be picky under the circumstances? True, I had rather liked the idea of using the magic device in my possession. Conversation with another person seemed commonplace when I might converse with lions or elephants instead. However, as the snake had very properly pointed out, other humans would be better qualified to help me meet my own requirements for survival.

But it was not so much the snake's excellent advice as his warning that convinced me to immediately withdraw and investigate the cave.

Besides, other people, even if only poor peasants or fellow travelers, might provide me with food and fire for the night. Of course, I expected when the snake said they were in the cave that they would be immediately within the cave, so when I entered the little room just beyond the cave mouth and found it dark and empty, I almost decided I had the wrong cave. But as I moved toward the front again, I stumbled and looked back, and saw faintly from a corner I had not bothered to investigate a glimmer of light.

No doubt I was only in the entryway and the lodgers dwelt in a more commodious room deeper within the cavern. The leather curtain that parted beneath my hand, bathing me in the faintly greenish light, seemed to confirm that notion and I almost called out to my hosts. But my father had taught me the wisdom of learning the lay of the land before announcing oneself, and this caution saved my life.

At first the room appeared deserted, but it is true that I could not see very well in the sickly lime-colored light shining off the very walls of the cavern. Massive shapes huddled around the walls, and in particular one huge lump crouched in the middle of the room, toward the back, but though they seemed solid and menacing, I simply could not form any other impression of their nature except that they were inanimate.

Even that impression was rapidly dispelled, how
ever, as from the central mass came a scratching, and a
click. I saw something jerk against the green-lit stone
behind it. I fell back two steps and heard the thump of
eight bounding steps apiece taken by a plethora of feet—
a pack of camp dogs belonging to travelers?

What faced me heart-stilled moments later was
nothing anywhere near so ordinary. Far from being
many dogs, it appeared to be, at first glance, one tiger

# Chapter
# 10

For only one pair of lamping
russet eyes, each larger than my fist, stared up at me
And only one voice grumbled in a deep growl that
threatened at any moment to erupt into a roar. I barely
took in its other tigerish attributes—the stripes, broad
cat face and rounded ears. I was busy noticing the other
important detail—the gleaming ivory teeth, a full set
So hard did I stare at those teeth that I was almost
unaware of the disorientation I experienced concerning
the remaining portion of the tiger. Without realizing it
I kept expecting to see another head.

For though I was not acquainted with tiger
specifically, Amollia had described them to me and
knew they were large cats similar to those who preyed
upon Yahtzeni sheep and to the leopard Kalimba. Fatima
had also spoken frequently of tigers. From her I had
also formed the picture of another species of ordinary
ferocious feral cat differing from its fellows essentially in
matters of coloring. Neither Fatima nor Amollia had
ever mentioned anything to indicate that the beast's
head would be as large as one of the silver platters upon
which meals were served to whole companies of people

or that it would have two clubbed and angrily jerking tails and no fewer than eight legs, eight paws and forty wickedly gleaming claws. I did not pause to count each of them, for I was engaged in counting teeth instead, but the general impression was indelibly inscribed upon my mind. And though I had no desire to observe the rest of the beast at closer quarters, I had no choice, for the monster pounced forward again, all eight feet in perfect coordination, as if it were a team of exquisitely matched horses.

While my eyes were wholly occupied with the fearsome aspect of the beast, my hands were serving me better, for they had freed the headcloth and one of them, of its own will, tremblingly shook the rag before the tiger's very nose. My other hand flew up to cover my face so I wouldn't see when the monster took off the first arm, headcloth and all, and also so that when it attacked me it wouldn't mutilate my face first. I dislike seeming vain, but I wanted what was left of my corpse to be recognizable. Perhaps word would someday reach my mother and she would light a fire in my honor. I waited for an eternity and when nothing happened, peeked out. The beast had stretched forth its neck, which would have done a bullock credit, and was sniffing. The noise I had been interpreting as a growl had changed to an equally loud and ferocious purring. Then without warning it sprang again—onto its back, where it rolled and writhed with all eight paws in the air.

"Greetings, beast," I said. My voice refused to rise above a whisper.

The cat jumped to its feet and bumped against me, sending me sprawling. "Greetings, bearer of the sweet smell. Greetings and welcome."

"Welcome?" That was not the sort of attitude I expected from a guardian beast.

"Welcome. What a treat to have you here. The King didn't tell me you were coming, but I'm sure he wanted to surprise me. So seldom does anyone really interesting come while I'm left alone to guard the palace. I thought at first you had come to steal the

treasure, or perhaps one of the lemons from the orchard of experience, and I was going to eat you. Ca
you imagine that?"

I hoped he took my generalized trembling for
negative shake of my head.

"But having smelled that lovely smell, I can te
you are a splendid sort of person—though I don
suppose you came to visit just with me?"

"Actually, I—"

"No, naturally, you did not, a person with a
important smell like that. You have no doubt com
visiting at the harem. Perhaps you are even to becom
one of the Div's wives. Oh, *are* you?" The idea sent th
beast into spasms of eight-pawed leaps and rolls.

I tried to look noncommittal as I said, "We'll see
Can you show me the way?"

"Certainly I can. Do you think I would guar
something without knowing where it is?"

I followed it, walking behind and between th
bodies. It turned its head to gaze at me, its big eye
slitted with pleasure, and in its purr another questio
was forming.

Quickly I asked one of my own. "Why two bodies
Did you start out as twins, perhaps?"

The purring halted for a moment and the tige
turned to face me. "*All* bitigers have two bodies."

"Truly? Forgive my ignorance. I didn't know."
was most sincerely contrite for the bitiger's purr ha
stilled and the teeth gleamed under the eyes. "I ha
only heard of the other kind."

I held out the rag to sniff again and the beast
purr resumed, as did its forward eight-pawed prance
"That is understandable. Bitigers *are* rare. And superio
We are a new magical improvement on the other sor
you see, and since we are a new species, there are bu
few of us."

"In that case, I am honored," I said. "But tell me
how is having two bodies an advantage?"

"That should be easy for one with such a wis
smell to understand," the bitiger replied. "Why, we ar
far more efficient than ordinary tigers, for we hav

twice the capacity for disposing of enemies, since we have two stomachs, twice the speed, since we have eight paws. But, unlike two-headed beasts, we have only one leader for both sections and therefore no dissent or question, when there's a decision to be made, who is in authority."

"And who are the enemies of bitigers?" I asked.

"Prey mostly. Water buffalo and gazelles and deer. And ordinary tigers—who are jealous of us. Then there are the enemies of the King of Divs—" But at that point the bitiger turned a corner and stopped, so that I all but ran between the bodies and into its neck. I stepped back and the beast roared "to let them know we are without." In a moment the stone slab before which we stood creaked and thumped aside, opening upon light and music and the smell of incense.

I entered slowly, still bemused by the strange beast growling encouragingly behind me. Selima's headcloth had worked extraordinarily well on the animal, who had behaved as if intoxicated by the saint's odor of understanding and benevolence. Could it be that bitigers, enemies of ordinary tigers and of most animals or folk that they met, were so rare, with so few of their own kind, that they were glad of companionship? One might think the two bodies would provide it for each other, but then, there was no second head to confer with or to comfort.

When I was beyond the stone slab that served as a door, it slid shut and I ceased musing about the tiger, and turned to wondering, now that I had managed to enter this place, how I would leave it. Furthermore, my headache, all but forgotten, began to throb again as my eyes adjusted to the brighter light in this room. It was a large room, a sort of gathering hall, with the usual deep richly colored rugs and opulent gold-tassled cushions and bolsters lying about. The walls of the cave were fretted and carved into beautiful patterns and soft rosy light rippled upon silken banners draped across the cavern ceiling. These banners did not quite conceal that which caused my pate to throb: the iron rings suspended from the ceiling, one for each of the ten or fifteen women in the room save one. These women were all gorgeously dressed, very beautiful of face and form, varied widely as to complexion and hair color. But their tresses were all similarly styled; amazingly long and worn loose except for the ends, which were bound to the rings.

Only one, a young girl, was without fetters. She sat in the middle of the room upon a beautiful cushion of apricot hue embroidered with gold and silver atop an ankle-deep silken carpet of lapis lazuli, aqua and palest topaz. Her slender fingers wore tiny silver cymbals. Her body was frozen in mid-undulation, her mouth still partially open. The music I heard at the door had come from her.

The other women sat or lounged upon cushions while doing needlework, brushing the portion of their hair they could reach (which must have resulted in frightful snarls), applying cosmetics, or chatting. They paid no attention to me at all but went ahead with their activities, seemingly oblivious.

"Do make sure the door is really closed," the girl said, a slight tremor in her voice. "The bitiger is supposed to be a man-eater but one never knows." I turned and shoved against where I judged the opening had been, but now the wall was as if it had never been anything but solid. The girl sighed an exaggerated, childish sigh, a not inappropriate gesture since she looked to be little more than just past the shedding of her first woman's blood. She flipped her raven curls and beetled her heavy black brows so that they met across the bridge of her nose. I thought the expression made her look rather like one of Saint Selima's sacred monkeys, but I have been told that to have a browline such as hers is to possess a feature of great beauty second only to a deep navel in erotic appeal. "Very well, then," she said briskly. "You can change yourself now into what you really are. Never mind them," she flipped a wrist negligently in the direction of the other women. "The rings deprive them, after a while, of all interest in anything outside of themselves. The King says it makes life more peaceful that way, though I find it rather tiresome at times to have no one but his former first wife, who isn't yet affected by her ring, to show the jewels and gowns and other presents he gives me. She's not very appreciative." She paused for breath and blinked her wide dark eyes several times before continuing. "I must say that is the most hideously horrid guise I have ever seen any of King Sani's folk assume but I suppose I'll have to get used to it. Only give me a hint. Are you truly female or are you some cute boy come to ravish me?" She giggled a little and hugged herself as she asked.

"I'm sorry to disappoint you, your—uh—Your Radiance," I began, keeping to the formula of following Aster's example with dangerous and potentially dangerous beings. If it worked with birds, why should it not work with females with the brains of birds? "But I am afraid this is my true guise."

"*That?*" she asked, her hand going to her mouth.

"This," I agreed.

"But it can't be. Look!" And she held up a hand mirror of silver and mother-of-pearl for me to behold my visage. I immediately saw her point. With a patch of hair missing above my right temple, the rest of it strewed about in a matted, spiky structure similar to the Simurg's nest, my face streaked with blood and scratched and dirtied and streaked again by the rains, my clothing torn and my face and arms scratched, reddened and swollen, I looked very much as if I had been flayed, buried for several days, and disinterred.

"I'm afraid it is," I said, wincing and handing back the mirror, reflective side toward her. "I have met with disaster today, you see, and stopped here to ask for directions and perhaps shelter for the night, for I have become separated from my companions. But before I continue, would you be so kind as to tell me why these women are tied by their hair?"

"I suppose it does look a little unusual," she replied. "But it's a sort of beauty treatment. Makes their hair grow longer. I may try it later but right now I'm readying myself for my wedding. I was just practicing the song and dance I intend to perform for the King on our wedding night. I shall wear this very outfit too. Do you like it?" There was very little of it and quite a lot of her to be seen but I nodded. She hardly noticed the nod, but once more inspected herself critically, including the ends of her silky curls, which she tossed back over her shoulder as if rejecting them before staring at me, her lower lip protruding. "Why is your hair that color? Are you very old? The only one of the King's wives with hair that pale is quite ancient. You are a frightful mess but you don't look that old."

"I am not old," I said in roughly the same tone of voice the bitiger had asserted that it was not an aborted set of twins, "I am Yahtzeni."

"Oh. What's that? Is it good or bad?"

"Goo . . . we're shepherds, warriors, traveling people from across many seas and mountains. Very far away but we don't live so differently from some of your folk except," I nodded to the women bound by their hair, going about their business as if they were one of the shadow plays Aster produced with her clever hands on the walls at night before Fatima's lamp was blown out, "that Yahtzeni men haven't so many wives." I started to add that we didn't have as many men either but her curiosity was quite sated and her vanity aroused.

"Our men don't have all that many either, usually—only four, if they can afford it. And they *always* love one the best—usually the youngest and prettiest." She smiled, dimpling, just in case I missed guessing who that person was in this household. "Only very important officials and kings, like my fiance, the King of Divs (He's said to call him Sani but I do think that's improper before we're married, don't you?) can have so many. But these others, why, he doesn't care a fig for them." She waved her delicate little hand with its long hennaed nails and fingers full of rings dismissingly at the women behind her.

"Obviously," I said. "Still, I suppose at one time he must have."

"Oh, I don't think so. They're all political alliances. You know, that one over there is the one I was telling you about, was the last one he had that was anything like a favorite. She's a princess of the Peris—they're these most awfully odd magical folk from the other side of the mountains. Have you ever seen hair striped in colors like that? And her eyes are strange too. Sani says Peris live for hundreds of years and he just got tired of hearing how much older and wiser she was. But then, her father helped him overthrow his father so he could win the throne. I suppose he let her get away with it for sentimental reasons."

"A moment, please," I said. "I thought the king of this land was a young boy. Are we not still within the realm of the same Shah who rules both Bukesh and Kharristan?"

"Certainly. We're not far from Bukesh at all—but Adar Shah is King of Tamurians only. He has no control over the Divs." She sounded quite superior about it, as if she were already queen.

"But please," I said, "what are Divs?"

"You *are* foreign, aren't you?"

I kept my mouth shut and my eyes trained upon her face, the soft shadows licking across it with the ebb and flow of the rosy light. I refrained from remarking that if she were to be carried off to our grasslands by one of our demons she'd be just as foreign there as I was here.

"Divs," she said, "are simply the most wonderful things there are—at least most of them, and I don't need to worry about the others because I'll be their queen and they won t dare trouble me. They can change themselves into any form at all. You should see the handsome one Sani—His Majesty—has chosen to marry me in."

"But that's not unusual around here, is it?" I asked. "I know a djinn who does the same thing."

"You must be mistaken," she said firmly. "Djinns cannot turn into something that is not already in existence, the way Divs can. They are only able to occupy existing forms. Djinns *never* create forms."

"How knowledgeable you are for one so young!" I

replied. I wanted to wring her conceited little neck but I had begun to realize who she was and that I would need her help, not only now but later.

"I think every bride should share her husband's interests. I mean, once I'm queen, I'm sure to be expected to help out with the ruling, because Sani can scarcely bear to be parted from me and well, just between the two of us . . . I have lately felt the urgings of my royal blood—my *real* heritage, telling me how a few matters around here should be conducted. I used to think I was a peasant, you know, and raised by peasants, and my friend the Emir of Kharristan did say often when he came to me for advice and comfort that I certainly had the common touch—but now, Sani calls me his princess and I feel sure that he, with his magical powers, knows something."

She admired herself in the mirror she had held up to me and was obviously pleased by the contrast. The little round mirrors attached to the strip of rose silk barely covering her ample bosom sparked light around the room as she turned to catch herself at different angles in the mirror. She smiled fondly at her reflection. "He also calls me Akasma, the climbing rose." She giggled. "I think he means something naughty by that, but I don't mind. It's pretty, anyway. You can't imagine what a trial it is to have a mother who insists on naming you something awful like Hyaganoosh. Can't you just hear people snickering if they call me 'Queen Hyaganoosh'?" Then she sighed. "All the same, I wish my mother were here to see me now. Not that the Emir hasn't been wonderful to me since I was orphaned—I suppose he *did* feel responsible since it was his soldiers who accidentally ran my parents down while changing the guard. It made my Aunt Samira very bitter against poor Onan and she didn't like it when I went to live with him, I know, but she could scarcely feed herself and that lazy, daydreaming cousin of mine. She thought I should marry him, but between you and me, mama always told me I could do better. Not that Aman's not well-favored, you understand, but he never brought me nice presents like Onan and Sani."

Maybe the presents were to keep her quiet so they could contemplate her charms in peace. Her tendency to chatter was every bit as pronounced as Aster's. Despite the disastrous consequences of his failure, I was glad Aman had not succeeded in winning her. Two such tongues in one household would be enough to drive everyone else into the desert. At least she talked to me, which perhaps meant she liked my company. And why not? I had given her no cause not to. The way I looked at the moment I was certainly no competition for her, and the obliviousness of the other women would be a great trial to this self-proclaimed paragon. Ears into which she could pour her chatter were more than welcome and since I needed to gain her goodwill without revealing too much, listening seemed the safest course.

"Would you have married your cousin if he had been rich enough to give you presents too?"

"He couldn't be as rich and powerful as Sani, could he? And he can't change forms—" She broke off to titter behind her hand. "At least, not by himself. Oh, Aman is such a buffoon! Do you know he crept into my private chambers when I lived with the Emir and gave me a lamp he claimed was magic? I didn't believe him, but I was so annoyed at him for endangering my position with the Emir that I called him an ass and—and something funny happened. Onan was coming and while I was looking for a place to hide Aman, he disappeared, but there was an ass right there in my garden!"

"Do you suppose that was your cousin?"

"Oh, no, how could it have been? Why, if I'd turned her precious son into an ass, I would have heard my Aunt Samira screaming all the way from her house on the other side of Kharristan! No, no. I've been told of such things, but that's not possible, is it?" Her pretty brow wrinkled with the strain of thought. "I mean, Sani is someone different. He is a genuine magic person. So, of course, what *he* does is real, but Aman with a genie and a magic lamp? No. I do not think so. Nevertheless, I gave the lamp to Onan for safekeeping. What if that genie crawled out of his bottle when I was asleep and tried to molest me?"

"Oh, you handled it properly," I said. "Very cunning. By giving the bottle to the Emir, you earned his gratitude as well, no doubt."

The smooth brow puckered further and the little mirrors shimmered with agitation as her wide brown eyes clouded with a hint of the anxiety a lamb with any measure of intelligence should feel upon entering a wolf's den. "Ye-es, except he wondered where I got it. That was when he decided I'd be happier here with Sani, and should come here to await the wedding instead of remaining with him—" She broke off, blinking ingenuously at me. "But you poor thing! Look at you! Starved and dirty and tired, and here I am going on about all the wonderful things happening to me."

I was so predisposed against her by this time that I decided she was not really being thoughtful but was merely disinclined to continue talking about a subject which made her uncomfortable, and grasped at any straw to change it. Whatever the reason, if indeed she had any, she reached behind her, picked up a small padded stick and struck a round bronze gong.

"We'll all have something to eat. It can be a party! But—don't you think you should wash first? There's a pool over in the corner, behind the striped-haired Peri. And perhaps you should remain inconspicuous while the servants are here. Sani doesn't really like visitors."

"I gathered," I said, thinking of the bitiger, and rose to wend my way through the ring-bound women to the pool, where I made myself at once presentable and less noticeable to the servants, who turned out to be large black spiders who scuttled into the room with trays on their backs.

"What are those?" I asked. I did not expect an answer for the talking among the women had neither ceased nor slackened. The Peri princess, however, had not been talking. She had been watching me in her own mirror while I washed my face and all other modestly available flesh before ducking my head to rinse the blood and sweat from my hair and scalp. The calculating gaze with which she now favored me caused me to wonder at Hyaganoosh's bland assumption that only the servants would report my presence. Why worry about spiders when there were jealous, deposed wives with which to concern herself?

"That," the Peri replied, pointing to one of the spiders scuttling toward us, "is my sister, Pinga. She wasn't beautiful enough to marry King Sani after he disposed of his old ally, our father, so he froze her into that shape and condemned her to serve as a slave. He does likewise with all of the less well-favored female relatives of his defeated rivals. He claims the spider's shape is a more useful one for women of unpleasing aspect, and as spiders they are less prone to servant's gossip. Unless, of course, he turns them back into their human shape long enough to question them." And with this she gave me a significant glance out of eyes that were clear and faceted as diamonds and reflected all of the colors in the room. Then, quietly, she stepped in front of me and stooped to receive a plate of fruit and cakes from one of the trays before the spider crawled along to the next woman.

When all of the women had been served, the spiders arranged themselves and their trays in a sort of honor guard around Hyaganoosh, who busily popped mutton chunks into her mouth and licked her fingers.

The Peri sighed and shook her head slightly. "How long it has been since I was as wise as that!"

I said, "Um," through a mouthful of apple, which gave me an excuse not to say more.

The Peri, however, was not in need of information from me, as she soon demonstrated. "So. Your husband is still an ass," she said, watching with a sidelong glance as I choked on my apple.

"How did you know about that?"

"Who do you think was Highest Highness before our little climbing rose came along? Any magic requiring shape-shifting to an unprefabricated body requires *our* help, you know. That trick your friend the djinn did may have looked so fast to mortals that dark-eyes over there missed it altogether, but actually, he had to send a message through the ethers requesting permission and filling out the proper forms before he could so much as add a hair to your husband's tail. I myself was accustomed to taking care of such matters, to spare Sani's energies for more important affairs. You see how grateful he was!" She reached up and tugged the combined blue and green stripes of her hair so that the iron ring to which it was bound creaked against the stone ceiling. "But then, Sani always resented my administrative talent. In a few months' time I will have no thought for the statecraft I learned at my father's knee, along with flying and vanishing. I'll be as oblivious as these other poor drudges. The ring does that to one after a while. With all magic gone, all interest in anything beyond the self goes too."

"You cannot help us then?" I asked.

"No. Even if I were free of this accursed iron and enjoyed Sani's trust once more, I could not change the wish. She who invoked it must—"

"I know, I know. Everybody seems agreed about that. I was just leading up to asking for her help when she called for the spi—excuse me, your sister and her fellow captives. But actually, I only stopped long enough to get directions back to the hunting lodge where Aster and Amollia and I met some—" I looked into the faceted eyes, which were politely waiting for me to finish another story their owner already knew well. "—Divs," I finished lamely. "You know about that too?"

She smiled smugly. "I have my spies."

"Then you will understand that I must see to that situation first," I said.

"You may have another problem, if you linger too long. If Sani returns and finds you here, here you will remain," she eyed me critically, "possibly as a spider. I do not know how you got past the bitiger, but dealing with Sani and the honor guard accompanying him to meet Emir Onan will be no piece of halva, believe me. You will not be so lucky as to find them out next time."

"Perhaps I can sneak past them."

"Impossible. A thousand gongs would gong and a thousand nightingales would cry out in the barrack even if you manage to work your wiles on the bitiger again. I developed the security system myself."

"Can you not help me?"

"I could," she said. "If I thought it would be worthwhile. And if I thought my help would be enough to keep you from bungling it anyway. You have no idea how vicious Sani can be when betrayed. I'm an immortal. Spending the rest of my life being tortured is therefore even less appealing to me than most, and while I am bound to this ring I cannot properly defend myself."

"I could cut your hair loose of the ring," I said.

"Umm—yes, I suppose you could. However, it would not serve," she replied, squatting beside a low table, upon which were pots, jars, sticks and bottles full of cosmetics. She began drawing lines around her eyes and offered me the pot when she had finished to her satisfaction. "Here, you could use a little color."

I thought that such severe shadow would only give one of my pallid appearance a corpselike aspect and declined. "Why would it not serve?"

"Because in my hair is half my power, and if you cut it you would be debilitating me even as the ring now debilitates me. You might as well cut off my arms."

I started to remind her that while her hair would grow and she could regain her power, she would steadily lose it while she was tied to the ring. But what did I know of Peri hair? No alternative solution to her problem or my own suggested itself. I watched in silence as she rouged her cheeks and lips and then paused, the rouge pot halfway to her cheek, her index and little finger extended stiffly as she froze. Throughout the caverns, the distant sound of gongs and bird songs echoed and the bitiger roared in greeting. The life which had drained from the Peri's face quickly returned and she dropped her rouge pot and snatched up another, thrusting it at me. "Follow my directions exactly or we are all doomed."

It was almost worth the danger to see the smugness melt from Hyaganoosh's face to be replaced by a frantic searching stare as her much-praised eyes first sought me among the other women and then darted back to the place in the stone wall where the slab would slide away at her fiance's bidding.

Both the Peri and I had meanwhile been busy coating my face with the ointment. This, as it turned out, was a special Peri-formulated vanishing cream that caused those not bound to iron rings to vanish. It was convenient and economical, because though the jar was small, one needed only to coat the face to have everything vanish. When the cream had done its work, the Peri called to a spider and, with some fumbling, refilled my invisible foodbag from the tray. The spider, still facing Hyaganoosh, must have thought the Peri's appetite had suddenly become ravenous from the rapid fashion in which the tray lightened.

No sooner had the spider scuttled back into place when the wall opened again, and the light of three additional torches illuminated Hyaganoosh in all of her guilty confusion. The other women were thrown, as I would have been had I been visible, into deep shadow.

The King of Divs was likewise streaked with shadow, but as I very discreetly slipped past him I could see that he was not in one of his more attractive aspects that evening. His head bore a ruff of orange fur around it, his nose resembled a boar's snout, complete with tusks, and his hands those of a large monkey.

Hyaganoosh cringed as he advanced on her, the gap widening between his guards and himself providing me with the opportunity to gain the corridor, where I paused to listen through the open doorway.

"So," the King said in a voice held with iron strength to low, soft tones, "has my little poppet been lonely while I've been away? Making friends with outsiders? Are not all of the women of my harem company enough for you?"

"But—but—your own guardian brought her here, Your Majesty. I assumed she came with your persmission."

"Where is she?"

"I slew her, Sani," the Peri answered from her corner, her voice sounding efficient and housewifely. "I am glad to know you concur, but you mustn't disturb yourself so. Naturally, as always, I see to it that your household is well-run in your absence. You can't expect a mere mortal girl to perform the tasks of one of us."

"And how, my sweet, did you manage to slay her with none of your powers?"

"I poisoned her food—even mortals may do so though it requires the wit to think of it." She looked pointedly at Hyaganoosh.

"And the body?"

"Pinga disposed of it."

Hyaganoosh gulped and nodded. I stood without, my wet hair causing me to shiver slightly in the drafty cavern corridor, and wondered which way to run. Hyaganoosh seemed to be wondering the same thing the last time I glimpsed her. The King stroked her cheek and hair and asked his treasure to forgive his harshness. His treasure looked up at him with an emotion more sensible than admiration—fear.

And at that moment the bitiger's single head rounded the corner, its growl plainly saying, "Ah, that lovely smell again. But where?"

I possess, as does any warrior of a wandering people, an unfailing sense of direction. I did not take the wrong path accidentally. But the headcloth-intoxicated tiger blocked the entry hall and the King and his guard blocked the harem, the only other room with which I was familiar. Short of abandoning Selima's useful headcloth to confound the bitiger, there was little I could do but seek to evade both situations and find another exit. This almost cost me not only my freedom but my life, for the cavern was a veritable maze of passages, and had I gotten lost within them, I might have perished before finding my way out. But like the entry hall, the passages were illuminated with a pervasive green glow, and though I was most puzzled to find myself in locations where I had never previously been, I was not lost.

Quite the contrary, for the gods were obviously with me—or if not the gods, Fatima's advice. Bewildered by the forks and side passages, possessing no knowledge that made one way any more reasonable or safe course to follow than any other way, I recalled the holy woman's admonition to turn right, and did so each time I had a choice. Therefore I suppose you could not truly say that it was by luck alone I came upon the tunnel opening into the starlit grove.

I stood for a moment in the passageway, catching my breath and surveying the scene before me. The grove was cupped in a small meadow in the palm of surrounding peaks, roofing the hindermost portions of the Div's palace. That this was the orchard of which Fatima had spoken was obvious at once from the faint lemon scent perfuming the chilly indigo night. The trees were ancient, huge, twisted with pale oblongs dotting the heavily leafed branches. Several of the branches drooped low enough that with a good jump I should be able to dislodge a lemon without much problem.

But suddenly in the passage behind me I heard an eight-pawed thump and a prowling growl. The bitiger had found my trail. Abandoning thoughts of pilfering lemons for the time being, I sprinted to the right, scrambling up a short steep incline beyond which threaded a downhill path. This I followed, running along it, sure that at every moment I would be devoured by one head and my carcass distributed evenly between two massive striped bodies.

But when I halted what seemed miles later, stomach churning, heart thumping, arms and legs too limp to sustain so much activity from the mid-section, no sounds of pursuit followed me. I hid behind a tree, wondering how to surprise the beast: leap upon its back and strangle it when it came near me again? Bribe it with a piece of the cloth? With such clear-cut and brilliantly thought out tactics, I was doubly fortunate that the beast never reappeared. The path led me down through low hills, angling, but never again forking, eastward of the Simurg's nest and the cave below it, into the jungle.

I plunged into the greenery, my feet squishing through the mud from the afternoon rain, leaving, as I had left all along, very visible tracks. I winced inwardly but wasn't about to go back and cover them. The Divs had been told I was dead and would not be looking for me and even the bitiger had apparently given up. Valiantly, I squished onward.

I did not cease putting distance between myself and the palace of the Divs all that night. At times the trees blocked the starlight, concealing the path. But the forks were for the most part clearly marked, and I always turned right. Toward morning the rain began in earnest again, soaking me. I tucked the headcloth carefully away, for fear that if it were washed by the rain, it would lose some of its precious stench. Its protective presence was the one source of comfort that sustained me—well, that and the food.

I was not to remain alone for long. Despite my precautions, the headcloth grew sufficiently moist to transmit fumes which soon won for me quite a following.

Though I intended to keep walking all night, the sky was still dark above the leaf cover when I dragged my right foot after my left foot a final time and collapsed, unable to move any longer. My eyes were so blurred from lack of sleep that I could no longer make out the path and began to fear I might lose it, and with it my life and the lives of Amollia and Aster, if indeed they still lived, and the humanity of Aman Akbar.

On the other hand, the thought occurred to me that while I was armed with the headcloth, the ointment and the knowledge of Hyaganoosh's whereabouts, I could leave the others to whatever fate had doubtlessly already claimed them and free Aman Akbar myself. To do so I would need only to persuade the animals to help me find him, whereupon I would smear him with the ointment and deliver him to Hyaganoosh, who could change him from an invisible donkey to an invisible man with the help of ... Wait! Hyaganoosh was not a witch. I'd need the lamp—still in the Emir's possession—and the stopper—still in Aster's—and while I might be able to use the ointment to obtain those items, the longer I thought, the more I wished I had Aster and Amollia to talk things over with.

Not that Aster would let anybody else talk. Still, her chatter made a nice background noise while a person thought. And she was clever. So was Amollia. I, on the other hand, was feeling distinctly unclever. And if I rescued Aman Akbar single-handed, while he would be grateful and loving enough for a while, in time he would probably elect to marry other women and I would be back where I started. Better, as we had decided with the Divs, to keep our household together. Loyalty prompted such a choice. And honor. And the sealed cork in Aster's sleeve. With all of this in mind, I finally fell asleep.

The monkeys woke me, pulling at my food bag. I was apparently no longer invisible. I seemed to have rubbed the ointment from my face during the night. But other than the hairy-handed thieves busy robbing me of the food I had stolen, I was alone. I snatched the bag back and the boldest monkey chattered angrily at me, flinging its skinny arms in the air and stomping its feet. When this behavior failed to cow me, it slung itself down on its haunches and looked up appealingly at me with round, betrayed eyes while the fingers of one paw picked timidly at the bottom of the bag. A great many other monkeys crouched or hung in trees nearby, watching me carefully.

"I can't feed all of you," I told the one picking at the food bag. "If I do then I'll have nothing to eat. There are too many of you."

Immediately the monkey turned its back on me and began chattering angrily at its companions, who fled into the trees—at least for the time being. I offered it a nut, which it held to its mouth and nibbled in a dainty fashion. It was not truly hungry, I understood, but had merely wanted to try cajoling me to see what it could obtain. This was made clearer when the little beggar next began fingering the gold bracelet that was Aman Akbar's wedding gift. There I drew the line.

One by one, its companions flitted back to me, demanded a treat and fled again when it wasn't forthcoming. Thus accompanied, I traveled for two more days. While the monkeys were more pesky than protective, they were company. When the road forked right, we followed that path and where it forked left, we continued straight ahead. At one point, the trees were crushed away from the path and broken, as if under some great weight, and we had to climb over them. All the while it seemed to me that we were traveling in quite the opposite direction from the "hunting lodge" and yet, somehow, twilight of the second day brought us to the river bank opposite it.

The lodge had undergone some alterations. The doorway had been smashed open. Several of the carved hoydens had also suffered dismemberment.

The sight of it, broken and to all appearances empty, left me feeling much as it looked—empty, remote, detached. I sat down on the river bank and just a short distance along the shore saw the mud move and fall slithering into the water. Once in, the mud slab twisted itself and opened to reveal a line of jagged but deadly teeth. A monkey high above me on an overhanging tree limb chittered its reproach.

On the opposite shore, another monkey flashed through the thin overhang and a line dropped from the top of one of the larger trees, a small brown body clinging to it. The monkeys accompanying me had often chosen this mode of travel. The vine swung across and the monkey dropped to my feet, its paw still clutching the vine. I understood that I was to take it, and did so, tugging hard to test my weight upon it. The eyes of the great lizard stared at me with lazy watchfulness. If the vine broke or I lost my grip, I'd get more than a quick bath.

Walking backwards for several steps, I jumped up, grabbing the vine as close to its top as I could, which wasn't far, and swung out across the river—well, almost across the river. Before I reached the far bank, the vine slowed, fell back, and hung over the center of the stream. The big lizard blinked. The damned vine wouldn't budge one way or the other, no matter whose curses I called down upon it. I was debating about whether or not to try climbing it to reach the overhanging branch from which it hung when the rescue party arrived. Several monkeys on another vine slammed into me from behind, nearly loosening my hold but ultimately

knocking me onto the opposite shore. My legs refused
to support me for a moment afterward and I watched
numbly as the lizard's porcine eyes stared wistfully at
where I had hung. The water running off the creature's
head made it look as if it were weeping. I was not
heartbroken by its disappointment.

Despite the building's deserted appearance, I
approached cautiously, assessing the size of the holes
and the position of the rubble—which seemed to have
exploded into rather than out of the doorway. The
monkeys grew quiet too, and peered anxiously into the
hole. But none of them offered to accompany me.

So I did what the women of my people do best and
simply walked forward, as if I were leading the sheep to
pasture or striking out for the next camp.

Plenty of rain and dusky light poured in through
the newly enlarged doorway. The rugs, candles, pillows,
tapestries, trays of food, all were gone. Remaining was
nothing but cold stone floor, weeds sprouting in the
cracks. The shadows in the corners moved and once,
just beyond the corner of my eye, a long fat tail
whipped away and into a wall. A bit of wind and dust
agitated itself into a dust devil and spun across the floor.
A ghost of candle smoke lingered near the walls, despite the brisk wash of rainy smell.

One of the connecting doors hung half open and I
kicked it aside.

Narrow stone steps clung to an inside wall. At the
top of them, a small circular room was pierced by light
from a window. Outside the window, a latticed screen
flapped back and forth, banging against the wall, its
fitful noise uncoordinated with the ring of iron on
stone. I stooped and glanced through the opening at
the rusting rings, groaning on their chains. The ends of
my braids were still attached to one of them. I stretched
to my full length and grabbed at my sodden hair,
pulling the ring toward me. Struggling with the wet
strands, I unknotted and detached every one of my
hairs from that ring. Not that I thought I could use my
hair again, but with all of the witchery abounding in
this land and the quantity of it that had been loosed

against my new family, it would have been extremely unwise to let items such as my hair, nails or less delicate personal sheddings lay around where my enemies could find them. Most of the enemies in question were so powerful they had no need of such items to damage me as sorely as they pleased, but there was no sense making it any easier for them than I had to. Stiff and soaked, I withdrew from the window. Below, the gray-brown river rushed past.

The rest of the room was as barren as the one below and I couldn't help wondering what its function was, other than as a platform for tormenting hair-hung women.

Returning to the main floor, I tried the door in the center of the back wall. A many-limbed idol clad only in a girdle of skulls dominated the room. A brown-stained stone altar with a convenient surrounding trough lay in front of the idol. The rain evaporated from my skin leaving a cold, goose-flesh chill. I touched the altar and examined my fingertips. No blood came away on them. The stains were old then. With blood on my mind, I returned to the main room and noticed for the first time the gore flecking the walls, causing the voluptuous stone maidens to look as if they'd been brawling.

The monkeys waited in the rain. I would find no tracks after all this time, I felt sure, and though this place—a temple certainly—made my spine crawl, it was the first shelter I'd encountered in days. I slept inside the doorway, but out of sight, behind one of the rubble piles. Using the headcloth, I asked the monkeys to warn me of anyone approaching. They wanted to know when I would return their various favors with more rice balls and fruit.

# *Chapter*
# 11

Marid Khan and Aman Akbar must have come while I slept, sometime during the night. Only two of the monkeys had seen fit to remain alert, and even with them shrieking at the top of their little lungs, it took some time to alert me. I had needed that sleep. Though I had some company in the shelter of the rubble, even the vermin were animals, and as such honored the scent of Saint Selima.

I heard the monkeys scream at almost the same moment I opened my eyes and saw shadows fall across the stone floor, each crack now distinct in the muted light of early morning. When the intruders stepped into the room, I was initially relieved to see that they were not the false princes nor anyone else I knew, but several men of Sindupore, dressed similarly to the villagers near Selima's shrine in dingy white loin cloths. On closer scrutiny, they were no less strange and far more alarming, for their brows beetled fiercely and they muttered to each other, sharp phrases and words exploding through the general hubbub now and then. Though I gathered that they were pilgrims to the skull-girded idol, their expressions bore no gentle reverence or even a reasonable degree of the practical self-absorption of the supplicant to such Yahtzeni deities as Fanya the Fertile Fodder Finder.

"Desecrated," one of them spat, and though I had the sense that his words were not spoken in any of the tongues I knew, I understood them as clearly as I did the Simurg, monkey or snake languages, no doubt through the benefit of Selima's headcloth. Perhaps because the newcomers were fellow human beings, no preliminary sniffing of the cloth on their part was required for me to understand what was in their hearts—if they possessed any.

"Indeed, indeed," said the largest among them, a hulking man whose torso and face hung with flab but whose arms and legs were corded. He smiled unamiably through a mouth devoid of teeth, and whistled most of his words. "But who would dare to desecrate the shrine of The Terrible One?"

"A fool!" another blurted, scowling at the rubble and emptiness as if it was a personal insult. "Only a fool would desecrate the shrine of the goddess of death and torture! Only a new sacrifice will redeem us."

With those words my suspicions were confirmed that despite the nubile maidens covering the temple walls, the resident goddess had nothing to do with fertility. I briefly considered a fresh application of the vanishing cream and a fast retreat, but hesitated.

"Are you volunteering, Gobind?" the husky man asked, smiling even more unpleasantly.

"To perform the sacrifice? Assuredly," the angry man replied. "Come, let us see if the goddess's image has been outraged."

The men crowded the door to the idol's chamber, taking turns entering and kneeling to the hideous figure. Those awaiting their turns shifted angrily and continued muttering. After a considerable time with one group wailing, cajoling, and apologizing at the idol, the groups traded places.

Those renewed by commune with their goddess milled restlessly outside the door, and I rose cautiously to the balls of my feet, poised to flee into the jungle the moment every back was turned and all eyes were intent upon the new group of worshippers. Such a moment did not come.

A monkey's scream cut through the human voices, joined at once by the cries of other monkeys. Two of the waiting pilgrims detached themselves from the group and wandered over to the doorway, gazing first toward the river and then to the right before disappearing, the noise of their bare feet slapping mud and splashing through puddles following soon afterward. Just as the slappings and splashings grew faintest, they began to grow louder again and both men padded back inside, gesticulating frantically to their fellows and whispering excitedly. The expressions of the others changed from hostile boredom to active hostility, and the lot of them, including those closeted with the idol, followed the first two outside and down the path. By the time they were well away enough that I felt it safe to pop out into the jungle and follow at a discreet distance, it was too late.

They had been gone for but a heartbeat or two when from the distance came the surging voices of the angry worshippers, a muffled curse, general scuffling noises, and a heartrendingly familiar bray.

That bray caused me to leap to my feet, my hand flying to my dagger, but I caught myself and jumped back behind the rubble just as the worshippers led the donkey and its limply flopping rider through the door. Against all probability, the donkey was indeed Aman Akbar. And his rider, when pulled down and thrown onto his back, where his bleeding head lolled upon the stones, was none other than Marid Khan.

"What shall we do with him?"

"What do you suppose? The goddess is great. She not only demands a sacrifice, but practically delivers one to us personally."

"Such a sacrifice must be performed in a special way," the husky man, who seemed to be something of a leader, said consideringly. "A very special way indeed."

The face of the one called Gobind softened into a smile of childish delight. It did not make him especially appealing. "Ahh, I think I know," he said, rubbing his hands together briskly. "You will recall the tale of the proud beauty who tried to escape her marriage to the Rajah of Kinjab on muleback?"

"No," the big man said flatly, plainly prepared to reject any idea not of his own devising.

"You'll like it," Gobind assured him. "What we do, you see, is kill the ass, slit it open, stuff the desecrator inside and force his head out the ass's bung hole. Then we let the flies and mosquitoes at his face, from which we will not have bothered to wipe the dung and ass's blood."

"I think I may be sick," said one sensitive soul. "It's wonderful! The goddess will be very pleased. We'll kill the ass upon her altar, won't we?"

"Yes, that will teach these foreigners to mess with *our* goddess."

Aman brayed breathlessly, his eyes rolling and his knees trembling, his hind legs dug into stone as the worshippers tried to drag him to the altar.

I could not let them do it, whatever the cost. They should know the truth. "Wait!" I cried. "These two are not the ones who defiled your temple. Rather it was three Divs seeking to—" I got no further, of course, before I too was seized and disarmed. I expected no better, really. I was hardly such an innocent that I truly thought an appeal to justice would interest these particular pilgrims. A Yahtzeni is taught from birth that there are two kinds of people. There are our people and then there are *those* people. One cannot even trust all of our people, much less any of the others. Still, I had married one of those untrustworthy outsiders, and now traveled among many others. Having gone so far, there seemed no choice but to go a step further and attempt to win over these new ones if it was possible thereby that I might preserve my lord from harm.

I did not change the minds of his would-be slayers, but I did delay them.

"Excellent idea, Gobind," the large fellow said, scanning me contemptuously. "But now what?"

Gobind's enthusiasm was not so easily quenched. "Why, we kill the woman too—the goddess is hungry for blood."

"I'm not a virgin," I said hopefully. "I'm a married woman."

"The Terrible One is not particular about that, being a female god," Gobind reassured me. "Your pain will be a sufficiently pleasing contribution."

Oh.

"That is all very well, Gobind," a man with a rather squeaky voice and a nervous manner said. "But we have only one donkey. Do we put him inside as we originally planned or shall we substitute her? I say watching the insects destroy a woman's face will be more entertaining than turning them loose on him."

"This is for the goddess's appeasement, not our entertainment," his friend reminded him sternly.

"If we are more entertained by one mode of sacrifice than the other, it stands to reason that the goddess will be similarly entertained," the squeaky one argued.

"What we really need is another donkey," someone else said reasonably.

"Ahh," the large one said, with leering wigglings of his black and wormlike eyebrows. "But if it is entertainment that is needed, there are far more entertaining ways of killing women than stuffing the best parts inside of beasts."

Having blundered on the side of honor enough for one day, I declined to make matters easier for them by explaining that Aman Akbar was my husband, in case they were sentimental sorts who would decide that we ought to be reunited.

They shoved me into the altar room, loading Marid Khan upon the back of Aman Akbar and pushing and pulling the pair in behind me.

"The goddess shall decide," Gobind declared, and, clashing the knife he had captured from me against his own, laid both before the idol.

"You know how she hates to be disturbed," the squeaky fellow said fearfully.

"For trivial matters only. This is her sacrifice. She shall determine the mode of death."

"Yes, only by the right and proper sacrifice can this desecration be avenged. These conquerors must learn they simply can't go about treating other people's goddesses in such a fashion."

I was out of sympathy with them completely. In fact, I didn't think they were religious fanatics at all—not sincere ones, anyway. They just liked to hurt people, but being mere villagers instead of soldiers or bandits were too respectable or cowardly to indulge their vice without some sort of religious sanction. This goddess probably was invented just to give them the license to do what we Yahtzeni have always had the courage to take upon our own heads, instead of blaming our actions upon the gods, who, as everybody who is at all honest with themselves will admit, have better things to do.

Thus I maintained a brave sneer upon my face as Gobind lit the brazier and dropped powders upon the fire and implored the idol to speak.

Thus my teeth all but fell from my gums when the goddess said, her voice echoing in properly doom-laden tones, "Grovel when you speak to your mistress, oh vile vomit of a deformed offspring of a monkey's slave and her master."

The worshippers at once and in unison groveled. If they had not been true believers before, they were instant converts. They slammed me down with them—an unnecessary gesture, for I was almost too frightened to stand. But something in that voice, for all of its stony, otherworldly overtones, was familiar.

"Is that any way to be, Terrible One, when we've brought you such nice sacrifices?" Gobind whined. "We realize you are naturally upset about the desecration of your temple but—"

"Silence! What sacrifices?"

"Why, this woman—you can see what a rare offering she is with light hair, for all that she seems uncommonly stupid. And this excellent donkey and his rider."

"How can I see them with you standing right in front of me? Have the woman stand."

My captor released my shoulders and I stood. I hoped the goddess was unacquainted with vanishing cream and its properties, for while lying on the ground, I had worked the little pot loose from my sash and had it ready.

"Turn around," the goddess commanded. I did so, thinking that this was a very fussy goddess. I was also stabbing my finger in the open ointment pot. Bringing forth a small gob, I reached out to Aman Akbar and, before those lying beside him noticed, swabbed around each of his eyes and down his muzzle. Abruptly, Marid

Khan hung suspended, collapsed across thin air. None of the worshippers stopped trembling or looked up long enough to realize that they now had only two sacrifices instead of three.

"Won't do," the goddess said as I turned back toward her. "Temple desecration is most serious business. If you think I'll be pacificed by a big dumb blond and a dead man, you're wrong. Nothing less than the personal sacrifice of each of your lives will please me."

"But great goddess, who will serve you if we all die—who will—"

"Enough. I have spoken."

"You have spoken," the hulking man agreed, rising suddenly. "But not with the voice of the goddess."

He was correct. The goddess spoke with the voice of Aster and, as usual, she had overdone it. I quickly dabbed around my own eyes, cheeks, and chin with another gob of ointment and with my free foot mashed the fingers holding my left ankle. I lunged and reached the crossed daggers a blink before the big man and Gobind, who crashed into the altar and each other as I sidestepped.

"For the sake of your skin, don't *argue* with her," the squeaky-voiced man cried, taking my disappearance and the fall of his companions as evidence of the goddess's wrath.

The big man angrily shoved at the altar's trough and the entire seemingly solid stone table slid easily aside. Very tricky, these folk who dwell in towns.

"Cease!" a voice cried, whether that of the Goddess Aster or one of her followers, it was hard to say, for the worshippers were clutching at the big man's knees and imploring him tearfully not to anger the goddess further. Aster's voice babbled boomily and imperiously but was lost in the melee. While everyone's attention was on the idol and altar, I groped until I found Aman and turned his head, pushing him toward the door.

As we neared the outer door, the sounds of the angry idolators dimmed just enough that the screams of the monkeys could be clearly heard. Also clearly audible was the tramp and jingle of the army approaching single file down the path to the temple. I saw a soggy silken litter just beyond the first two soldiers, who wore the uniforms of high-ranking officers in the guard of the Emir Onan. For a moment I forgot I was invisible and my heart plunged.

By the power of the headcloth, Aman Akbar understood what was in my heart and cried out to me, "Fear not for me, Rasa, my wife, but save my lovely Aster. These rabble will feel my hooves and teeth if they attempt to thwart you, for even as I have rescued you before, I will not stint to do so again, though it cost me my life."

"Fine," I said. "You may well save me from the first two, O Lord, but that is an army and you are but an ass and upon your back you bear one who cannot defend himself. On the other hand, you and I are both invisible and can easily flee. Therefore, fly into the jungle while I seek to deliver Aster from the idolators within and perhaps we can bypass this situation altogether."

"Very well," he said. "I suppose no harm will come to you while your beauty is so concealed. But if you need anything—" I lost the rest in the pound of his hoofbeats, as nearby fronds parted to admit the jouncing body of Marid Khan. The head of the first soldier's horse was less than a stone's throw from the temple. I dashed back inside, bedazzled for a moment by the change in light.

Fighting my way through worshippers who fell before my knives in superstitious awe, I reached the altar. The big man was prevailing, and with all his strength pulled Aster's arms, dragging her as far as her hips from the open hole. Barely visible at her trouser legs, two black hands clung to her ankles.

"Unhand me, faithless one!" Aster screeched. "Don't you people believe in human incarnations of your gods?"

They apparently did not, for none made any reply save a distinctly irreverent low snarling sound.

I dispatched the big man with a knife in his ribs and the others—or anyway, those who had survived my entrance—scrambled from the inner sanctum.

Aster slapped at Amollia's hands and Amollia released her, crawling from the hole after her. The irises of her eyes were surrounded entirely by white and she trembled. "What—who—"

Aster shrugged and adjusted her jacket. "This goddess is obviously misunderstood by her worshippers. She may be goddess of death and suffering for such swine as they, but she appears protective of her fellow females. Perhaps we should burn an offering—"

"I'll be only too happy to let you cook the next time it's safe to do so, and accept your homage in that fashion," I told her. "But for now, we must escape the Emir's army, awaiting without, and join our husband. This way!"

"Which way?" Aster demanded. "Where are you?"

"Never mind!" I snapped. From outside came the sounds of men dismounting. "We cannot leave now by the front entrance. Quickly! The upstairs window!"

Amollia beat the rest of us and had a leg out the window before Aster and I had reached the second floor. From around the corner, near the front entrance, curt commands were spoken and vehement denials and accusations spilled forth from the goddess's rejected suitors.

Amollia hung indecisively out the window. The river was a long way down and muddy. To dive in might be to lose her life stuck in the mud. She had not seen the soldiers and so far she was not frightened enough to attempt it. She pulled her leg back and sent a sick look down at Aster, who stood on a lower step and peered out over the bottom ledge.

"Don't jump," I whispered. "I'll find something we can swing across on. Keep quiet. Stay hidden, but stay near this window."

I had once more remembered the advantage of being invisible. I didn't have to hide. I was already hidden. I could move freely among the soldiers without detection. I could spy upon them and learn their plans and leave whenever I chose. I thought I would skip the spying and stick to leaving—and quickly. But first I needed to find the monkeys.

Beyond the ruined doorway the jungle clearing was choked with milling horses and camels decked in silk and tassles, robed Kharristanis with curved blades drawn, a bright palanquin and several bearers of the same type as the men I had just vanquished.

Also those same men, or those who had retained their facilities, trembled before none other than the Emir, whose brocaded figure, spotless bejeweled turban, and well-oiled mustache and beard and whose perfume outstunk every flower in the jungle. Among the soldiers, the riffraff, and the animals, he looked awesome as a king.

I was sure this illustrious person would have something enlightening and educational to say, but much as I wanted to eavesdrop, I declined for the moment in favor of finding a vine suitable for my co-wives to use to transport themselves across the river. So I left the soldiers and the Emir abusing the natives and wended my way deeper into the jungle, strangely quiet now. I had scanned the trees in vain for monkeys and was about to decide to try to steal something from one of the soldiers when a pointed finger tapped me on the pate and I looked up to see the wide troubled eyes and wrinkled mug of one of my erstwhile companions. Pulling forth the headcloth, which retained its smell despite its invisibility, I made my need known to that creature and together we skirted the building, selecting a vine from the wall farthest from the soldiers. The monkey then scampered up the erotic carvings and gave the vine to Amollia, who held one end for Aster while I held the other and she swung herself down and across to the wall where I stood, just above the shore of the river. Afterward, Amollia anchored the vine to one of the iron rings and slithered down to meet us.

The monkeys, more than any other creature I had occasion to deal with, had a relay of messengers, and what one monkey knew soon every monkey in that part of the jungle knew also. No sooner had Amollia arrived than a monkey delivered a vine from the far shore, as courteously and solicitously as a bride presenting her husband with his first meal.

Amollia put the vine in Aster's hands. "You're the lightest," she hissed.

Aster did not argue the point, but grabbed the vine and swung across. Amollia regarded the jungle behind her and to the left with great suspicion. "What are you up to, barbarian? You should go next."

"I can't," I hissed. "I have to help Aman Akbar and Marid Khan cross."

"I'll stay and help."

"You're not invisible," I said. "And I can't spare any more ointment."

"Very well. But if you aren't across in a very short time, I'm coming back after you."

"If you do, try to bring a few of Marid Khan's brigands," I suggested. "I'm not sure how much help you'll be alone."

"Your faith in me is touching."

"Go!"

The monkey messenger delivered the vine once more and she clung to it, rocking back twice before swinging smoothly across.

For the time being, Aman Akbar was safe, though how long Marid Khan would survive his injuries I knew not. Neither did I dare to make the Khan invisible, for I had very little of the ointment left and if I was to have enough to execute the plan I had for freeing us all from the Emir's schemes and those of his ally, the King of Divs, each dab would be needed. I could only hope that once the stuff was applied it would continue lending its magic properties to its wearer until rubbed away. I would need to be very careful indeed.

The Emir strode into the temple, despite the imploringts of the goddess's devotees, who whimpered that the Terrible One was not in good humor today and perhaps the illustrious one would care to inspect the temple at another time. Their solicitousness was less for the Emir than for themselves, for if anything happened to him, they feared—no doubt correctly—the guard would avenge him upon their persons. The Emir also addressed—and abused—another party, who answered with familiar oily tones.

"And what of our allies and their task, o djinn? I thought you would have my heart's delight wrapped and waiting for me here, together with the object she bears which will cause you to submit yourself to me finally so that I may have the obedience you owe me as owner of the bottle."

"Master, I know only that the two women were hanging by the hair when you summoned me and the one you desire was imprisoned and contemplating the fate of her rebellious sisters. Had I had longer to inspect the manner in which thy wishes were being attended to by those Divs, the results would have perhaps been more to thy liking. How often must I implore thee not to drag me through the cosmos so often?"

The worshippers gabbled at each other fearfully and the Emir turned to regard them sharply and said to the djinn, "It would be to our mutual advantage if this pestiferous refuse was questioned regarding what has passed here."

"Am I to take such a remark for a wish, master?" the djinn asked slyly.

"You are to understand that it would be to our mutual advantage to learn what questioning would teach us." The Emir patted a bulge in his sash. "It would be a pity if harm should befall me through lack of knowledge and I should accidentally *break* certain objects."

The djinn sighed and looked affronted. "Hearing and obeying." Rapidly, he questioned the men.

Gobind answered with a question. "Ah, mighty one, is it by your design and the design of your exalted master that imps destroyed our sacred carvings and loosed upon us the demon woman who posed as our goddess and her phantom servant?"

"It was not," the djinn replied, "but both myself and my exalted master would be most edified to hear what you have to say regarding these manifestations."

Gobind supplied him with a false and unflattering version of what had happened.

The djinn relayed the information to the Emir, who considered for a moment, then said, "Tell them that the apparitions they have seen are wily demonesses loosed upon them by an unscrupulous fisherman. Tell them that these demonesses have stolen from me an object of much value."

"What object might it be that has been taken from the Prince Among Princes?" Gobind asked, his voice fairly warbling with greed.

The Emir understood well the greed, if not the untranslated sense of the words, for his answer, while seemingly casual, showed consideration of his listener's dubious sensibilities. "Say that it is a magical thing which can impart great harm to he who would use it badly. Explain further that one would not think it so to look at this object, for in appearance it is but a simple bottle cap, decorated with an ornate seal. Tell them that my true reason for seeking it isn't so much the intrinsic value of the thing as that the poor stupid women might harm themselves or someone else while using it."

"The Light of the World need not concern himself for those women," Gobind answered ruefully.

"The Light of the World," the djinn said, sounding very much as if he would choke on the words, "says that he is concerned for not only the women, but that they will use the power of that object to destroy other places holy to your people, whom he reveres and respects. He wishes me to tell you how this situation grieves him, and bids me tell you that he was even this day on his way to seek the young King and persuade him that your gods should be honored with our own. Therefore, this matter of the demonesses is twice as troubling to someone of such—" The djinn tried to swallow, and could not, and coughed out the last words, "—generous conscience. He needs to find the women."

Gobind, moved by the content of the speech and oblivious to the tone in which it was delivered, crawled over to the Emir and kissed the ground in front of him. "You will prevail, o great one. As for the women, surely they cannot be far from here. Though my brothers and I finally drove their defiling presence from our altar, they may still lurk nearby, waiting to desecrate it again. It is more likely that even now they cower in the jungle, fearful of our wrath."

I felt like showing him how fearful I was of his wrath, but had better things to do. Locating an invisible donkey carrying an unconscious man in the middle of a jungle while surrounded by enemies one does not wish to alert is no easy task, even for a woman who cannot be seen. When the Emir's second-in-command bellowed to his subordinates to fan out and search the jungle, I grew frantic—so frantic that in stumbling back through the trees where I had left Aman, I nearly tripped over him and his cargo before realizing I was in his presence.

I had hoped to learn more of the purpose of the Emir's visit and perhaps to purloin the djinn's bottle while I enjoyed the advantage conferred upon me by the vanishing cream. However, the search and Marid Khan's tortured breathing and drained, bloodied face, once smooth as milk and now blotched and bumpy with insect bites, convinced me no time was to be lost.

I whispered to Aman Akbar, "In the river, beloved. And quickly. I will hold your passenger upon your back and your strength shall pull us across."

The water was sluggish and shallow, only chest high at its deepest on me, but there was a strong undertow I doubt I could have resisted alone. I kept a nervous eye out for the big lizard, but it and its cousins did not molest us. I cautioned Aman Akbar to keep his head above water so that the ointment in his eyes would not be washed away. The headcloth I tied around my neck so that its sacred scent would not be diluted.

We were but the length of two tall men from shore when the soldiers saw us and shouted. "Behold! Someone is in the river over there."

I dared not look back but presently the sound of a blow carried across the water.

"Lout! Don't you know live women from one drowned man?"

"Still, we should tell His Excellency."

I guided Aman into tall reeds near the banks,

within which Marid Khan's limp body could be concealed, as if it had drifted there of its own accord. I slid the nomad chieftain from my husband's back so that a body would not be seen to float in midair from the opposite shore, although I would have liked to have heard the conversation that would follow such a discovery. He was heavy and slippery to pull through the tangle of undergrowth, but as soon as we were well-concealed, Amollia and Aster found us and aided me in remounting him upon Aman's back. Thereafter we fled, with all possible haste, cutting through the jungle with the sacrificial knife of the idolators, bearing right until our path intersected with a trail.

When night fell with no evidence of pursuit, we thought ourselves safe. The monkeys scouted before and behind for us and reported no other human in either direction. The supernatural aspects of our behavior had no doubt alarmed the enemy host and convinced them that we had (as two of us had indeed) vanished into the ethers.

Nor were our enemies the only ones unnerved by such aspects. Twice Aster stepped on my invisible heels, and I kept getting brushed in the face as Aman Akbar flipped flies from his invisible body with his invisible tail.

"Can't you show yourself now, Rasa?" Aster asked, nursing the toes of her right foot, with which she had just gouged a large piece of flesh from my ankle. "After all, you're among friends. It's unfair that Aman Akbar has to see the rest of us with our hair mussed, our faces dirty and bloodied, and our clothes torn while you hide so conveniently."

"Aster," Amollia said quietly but firmly.

"Well, it's true. I don't know who she thinks she is to just disappear like that and then run things when she won't even face a person."

"I will not waste more of the vanishing cream just to appease your wounded vanity, little sister," I said. "I am trying to make the spell last until we gain the Div's cave once more."

"Cave? What cave?" We had been so busy being quiet and tense while trying to elude the Emir's forces that we hadn't done much talking. I told what had befallen me since the bird made off with me, and of meeting Hyaganoosh and the deposed Queen of Divs.

Aman Akbar snorted that he could see no reason for us to endanger ourselves by reentering the cave. For his part his faithless cousin Hyaganoosh could hang by her toes and he would not mind.

"If you command it, Lord and Master," I said like a good obedient wife. "We will, of course, choose another path. But the fact of the matter is that without your cousin's help we cannot free you from the spell. Also, we owe a debt to the man you bear upon your back, and it is in my mind that the Queen of Divs is the closest person who might have the skill to aid him."

Aman Akbar said something rude—an ass's expression he had no doubt picked up among the pack animals, and that concerned me, for I hated to think that he might be becoming more and more like a donkey the longer he looked like one. Nevertheless, he conveyed the impression that however reluctantly, he agreed with my reasoning.

The chattering of the monkeys took us by surprise, but they too had been surprised, for they had been alert for signs of humans, and the rapid pattering behind us was four-footed. Amollia, guarding our rear, turned with knife in hand to face this new threat. Before she had attained her defensive stance, however, the animal sprang from the bushes and leapt upon her, its tail lashing with excitement, loud rumblings rolling from its throat.

Amollia deflected her knife at the last moment and embraced her old companion, both of them behaving in a sloppy and sentimental manner that seemed to disagree with the cat as much as it did me, for the animal emitted a great belch and burped forth a cloud of smoke which caused Amollia to swat the beast to the ground as she coughed.

The genie gathered himself together and bowed with his usual superciliousness. "Gracious ladies, former master, how it cools my eyes to see you reunited and to know that I have played no small part in your happiness."

"And the prevention thereof!" Aster cried indignantly. "How dare you appear in your serpentine guise only to disappear without lifting a finger to help us! Why, had the bird not carried Rasa away and had our poor elephant not intervened to drive away the fiends *you* set upon us we would all of us be dead."

"I have always said the worst part of dealing with women, old master, is that they exaggerate so and bend everything completely out of proportion. They are far too imaginative and oversensitive to understand complex situations."

"Do you mean to stand there and look pompous all day, rotund one," I asked, "or are you going to explain yourself?"

"Tsk, tsk, tsk. Impatience. Another problem you women have. But I'll say this for the three of you. You are faithful wives—" This praise being received less enthusiastically than he deemed it merited, he added in an aside to the air between Marid Khan and the ground, "though perhaps in truth they did take a bit long to reject the advances of the conjured creatures I set upon them, former master. Still, they did better than most of their sex, and for that reason I shall render unto your party the benefit of what assistance I am able to provide without compromising my professional integrity."

"When you approve of us, fat one, I begin to wonder where I went wrong," I said. "I didn't notice any of this assistance of yours handy when the bird was carrying me off after having nearly yanked my hair from my head. All you did was hiss in my face."

"A face much improved by thy new cosmetic, if I may say so, dear lady," he replied nastily. "As a crude barbarian, thou naturally wouldst fail to comprehend the intricate machinitions of fate. But ponder upon this: had the bird not delivered thee from the hands of thy tormentors, wouldst thou have found the cave of the Divs? Wouldst thou have gained the aid of the vanishing cream and thereby delivered thy companions and thy

husband from their oppressors? What a selfish creature
thou art, to seek to escape a moment's fear and discomfort at the expense of making thyself useful to those who
need thee."

"Suppose you explain this fate of yours to the rest
of us foolish females, if we are so lacking in understanding," Amollia suggested with a soft amiability be-
lied by the sparks in her coal-black eyes.

"Yes, and also where was all of this help you were
supposed to be giving us."

The genie's face was as clouded as his entrances
usually were. "I see that I am not believed and yet, I
speak the truth. No one could be sadder at the inconve-
nience your family has experienced in the hands of this
wily prince, and I prevented what it was possible to
prevent. You must bear in mind that even a djinn has
not the ability to be in more than one place at once,
and you flighty women delayed me to no end when you
made your way across salt water, over which we of the
djinn cannot traverse, and came unto this land. I had to
travel overland, around the sea, to reach you, and that
was no short or easy task. At the same time, I could not
abandon your husband, ensorceled as he was by my
own spells and in the hands of those who knew him not.
Also, I was continually at the beck and call of your
enemy, the Emir, who holds the bottle containing my
soul. As I have already explained, were it not that the
seal to this bottle is in your hands, I would not have
been able to assist you as I have done."

"In that case, I'll throw it into the bushes immediately," Aster said tartly, reaching into her sleeve. I
knew she was only threatening, but the djinn did not
and held up his hands as if he thought she were going
to throw it at him.

"Do so, lady, and never wilt thou behold thy
husband again in his true form. Let me but continue
and I shall show that no one was ill-used by me. For
your sake I have stretched myself very thin, and this is
all the thanks I get." His tone was so lugubrious that I
almost clucked my tongue with mock sympathy, but
restrained myself. "For know that after I departed thy

presence in the tents of the nomads, I was called to the Emir, who waxed exceedingly wrothy when I explained to him that I could not force the three of you to return with me on account of the very seal he craved. Ordinarily, that person would be my master, for it is the seal that binds my soul to the bottle. As I tried to explain to thee and thy companions previously, Holder of The Seal, in this case thy possession of the seal while the bottle is yet in the hands of the Emir presents me with a conflict of interests. I can serve neither of you directly, nor use my full powers to help either of you prevail against the other.

"When the Emir learned that he did not control me fully, he flew into a rage and would have broken my bottle and destroyed my soul, but I convinced him it was better to attempt the stratagem involving the Divs. Further, it was arranged that while the Divs delayed you with dalliance (or whatever proved necessary), the Emir and his men would travel forth, meeting both yourselves and the allied Div henchmen at the temple. In this way, by the time His Eminence arrived, your persons, if not the seal itself, would be at his disposal. Had the Divs failed to obtain the seal from you, the Emir could have taken it personally, for he is under no magical restraint. Since my plan coincided with his own for traveling here to attend the wedding of the Div King to the Lady Hyaganoosh, after which he planned to use the magical influence of his ally to subvert the young King, I was able to cajole him into adopting it. For my part, I must not let him know I oppose him in any way. That is why I entered the snake to converse with you, when the minions of your enemies were close at hand.

"Likewise, when I saw that the nomads had cast you out for having traffic with me in my true and terrible guise, and that my former master was helpless among them and without your protection, I entered from time to time the body of thy cat, dark one, to prevent thy husband from coming to harm among the wanderers. Not that he stayed among wanderers long. As soon as the noble Marid Khan discovered that you women were missing and the *ar* was thereby broken, he mounted upon the ass, and, with the help of myself within the cat, came straightaway here to offer you his continued protection. That is why it took me so long to come overland. I kept having to backtrack to allow them to catch up with me."

"How good you are to us," Aster spat.

"Next he will be saying it was not our elephant who saved us from his henchmen, but himself within the elephant," Amollia sniffed.

"What elephant?" the djinn asked. "Just like a woman to throw in irrelevancies and confuse my tale."

"The elephant we obtained in the wise woman's village," Amollia said. "Those persuaders you arranged to trick us into relinquishing the seal were about to kill me when they saw that Rasa was gone and Aster would not give them the seal. They picked at me with their magic, dissolving my jewelry from my body and warning Aster that my skin would go next. Fortunately, our younger sister is of a delicate disposition. She screamed when it seemed they would actually do such a thing."

Aster shrugged. "It only makes sense to scream sometimes. Otherwise, how is anyone to know a person is in trouble?"

Amollia sighed deeply, and nodded. "That is true. Our elephant heard her and charged in with a mighty trumpeting, his great feet causing the ground to tremble, his mighty body breaking through the very walls. He lifted the Div and smashed him against the wall. He trod upon the one who resembled you, Rasa. But he who wooed Aster was quicker than the others and hurled a spear into the poor beast. It ran away in terrible pain—straight over the man who wounded it. We two fled into the jungle and concealed ourselves, and later that night, a flock of giant vultures descended in front of the temple and turned into men. When they left, they carried the other three with them on their backs."

"That explains the ill humor of King Sani," I said, remembering the Div King's grimness.

"When they left and the rain began to pour harder,

we returned to the temple to try to find food. In our search we discovered the idol."

"We knew not what she might be goddess of," Aster said. "But I deduced she might be the one favorable to weary travelers and so the food upon her altar had been left for the same, namely us, just as offerings at Fatima's shrine go to the monkeys, snakes and tigers. Therefore, at my urging, we ate that food. I've been wrong before. While I was chasing a garbanzo bean, I happened upon the pit under the altar. You can stand up full length inside the idol and speak through the little tube. I think the fat man knew all about it."

"Speaking of food," I said to the djinn, "we have all been without today. I don't suppose you could—"

"That would be unethical," the djinn replied. "Too helpful. If the Emir discovered I had aided you in so direct a fashion, he would hasten to put glass splinters in my soul."

"Is that so?" I asked, suddenly glad I was invisible. I didn't like to tremble with rage in front of so many people. "What do you suppose he'll do to ours if you don't help us? He has not only his army and all the Divs and all their power but you as well. Your so-called kindly feelings toward us are as nothing. Very well then," I ended ominously, not considering what the effect of my disembodied furious voice would be on my companions.

"What are you going to do?" Aster and Amollia asked in unison. Aman Akbar nipped me smartly.

"Regain the accursed bottle without delay," I answered. "I would have done so before except that I was more concerned with preserving our lives."

"Pray continue being concerned for them some-what longer then, O sister," Amollia said. "For the magic we possess is as nothing compared to that of the Divs. And we dare not wait to find aid for Marid Khan," she cast her eyes down at the twitching shoulders and fly-bedeviled body of the formerly dashing brigand prince. "Even now he is near death."

"Excuses," I fumed, my anger at the djinn's contrariness overcoming the good sense in Amollia's argument.

"A Yahtzeni warrior does not listen to excuses—" Before I made myself a greater ass than Aman Akbar, my speech was prevented by a yodel bursting upon us from the tree-tops. Looking up, I saw black veils sailing overhead like the wings of some great crow. This vision was accompanied by the screechings of many monkeys and at first it looked as if the veiled figure was swinging toward us on the vines. Nor was I the only one to fall prey to this misconception, for the notion of persons swinging through the trees with monkeys and bellowing loud cries has persisted in the region, and spread even unto Amollia's land. Who would dream that such a story could be born from the rather comical sight of an ordinary elderly mother flying to her son on a prayer rug activated by her religious fervor, or that the apelike cries she was reported to emit were nothing more than the desert woman's traditional half-joyous, half-mournful trilling, the zaghareet?

The carpet settled among us, and she looked about her in a perplexed and impatient fashion. "Where is he?" she asked, looking from the djinn to Amollia and Aster. "Where is my Aman? What have you done with him? Fatima said the monkeys had found him and would guide me to him if I sent my prayers to God from this rug. He must be nearby."

Aman brushed past me and all but knocked Marid Khan from his back in his haste to reassure his mother.

The djinn meanwhile grew frenzied and smoky, crying, "Oh, foolish woman! Oh, betrayer of my soul! Now you have done it. Why cannot members of your feeble and weak-minded sex leave matters alone?"

"*What* are you babbling about?" Aster demanded. She looked no happier to see Um Aman than I was.

"In flying straight here, she has as much as led the Emir to us. Such a carpet as that may be observed from miles around and most particularly would have been visible from the temple. You must hasten or your enemies will be upon us like jackals on a corpse before the moon has risen."

# Chapter
## 12

Midmorning the following day, shortly after we had taken the fifth right-hand fork in the road, the thudding hooves of the Emir's horses pounded behind us. We had been traveling all night on foot, for we dared not risk using the prayer rug and attracting more attention. The last faint jingle of harness faded down the left-hand road before we had traveled more than an arrow's flight from the place we had been when the first horse approached.

I swore, the djinn looked pained, and Aster cried, softly, "We are lost!"

"No so," I said. "I'll enter as I left, through the lemon grove. The rest of you can wait until I return with Hyaganoosh."

But as we stood on the rocky plain overlooking the lemon grove, Amollia turned to me. "Rasa," she said, "it is in your mind to do something foolhardy, is it not?"

"I mean to recapture the bottle," I said. The djinn, who had wafted along beside us as we ran, studied me carefully. I gave him a hard look and he discreetly dissolved into smoke and blew away.

"I shall go with you," Amollia said. "You will need assistance." Her face was set and determined, her black eyes level and sober, though they stared slightly to the left of me.

Extracting the ointment pot, I dabbed my finger in very lightly. She recoiled for a moment when she felt my invisible finger swab around her eyes and down her cheeks, and then faded, but not all the way. I could spare no more ointment, for I needed enough to disguise Hyaganoosh. Amollia wavered before me, her translucent darkness giving her the appearance of a colorful spectre. In the dimness of the cave she would be very difficult to see.

"Stay right beside me," I cautioned her as we slipped through the grove and faced the long, green-shadowed passageway.

"Here," she said, and handed me the end of her sash. Where the garment stretched between us, it was invisible, though the parts attached to us were not. "I cannot keep beside you unless I know where you are."

From the ledge above, Aman Akbar brayed. Aster and Um Aman leaped to support the body of Marid Khan as it slid from our husband's back, joining the carpet on the ground, and Aman began trotting down into the grove. We ran quickly back to meet him.

"Husband, what are you doing?" Amollia asked, stroking his ears.

I gave him the headcloth and he shook his head. "No wives of mine shall risk themselves for my sake without my help."

"But, husband," Amollia said softly, "the life of Marid Khan is upon our heads. He and the rest of our family will need you sorely if we fail. Are you not honor bound to protect them? And is it possible for you to be in two places at once?"

Aman snorted and laid back his ears. "Argue if you will, beloved, but this matter must be as I say, for a wife must be obedient to her husband, for God has made the husband superior to her. So it is written."

Amollia's hand fell to her side and she regarded him with a faint quizzical frown. "Truly?" she said, her tone more amused than cowed. "My people see it that man is of the rhino but woman of the crocodile and neither has anything to do with the other and indeed neither speaks the language of the other. Therefore, not only can there be no true commerce between them, but there can be no superiority or inferiority—only misunderstanding."

Aster, looking extremely anxious, had scrabbled down the hill behind us. "Sounds reasonable to me," she said. "Not that the Master of our philosophy would agree, but he never has a good word for women anyhow."

"Until we have that bottle, the Emir is superior to us all," I pointed out. "Do you want me to try the plan my way, husband, or shall we simply submit ourselves to his mercy now?"

"Never," Aman shook his mane, rolled his eyes, and showed his teeth. When none of us trembled with terror, he gave himself another shake and sighed deeply, saying, "Very well. I suppose there is no need for a dung merchant to marry a battle maiden if he behaves like an ass when she practices her craft. Do as you will, my fearless love. I will protect the others." And he turned and trotted sadly back up the hill, Aster in tow. Their steps dislodged a shower of droplets from the leaves of the lemon trees.

The floor of the passage shimmered with a coating of mud and water almost ankle deep. We had already turned right twice down two more passages without encountering anyone, when the noise began. I had only a moment in which to wonder why a bird was loose in the caves, when that bird was joined by nine hundred and ninety-nine others and the promised thousand gongs, warbling and bonging rebounding off the walls of the passages, turning corners and attacking us with the force of clubs. The slip of shadow that was Amollia slunk against the wall, hands to ears. I did likewise and hoped that continuing right turns would quickly lead us back to the women's quarters.

The heavy tread of running feet splashed through the corridor ahead of us, straight for us, and passed. The feet were unshod and similar to those of the elephant, attached to monsters wearing the silvery livery of the Div King. They bore no arms, but were equipped instead with horns in the midst of their long blunt snouts, long tusks protruding from gray leather lips, and large yellow teeth. Their lolling tongues were broader than a man's shoulders, and their own torsos were only slightly larger, being basically in the shape of men. They waved taloned paws before them and their forked tails whipped at our legs as they passed. Never had I beheld such a various collection of malformations.

These creatures raced past us at every turn until the corridors seemed as filled with them as they did with water. And all the while the gonging and warbling never ceased. Down one last corridor, the water covering the floor grew shallower until it dried up completely, the lengthy distance of a broad stretch of unbroken wall. Certainly this had to be the same wall that had opened into the harem but how had it opened? Amollia crashed into me while I stood there wondering. From the tunnel to the left came the heavy pounce of eight clawed paws. I rammed my finger against the door but to no avail.

I felt fingers at my belt and Amollia fanned the now translucent headcloth before her.

"Greetings, wraith of the wondrous fragrance," the bitiger growled.

"Greetings, grandest tiger of any jungle," Amollia replied courteously.

Hollow voices echoed from the entrance chamber. "Hear the beast growl and rumble? What do you suppose it's onto?"

"Could have captured something. Let's go see, shall we?" And elephantine feet thumped the cave floor again.

"Oh, great bitiger," Amollia said plaintively. "Do not let those creatures find me."

"Except for your smell, there's not much of you to find," the bitiger said. "Who are you? Are you related to that other who smelled similarly?"

"No, great bitiger. I am but a simple ghost, the spirit of one of the King's former wives. I can find no rest until I have regained a talisman which was not burned with me when I died."

"Happy to oblige," the tiger said, and roared the door open again for us. Amollia slipped immediately into the shadows and I shut the door in the bitiger's striped and bewhiskered face while it gazed with greedy golden eyes at the captive contents of King Sani's harem.

If the ladies had been engaged in primping before, they were in a veritable orgy of it now, with cosmetic pots, sticks, jars and bottles flying from hand to hand and spiders bearing trays of brilliant gems from which light shivered and splintered, and gorgeous gowns deeply trimmed in sumptuous embroideries and swirls of gold and silver thread embellished with jewels, feathers, ribbons, coins, fringe and all manner of ornamentation.

Hyaganoosh still occupied the center of the harem, but she had changed. She was more decorously dressed than before, in many layers of robes and gowns of varied hues and patterns, flowers upon birds upon teardrop swirls of rough and smooth textures, of fine fur and shimmering silk, and gossamer like butterfly wings. But her hair was dressed most plainly, save for a thin diamond chain dropping a thumbnail-sized pendant between her eyes. The rest of her tresses were now strung up behind her from one of the iron rings. Moreover, a frightened and bewildered look had invaded her eyes, from which self-satisfaction had fled, to be replaced by a certain vagueness common in the expressions of the others.

Avoiding her, I tugged the end of Amollia's sash and pulled her toward the Peri.

She looked straight at us, her faceted eyes glittering. "That's a singularly sloppy job you did of vanishing your friend," she said to me. "Why have you returned? Do you wish to undo me when I have already attested to your demise? I warn you, I will see to it personally that I was telling the truth before, if you endanger me."

"No, Queen," I said respectfully. "We seek only to remove your rival long enough that our husband may be released from her curse."

"And I suppose you have no interest at all in the bottle borne hither by that slug of an Emir?"

Amollia's grin, even half-transparent, shone in the dark. "We would not refuse the item should it come our way, O Queen," she replied. "But there is one more matter upon which we desire your help, and that is the healing of a young man who aided us earlier and who now lies wounded—"

"And I'm to do this with the great art you are certain I possess?" the Peri asked ruefully. "You confuse shape-shifting with healing. The two are as different as pomegranates are from grapes."

"That may be so, Lady," Amollia said in her most persuasively reasonable sibilant voice. "But from Rasa's tale, you are more than a simple shape-shifter. You have officiated lo these many years as Queen and Lady of these powerful people and all have looked to you for guidance and nurturing. Surely healing entered into your duties."

"Not necessarily," the Peri said, her eyes flickering with indecision. "While the Divs are not immortal in the manner of my people, they are long-lived and heal quickly."

"Ah, but they can be injured!" Amollia said. "For I myself saw three of them all but destroyed by an elephant."

The Peri shrugged and looked away. "I know nothing of this."

"And yet you know of the Emir's presence and the bottle," I said.

Her faceted eyes flashed back to me, sternly. "My husband was suspicious of the story I made in your protection. He chained his little favorite even before the wedding and has threatened to bob my hair if the slightest irregularity occurs again."

"And you would let him?" I asked.

"What can I do?" she replied. "My powers, save a few external ones such as the cream, are dwindling daily."

"We can still release you," I said.

"Only by cutting my hair and that would destroy me."

Amollia shook her head. "Not at all. If Rasa will give me a leg up and you can stand it, I'll have you free soon enough."

The Peri hesitated for only a moment before agreeing. Amollia sprang from my hands to the Peri's shoulders, but almost immediately grasped her hair high up its length, climbing hand over hand, her legs scissoring the locks, whose colors glowed through all of her limbs, until she gained the iron ring. Rainbow strands slid

over and through her fingers, the length of hair slackened
and fell. Amollia dangled fully visible for a moment
from the heavy ring before swinging twice and leaping.
She landed rolling at my feet.

Instantly, the Peri was transformed. Her hair curled
and twined constantly, charged with power. Her eyes
gave off sparks. She stretched and smiled, but the smile
was not especially kind. Her knuckles popped as she
stretched her fingers and for the first time I noticed
how long and clawlike were her nails. Pointing to
Hyaganoosh she said, "You have a quarter of an hour to
remove her and yourselves from the caverns before I
give you to Sani. With my powers renewed and her
gone, I will be queen again and I must not be remiss
in my duties. Go!"

I did not argue. Suddenly I saw the sense in that
coupling. King Sani and his Peri wife, humble and
helpful while captive and frightened, arrogant and curt
when she was once more in charge, seemed made for
each other.

Amollia dusted herself off and bounded across to
Hyaganoosh, who cowered with her fingers pressed
against her teeth while the translucent fingers unknotted
her hair. I spoke to her quietly. "We need your help for
but a moment. I will now rub something upon your face
that will cause you to vanish. If you will come quietly
and aid us in undoing the harm you have done, you'll
be free to return. If you give us away, I'll kill you. Is
that clear?"

She nodded and gulped. I applied the last portion
of cream to her eyelids and cheeks. Before she
disappeared, Amollia had freed her from the ring but
had twined the length of her hair around her own wrist
and arm. "Come now, little sister, come with us and you
will soon be back in time for your wedding. Do not be
afraid." Hyaganoosh looked only minimally reassured
before she vanished and, with her between us, we
made for the door.

Before we reached it, it swung open of its own
accord. A distinguished and regal-looking person stood
framed in the opening.

"Sani!" Hyaganoosh breathed. I pressed my knife into the side of her. The man looked all around him, his eyes changing gray to brown to black to gold to green to blue to gray again.

"Greetings, my Lord of a Thousand Shapes," the Peri said smoothly, her hair crackling out behind her as if charged by lightning, her eyes casting splinters of color around the room.

The Div King tried unsuccessfully to look unsurprised, but stumbled slightly over his feet, which resembled those of a toad. No doubt he had found them handy for sloshing through the water-filled tunnels when investigating the gongs and warbles and had forgotten to change them back to suit his new visage.

His forward momentum gave us a chance to slip past him and the guards who stood on each side of the door outside the harem staring as far forward as beings with eyes on either side of their mouths can stare. Standing in the middle of the tunnel, his form straining toward the harem door, was the Emir Onan. Breaking loose from Hyaganoosh, I shoved both her and Amollia forward. I could say nothing, and only hoped Hyaganoosh would not cry out until I rejoined them and that Amollia would have the good judgment to keep turning right until the two of them were free of the palace.

The Emir crept closer as the voices rose inside the harem.

"And what have you done with her, my dove?"

"I? I have done nothing," she replied. She added cryptically, "Why don't you ask your house guest, the Emir, where she could have gone?" I thought at first she only meant that the Emir was the one who could explain why we would kidnap Hyaganoosh, and by fobbing the question off on him would give herself time to build her power and think how to retain it, but I failed to give her enough credit. The wily Queen instead used one suggestion to divert her husband's suspicion to the Emir, discrediting both her rival and the man who had introduced the chit who displaced her.

When the King stepped back outside the harem and the door swung shut on the smug face of the Peri, I took advantage of the seeds of dissension she had already sown.

The King changed his aspect to the boar-lion cross I had previously seen as he addressed his guest, "I see, tail of a dog, that you have eavesdropped upon my conversation with my Queen, who has discovered your duplicity. What have you to say for yourself? You who offer tribute and withdraw it before it can be sampled?"

"My Lord, I assure you, I—" he began, and at that moment, while the Div King faced him, I slipped my arm between them and parted the folds of the sash spanning the Emir's belly. Grasping the neck of the bottle, I jerked it toward me and retreated quietly to the side of the tunnel, holding my breath. The Emir's face did a color change worthy of a Div as he patted and pounded at his middle, sputtering, "See here, my Lord. Allies we may be but I have not seen that girl since I sent her to you and you have no cause to steal from my person my own private property."

"Steal? I, steal? Watch your tongue, thief!"

"May I remind Your Majesty that we are allies!" the Emir exclaimed. "And that my army is no less mighty, though somewhat less fickle of form, than your own. If you will just be so kind as to return my bottle, I will be happy to help you hunt for the missing woman."

"Allies, hah! What sort of ally is one who cannot be trusted?"

"I don't know. I would ask the father of your Queen, great Sani, but I understand he—"

At that point I crept down the hall, leaving them to break or maintain their alliance as their treacherous dispositions dictated.

I had passed the first three right-hand turns before the gongs and warblings began again. Soldiers stomped past me on their elephant feet, but they always took the left-hand turns and I the right. At one point I heard an eight-pawed splash and heard a ferocious snarl. Looking back, I saw that the snarl was largely composed of frustration, for the beast hated water, and no sooner took a pounce into the stuff than it sat down, trying to keep one rump dry while propping it on the other rump and licked at each of its eight paws before rising. Furthermore, its sense of smell would be impeded by the water. Thus I passed once more unmolested into the rainy afternoon, where a now visible Hyaganoosh and Amollia waited with the others.

I wiped the ointment from my own face with my sleeve, so they could see my triumphant expression and the bottle I held in my hand.

The bottle and the seal were soon reunited. I took the precaution of retaining a grip on both as Hyaganoosh meekly placed her hands on the bottle and we removed the plug we had just inserted.

Aman Akbar shoved his nose between Um Aman and Aster, who crowded forward as the djinn smoked forth.

The demon laid his finger to his chin and bowed, saying facetiously, "Now, I just *wonder*, dear ladies, how I may be of service to you?"

"Tell him," I said to Hyaganoosh.

"Tell him *what*?" she cried pettishly. "I don't know what to say to him. You've disgraced me, making me look at a strange man without my veil or anything—"

"Fear not, Treasure of Princes," the djinn said gallantly, "for I am no man but—"

"Tell him to turn Aman Akbar back into a man."

"Aman Ak—but—but—" she stammered and looked appealingly at Um Aman, who glowered at her.

"Do as you're told, Goosha."

"Oh, very well, but I don't see—"

Um Aman gripped her by the elbow so tightly the skin of the old woman's knuckles blanched.

"Turn Aman back into a man," she said very quickly.

The girl babbled her words so quickly I thought for a moment she'd botched them. But the djinn nodded and dispensed from his forefinger a cloud of smoke which enshrouded the donkey. When the smoke drifted away, in place of the ass Aman stood, supported by two human legs rather than four donkey ones. He was clad as he had been when he disappeared into the Emir's palace. His ears had been returned to shell-like smallness. His eyes were reduced from donkey largeness and brownness to human largeness and brownness. Aster flung herself at him, of course, but Um Aman was there clutching him before her. Amollia smiled at him with joy and fondness. Aman himself looked rather dazed for a moment. He patted himself with the beautifully shaped hands he had just regained and gazed across at me with an expression so full of fathomless intensity that it was painful to meet his eyes. I grinned at him foolishly and he grinned in turn, and beamed down at the other three. Then behind him, Marid Khan groaned. Aman blinked and shook off wonder with a still somewhat donkeylike toss of his head and turned toward his injured former rider.

"For your second wish," I quickly informed Hyaganoosh, "you can tell the djinn to heal Marid Khan."

This time she did not hesitate, but repeated my demand at once. Afterward she said petulantly, "If it's true I only get three wishes, that one shouldn't count. It was really yours."

I smirked at her.

"If you women are quite done," Aman Akbar said, "there is a serious matter to be taken care of. If the Emir and the Div King are plotting against the Sultan, I must warn him immediately. Therefore, the djinn must dispatch me at once, in suitable apparel and style, naturally, to the palace, where you will join me and we will enjoy the King's gracious thanks together."

"May I remind you, former master, that all of your wishes are used up."

Um Aman wrenched the bottle from Hyaganoosh's limp grasp and my own. "Do as my son says, ifrit. Did you not hear him say the matter is grave?"

The djinn rolled his eyes heavenward and in one wink Aman Akbar was clothed in lime green satin embellished with gold and in another wink he was gone.

"Now then, djinn, you must honor the second part of our husband's wish and take us to safety—" Aster began before the reflection of Aman's image was yet gone from her eyes.

"In a moment, little sister," Amollia said. "Wai

first, while I pluck the lemon we promised to take the King for Fatima—" And she tripped down the hill, Kalimba trotting along at her side.

At that moment the ground beneath us rumbled and Marid Khan cried out an alarm. I ran down the hill to pull Amollia back and Aster ran after me, babbling unintelligibly. A dripping bitiger padded into the grove followed by soldiers in the livery of the Emir, who seemed to be chasing the two-bodied cat. Kalimba bristled and stood with all four paws planted.

The Emir appeared and Hyaganoosh gave a little shriek. Um Aman shouted, "Ifrit, obey my son's wish as if it were mine," and tackled Hyaganoosh.

Selima's carpet snapped open and scooped up first Aster and myself and then Amollia, who had already snapped off a fruit and started back up the hill.

Kalimba leaped onto the carpet after her. Hyaganoosh and Um Aman rolled over and over down the hill as the carpet rose steadily toward the peaks. I saw something roll, shining, from their embrace and the djinn's smoke streaked down toward it, wrapped around it, and twirled it upward, arching high above our ever-climbing carpet, into the neighboring mountains. Thus did the ifrit seek to guarantee that he would be bothered no more to grant wishes to any of us.

# Chapter
# 13

Amollia kept looking back toward the grove even as we sailed over the jungle and fields toward the rain-wet city in the distance. Her face was sad and quiet.

Aster grumbled. "The djinn might have at least provided a parasol," she said, wringing out her hair and sleeves.

Both of us ignored her. "Poor old lady," Amollia said. "She was so determined to save that worthless girl from dishonor—and to think, she used her last wish for us."

"If that even more worthless demon had done as he was told, the wish would have saved her and the girl also," I said sourly. "I don't know what we're supposed to tell Aman about this. How can I explain that I left his mother in the hands of his enemies?"

"Oh, really, Rasa," Aster said, "you act as if someone put you in charge of everything. I wouldn't concern myself with that tough old hen. If the Emir gets his hands on her, he'll quickly wish himself rid of her. Besides, maybe Marid Khan saved them. You weren't the only warrior there, you know. Now, come on, both of you, cheer up. See you, the domes of the city are upon us! Soon we will be sitting in our own perfumed garden full of exotic flowers. We will sip sweet drinks and have lute music played for us while we try on silks and brocades and wait for Aman to return ahead of a whole train of slaves bearing baskets and baskets of beautiful gifts from the King."

She was right about the garden, at least, but had figured without the djinn's mistrust of lone females and his prudery. The rug settled softly in the middle of an extremely lovely garden, surrounded by high fretted walls and arched and scalloped doors and windows. The flowers were laid in fanciful patterns and the trees trimmed into the shapes of frogs, mushrooms, little horses, all sorts of ridiculous shapes trees were never meant to assume. Also, however, many of them were left tall and broad and sheltering, bearing cool-looking moss up their sides and long streaming branches like a woman's hair dressed with silvery coins, fanning in the breeze. Tiles of blue, green, red and gold lined sparkling pools full of golden animals spraying water and paved the pathways between ornate beds of roses. Hedged borders also flamed with bold tropical blooms of which a single blossom was larger than a whole bouquet of our little plains violets or wild daisies. In the middle of all of this glory, surrounded by drooping trees, stood a latticed and carved pavilion.

Aster threw us each a look that said plainly that she had told us what to expect and stepped off the rug.

Kalimba growled warning, so that we heard the laughter and voices before they were upon us and were able to dive behind a flowering hedge. Aster looked indignant. "Probably just our slaves come to see if we need anything," she muttered. But that was just wistful thinking. We were all sufficiently accustomed to trouble to be wary, and she watched as anxiously as did Amollia and I as six guards of a girth sufficient to make the djinn look meager strode down the dainty pathway followed by half a dozen women, dressed in white robes and bearing bronze ewers on their heads. Not a drop sloshed over the side. These women swayed their way down the path to the pavilion. Behind the last of these came the rows of laughing, chattering females all clothed in rich and colorful garments. Most of these ladies looked strangely short.

Their laughter and high chirping voices carried out into the garden. Though the pavilion had no windows, the airy dome was supported by a wooden lattice separating dome from walls, and all sounds floated out through the diamond-shaped holes.

Aster was swearing in her native tongue again, her face screwed up like a monkey's with the vehemence of her curses. We both stared at her.

"Can't you see? That misbegotten son of a she-goat djinn has not sent us to our own palace, but someone else's! No doubt the King's, where he reasons we will be unable to entertain hoards of men while awaiting Aman Akbar. The *fool!* Landing us here like this, in these tatters and rags, he endangers our very lives! Why, the guards will take us for thieves."

Amollia smiled for the first time since we had left Um Aman rolling down the hill in Hyaganoosh's embrace. "Why then, we must see if we cannot find a way to introduce ourselves to the ladies without arousing the interest of the guards. Surely one of them will be disposed to help us. Let me see if I can discover how best to accomplish it." She motioned us to follow, but patted her hand low to the ground, and we kept below the level of the hedges, our eyes always on the guards, until we were able to gain the cover of the dripping trees surrounding the pavilion.

Amollia was up the first of these in less time than it takes to tell, but when she tried climbing out upon the branch nearest the carving, it bobbed dangerously. She crept back, summoning Aster, who swarmed up and past her. The limb readily supported Aster's smaller form, and by steadying herself with her fingers in the lattices, she could lean forward and peer through the holes. For once she was silent, but soon she leaned back and grinned at us.

Thereupon she pulled gently at the lattices and the delicate strips broke off in her hands until she had made a hole no larger than my head. The limb protested, groaning and dipping, but held. When she had discarded the strips which were warped and rotting from the damp weather, she slipped out of her gown and undergown and, naked, wiggled her way through the window.

Amollia grabbed at her ankle but too late for she slid away, slippery as a serpent, and Amollia was too big to pursue her. Kalimba growled and leapt halfway up the tree to join them but Amollia waved the cat away, and with a clicked exclamation that sounded like disgust to me, she backed down the tree again to stand beside me, studying the hole, waiting for Aster to return.

In a few moments Aster did just that, poking her head around the corner of the door, and then her hand, waving her fingers in a downward cupping fashion to summon us. Warily, we joined her, finding ourselves in a sort of anteroom where several ewers, towels, and assorted stacks of clothing waited. "It's a bath house," Aster giggled. "Quickly, disguise yourselves," and helped us as we too removed our clothing and followed her inside.

I cannot say I felt enthusiasm for entering the enemy's camp, as it were, naked. This was, no doubt, the private bath house of the King's harem, but the women here were as unlike the bored and voluptuous beauties of the Emir's apartments as they were unlike one another. None of us appeared out of place, for there were several women darker than Amollia and of like stature, and likewise, several far paler than myself, and with lighter hair. Aster, as usual, blended in, the only significant distinction being that most of the females around us appeared to be either somewhat older or very much younger than ourselves. I thought at first that the King must have begat a great many daughters, for most of the women in the pool were little girls, of no more than twelve years, shrieking and splashing and ducking each other. Like the older women, these girls were of diverse races, which puzzled me until I recalled that the King was not a man but a boy. These children must be his wives or his espoused wives. Or perhaps concubines-to-be? And the older ones his aunts and sisters or former members of his father's harem? Since possession of women was deemed among these people to signify wealth and power, I supposed a child-king might need the girls as symbols, even if he was too young as yet to need them for any other reasons.

Children are curious. Before long one of these miniature houris had befriended us. Aster told her we were the wives of an influential man who was having an audience with the King. She cunningly explained that our baggage camels had been lost in a sandstorm and our husband delayed while looking for them. Because of his exalted position, we had been invited—she didn't say by whom—to lodge with the King's ladies. She wondered with decorous wifely concern if the girl could tell us from whom we could make inquiries regarding our husband's safety.

The girl, Zarifa, interrupted this story many times with tales about the antics of her ponies and goldfish. Amollia drew her out maddeningly by asking playful questions. In the end, however, the effort was worth it. Our new acquaintance turned out to be none other than the King's favorite sister and niece to the acting Sultana. She was a nice enough little thing, despite her lofty title and runaway tongue. When we emerged from the baths, she had us dressed in fine clothing. As soon as she saw Kalimba, she insisted that we be lodged in her personal quarters. Amollia persuaded Kalimba to allow herself to be stroked and the girl returned the favor by persuading her aunt to grant us an audience.

The Sultana's court was large enough to pasture forty goats and a horse for a week. None of the adult ladies looked as if they would allow anything so odoriferous as a goat anywhere near them, however. I was very glad we had availed ourselves of the baths, fortunately late enough in the day that the rains had begun again, cooling the air, preserving the beneficial effects of the soap and water. Despite the grandeur of the court, dishes were set here and there to catch water leaking through the ceiling. Once a salamander scuttled across the tile: no one bothered it. Either it was beneath the notice of these folk or its businesslike progress convinced them that it should be able to proceed unmolested.

Princess Zarifa explained the disrepair of the baths and the apartments by saying that the palace was a makeshift affair built on the ruins of the palace of the native prince who had ruled here before being conquered by the Sultan's father. The baths, which were very old and fed by natural hotsprings, had been left standing more or less as we now saw them, since bathing is important to True Believers. The King's main audience chamber and apartments had been remodeled and other parts of the palace were still under construction, but the women's quarters were saved for last, since either special eunuch craftsmen had to be obtained or else the women had to be removed. I wondered why everybody didn't just put their veils on, but apparently that expedient wouldn't have been sufficient.

The acting Sultana was the central gem of this setting, but she didn't seem to fit. She was herself a royal princess, a paternal aunt of the King who was actually only half-brother to Zarifa. She didn't seem to care much about ruling, for she yawned all during the audiences prior to ours, and she didn't really have the hang of it either. She kept interrupting her petitioners with irrelevant questions about where they had gotten the material for their dresses or if they knew a good bootmaker locally. I felt she mostly asked these questions to keep herself awake. Zarifa whispered that she was chosen Sultana because she was barren and therefore presumed to have no partisan interest in who obtained what favors and privileges. Her face was round, with a little more chin than a Yahtzeni woman ever has the good fortune to acquire. Her brows were scanty and arched high over wide eyes a bit popped and staring, as if she didn't see well. She unfortunately emphasized them by lining them with kohl, which was favored by the women of the desert and was said to be beneficial to the eyes, but which in her case made the problem more prominent. She dressed well, of course. Her gown was the same shimmering blue as that found in the tails of peacocks, with a scarlet undergown, and her hair, not gray enough that I could discern it from our waiting place by the fountain, was braided under a jeweled cap.

At last it was our turn to speak with her. Zarifa, eager to act as tutor to three adults, had instructed us to approach the dais upon our knees, not to speak until spoken to, and to back away when dismissed.

The Sultana's eyes popped a little wider as she inspected us. "My niece tells me you ladies seek my help, and through me, the help of the King? Is that right? I believe there was some—er—travail you have recently encountered."

We had all been so impressed by the Princess on the perils of speaking without being asked that as one woman we dipped our heads to indicate that the Sultana had the straight of it.

"Oh, dear," she said, and leaned forward, whispering, "Are you going to bow and scrape all afternoon or are you going to tell me about it? I haven't the faintest idea what to ask you. You'll have to tell me what you want to say." Aloud she said, "Falidah, please fetch some cushions for these ladies. And—and some cakes and sherbet, please."

Cheered on by the promise of food, Aster told a much-embellished and highly colored version of our adventures thus far, carefully pruning the facts to coincide with the story she had told Zarifa of lost baggage camels and influential husband.

The ladies relished the part where, according to Aster, we (all except her of course) came much closer to being ravished by Marid Khan's men than was actually the case. Marid Khan himself she cast in the role of deliverer, which was more or less true, and so spared his reputation for later. The women's eyes all but bugged out of their heads as she described our flight to the shrine on the magic carpet, especially when, as a grand dramatic gesture (previously agreed upon among us), she presented it to the Sultana and commended it to the King in the name of Fatima.

At the mention of Fatima's name, however, the atmosphere in the audience chamber cooled considerably. With only a brief last glance at the marvelous carpet, the Sultana indicated with a flick of her finger that it should be rerolled.

"This is a most amusing tale," she said, rising. Her jaw was set and her voice was hard. She sounded anything but amused. "However, I fear the rest of it must be delayed until tomorrow. I am weary, and need to rest before my nephew visits me this evening. Leave me."

We were escorted back to the Princess Zarifa's quarters, and refrained from speech until we were alone.

"I don't understand!" Aster said. "I had them in the palm of my hand!"

"You spread the sap too thick," I said. "Why not just tell the Sultana the truth? You didn't even ask that she send someone to rescue Um Aman and Hyaganoosh."

"It's too bad about the old woman, but she probably was killed right away. And when did Hyaganoosh ever worry you or me? A person has to look out for herself in this world. What I'd like to know is why the mention of Fatima's name should cause such a fuss."

Amollia stretched out on a ruby-colored cushion beside Kalimba and flexed her fingers over her head. "I have a notion about that, Aster, and I would not tell you what it is while within these walls. But I think we must bear in mind Fatima's injunction to give her other gifts to the King personally, and not through any of these women."

"But we won't be allowed to speak to the King personally!" Aster protested.

"Perhaps we should get the treasures to Aman then. I wish while the djinn was tampering with our wishes to protect us from our own immoral impulses by landing us in the King's harem rather than one of our own, he would have thought to protect us as well by providing us with calling cards or credentials instead of merely plopping us down in here like vagrants. Our social connections don't seem to have impressed our hostess in the right way."

# Chapter 14

The young Princess was much cooler toward us that evening. From this I gathered she had taken the blame for our awkward presence. It seemed only civil to apologize, and I could see that that was what Amollia wished to do too, but we couldn't attract her attention long enough to speak to her. She and the maids had billowed into her chambers chattering about a gift an exalted subject prince had sent before him to announce his presence and implore an audience the following day. The gift consisted of a troupe of three dozen nautch girls, all of extraordinary beauty, grace, suppleness, voluptuousness and accomplishment. They had suddenly danced into the audience chamber and undulated greetings to the King from the prince. The King, young enough to be charmed and old enough to be inflamed by their charms, had not had the intrusion punished, but had installed the dancers in the rooms vacated by the former maids of his late mother. Zarifa had seen the dancers. She and her women spent some time enbroiled in a discussion of what sort of beauty treatments it would take for them to look like those dancers.

Finally the child settled down to have her hair brushed, and Amollia and I were able to tender our apologies. The girl shrugged, smiled a precociously false smile and began slyly to interrogate us about Fatima. We told her the truth. That Fatima was a holy woman who had befriended us, had given us gifts to deliver to the King and that she kept the shrine of Saint Selima.

"These holy persons are very wise, of course," Zarifa said with a yawn which probably was not feigned. "But they can be a little crazy sometimes too. She never mentioned, for instance, that she wanted to send gifts here because she used to live here?"

Aster was not to be outdone in slyness by a chit like the Princess. "She mentioned living in a palace somewhere once but didn't think much of it. She seems much to prefer monkeys and holy relics. Palace life can't have been pleasant for her. She was little more than a slave, from what she told us."

"Ah, is that what she told you? That she was a slave? She didn't say how she came to leave the palace?"

"To follow her saint, I believe she said," I interjected. I saw no reason to mention the baby. That was obviously a personal matter and painful one for Fatima. No need to confide it to a stranger too young to know from whence babies come.

Zarifa's expression softened and some of her former friendliness returned. "Don't worry about this too much. My aunt was interested in your story, but she is unaccustomed to as much responsibility as she has now and tires easily. She'll hear the rest tomorrow. Be sure and give her all of these fascinating details you have told me. We do love hearing about new people here. Those dancers for instance—"

For my part I was irritated by the arrival of these dancers and the man who had donated them, whoever he was. He would no doubt manage to occupy the King all day and thus interfere with Aman's ability to receive an audience. Nice clothing and perhaps a fine horse or two could not compete with three dozen dancers, a royal title, and the gods only knew what else.

As well, perhaps in the meantime we could contrive a way to send Aman the gifts Fatima wished to bestow upon the King. With that responsibility dispatched, we should be able to wait in relative comfort until matters were resolved one way or the other. We had only to be very cautious in what we said about Fatima.

Like Amollia, I had my own suspicions about why the holy woman was a touchy topic, for evidently this was the very harem in which she had dwelt before leaving to follow Selima. Some scandal no doubt lingered because of the baby, though how it could blacken Fatima's name when she was the one victimized escaped me. But no matter what the problem was between Fatima and the King's ladies, surely the Sultana would be able to see, if Aster could manage to work in the rest of our story without contradicting the lies she had already told, that we were only interested in justice and in having our family restored. Perhaps she'd even intervene with the King to have the Emir punished for abusing his governorship.

With such an enemy still at large, I belatedly felt almost thankful that the djinn had sent us to a place where we were so well defended both by men-at-arms and by the King's position. If only Aman Akbar were as safe, I would have wanted for nothing.

The attack began gradually, while the palace was still and no one was vigilant enough to help until the worst of the damage was done. It began for me when I jerked awake kicking, the top of my foot aflame with a burning itch. All ten nails of both hands did I rake across the area in an attempt to end that jangling itch, but it burned all the harder for that, and was at once joined by another, on my ankle, and yet another, on the other foot, so that I could not move fast enough to scratch both at once. To my right Aster cursed incomprehensibly and sat straight up, clutching at her midsection, digging herself with her nails. Amollia sat up too, scratching furiously.

Aster cursed again. "What kind of country is this that the harem of the very King is infested with bedbugs?"

From the adjoining apartment, Zarifa whimpered and her snuffling and scratching joined ours, as did the tinkling of her bell as she rang for her maid. Ringing did not produce fast enough results, so she screeched, "Jamila! Jameeela!"

I did not note when the maid arrived, for I was too busy trying to douse the verminous fires lighted in my own flesh. Accustomed as I was to the pests dwelling among my own people, never had I experienced such itching. Now, indeed, I could not discern which fires were from the bites and which from the self-inflicted scratches. The maid came, half rolling into the apartment, digging at herself and crying. Weeping and lamentations in a choir of female voices erupted around her as she pushed open the door, backing up against the edge of it to scratch a place on her back, rubbing up against it like a vastly irritated cat.

"M-my lady," she stammered.

"Attend me!" Zarifa screamed. "Do something!"

"I am, Lady, but it isn't helping. Could you scratch there please?"

I freed a hand long enough to minister to the shoulder blade in question and drew the woman into the room, shoving her toward Zarifa as I stumbled into the hall. It is hard to walk when you must stop in mid-step at each step to scratch your foot so it will function without twitching.

The volume of the moans and wails and the steady scritch-scritching of a thousand hennaed and manicured nails upon carefully tended flesh told me of the monstrous magnitude of this attack. I wished to question the other occupants, but even could I have formed intelligible questions in spite of my agony, I felt the other women of the harem were not entirely kindly disposed to we who belonged to Aman Akbar. Therefore I hobbled back inside. Amollia had made her way to the niches containing cosmetics and unguents and was frantically daubing anything moist all over her body. The maid, no doubt wearied of Zarifa screeching at her, now took the opportunity to screech at someone else.

"Filth! Excrement! Don't defile the Princess's ointments by placing them upon your own wretched skin. Give them to me—ah, God, how it itches!"

Amollia bypassed the maid and, once somewhat relieved, began slathering perfume, ointment, bath oil, henna, whatever was handy, upon the rosy welts and bumps covering Zarifa's body. The child flailed about so trying to expose all of her hurts for treatment at once that she hindered Amollia's aim. I went to aid them and also to acquire some of the ointments for myself. Aster had found another jar and was contorting herself every which way trying to reach parts of herself that no human is fashioned to reach.

Amollia turned to the maid, "Surely there must be more supplies of these. Where are they?"

The unguents were exhausted, bottles, vials, and jars scattered like old leaves across the rich carpets and all of us exhausted. Zarifa wept as only a child injured and betrayed without explanation can weep, her eyes as red as her scratches, Amollia's eyes drooped and her fingers curled convulsively, Aster still scratching. The maid ran from the room, daubing herself with the dregs from a discarded jar. She seemed long in returning, which may have been only my imagination, but probably, from the look of relief upon her face, was because the faithless creature had taken time to treat herself before bringing further succor to her mistress.

No sooner had she arrived, however, than she began criticizing our efforts. "Dolt! What do you mean using henna on the lady's skin! Why, she'll be dyed that way forever! I shudder to think what the Aga of Girls will say when he sees this! None of the others are so bad as we, but all are afflicted."

"If the place is so infested, why hasn't something been done?" Aster said. "Ladies of quality in my country take more pride in their complexions than to allow such sloppiness in housekeeping."

"How dare you!" the maid said. "Think you this is

a typical night? Why, even the Princess Zarifa would look like a hag if each night were as this one. It is a plague I tell you, brought on by you evil women. My mistress, my child, have I not warned you your trusting nature would bring calamity upon your head? And now upon all of ours?"

"Don't be a fool, Jamila," Her Highness sniffed. "Calamity doesn't itch like this." She scratched her scalp, which immediately provoked the same response in the rest of us, and so in unison did we scratch that Zarifa began to laugh even as she wept.

My bites were lessening as the maids ran to fetch water and more unguents, and I thought the incident over, until suddenly a new wretchedness itched its way across my stomach and I jerked my gown up, scratching. Amollia held my hands, and Aster smeared some ointment across the area.

"Gods, what is it?" I moaned, still trying to scratch. No nit, no flea, had ever had such a bite.

"It—it looks like a butterfly," Aster said, plucking something from me and holding it up to examine. The wings were tinged with as many colors as the Peri's hair, but the creature's beauty didn't prevent me from wishing to grind it beneath my heel. Aster dropped it, thinking it dead, but astonishingly it had survived all my scratching and pounding and flew away. Now both Aster and Amollia stared at my poor stomach. Before I was able to look too, Amollia snatched my gown down.

"What is it?" I asked. "Did I eviscerate myself?"

"There's a message there," she said.

"A message?"

"Scratched into your skin."

"What does it say?"

"Beware the Revenge of Sani," Amollia answered.

"And the butterfly?"

"The Peri Queen did us one last turn."

"I wish she had been a little more direct in her methods," I said, smearing on some more ointment.

"And a little more prompt," Amollia added.

\*       \*       \*

We women were gathered in the Sultana's audience chambers while the eunuchs fumigated the quarters. We spent much of the morning rubbing lotion on each other and scratching ourselves. The Sultana announced that by God's mercy, the King had been spared our nocturnal tribulation. Neither had the men's quarters been affected. To compensate us somewhat for our suffering, the King was going to allow us to attend the elephant fights he customarily held at noon. I had trouble working up any enthusiasm. I felt like fighting something myself.

The heat grew as morning waned and made the itching worse, despite new applications of medicine, and some of the children cried and quarreled. I sat on my rump with my knees drawn up to my chest and my chin upon them, wondering why the Sultana, once her preparations had been made, retired behind the curtains of her dais and left the rest of us to our scratching. Why not have Aster finish her story? The diversion might be welcome to those who had not heard it—or her version of it anyway. But the occasional sidelong looks I spied on faces that rapidly turned away as I confronted them and the amount of space on all sides of us in that crowded place told me that drawing attention to our difference that morning might not be such a good idea. As outsiders we were suspect, although our welts and bumps were as evident as everyone else's—more so on me, with my fair skin, no longer fair but ruddy with the ruts of my nails. It was a very good thing for us that our hostesses, whom King Sani had punished for harboring us even as he avenged himself upon us, had not yet heard about our encounter with the Div King, nor been close enough to read the warning scratched into my skin.

After noon prayers we were collected by six of the eunuchs, the unmanned men who were deemed safe to guard women. With their scimitars swinging from their sashes and not entirely ceremonial pikes clutched in their fists, they conducted us through a maze of tunnels, corridors and secret staircases interconnecting in such a

way that we might travel from the harem to the main
portion of the palace without meeting or being seen by
outsiders.

The balcony onto which we crowded was topped
by a silken canopy from which hung an all but transparent veil. To our right was yet another balcony from
which the King would view the entertainment. I could
not see him since the other women crowded back and I
thought it rude to do as I wished and elbow them out of
the way. Aster, however, had no such compunctions,
and used her elbows and hard little head liberally.
Following her, I peered over her head at the young man
on the throne. In his cloth of gold jacket, trousers and
turban, all embroidered with pearls and topazes, topped
with a pair of enormous red plumes, he looked rather
like a richly set ring from which the central jewel is
missing. He could have been no more than twelve
years old, but his face showed no childishness, except
in the pout of his mouth and the puffiness of his cheeks
and hands. On either side of his richly carpeted and
cushioned dais two servants fanned him with fans of
peacock feathers whose handles were gold and whose
eyes were set with sapphires, turquoises and emeralds.

The courtyard spread wide and flat for a space
about as large as that of the Sultana's inner court before
terracing in marble steps down to the river. Everything
was colored vaguely pink by the veil billowing stickily
against us as the hot wind struck it, but the pinkness
did not wholly disguise the gray of the skies, swollen
with the impending afternoon rains. The bright raiment
of the courtiers, the golden canopies, the vermillion
rugs, looked brave indeed in the face of such skies and
the sluggish dirty river.

The people below were a blur—so many turbans
and sumptuous robes, a few spears sticking up, a flash
of jewelry. People stood still for the most part, making
only small movements when they swatted flies or straightened an errant drapery. A low murmur had rippled
through the crowd, but suddenly stopped. A gong
struck and two elephants marched from separate gate-
ways into the courtyard.

That one of them was far from well was immediately evident. While the one on the left pranced with high pudgy knees and an uplifted trunk, the one on the right drooped, big feet scuffling the half-dried mud, ears dangling, trunk dragging. As both beasts turned to salute the monarch, this second beast gave up and toppled over onto its side without so much as a groan. The mahouts—or elephant keepers—ran forward, prodding the poor beast with their sticks, trembling all the while—from where I stood, even through the veil, I could see the gooseflesh and the hairs standing upon their necks.

After several minutes of futile activity, the eldest of the mahouts, a man with the aspect of one who has spent many years watching and listening for danger signs in creatures who might crush him, sank to his hands and knees and crawled to the balcony.

The King's voice was impatient, pitched low as if he were trying to sound more manly. "Speak, Keeper of Elephants. What ails the beast?"

"It is dead, Your Majesty."

"Obviously it is dead. What I wish to know is why it is dead. Two live fighting elephants were ordered, not one live and one moribund."

The man's spine twitched as if he could already feel a lash and he said something in a choked voice.

"Hmph," Aster said. "You'd think as august a personage as the King would have someone else handle a matter like that."

One of the younger girls replied, sniffing a little at the implied criticism, "His Majesty takes a special interest in his elephants and besides, he had the most recent vizier beheaded last week. He hasn't chosen a new one yet."

The mahout mumbled something so low one might have thought he could now feel his head already disconnected from his body.

"What was that?" the King demanded. "Speak up."

"I said, Majesty, that the elephant became ill only as it walked through the gate. When I selected it, it was as fit as the other beast."

Beside me, one of the older women stuck the fingers of her hand straight out in the gesture against the evil eye.

With mock patience the King said, "Elephants do not perish for no reason twixt gate and courtyard." The man before him simply shook harder. "Very well, remove the body and return the other beast to its stall."

From the back of the crowd, a subtle stirring arose, and as the mahouts and the army of slaves that suddenly appeared began swarming around the great gray corpse like so many large flies, a brace of soldiers in the King's purple livery marched forward, followed by several in depressingly familiar uniforms. Two of these soldiers carried a litter and at the proper distance from the King's balcony, set it down. The Emir of Kharristan crawled out onto the ground, and forward, genuflecting before the throne."

"Onan Emir, my father's former wazir, what have you to say?" the young sultan demanded. He remained petulant, but though his tone was only slightly more welcoming to the Emir than it had been to the mahout, he strained forward a little on his cushion and his eyes lost some of their fixedness and surveyed the Emir's face with something like eagerness.

The Emir, gorgeously clad in silver pantaloons, a rose-and-silver jacket sashed with violet, and a violet-colored turban plumed with rose-colored feathers held in place with a whopping great amythest, pressed his face deeper to the ground and then looked up at his King with eyes as sad and melting as if he had just lost his best friend, if indeed he had ever had one. "I am desolated that Your Majesty's pleasure has been interrupted. I was going to request an audience at a later time today to present you with some amusing trifles, but I wonder if perhaps, in view of the sad turn this diversion has taken, Your Majesty would not prefer to receive my presents now."

"Gifts?" the boy king asked, his voice lilting with the greed of any child promised a present. "Aha! You were the one who sent the dancing girls then!"

The Emir looked genuinely confused for a moment and his brow knotted. Then it smoothed and he smiled ingratiatingly and made a complex gesture with his hand. "A trifle, Majesty. I hope they pleased you. What I have today is perhaps of higher quality and more useful than dancing girls. It is some of the tribute due you from your loyal subjects in Kharristan. As you know, Your Majesty, the city was specially entrusted to my care by Late His Majesty, your father. One small portion of the riches I have gathered for your edification do I wish to bring forth now to cheer you. With your permission?"

"Granted."

The crowd parted and a small pavilion I had observed in the distance rose and moved forward. Underneath it was an elephant, its tusks rimmed with jewels, its face and trunk painted with gold and vermillion designs, its back silken clad and tassled.

"Within the howdah, Majesty, is another small gift. Two female slaves, a beauty I hope you will find worthy of your attention and her old aunt and attendant. Also, this fine fighting elephant to replace the one missing. And, if you care for entertainment yet this afternoon, I have succeeded in capturing a notorious bandit chieftain who has been plaguing your loyal subjects. Perhaps his execution could provide—"

"Is that all?" the King asked, disappointment plain in his voice.

"Oh, no, Your Majesty. There are also jewels and fruits, spices, carpets, silks and brocades, all of the other usual fare. With your permission I will bring forth the bandit—"

The King nodded and, after a brief scuffle, several soldiers marched forward, pushing ahead of them the bedraggled form of Marid Khan, whose turban rolled from his head as they threw him to the ground, well behind the Emir. The curtains of the howdah stirred and from within came a small cry.

"What is this man's name?" the King asked.

"He calls himself Marid Khan, Your Majesty."

The Sultana, enthroned on her own dais two ladies down from Aster, turned to her and asked in a low voice, "Was not Marid Khan the name of your husband?"

Aster bowed as low as she could in the crush of other ladies, "No, Madam. My husband's name is Aman Akbar. Marid Khan, the man accused of being a criminal, was twice our deliverer. The Emir Onan is the brute who has deprived us of family and fortune."

"I see," she said. She did not sound particularly sympathetic. She spoke briefly to one of her servants and the woman wound her way to the back of the balcony.

The King was regarding Marid Khan without much favor. To the Emir he said, "It appears you have all but executed this man yourself. He wouldn't make a very lively show."

The Emir hesitated in his answer and the King sighed, fidgeted, and said, "Perhaps if he rests in the dungeon overnight, and receives a good meal, he'll revive a bit."

"Your Majesty is very wise," the Emir agreed, genuflecting again.

"Yes, yes. We will receive your other gifts later. Now, we are hungry." He snapped his fingers and a servant crawled to his elbow. "The Emir will join us for refreshments."

Sighs of disappointment emitted from the ladies around us, who, from the chatter, found Marid Khan well-favored and were looking forward to watching him die. Instead, we were herded back down the stairs and the corridors and the tunnels to the gardens, which were hot and oppressive.

I tried to ask where the new slaves would be taken but Zarifa, no longer amused at our novelty and worn out from the long night and heat and letdown of the day, snubbed me. We sat and stewed in the heat while the afternoon court began, the Sultana looking as if she hardly knew what to do with so many extra women now that the King had called off the entertainment.

Zarifa's fertile young mind was not at a loss for

ideas, however. "Please, Madam," she said to her aunt when the latter had acknowledged her, "we have heard much and seen nothing of the dancing girls the Emir gave His Majesty yesterday. How did they fare during the troubles of last night? Are they well? Perhaps if they escaped injury, they would dance for us too."

Everyone seemed to think that a splendid suggestion, but when the messenger returned, it was to say that no trace of the women had been found in the quarters allotted to them. However, neither did the quarters appear to be infested, so perhaps the King and the Emir had sent for them.

Thereupon, the Sultana beckoned to Aster, and said, "I was most concerned by what you told me earlier. The Emir appears a cultivated and superior sort of man, a valuable subject, whereas the man you spoke of as your protector appears to be a scoundrel, and we have yet to see this husband of yours. I confess I am most confused by all this, but I really shall try to be fair. Please finish your tale and leave nothing out."

"Illustrious Madam," Aster said, taking a deep breath, "your goodness and kindness in hearing such unworthy strangers speaks highly of the justice available to the helpless in this, my newly adopted land. My co-wives and I are grateful for your mercy and hospitality, and your willingness to be informed of the wrongs done to ourselves, humblest among your subjects." She licked her lips and watched the Sultana's face, to see if the flattery promised her a better hearing. The Sultana discreetly scratched her knee.

Aster took another deep breath and began, "As I recall, I was relating to you how after leaving the wise woman," and she wisely refrained from mentioning the name of Fatima this time, "and leaving our husband's mother in her charge, we ventured forth into the village where we rented from a certain man a certain elephant, and upon the back of this beast made our way into the jungle."

The Sultana settled back into her cushions, her mouth still wrinkled with irritation at one corner but her eyes now upon the face of Aster, whose graceful gestures and expressive voice began once more to capture the attention of the court.

Once our co-wife was properly warmed up, no one noticed Amollia and me any longer. Amollia tapped my arm, and as unobtrusively as possible, she, her cat and I slipped behind the fountain and onto the steps leading down into the garden.

"We must warn Aman Akbar," she said, and her jewelry jingled slightly because in spite of the heat she was shivering.

"A very good idea," I agreed. "We have only to find him. Why do I feel that we won't be permitted to leave?"

"I don't know. No one has accused us of anything, but I too feel that this place is less wholesome for us than before. Perhaps they want us to give evidence in Marid Khan's trial?"

"Perhaps they want us to share his execution," I said. "Any ideas?"

We sat in silence for a fair time. The drone of Aster's voice and the occasional gust of laughter or talk from inside harmonized with the tinkling of the fountains and the songs of the many varieties of birds inhabiting the gardens. Once in a while one of the guards shifted at his post, and I heard one swear. The gardener was visible in the far end of the garden, on his hands and knees, weeding a bed of marigolds.

"We may not be able to leave, but I think they would not be able to stop Kalimba," Amollia said. "If we use the cloth to speak to her, she could warn Aman Akbar."

"Only if we send the cloth along so that they can understand each other." She stared at me sternly, and I realized that I was reluctant to give up the power of the cloth. I shrugged, and started to pull it from my sash. "I suppose there aren't that many beasts with which to use it here."

"It is in my mind that we must send him another thing," Amollia continued carefully. "That charm given to Aster by Fatima to give to the King. I cannot help but wonder if the King is not the baby from whom Fatima was separated. If the charm has significance for him, then our husband should be the one to benefit from its influence."

It was a lot to ask of an animal, to bear two treasures through a crowded city and track one man. In the wild, perhaps, the cat would have had little trouble finding Aman's scent among the others, but in the reek of a city? Amollia's eyes steadily met mine, her mouth set in a determined line. I handed her the cloth.

When she returned to the balcony to wait for Aster, I sat staring across the garden, watching the water splash, the lilies and lotuses bob in the pools. Ranks of pillars supported an outcropping of roof on three sides of the garden, and from between two of these pillars in the section directly across from me emerged three figures—one of the eunuch guards, a huge man, and two women, both heavily veiled. One of these was Um Aman: I recognized her at once despite the veils, since even within the folds of the veil her characteristic way of arranging herself identified her. The other, almost as certainly, was Hyaganoosh, from the way my mother-in-law was bullying her.

I was deciding whether it would be more prudent to rise and greet them or to slink back inside and see what happened when the columns of darkness inside the pillared recesses shifted. For a moment their shapes resembled those carved temptresses on the walls of the temple—impossibly full-bosomed, narrow-waisted, full-hipped and supple in movement, for they were moving, and then, as the trio neared the center of the garden, the shapes altered, dropped, lengthened and crawled forward, the blackness brightening to brown as they whispered through the tall grass and bright flowers. Near the far wall, the gardener whooped and waved his arms, and one of the shapes turned back upon him.

Snakes. More damned snakes. Who had let them loose in the garden? I hollered a warning to the eunuch and he looked stupidly about him, eyes scanning columns and fountains and missing entirely the menace no higher than his ankles.

Hyaganoosh, whose eyes were downcast because she was still being scolded, was more apt and screamed as if already bitten, pointing. Whereupon the eunuch saw the snakes, or some of them, and drew his scimitar. Hyaganoosh and Um Aman, noisily but with a sort of well-accustomed calmness, began shaking their veils, hollering, stamping their feet, clapping their hands and making all the noise they could to frighten the serpents away. This struck me at that time as being very brave and rather foolish, but since then I frequently have seen snakes dispersed with such racket. Country women such as Um Aman and her niece were doing what they ordinarily would do. The snakes, however, were not.

Rather than fleeing, they were attacking, and those at the forefront coiled and reared, their hoods spread, two or three serpents focused on each of the people. The gardener was also creating a racket, but it cut off abruptly and turned into a cry of terror.

I'd been so busy watching the figures in the distance, I hadn't noticed the movement on the steps in front of me, but a pair of slitted eyes fixed mine, and a red tongue flickered in and out. I swung my legs out of range without wondering whether I was faster than the snake, snatched up the nearest object, which was an ornamental bronze urn, and smashed at the hooded head, which sank with a final sharp hiss, and a surprisingly hard clunk as the jaws hit the marble step.

Behind me came other cries and gasps but as the ladies peered over the balcony and ran to the head of the steps, I plunged into the garden, braining any serpent I saw. The eunuch cut circles around himself, but Hyaganoosh and Um Aman, in the necessity for staying out of range of his blade, were apart from him and unprotected. I laid about me with my urn and those I didn't kill seemed by my efforts discouraged, for they slunk away toward the pillars again. By now the gate guards, or some of them, had joined us, and pieces of cobra and spurts of cold blood flew about the garden. The gardener stood howling among his marigolds, his trowel lying uselessly beside him. I crossed the distance between us in three leaps spanning four snakes and parts of two more. The gardener's face was whiter than the marble steps and two long streaks ran down his right leg—one the jerking body of the cobra whose teeth were embedded in his calf and the other a stream of blood seeping from the wound. I had to pull the living snake's head out of him before I could behead it with the trowel. When the tail whipped around me and the bloody mouth snapped I thought I would be killed before I got the job done, but in the end it was pieces of snake lying before a whole Rasa, upon whom the body of the gardener flopped for support.

No more snakes menaced any of us. The eunuchs, Hyaganoosh and Um Aman all stood staring around them. The pieces of cobra seemed to evaporate before our eyes while the others twisted into shadows similar to those I had seen at the beginning, and shrank further—one I am sure became a spider and crawled away, but with the gardener leaning against me I couldn't very well pursue it.

Most of the ladies on the balcony fled back inside but a few braver ones, including Amollia and one of the Sultana's servants, rushed forward to help. Four women surrounded Um Aman and Hyaganoosh, and I dragged the gardener toward them. Amollia met us, and started to speak to me. But, glancing at the gardener's leg, she dropped to her knees, demanded and very surprisingly received, a knife, I didn't see from where, whereupon she cut away the fabric and sliced the poor man's leg where the snake had bit him. She proceeded to kiss him on the leg and I tried to pull her away, thinking that surely if these people frown at a woman being seen by a strange man without a veil, they'd have fits to see her kissing his knees. I kept forgetting the men in the harem supposedly weren't true men. When Amollia raised her bloodstained mouth, I recoiled momentarily, and wondered fleetingly if the woman I'd come to regard as a friend wasn't after all a monster like the drinkers of blood I had heard of from passing tellers of tales. But Um Aman slapped my hand away when I would have restrained Amollia, who spat out that blood and went back for a second taste.

"She's drawing the poison. Don't interfere. She also could easily die but it is the only way."

But I had to look away, while everyone else watched, and the gardener's fellows supported him against them while Amollia worked over him. That is why, I suppose, I alone saw the spotted cat with the rag around its neck leap to the roof of the palace and pad away, something golden glinting in its fur.

Though Hyaganoosh and Um Aman were now the King's slaves, whereas Amollia, Aster and I were still supposedly "guests," even while being watched like prisoners, everyone seemed too preoccupied by the topic of how the cobras had entered the garden and what would have happened if they'd gotten onto the balcony or into the women's sleeping quarters to pay us much attention. Zarifa gave us a small, tired, but quite deliberately friendly smile and left us alone, and several of the others seemed to have softened in attitude toward us. I also overheard a group of women trying the idea out on each other that we were the cause of the snakes and the bedbugs and were bearers of the evil eye and should be driven out or, better yet, killed.

We were able to visit with Hyaganoosh and Um Aman briefly, through the intervention of Zarifa, who had them brought to her quarters and then had the grace to leave us alone together. Um Aman looked drawn and tired, but quite unexpectedly embraced each of us. "Poor old mother," Aster said. "That Div King doesn't seem to know who he's mad at. I thought it was us, last night, but today he went straight for you."

Hyaganoosh edged forward slightly, and offered in the tone of an expert sharing her knowledge, "Divs do change, you know. It's what they're for. They're in *charge* of change, which is what makes them so fearsome. Just when you have things the way you like them, the Divs get bored and change everything around. They'd bother people more if only they could make up their minds quicker, you know. That's why the Peri woman had so much power over Sani. Peris aren't as fickle-minded as Divs."

"They change too, though," I said drily.

"Well, yes, I guess it must seem that way to you," Hyaganoosh said. "But naturally she was much nicer to you than to me. I'm sure she's ever so glad you took me away from Sani. I am too, now that I'm here and have seen how awfully jealous he can be. My goodness, sending snakes after a person! And it wasn't even my fault."

We told them of the vermin of the night before, and the warning on my stomach.

Hyaganoosh was unimpressed. "That Peri is so two-faced. She may have warned you, but who do you think told him where you were? Though I'm sure she thought I was here too last night."

"And so we would have been," Um Aman said. "For the Emir possesses magic that can make his horses run three times faster than ordinarily. But halfway here, we came upon a rogue elephant."

"Oh, it wasn't really," Hyaganoosh said. "It was just lost and it didn't like men. It took a real liking to you though, Aunt Samira."

Um Aman shook her head hopelessly. "Vermin, snakes. What next? I wish to God Aman had never found that accursed bottle. Because of it he was turned to an animal, you, my daughters, may die in a foreign land far from your people and I, too, far from my friends and home. My niece," she glared at Hyaganoosh, "is corrupted, the honorable Marid Khan, for attempting to defend Hyaganoosh and me from the Emir's men, is captive and scheduled for execution and his people will lose a fine leader." We all had gained her approval, it seemed, now that she deemed us doomed.

Amollia was sick the next morning, vomiting and shaking, and remembering Um Aman's caution, I feared the poison from the gardener's leg had crept into her system. But everyone else agreed that the poison would have acted faster.

For that matter, I did not feel entirely fit myself. I was out of practice fighting anything, and whanging a brass pot on the heads of vipers is a strenuous business. My right arm ached, my shoulders and neck throbbed, and I felt a little sick remembering the cobra taking its supper out of the gardener's leg. I had not had vast experience with snakes before, especially of this variety, but was beginning to consider them untrustworthy. I shivered just thinking of the look in the eyes of the one on the marble steps.

By that time, the entire harem was quite a lot worse for the wear. My sleep had been disturbed not only by my own troubled dreams, but by the mumblings and occasional cries of Zarifa and her maids. From down the long hallway the sound of bodies turning from right to left, stomach to back, curling and uncurling, trying to get comfortable, trying to kick off the snake phantoms in their nightmares.

Thus I was more than grateful when Zarifa's nurse offered to sit with Amollia while Aster and I joined the others in the baths.

"The Sultana feels the taking thereof will be most efficacious for all today," the nurse, Sula, said politely. But a hint of something else was in her voice and eyes as she added, "And naturally, it being the third day of your stay and you being in need of returning to your own homes and duties, you will want to be clean to start your journey."

Um Aman and Hyaganoosh fell in with us as we strolled along behind the others through the west garden to the bathing pavilion. I mentioned the nurse's remark and Um Aman nodded gravely.

"Three days is the customary length of a visit, though by no means a hard and fast rule." Her black eyes snapped as a group of tardy women rustled past, swinging wide of the path to avoid us, pulling their skirts close to their legs and turning their heads away until they had joined others farther up the path. Two made small spread-handed gestures as they passed us.

Aster spit after them and grumbled, "If Aman doesn't speak to the King soon, we will leave here only to join Marid Khan in the dungeon guest-house. In trying to explain to these ninnies the intricacies of our situation, I'm afraid I may, in some small insignificant way which will be blown all out of proportion by our enemies, have implicated us."

"Besides which, you would naturally not rejoin Aman without me," Um Aman said. "What would be the good to him of regaining all he owns if he should lose his mother in the process?"

Aster dropped back a step and made a face to me that indicated she was biting her tongue. Hyaganoosh covered her face from nose down with her sleeve and made a choked noise that could have been, but was not, a sob.

The steam rising from the baths was scented with perfume, sweat and the pungence of the green mossy growth lining the pool's sides and bottom. Servants wandered around the edges carrying their trays of oils and unguents, bearing pitchers of fresh water for rinsing hair. The pool seemed more crowded to me than it had been initially, and I also thought there were more adult figures than before. Quite a few of them, in fact. Leaving Aster in fervent discussion with Hyaganoosh, I allowed myself to wade and drift over to the corner most occupied by taller figures. Even from the middle of the pool, I could see that these were strangers, and judging from the unusually voluptuous aspect of each, I knew which strangers. These were the Emir's dancers. My curiosity satisfied, I started to drift back to my companions, but one of the women caught my eye and waved at me to stop. She glided toward me, bearing something in her fingers.

"You are Rasa, the foreigner who fought those dreadful snakes yesterday?" she asked. Her voice was strangely husky and her eyes were odd, though no man would have found anything odd about the rest of her. She and her group were the first flesh-and-blood women I had ever seen who came close to matching the temple carvings in beauty. I suddenly wanted to find a robe and hide myself. As if reading my mind, she said, "I thought that was the most wonderful thing I have ever seen anyone do. We are all of us so sheltered, having been raised in the Emir's harem since we were children, and we are most dreadfully afraid of snakes. It occurred to me that all of that fighting you did might have made you a little sore today, so I thought—that is, my sisters and I thought—we would like to share with you some of this liniment we dancers use for sore muscles."

I took the little vial from her and thanked her, feeling that I was too quick to judge against someone just because her eyes were different and she was so beautiful she made me feel like a boy. The gesture seemed the kindest anyone had made toward any of my party since we arrived and I dipped my head briefly and mumbled thanks and turned away, embarrassed.

When I told the others, Um Aman sniffed and said some people who sold the wrong things for a good profit could afford to be generous, but since I could partake of the baths and Amollia couldn't, perhaps I should save some of the liniment for her instead of hogging it all to myself. For once I felt the reprimand was warranted. I felt so ashamed that I decided to dress again and take the liniment back to Amollia immediately, so that she might be somewhat relieved by the time the rest of us returned from bathing. I was also still not entirely convinced that the poison was not responsible for her condition and now that Um Aman had mentioned her again, I felt I needed to check on her.

Or at least that was what I thought was the source of uneasiness gnawing at me.

The rain-damp morning air, freshened with grass and flower smells, was welcome after the cloying miasma of the baths. I strode briskly away from the pavilion toward the sleeping chambers with a stride determined enough to discourage questioning or interference.

I got both, but not from the guards or other harem authorities.

For I had taken but two or three of these brisk, discouraging steps when the great willow tree standing between pathway and wall jumped, showering me with enough water that it appeared I had been bathing with my clothing on. I whirled, dripping and angry, feeling half ridiculous when I saw two pairs of eyes glittering down at me from among the leaves and I cursed inwardly that I was unarmed.

"Rasa—" Aman said from the tree.

"Aman? My Lord? What are you doing up there?" I asked, whispering and parting dripping stems to try to see him. He lay on an upper branch. Kalimba stretched comfortably on the branch above him. He did not look comfortable at all and his new djinn-manufactured brocade clothing was soaked and soiled.

"Trying to gather my family, what else? Have you been here all along? I suppose it was too much to hope the djinn would keep you safe where I could actually *find* you. I was beside myself with worry until Amollia's cat sought me out and—er—explained the situation."

"Yes," I said excitedly. "Oh, Aman, I am so glad you've found us. The Div King has sent snakes and fleas to torment us and the gods only know what he'll try next. Amollia is ill and your mother and cousin were captured and given as slaves to the King and—"

"Yes, yes, I know all that. And that poor Marid Khan, who isn't a bad sort of fellow at all when he's not after one's womenfolk, is to be executed today for trying to help us. I was in the crowd the other day when the Emir preempted not only my turn but that of all the other common folk seeking justice from the King to present *my* family as tribute. Oh, Rasa, what am I to do?"

"Do?" I asked, as dumbfounded at being consulted in the matter as I was at a loss for an answer. "Do? Why—why—you should give the King the charm, I suppose, and tell him the story and explain how the Emir had no right to enslave your mother and Hyaganoosh and—"

"Be sensible, will you? I cannot very well do that if I can't even see the King, and I have already told you I cannot. No, I must help you all escape and we must flee the country and start anew elsewhere."

Though I had not really expected him to follow any suggestion of mine, I was irritated by his immediate dismissal, but strove for patience. "Very well, My Lord, if you insist that is what we must do, then I suppose we must. However, the charm was given to us by a holy woman to give to the King and we are under an obligation to do so. Therefore, if you can find no way to give it to him, give it to me and I will attempt to see that he receives it before we leave."

"A holy woman, you say? It wouldn't do to offend her along with everyone else I've managed to offend lately, would it? Just a moment." He fumbled on the tree limb, using both hands and ducking his head to try to pull the pendant off over it. The branch wobbled.

"Aman—" I began.

"I have it, I have it," he replied impatiently, and he would have had, except that the first scream burst from the bath pavilion then and the great lizard—the crocodile—slid out the door, snapping its jaws and looking around, its nasty little eyes gleaming with triumph when it spotted me.

# *Chapter 15*

Aman fell out of the tree and Kalimba sprang down after him. The crocodile slid toward me, snapping, its powerful tail whipping the grass, smashing the tiled path. One shrill scream after another split the air. Aman drew his sword and hacked at the crocodile. The sword broke on the animal's horny back. The broken end clattered across the tiles. The lizard forgot about me momentarily and snapped its great jaws shut where Aman's leg would have been had he not danced backward. I dove for the broken sword piece as Aman flew back up the tree. He was unable to gain even the lowest solid branch, and clung to the trunk, his eyes wide. The crocodile, taking its time, climbed halfway up the trunk with its stubby front legs, jaws snapping, tail thrashing. I timed the tail. When it thrashed to the left I dove in from the right and drove the blade into the beast's belly, cutting my hand with the raw edge but also doing enough damage to the lizard that it fell from the tree and rolled over. Dodging tail, claws and jaws, I padded my bleeding hand with a wad of my gown and shoved the blade upward, finishing the animal off.

Aman's hands were shaking as he climbed back down, but when I turned and raced for the bath house, he was right behind me.

We were prevented from entering by all of the naked ladies now scampering and screaming out of the pavilion. I saw that some of them were bleeding already. I feared to see what I would find inside.

Aman was at his masterful best slipping along the side of the pool behind me, shouting orders and picking up girls and women bodily and flinging them out of the range of snapping jaws and toward the door. Most of the women were out of the pool but no less than five crocodiles in the water had Um Aman, Aster and Hyaganoosh trapped against the edge while beyond us, not even interested in the remainder of the fleeing women, three others slunk-slid-waddled around the edge of the pool to separate the three trapped women from that avenue of escape.

Aman pushed the last slippery back end out the door and shoved the butt of his blade in a crocodile's mouth.

"Aman, your knife!" I cried, for I had nothing and could spot no potential weapon amid the steam and water flying from the booming lizard tails.

"I—it's in my other clothes!" he wailed, and the crocodile's mouth closed on his broken sword and it disappeared even as the animal splashed dead back into the pool.

The three crocodiles heading for Um Aman, Aster and Hyaganoosh, turned and advanced on us as Aman backed away from his other adversary. The five in the middle stopped lolling in the water and advanced in earnest upon Um Aman, who was calling down curses upon them, Aster, who was alternately hiding her face against Um Aman's hair and hollering something unintelligible at the crocodiles, and Hyaganoosh, whose head lolled listlessly upon her neck, her hair streaming over her face.

I would like to say I attacked the lizards and saved my friends but that is not what happened. Two of the lizards from the edge slithered toward me at once and in trying to leap aside, I succeeded in avoiding being devoured for the moment but the body of one of the beasts knocked my feet out from under me and I plunged into the pool.

The five crocodiles who formerly menaced Um Aman and company now menaced me. My hand was bleeding copiously. My sword was gone. I was half-drowned. The only hard object I had at hand was the little liniment bottle the Emir's dancer had given me and this I pulled from my sash and threw awkwardly at the beasts, hoping wildly that one of them at least would choke on it. It bounced on their backs, the stopper flew out, and sizzling liquid spread all across their warty hides. Wave after wave of oily water engulfed me, as the middle of the pool churned with cooking, thrashing crocodile. When the forms changed I do not know, nor did I hear the voices of the guards as they burst in and killed the remaining crocodiles. I was pulled half dead from the pool by one guard, bundled in a robe, and delivered with all of the others to the Sultana's court. I saw only in a daze that the crocodile bodies shifted and shrank briefly into the bodies of human women, the dancers, into the bodies of cobras, into human form again, to disappear briefly and reappear as something neither animal nor human but more like the combination of forms assumed by the guards of Sani the Ever-Changing. I looked away as I was carried through the door, but glanced once more over the shoulder of my rescuer and this time it seemed to me that there were no bodies inside at all.

*  *  *

The King wanted to have Aman Akbar gelded on the spot, before he was tortured or executed or any of the other things the King considered it proper to do to the man who had illegally entered his harem and viewed the nude bodies of his women. The Sultana and Zarifa, who had been in the baths when the crocodiles appeared seemingly from nowhere, and who had been saved by Aman's rescue efforts, convinced the King that such an action was unnecessary cruelty. Being stomped to death by elephants along with the other criminal, Marid Khan, seemed to them more than sufficient punishment. The King didn't like it, but Zarifa, of whom he was fond, said she would never speak to him again and the Sultana said that she didn't like to go against him of course but really, in this case, she felt that there were extenuating circumstances he had not heard such as the fact that the man was clearly there only to find his own wives.

The four eunuch guards who held Aman Akbar down, their knives poised to make him one of their number, relaxed, and he was allowed to do likewise and rise to a merely prostrated rather than totally flattened position. The King pouted, but presently brightened.

"If this man was in my harem because of his wives, they must have let him in. Therefore, they should die with him." That seemed to cheer him to no end. "Oh, yes, that will be wonderful! And you say the Emir's slaves are his cousin and mother? They too, shall die! We will have one-two-three-four-five-six-seven, counting that fellow from yesterday. Yes *seven* executions instead of only one today! Seven! An auspicious number, isn't it, Aunt? Oh, that will be wonderful! People will talk of it for years! Tell the executioner to tell the Keeper of Elephants I want my very biggest and newest elephant to do it—the women first, one at a time, then their husband and then that other fellow—whatsisname?"

I must say on behalf of the King's ladies that they were aware of the injustice perpetrated on us and protested bitterly, with lamentations and wailings and farewell zaghareets as we were led off to the dungeons to await our doom. While we were there, one of the eunuchs, who had been early on the scene and actually saw the crocodiles and knew that we spoke the truth, brought a pile of rich clothing and jewels as a parting present from our hostesses, who wanted us to be able to die well-dressed. Hyaganoosh solemnly picked out the richest raiment available, saying a girl should always look her best, but the rest of us found in the pile our old clothing and decked ourselves in that. Um Aman was grateful to find her abayah in the pile, for she intended to die with her veils on.

The executioner was also the gardener, an odd little economy in the midst of so much opulence. Though this was not the same gardener as the one Amollia had attempted to save from the snake bite, he said that he was the man's brother and stood with us, among a circle of guards, commiserating. Personally, I didn't see him as an executioner. He seemed much too sensitive.

He had good news for us women. We would not be stomped to death after all, as the Keeper of Elephants had finally persuaded him and he had been able with great difficulty to persuade the King's chief servant who finally persuaded the King, that seven stompings was too hard on the elephant. Two would get the point across. We women were to endure the traditional death of adulteresses and be sewed into silken bags and tossed into the river instead. What he wanted to know, since we had been so kind to his brother, was what color silk we preferred—he had arranged that we might have our choice.

He also said that it wouldn't hurt too much from what he had seen of the ladies his late brother had done for in the past, and if we went quietly and didn't struggle all would be well and we wouldn't suffer. Well, not for long anyway. I said they might as well have let me drown in the pool among the crocodiles since they were going to do it anyway. He seemed shocked. Without a trial? That would go against God's law. And I really mustn't go on about those crocodiles. The King was most angry with his women for lying about them, because there were no bodies present in the pool. Perhaps there would be the need of more silken bags later. I glared at him and said he was horrible and he looked offended. He really was grateful that Amollia and I had tried to help his brother and wanted us to like him.

"What do they do in your land, lady?" he asked, and snapped his fingers for the first of the silken bags as the elephant was led onto the field beyond.

"Do? Herd sheep mostly, and fight," I replied.

"I mean about executions. Anything special for adultery? Treason? I'm new at this, you know, and the King is fond of novelty, as boys are."

I felt dazed by the events of the day and the man's attitude, but answered civilly enough. "No, nothing special, just simple cutting—you know, the usual."

"Nothing exotic?" the man asked, disappointed but trying not to sound disapproving.

"Sorry. We're simple people."

"It can't be helped, I suppose. Now then, off with you to watch while the Keeper of Elephants does for your husband. The King wants you to watch, and it is quite a sight. The Keeper, Faisal, always makes such a fine display and he's going to try especially hard today is my guess to make up for yesterday. Ahh, yes. Look at that beast!"

When we had been bundled onto the parade ground and our feet encased to the knees in weighted silken sacks, a different color for each of us, we had a fine viewpoint for the whole affair, or such as we were to be alive long enough to witness. Aman and Marid Khan were staked to the ground, several lengths apart, so that all the excitement didn't happen at once. The King sat on his balcony, the Emir smiling on the cushion beside him. From behind the pink curtain came more wailing and sobbing. Um Aman was praying to herself. I couldn't see because her veils were drawn about her, although none of the rest of us were permitted to cover our faces. I suppose they figured because she was a mother and not too comely they could grant her final privacy.

Hyaganoosh and Aster were supported by each of the arms of one burly guard. Amollia stared straight ahead, her face that of an ebony idol. Kalimba was nowhere to be seen. At least someone had escaped the King's idea of justice. The crowd pressed on all sides, restrained by ranks of splendidly uniformed guards. The King sported a new purple turban with jeweled peacock feathers that matched his fan. I didn't notice anything else, for the elephant lumbered onto the field.

The beast was, from its decorations, the same who had been presented to the King by the Emir. His trunk swayed rhythmically between his silver-capped tusks, ears fanning majestically under a little elephant's caplet of bells and tassles, the whole of which would have made a cloak for Aster. The elephant was led by the mahout, not ridden, toward the white cloth upon which lay Aman Akbar. This cloth had been spread, I supposed, to protect the grass from too much nourishment and also for the purpose of displaying to the court the maximum amount of gore.

The mahout tapped the elephant behind the knee and the beast raised its foot over Aman's outstretched legs.

Aman's head raised, his neck tense, as he looked up into the mouth of his destroyer. He did not flinch, but I did. To be pinioned, unable to defend him was more than I could bear. His image blurred before me and my throat tightened so that I thought it would burst. Amollia's hands flew to her mouth and she cried out. The elephant stepped back, knocking the stick out of the mahout's hand and lowering its foot safely on the grass. The mahout urged it forward again.

Amollia turned to me babbling. It took me a while to make out that she was saying the elephant was none other than *our* elephant, the one we had obtained in Fatima's village. When it was in position to crush Aman again, she cried out once more, but this time a guard clamped his hand over her mouth.

The elephant, looking over at us, saw this. Knocking the mahout aside, the great gray beast stepped daintily around Aman and thundered toward us. The crowd

scattered and the guard had sense enough to release
Amollia. The elephant felt her hair with its trunk, and
satisfied, stood near us, looking around as if daring
anyone to threaten us.

The King was pounding the balcony rail with his
fists. "Don't just stand there! Get another elephant! Kill
that one!"

Into the gap created by the scattered crowd bounded Kalimba, followed by a white-clad figure whose
every step was punctuated by the thump of a walking
stick. The few people who were in her way quickly
removed themselves.

Admonishing black eyes pierced the balcony and
the King retreated to a sitting position. The same gaze
swept us all, and even the elephant hung its head.

"Well," Fatima said, "I suppose if you want something done you have to do it yourself."

The hush following the elephant's defection and
Fatima's arrival was broken by the King's angrily gar-
gled order, "Silence that old woman! Who does she
think she is, anyway?"

The guards were not too eager to obey and hesitated.
Fatima turned to me. "Haven't you given him the
charm yet either? It's plain he hasn't tasted the lemon."

"Aman has the charm," I said.

A voice called to the King from the pink curtain
and again the guards delayed while all eyes turned to
the balconies once more.

"What did you say, Aunt? Must I clear the balcony?"

"I said," the acting Sultana's voice was hoarse, as if
forced through an unwilling mouth, "that woman is
your mother."

"I've had enough of women's nonsense for one
day!" the King said petulantly. "Clear the balcony!"

"If—if you do," the voice said, "before you can, we
will tear aside the curtain and every one of us will show
her face to the populace."

The crowd cheered and the King turned scarlet.
Fatima did not let any grass grow under her feet while
the Sultana bought her time. She was standing over
Aman and had the necklace from his throat in the wink

of an eye. This she handed up to the King on the end of her walking stick.

"Your Majesty, Abad, my son," she said, very patiently for her. "You are the Defender of the Faithful. We, the women who love you, seek only to help you avoid a grave injustice and to execute your duties and your enemies, not your friends. Only hear me, and the witnesses here today, and you will see that you have been tricked by that man beside you."

The King didn't seem to know what to say or which way to look. He opened his mouth to storm in the way he believed regal, and looked into Fatima's eyes and saw something that made him stop. He started to speak again, and looked back at her, and stopped again. "But, my mother is dead," he said in a small voice more appropriate to his age than any I had heard him use.

"Examine the charm," she said firmly. He took it from the hook and shook his head, then patted his chest in a puzzled way. "It is not the one you have worn since babyhood, my son, the one I placed upon you after securing the promise of your foster mother that if I left you in peace she would see that you wore it always. It is the other half. The half I have worn. The half I sent with these women, along with the sacred carpet of Saint Selima and another, precious gift, as my legacy to you. But the man beside you, the thief of the sacred carpet, the ally of the godless being who loosed catastrophes upon your helpless women and sought to slay my messengers, has prevented my gift from reaching you. I beg you, with love, to accept it."

The Emir whispered to the King, gently, and the young man shook his head violently, and with great effort stared down at Fatima. "Woman, I do not know you nor do I know why you support criminals and adulteresses against my faithful Emir but—"

"Oh, balderdash," Fatima said. "I knew I couldn't pull this off alone." She turned to Kalimba. "You'll have to tell him. My own son and he won't believe his mother."

The cat coughed several times violently and smoke curled from its nostrils. The smoke gathered into a familiar shape and as two of the guards swooned and a great part of the crowd screeched, the djinn appeared, genuflected as well as he was able with an ample middle and no feet, and floated upward to address the King.

"Your Majesty, please believe me that I sympathize with your attitude toward recalcitrant females. However, in this case, I fear that yours are not reacting with their typical inane hysteria. I have observed this matter from start to finish and now, as a free agent, a subject of a parallel and complementary people whose duty it is to educate mortals whenever possible, and as a true believer, I feel it incumbent upon me to mingle with mankind one last time in order to acquaint you with my knowledge. Only ask this scoundrel beside you once more, in the presence of your ladies behind the curtain, about the so-called present he sent to announce his arrival."

The King turned to the Emir who stammered, "D-dancing girls, wasn't it, Your Majesty? And very fine ones too, you said. I thought you were pleased."

The pink curtain agitated and though the Sultana did not again address the King directly a messenger presently arrived and whispered to the King. Meanwhile, a guard moved to the Emir's side.

"Onan Emir," the King said, turning from djinn and guard, "My Lady Aunt says that your dancing girls turned into crocodiles and tried to eat my harem. What have you to say? I for one find it amusing, since neither dancing girls nor crocodiles are anywhere to be found now."

"Amusing?" Aster had snapped out of her fearful trance some moments ago and watched the scene avidly. Now she rolled up her sleeve, pulled forth a yellow oblong and cried to the djinn, "Old Uncle, catch!"

The djinn fumblingly did so and stared at the fruit with some distaste before proffering it to the King, who flattened an upraised palm at it.

"My son, this fruit is my other gift. Only eat it and you will see the truth of this matter," Fatima said.

"You seek to poison me," the King said. "Guards!"

"Nonsense!" she said, "I'd eat some myself but I'm

a wisewoman. It would be wasted on me. Ask your friend the Emir to test it. He can use it."

The King's face grew cunning with the look of a child about to pull the wings from a moth. "No. I have a better idea. Try it on the prisoner. The one all of you women and even my elephants seem so intent upon preserving. If he survives it, I will eat it."

The djinn snapped his fingers and Aman's bonds in the same gesture and our husband sat up. The djinn waved his hand to summon Aman. Aman glanced at us. As one woman, we nodded silently, and he marched forward, head high, received the lemon from the djinn and bit into it, whereupon he puckered sourly, swallowed hard and said, "Ummm," bobbing his head encouragingly at the King. Then gradually, his expression altered and he looked at the djinn, at Fatima, and at us wonderingly and said, "God be praised. I never realized that before."

"Never realized what?" the King said impatiently. "Are you dying?"

"No, Your Majesty," Aman answered. "Far from it. In fact, I feel—I don't know how to describe it, Your Majesty."

"I command you to do so," the King replied. Aman shook his head ruefully and handed the lemon to the King, who angrily tore it in two and began sucking it and shredding it with his teeth.

He stood with his arms folded across his chest, a defiant look in his young face, for a short time. Then with an impatient gesture he pointed his finger at us, opened his mouth, and lowered his finger again, a blush creeping from his collar to his hairline and a sheepish look replacing the stubborn, angry one he had worn ever since the elephant refused to crush Aman Akbar.

"Captain of the guards," he said at length.

"Your Majesty?" the Captain ran and crawled at the same time, his progress ending in a genuflection before the balcony.

"Send my subjects home and bring all the principals to the audience chamber. See that my ladies are in attendance behind their screen, and have another screen, for privacy, moved close to the divan so that my mother and her female friends may present their testimony."

When he had heard the stories of Aman Akbar, Marid Khan, his aunt, Zarifa, Um Aman, Fatima, Hyaganoosh and the djinn, the King questioned the Emir. "We will forget for the moment, Onan Emir, that by the testimonies of no less than four Kharristanis, you have misused your power and taken from my subjects wealth to be used for your own enjoyment. The more immediate question is of a more seriously treasonous nature. Why did you send me sorcerous dancers who would change into crocodiles and try to eat my ladies? I am forced to believe that this was no random or accidental enchantment, for it happened, if what the wives of Aman Akbar and my own sister tell me is correct, no less than three times and on the third occasion one of these dancers gave the Lady Rasa a caustic liquid represented as a liniment so that she would destroy herself before the dancers menaced my harem. By trying to remove the one woman among my own capable of defending the others, the dancers showed their premeditated evil intent. I can only assume it was at your instigation."

The Emir's stomach spread against the carpet as he pressed himself deeper into it in an ardent salaam. "Majesty, I am guilty of no such heinous crime, only of a small and insignificant desire to appear pleasing in Your Majesty's sight. When you told me dancers had been sent to you in my name and that you were well pleased with them, I accepted the credit, but in truth I had nothing to do with it. If you do not believe me, you may ask the same Lady Hyaganoosh and the gracious matron who accompanied her from the palace of the Div King. Yes, you may even question the bandit Marid Khan. If they are the honorable people you believe them to be, they will tell you that I dispatched no such dancers. Indeed, Sani the Ever-Changing and I parted on such bad terms that he would have vouchsafed me no subjects of his as presents to you. It is instead my belief that he sent the dancers himself, in my name, to shame and implicate me and to punish not only myself but the Lady Hyaganoosh, who fled from him when he abused my gift of her person by mistreating her and her cousin's family, who aided her in her escape."

Much as I hated to aid the wretch in any respect, I was forced in all honesty to mention the Peri's warning scratched upon my stomach, and Aster elaborated. The King sighed and nodded sadly.

"Though it would give me much pleasure to continue the execution as scheduled, I must concede that on the surface it appears the crimes of the dancers were not of your contrivance. Your presence in the home of my fellow monarch, the King of Divs, is not yet explained however."

The Emir babbled something about being an old friend of the family, gifts exchanged, that sort of thing. The Emir had been just stopping by to see how Sani liked his new bride. Then, naturally, he, the Emir, would continue on the short distance farther to Bukesh and present his tribute.

"And the Lady Hyaganoosh then was not presented to me first?" the King asked, looking petulant.

"Well, not exactly, Your Majesty, but—"

"And her Aunt, Um Aman, was a free woman and not a slave for you to give to anyone?"

"She had become a prisoner through her attempts to—er, no, Your Majesty. I mean, yes, Your Majesty, she was a free woman formerly."

"I cannot accept them then. Um Aman may return to her son's household and the Lady Hyaganoosh, if she wishes, may reside here until my Aga can contract her a good marriage." The young King rubbed his eyes with the heels of his hands and one of his slaves stopped fanning long enough to rub his neck, a familiar gesture to which the prematurely experienced King offered no objection. "As for Marid Khan—" the King continued after a moment. Marid Khan crawled forward again and kneeled. "You admit to treasonous banditry, do you?"

"If it please Your Majesty, against none but the Emir of Kharristan only, this ruthless tyrant who beggared my people. We sought only to regain our own. He ha stolen and looted with all manner of magic tricks from all and sundry and—"

"I have already heard your accusations, Marid Khan. There is no evidence of this, however."

Fatima leaned forward and spoke through a leaf-shaped hole pierced in the fragrant sandalwood screen that shielded us from the eyes of the men. "There is the carpet of Saint Selima."

"My mother has mentioned this carpet before. I would see it." A low murmuring filtered through the fretted marble behind which sat the Sultana and the rest of the harem and presently a pair of eunuchs brought forth the rolled carpet and unrolled it at the King's feet. "And you say it flies?"

"I myself have seen it do so, Your Majesty, when the djinn used it to transport the three wives of Aman Akbar to the refuge of your seraglio," Marid Khan answered.

"Normally, it can be done only by a very devout person, such as Um Aman or myself, however," Fatima added.

The djinn wafted forward bowing. "If it please Your Majesty, *I* am a very devout person. It was my sense of fairness that caused me to return, though I was finally free of mankind, having flung my bottle far into the mountains where, lying unstoppered and unmolested in the nest of a bird, it is safe from tampering hands. Though I may rejoin the djinnia who disport themselves within the ether, I recalled that I had not exactly fulfilled all of the wish of my former master's mother, since the carpet I had employed to scoop up all of the concerned females was unable to collect the old one and her niece. For that reason I returned to the city, where I borrowed the form of the spotted cat and used its natural powers to seek Lady Fatima and bring her forth. The carpet is very sacred and I can testify that it was stolen by the Emir, and was in his possession when first I entered his—er—employ."

The King nodded, but by now his plumes were drooping with the weight of all of the evidence and testimony he was having to assimilate. Being a wise and just King is a good deal more difficult than being a capricious and cruel one. "So, we agree the carpet is holy, the Emir is a thief, and my mother is holy, but truly, Marid Khan, I do not see that that excuses you from turning bandit—"

"Your Majesty, we of my people do not consider our acts banditry nor ourselves treasonous. We were a separate people in the time of your father and mine, one of the desert tribes who allied themselves with your father. Our alliance was sealed with the gift of my father's own sister to your father, I am told, for it happened before I was born, and when word reached us that this aunt of mine was no longer in the harem, and had probably been slain by her rivals, my father was understandably insulted. Still, we honored the alliance until this rogue of an Emir was sent to govern Kharristan and would have robbed my people of all they possessed. We simply taxed him and his subjects instead."

Beside me, Fatima let her breath out in a sharp little puff and her plump hand flew to her mouth. "Oh, dear, I always meant to send a message, but it is a most inconvenient procedure with the sea between the jungle and your desert, Marid. And by the time I was settled at the shrine, I was sure your father would have died and it didn't seem important anyway, with Selima's work so pressing. Do forgive me and er—Your Majesty, son, may I present your second cousin, prince of my people and the people of your legacy from me, who, if they're doing all that badly, you simply must do something for."

The King sank lower into his velvet cushions and mopped his brow with the back of his hand, despite the peacock fans and the cool monsoon breeze blowing in through the open arched windows.

"I think under the circumstances we can pardon Marid Khan and restore his people to their former prominence. That takes care of about everything except what troubles me most, and that is that I still see no way to save the honor of my women and the life of Aman Akbar, for by invading my harem baths, even for such noble reasons as you claim, you have sullied them and myself by implication. I could simply castrate you and give you a government post, I suppose, for as a eunuch, even after the fact, you would have committed no serious breach of—"

Aman, also kneeling before the King, blanched. His melting brown eyes strayed longingly and apologetically toward the screen. Um Aman dug her nails into her abayah-covered elbows and her knuckles turned white. Her lips disappeared into a tight, pleated line and her black eyes glared straight ahead. Amollia closed her eyes and looked as if she would swoon. Burning, bitter liquid rose in my throat and choked me, receding only as I grabbed Aster, who was rising, ready to knock away the screen and berate the King—or so it seemed from the red flushing in her cheeks and the wild gleam in her eye.

Aman was speaking, "Your Majesty, though I understand that I have offended your honor, I must ask you to consider that mine was likewise offended: my wives were taken from me. I sought only to regain them. We were married a very short time when I became an ass. They are young and faithful and far from their homes and if I am made a eunuch, will have no man to do for them what a husband should do, and will be doomed to barrenness. Therefore, for their sakes, I beg you to let me divorce them and then, if you are merciful, you might ask the djinn to turn me back into a ass. I would prefer to be a whole animal than half a man and as an ass I would be no more of an offense to your ladies than as a eunuch."

Aster sat down again sharply. But as if it was unconnected with me, I heard my own voice saying, "Your Majesty, whether man, donkey, or eunuch, my husband is my husband and I will not be parted from him, having come this far. If you have him turned into an ass, I would be likewise transformed—"

Aster turned on me. "Don't be silly, Rasa. Who would take care of him then? Do you think I want to herd both of you?" Turning back to the screen she said, "Your Majesty, with all due respect, I simply do not accept such a solution. Aman Akbar didn't rape your wives, he saved them from being devoured by crocodiles. Lemon of experience or no lemon of experience, you aren't being very reasonable. The Emir is your enemy, not Aman. If anyone should be cut upon or transformed or mashed, it is not my husband but that fat toad."

"One dishonor does not wipe out another," the King said. "I know that now more than ever—"

From behind the marble screen, the Sultana spoke again. "Even so, Your Majesty, there must be another way. For my part, I would be as dishonored by the execution, mutilation or transformation of this brave man for saving my life as I would be by running naked through the streets of Bukesh and showing myself to every mahout and camel driver among your subjects." Murmurs of assent, with only one or two gasps of, "oh really, now, I wouldn't take it that far," buzzed from behind the screen.

"There is one other way, my son," Fatima said. "Among our people, the people of Marid Khan, women are not veiled with the tribe, for we are all one family. If Aman Akbar is transformed, not into a eunuch or an ass, but into a family member, the shame to your women will be wiped out."

"But that is not possible," he said.

"It is if you marry the Lady Hyaganoosh, who is his cousin."

He thought a moment and shook his head. "But I cannot, for to do so would be as dishonorable as to leave the stain unredeemed."

"Your Majesty?" Hyaganoosh's voice was small and girlish and cajoling.

"Yes?"

"Your Majesty, I know it is immodest of me to say so, but if you should in your wisdom decide that the thing for me to do would be to marry your cousin, Marid Khan, the great desert warrior and leader of his people, and if it is only your unwillingness to betroth me a third time without consulting my wishes or my people, I just want to let you know that I would happily bend myself to obey you if it would facilitate a solution to this problem. Aman Akbar really isn't a *bad* sort."

"It is most unseemly for a woman to speak for herself about matrimony without the consent of the head of her household," the King said severely.

"Your Majesty," Um Aman said. "Hyaganoosh is but a girl. Forgive her impetuousness. Her parents were murdered by this slime of an Emir, who also murdered her father's brother, my own dear husband, who had he lived would have adopted the girl. Therefore, I consider myself her adoptive mother. Aman Akbar is the head of my household. Therefore, you might say that if he is not to be Hyaganoosh's husband, he could be in place of her brother."

"The connection is not close enough."

Fatima spoke. "It is if you, my son, allow me to make the same arrangements in regards to Marid Khan. If he is your adoptive brother, therefore Aman Akbar is your brother-in-law if Marid Khan and Hyaganoosh wed. He was also, you will recall, husband to three of the ladies in the incident, son of one, and as brother of another, in-law to yourself and the Sultana, the stain is considerably bleached."

The King shook his head slowly. "It is too complicated. We will never be able to explain it to anyone outside this room."

"There is one other way, my son, but it will look even stranger to outsiders," Fatima said. "Um Aman is a widow. You have been given her as a slave, a potential concubine. Therefore, it seems to me that you may take Aman Akbar as your adoptive son."

Um Aman was sputtering and grunting and didn't seem to know where to look. The King's mouth hung open with consternation.

"However, since by your adoption of Aman Akbar, you would have a son of Um Aman, and the only son you are likely to get from her, she could be released as I was to return home, which is what you have already decided to do."

The King scratched his head and his turban slipped

forward. "It is still extremely complicated and I know if I think about it very long I shall think of some very good reason why it will not work. But as I do not intend to think about this any further, but to retire with my ladies and reap the benefit of some of the new experience I've gained from the lemon, I will place my seal upon the proper documents and consider it done. Only one further matter do I need to take care of and that is to place my newly adopted son upon the divan of Kharristan, where I am sure he will rule wisely—at least, he can hardly do worse than has already been done. And some fitting punishment must be devised for the Emir. I wonder if the elephant is still ready?"

The djinn bowed low again. "Your Majesty, if I may be so bold. Our law delights in appropriate punishments and I would suggest one for this man who insults innocent women, murders the people he is sworn to protect, and has honest men changed into donkeys while—ahem—ignoring the magnificent treasures he obtains by the downfall of those same honest men. Such a man should not be slain, but should be imprisoned, as I have been, in a bottle, and made to grant three wishes to the first person to find his vessel and release him. He will never be free again until someone shall freely agree to take his place—"

"Oh, I *like* that," the King said, boyish delight flickering once more in his eyes. And before he had the words out, the djinn had done it and disappeared.

These days I almost wish Aman would take more wives, for though we have many servants, and eat fresh food every night, the running of such a large household, and one in which we must so frequently entertain heads of state and delegations from allied peoples, is a grievous burden. Amollia has weaned her first baby, the one who made her sick that day in Bukesh, and has started another and Aster is so big now she is unfit to do anything but criticize my attempts at telling our tale. There are wonderful stables, and my husband solicits my advice about these as frequently as he does about the discipline and maintenance of his guard. I have barely had the time to learn to read and write while coping, and I miss Um Aman as well. Like Fatima, she found the harem life didn't suit her and she too has become a holy woman, and has dedicated herself to Selima's sacred animals in our part of the world: camels, scorpions, snakes, the elephant—still the property of the jeweler but still rented to us—and most particularly asses.

Hyaganoosh and Marid Khan are frequent visitors. Hyaganoosh entertains us with tales of the nomadic life, to which she has become surprisingly attached, while Marid Khan consults with Aman Akbar about the difficulties of governing. Amollia is of great help to our husband in these matters of diplomacy, and tells stories to her baby of how his grandfather, the Great Elephant, handled this or that problem in her native land. I have yet to have a child, but Aman shows no sign of wishing to put me away because I am barren, and indeed, we are much together these days, trying to alleviate my condition, while Amollia and Aster are unable to perform their marital duties.

In his new wisdom, Aman is careful always to treat us equitably. He gave Amollia a new gown and a rope of deep sea pearls when she bore her son, and both she and Aster received a rope of gold coins each time they became pregnant. I got mine when I bought the first string of horses, and a strand of turquoise when our army defeated that of a disaffected desert tribe. When the alliance was forged, my husband sent to the King and requested an elephant, which he has sent in the care of a number of his guard to my father, with the regards of the King. That will show my mother's cousins.

## ABOUT THE AUTHOR

ELIZABETH SCARBOROUGH was born in Kansas City, KS. She served as a nurse in the U.S. Army for five years, including a year in Viet Nam. Her interests include weaving and spinning, and playing the guitar and dulcimer. She has previously published light verse as well as three other Bantam novels, *Song of Sorcery*, *Bronwyn's Bane* and *The Unicorn Creed*. She makes her home in Fairbanks, Alaska.

Coming in 1985 . . .

# THE
# CHRISTENING
# QUEST

by Elizabeth Scarborough

Return to Argonia, magical land of BRON-
WYN'S BANE, with Bronwyn's brother and
cousin as they journey to Miragenia to rescue
Bronwyn's first born child. This delightful tale
of fun and adventure will be on sale in
late-1985 wherever Bantam paperbacks are
sold.